PRIDE, PREJUDICE, AND OTHER FLAVORS

Also by Sonali Dev

A Distant Heart
A Change of Heart
The Bollywood Bride
A Bollywood Affair

PRIDE, PREJUDICE, AND OTHER FLAVORS

A Novel

SONALI DEV

WILLIAM MORROW
An Imprint of HarperCollins*Publishers*

P.S.™ is a trademark of HarperCollins Publishers.

PRIDE, PREJUDICE, AND OTHER FLAVORS. Copyright © 2019 by Sonali Dev. All rights reserved. Printed in the United States of America. No part of this book may be used or reproduced in any manner whatsoever without written permission except in the case of brief quotations embodied in critical articles and reviews. For information, address HarperCollins Publishers, 195 Broadway, New York, NY 10007.

HarperCollins books may be purchased for educational, business, or sales promotional use. For information, please email the Special Markets Department at SPsales@harpercollins.com.

FIRST EDITION

Designed by Diahann Sturge

Library of Congress Cataloging-in-Publication Data has been applied for.

ISBN 978-0-06-283905-3

19 20 21 22 23   LSC   10 9 8 7 6 5 4 3 2 1

For Rohit.
Mamma and Papa (and the phul *and* taare*) were*
right after all: the only thing we'll have forever is
each other. Thanks for being such a sister to me, my
darling brother. I would not be me without you.

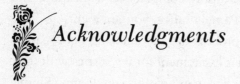 *Acknowledgments*

When you love a book as much as I love Jane Austen's *Pride and Prejudice*, little bits of it leak into all your work. So first and foremost, my deepest thanks to Ms. Austen for planting the seed in me for wanting to tell stories about how love finds its way around the divisions and norms of the world we live in. I'm going to start with alerting you, Dear Reader, that Trisha and DJ's story is only loosely inspired by the themes that Ms. Austen explored so very deftly. There are no daughters to be married off here. Only imbalanced power dynamics and preconceived notions to be navigated. And I thank you with all my heart for going on this romp with me afresh.

As with all stories, this one was a tangled yarn ball of ideas when I first started working on it. I would never have unsnarled it without the help of both my editors. Thank you, Priyanka Krishnan, for seeing the story beneath the surface and helping me dig it out, and Tessa Woodward, for taking my hand with such kindness and helping me polish it into beauty. Speaking of beauty, the art director and the art department at William Morrow found a way to turn the spirit of this book into cover art, and I am in awe. Which can be said about the entire team at William Morrow, who exemplify competence, dedication, and warmth. Especially you, Pamela Jaffee, you are a gift.

The backbone of my process are my amazing beta readers who perfectly balance their excitement for my stories with their undiluted critiques. I am so very grateful to you, Joanna Shupe, Piper Huguley, Gaelyn Almeida, Robin Bradford, Kalpana Thatte, Emily Redington Modak, Robin Skylar, Tamar Bihari, and Heather Marshall. An extra special thanks to Kristan Higgins, Barbara O'Neal, and Damon Suede for their masterclass-level input; to my parents for reading and loving everything I write; to Kavi Singh and Reshma Nanjappa for the benefit of their Englishness—DJ and Emma were doubly fun to write because I know you two fit cows (yes, I used that wrongly, I know!); and to Nishita Kothary, MD, who graciously swallowed her cringes at all my medical questions (and fantasies). A lot of the medicine in this book is fictional, but whatever grain of authenticity it is built on is thanks to her mad brilliance.

Lastly, my biggest thanks to the loves of my life: Manoj, Mihir, and Annika, for that unforgettable trip to Southall—daytime drunks, missed bus stops, bling-filled bazaars, and all. I promised you it was book research, and look, it really was!

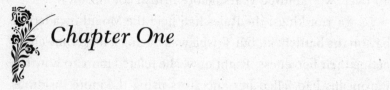

Chapter One

So much about the world baffled Dr. Trisha Raje, but she was never at a loss for how to do her job. Telling a patient her tumor was not fatal should have been the easiest thing, but Trisha had no idea how she was going to manage it. How on earth did one tell an artist that she was going to go blind?

Trisha stood frozen in Stanford's neurosurgery ward, staring down the passage that led to her patient's room. But instead of the clinical gray floors and walls lined with locally sourced artwork, what stared back at her were memories of marble arches inlaid with peacocks of emerald and lapis lazuli. The smell of ancient sandalwood and salty ocean air permeated her lungs, displacing the mild tang of disinfectant.

This wasn't the time for falling down the memory rabbit hole, but Trisha needed something to ground her and nothing did that quite like her family's ancestral home thousands of miles away. Wrapping her arms around herself, she tightened her hold on the memories and pulled them closer. The Sagar Mahal, or the Ocean Palace, with its three hundred rooms overlooking the Arabian Sea, was the seat from which Trisha's ancestors had ruled the kingdom of Sripore in western India for over two hundred years before British colonization.

As warrior kings, the Rajes had held the Mogul invaders at bay on the battlefield, but Trisha was having a hard time channeling their fierceness. Right now, she related more to how the Europeans had felled her ancestors using the more insidious violence of commerce to infiltrate and steal their land. In a befuddling twist of history, the rulers of the many kingdoms that made up modern-day India—the Rajes included—had found themselves stripped of their power and shoved into the role of figureheads, paying taxes to the British Empire.

In return for his indentured allegiance, the eighteenth maharaja, Trisha's great—add four more greats to that for good measure—grandfather, had been allowed to retain his title and their beloved home and all the royal properties associated with it. So Trisha had him to thank for spending every single summer of her childhood in Sripore.

Trisha's mother had insisted upon her American children staying connected to their royal Indian heritage. It was her way of holding on to the home she'd given up when she'd married their father and migrated to America. Trisha's father for his part had gone along with it so long as their heritage didn't interfere with their assimilation. To His Royal Highness Shree Hari Raje—HRH, as his children liked to call him behind his back—their royal lineage was their past, it was history. Their identity as native-born Californians was their future; it was the history he fully expected them to make.

To Trisha, medicine was where both her identities crossed over inside her, much the same way that the two optic nerves crossed over at the chiasm—the hallowed spot in the brain where her patient's tumor was tragically located. Which meant that Emma Caine was going to lose sight in both eyes when Trisha performed the surgery that would save her life. In her five years of performing surgery, this was the first time a patient of hers was going to go blind. The irony was cruel.

The year Trisha turned thirteen, her family had been on their annual summer trip to Sripore. As was his routine, HRH spent most mornings visiting the many royal charities. His pet project was the orphanage for blind children that his father had built just before he died.

Trisha was the only one of the children he had asked to accompany him to the orphanage that day—a rare treat she had rubbed in her siblings' faces. Subtly of course. The Raje children were expected to be dignified in all things, and tormenting one another was not an exception.

At the orphanage Trisha had followed her father up the gray cement stairs where the headmistress greeted them with a welcome party of children lined up along the hallway in their white-and-navy school uniforms. One of the girls, roughly the same age as Trisha, had stepped up to her. She had reached out and touched Trisha's face, traced her brows over her glasses, her cheeks, her jaw. Her hand had smelled of paint—chemical yet earthy; her touch had been moist and cool.

"You're pretty," she had whispered with a smile that wondrously reached her eyes where her pupils were sheathed in cloudy white film. Her shy voice had been at odds with the bold touch of her hand, the unselfconscious whiff of her breath, and when she had stepped away, Trisha had felt punched in the chest by a feeling she couldn't place. An empty, hungry restlessness that had knocked her completely off-balance.

For the rest of the visit she had felt like a balloon with a leak, pressure siphoning out of her pores and slipping through the silk kurta her mother insisted she wear for public appearances. She had carried the feeling back to the palace with her, like a parasite inside her body she couldn't expel.

Hours later, her father had found her hiding in the room she shared with her older sister, Nisha, curled up on the four-poster bed the rajkumaris had slept on since the first maharaja built the palace in the 1600s. Often at night, her brothers and sister and cousins gathered on the huge bed and pretended it was a battleship from which they conquered the world. The warmth of the teakwood posts had a way of stealing into Trisha's bones, and the quilted silk of the coverlets had a way of anchoring her until she felt invincible.

But that day Trisha had felt afloat on it, unanchored. Unable to bring herself back from the gray-washed walls of the orphanage. From the sightless children working in rows at the long workshop tables under ceiling fans that turned the summer air with a ponderous buzz and scattered the smell of ink and shaved wood around the room. They had stamped and glued, the rhythm of their movements keeping time to their chatter as knickknacks and toys gathered into piles in the baskets beside them.

"What about today bothered you?" her father had asked when he found her. Back then he still cared to come looking for her when she was lost.

Try as she might Trisha had not been able to articulate what she was feeling.

HRH had lowered himself into the armchair next to the bed and waited. The quintessential prince, his spine straight but not stiff, his strength at once shaming her and making her want to be just like him. God, she had wanted so badly to be just like him.

"It's important to identify what bothers you," he had said in that beautifully clipped diction that always became more pronounced when they were in Sripore. "If you can't pinpoint what bothers you, how will you fix it?"

He'd waited, his silence insisting that she move her focus from wallowing in her sadness to defining it, turning it active and curious instead of passive and consuming. Finally, it had come to her. What she was feeling was anger. Rage that only felt like sadness because it made a horrid mix with helplessness.

"They shouldn't be blind." She had sat up, blinking away her tears, embarrassed by how they pooled where her glasses dug into her cheeks. "Those children should be able to see. It's not fair!"

Leaning forward only the slightest bit, he had thrown a pointed glance around the gilded room. "Families like ours don't get to complain about the unfairness of how fortune is distributed. Guilt is a waste of time. The fact that you have the things you have isn't wrong. Not understanding what you have is. You do understand what you have, right, beta?" He'd paused until she acknowledged the meaning in his brown gaze. "It's not just sight or comfort. What you have is that

brain, and access to resources. But even more important than
that is the thing you felt today. That compass inside that told
you something wasn't right. That is your greatest gift. So what
are you going to do about what you felt today?"

She'd drawn her knees into her chest. "I'm not God, Dad.
What can I possibly do to make someone who's blind see?"

He'd smiled then, one side of his mouth lifting. "Well, say
you did have that power. What would you need to know to
help a blind person see?" He'd held out his monogrammed
handkerchief. He only used those in India, where the servants
laundered and ironed them and arranged them on the clothes
butler with the rest of his dress for the day.

Trisha hopped off the bed, her heart racing as though she'd
run up the cliff all the way from the beach to the palace. She
took the proffered piece of cloth. It smelled like the palace,
like sandalwood and history, and yet somehow it also smelled
like her father, all-American like the Californian summer,
gravelly earth and fresh-cut grass.

"I'd find out the cause of their blindness." She lifted her
glasses and dashed away the wetness.

"Bingo!" This time his smile lifted both sides of his mouth
and lit up his eyes. His proud smile, the one Trisha lived for.
He cupped her cheeks and dropped the fiercest kiss on her
forehead, making joy burst inside her. "That's my girl. Go find
the cause. Then find out if their blindness can be fixed. Then
do something with what you find."

She had. She'd gone back to the orphanage. It had taken
that entire summer, but she'd met with the doctors, procured
the reports, and pored over them with HRH while her siblings

and cousins lay on beach blankets by the crashing ocean and played rummy and Monopoly with the staff. She learned that a lot of those children had early-cataract-induced blindness. Some had retinal dislocation. Issues that had surgical fixes that the orphanage could not afford.

When they came home to California, Trisha had organized a mission of ophthalmic surgeons across the Bay Area to work with the doctors affiliated with the orphanage. Then she had convinced her mother to put together one of her fund-raisers and they had raised enough money for fifteen surgeries. By the end of that year, six boys and nine girls had regained their eyesight. There had been another four children who hadn't been blind from birth. Their blindness had been related to the brain and none of the surgeons had been able to come up with solutions for it.

The project had gone on to become a global charity that performed eye surgeries. Her aunt who ran it had named it "Trisha for Sight." *Trisha* was the Sanskrit word for "thirst."

Trisha had gone on to choose skull-based neurosurgery as a specialization. She had never even considered anything else. Now here she was, the youngest member of Stanford's neurosurgery team, and all she could think about was the blind girl's hands on her face and how, try as she might, she couldn't remember her name. And the fact that she had no idea how she was going to tell her patient that she was going to go blind.

Standing outside Emma Caine's hospital room, she took a deep breath, and reminded herself that Emma had received a terminal diagnosis before she came to Trisha. Every surgeon Emma had gone to before had deemed her tumor inoperable.

When Trisha had figured out a way to operate on the tumor, no one on her team had been surprised. The word *genius* might have been tossed about amid cheers. And not for the first time either.

It wasn't like Trisha minded the label. She did love her work with the combined intensity of every single star in the sky, as her grandmother loved to say. Problem was, the word *genius* suggested ease. There had been nothing easy about developing the technology that was going to save Emma's life. Trisha had spent every waking moment for the past five years thinking about how to operate on tumors growing on brain tissue without damaging the brain tissue. Actually, that wasn't true. It wasn't just her waking moments; she spent most nights dreaming about her work too.

Trisha pushed into Emma's room and was greeted with a far-too-hopeful smile, and a very British "Hullo there, Dr. Raje!"

Emma had always said Trisha's last name perfectly, without Trisha ever having to help with her usual "it's Ra-jay just like the bird blue jay."

Despite the electrodes stuck to Emma's chest that fed her vitals to machines, despite the fact that she'd been in and out of hospitals for months, energy exploded out of Emma like the profusion of curls spilling from her high ponytail.

From the moment Emma had first walked into Trisha's office and declared that she wasn't ready to die, her case had consumed Trisha. Her almost fearlessly detached determination to beat her illness made her unlike any other patient Trisha had ever treated.

For the hundredth time that day Trisha reminded herself that she was going to save Emma's life.

"I have something for you, Dr. Raje." Emma's heterochromatic eyes—one brown and one nearly black—shone with excitement as she pointed to a gift-wrapped package propped against the wall next to the bed.

Someone must have brought the package in, Trisha realized with relief. That meant Emma wasn't alone today.

"Is your brother here?" Trisha asked, looking around the room in one of those ridiculous reflexes that followed a question like that, even though the room was obviously empty.

Emma had come to Trisha because Emma's brother was an old friend of Trisha's cousin Ashna. This happened a lot. Sometimes Trisha thought of her family's network as an actual fishnet that stretched all the way around the globe. She was constantly seeing patients referred to her by someone who knew someone who knew her family. When Ashna had heard about Emma's diagnosis from her brother, she had insisted Emma come to see Trisha, believing—correctly so, thank God—that Trisha would be able to help her.

Ashna and Trisha were the only two people in the family who had skipped inheriting the Raje social-charisma gene, so Trisha couldn't help but be curious about this mythical old friend of Ashna's. But she had yet to meet Emma's mysterious brother.

"He had to go to work, but he was here earlier." Emma always got the fiercest look in her eyes when she talked about her brother.

According to Ashna, when the man had found out about Emma's tumor, he had actually quit some sort of fancy job in Paris, packed up his life, and moved here. Granted, Emma had been given six months to live by the doctors she had seen before Trisha. But still, there was something insanely noble about making that kind of sacrifice, something crazy large-hearted about setting aside the life you'd built when your family needed you.

There had been a time when Trisha's own brother Yash would have dropped everything to help her, too. But that was before Yash's dreams had become the only thing that mattered.

"I can come back when your brother is here." Trisha picked up the package Emma was pointing at. "And you didn't have to get me a present!"

"Open it," Emma said, veritable sparks of excitement shining in her eyes.

Trisha stroked the thick handmade wrapping paper before peeling off the tape with care. Tucked inside was a canvas. Trisha reminded herself that an artist's sight was no more precious than anyone else's as she stared at the thickly broad-brushed oil painting and blinked as the vivid strokes swirled and danced forming what looked like . . . oh! Was that a fleshy orchid?

Nope. No. It was something a little more human than that.

Definitely a . . . umm . . . vagina? It was angled to look like lips, but there was no mistaking it, especially not if you'd studied anatomy. And they were . . . well, they were popping the cap off a bottle of Sam Adams.

For a full minute, all Trisha could do was blink at the painting like some sort of buffoon. Her face warmed and her lady parts, well, they did more than just warm—they clenched in the most mortifying way.

Emma grinned. "I call it *Vagina Before Head*."

Something like a cough choked out of Trisha. "It's . . . It's . . . "—*vivid?*—"wonderful . . ."

"It's inspired by you," Emma added, humor quirking her lips.

This time the laugh Trisha was trying to swallow burst out. If only Emma knew the truth. Given how much use Trisha got out of those particular muscles, popping anything with them was delusional at best. If not for the few and far between under-the-sheets sessions of surgeon-on-surgeon with Harry, things might have even started to atrophy.

"Thank you?" she said on a gulp, making Emma laugh until she teared up.

And it sobered Trisha. Her fingers stroked the painting, tracing the strength that Emma had harnessed with her brushstrokes. Once you got over the initial shock, it was an incredible piece. Not only had Emma understood and captured the force and mechanics of the action, but she'd topped it off with an almost operatic humor.

Maybe it was time for some Kegels?

For anything that made her feel stronger.

What was wrong with her? The news she had to deliver was *good* news, dammit!

Emma had to have seen something in Trisha's face because the amusement in her dual-colored gaze fizzled. "The results for the scans came in, didn't they?"

"Yes." Trisha pulled up a chair and sat down next to Emma's bed. For the first time in her life she envied her siblings their ability to tiptoe around feelings, to understand the darned things.

"Spit it out, Dr. Raje. I want to know." Emma's voice was adamant, her gaze steady.

Trisha did as she was told. "We knew there was a good chance that the tumor would be too close to the optic nerves. It isn't just close, it's wrapped around the nerves. Around both of them where they cross over."

Emma looked away. Her eyes sought out Trisha's hand, the one that was gripping her painting too tightly.

She said nothing.

Maybe Trisha should have waited for her to not be alone. Where the hell was this noble brother? "It's still operable and the prognosis is encouraging. But there's just no way to save the optic nerves." She almost apologized, but it was ridiculous to say sorry for keeping Emma alive. "The surgery is our best chance to save your life." All because Trisha had done nothing for years but work to make the impossible possible. "The robotic technology we'll be using is spectacular. It can remove tumor tissue with minimal damage to brain tissue. It's . . ." She trailed off when Emma bit down on her lip and squeezed her eyes shut.

A knock sounded on the half-open door, and the level of relief that flooded through Trisha bordered on pathetic. Her boss strode in, bringing with him his signature air of warmth and understanding.

"How are we this afternoon, Ms. Caine?" Dr. Entoff slid

his hands under the sanitizer dispenser, then rubbed them together like one ready to fell demons on Emma's behalf.

The poor man had tried hard over the years to teach Trisha some of that charming bedside manner. But if all her mother's training had been wasted on her, there wasn't much hope that anyone else might succeed. Trisha had never understood the big brouhaha over doctors' bedside manners. She understood tumors. Those she knew exactly how to navigate, and destroy. Shouldn't that be enough?

"Oh, I'm just peachy, ain't I?" Emma snapped, her British accent sharpening to a bite. "Dr. Raje here just told me that I'm going to go blind."

Dr. Entoff patted Emma's hand, making the exact right amount of eye contact. "I'm truly sorry, Emma. We can't control the location of the tumor, but we sure can remove it so it stops being a threat to your life."

Trisha felt another rush of relief. She had spent all morning convincing her boss that the procedure was the right way to go. The new technique was still experimental, and convincing Entoff to use it on this case hadn't been easy. A failed surgery would lead to bad press and bad press could kill the funding for further development of a technology that was going to save thousands of lives. But Trisha believed in this surgery enough to risk her career on it.

Emma's only response was a belligerent thrust of the jaw.

Entoff made his way to the workstation and calmly started clicking through Emma's records. "I know it's a lot to take in. I would urge you to take some time to process this news.

Discuss it with your family. We don't need to make any decisions today. There are a few other experimental treatments that can slow down tumor growth and possibly impact life expectancy."

Wait, what? Bedside manner was all well and dandy, but what fresh rubbish was this? Even if Entoff was only trying to keep the patient from going into full-blown panic, none of these experimental treatments were real options. Even if they did slow growth, without the surgery, the tumor would eventually get large enough to kill Emma, and the larger it grew, the smaller the chance of success with surgery would become. Giving her false hope just to make her feel like she had options made no sense to Trisha.

Before she could say anything, Emma turned a suddenly furious gaze on her. "Dr. Raje seems to think the surgery is my only option. Are you two not in agreement then?" Her tone had all the raw force of a bottle-cap-popping vagina.

Dr. Entoff channeled all the cool counterpressure of a beer bottle, and Trisha suddenly felt very much like a bent-up bottle cap. "We are in agreement that the surgery is the best option. But the technology is seminal—and if you feel like you want to explore other options, I want you to know that we will help you do that." He threw Trisha a placating look and she forced herself to swallow her objection. "Having said that, I want to be clear that Dr. Raje has been working on the technology for years, and if she believes it's ready, I would put my faith in her."

The look Emma threw Trisha was a punch to the gut. "And you think losing my sight is my only option, Dr. Raje?"

Trisha met her gaze. "Yes. Removing the tumor is the only way to save your life. And we can't remove the tumor and also salvage your optic nerves."

Emma looked at her painting again, and Trisha tried to ignore the desperate pain in her eyes. Skirting the truth was not her job.

"I need to think about it," Emma said finally.

Trisha stood, hugging the painting to her chest. But before she could get out the arguments that rushed up her throat Dr. Entoff cut her off.

"Of course," he said. "We have more tests to run before we can schedule anything. Dr. Raje will go over the details of the procedure tomorrow and answer any questions you have."

Again, Trisha almost objected, but then she thought about the noble brother. Maybe if he were present it would be easier to make Emma see sense.

Instead of responding, Emma stared off into the distance, no longer willing to meet Trisha's eyes. For the first time since they'd met, instead of hope, despair wrapped itself around Emma, and it caught at something inside Trisha like a sharp hook piercing skin.

"Take heart, Trisha. We're saving her life." Her boss patted her shoulder kindly as they took the elevator to their offices. "Sometimes you need a soft touch."

Trisha forced a smile. A soft touch hadn't gotten her where she was.

They stepped out of the elevator. "That's better. Now let's turn that smile real, shall we?" He pointed to the surgeon's lounge. "Care for a cup of coffee and some good news?" His grin was so wide, Trisha stopped midstep and turned to him. She knew what he was going to say even before he opened his mouth. "I just talked to the foundation director. He's been trying to reach you. Your funding was approved."

Trisha slapped her hand across her mouth but a squeak still escaped her. And then another one. A ten-million-dollar grant, for shit's sake! She had just won her department its largest grant in history. They were going to fund the most ambitious multicenter clinical research for robotic brain surgery ever conceived.

"This proves that the rumors are true," Entoff said. "We have a genius in our midst!" He had never made her work for his proud smile, but the one he was flashing at her now—the one that made him look like a man who was blessing the day he hired her—it made her want to pump her fist in vindication and shout *Yes! Take that, Dad!*

Instead, she took the hand he held out and thanked him for being such a great boss and mentor.

"No, Dr. Raje," he said through that proud smile, "what I am is a very lucky boss."

Damn straight! she wanted to yell. But she thanked him instead with all the poise she could muster.

Coffee was probably a bad idea given the adrenaline racing through her, but she took the cup her boss handed her, thanked the two colleagues who congratulated her with somewhat less enthusiasm, and carried the cup back to her office along with Emma's painting. The first thing she did there was push the door shut and let out one woot . . . okay, two! But her heart wouldn't stop racing. She'd done it. She'd done something no one else had ever done before her.

Without thinking about it, she dialed Nisha's number. Her big sister was the only person who really understood how hard Trisha had worked on her grant and on this case. Her call went straight to voice mail. Right. Today was the big day.

Or more accurately, today was yet another big day. Tonight was yet another preannouncement shindig for her brother. Possibly the tenth "small celebration" Ma and Nisha had organized in the four weeks since Yash had decided to finally announce his candidacy for governor of California.

Within the last five years the venerable U.S. Attorney for the Northern District of California, Yash Raje, had foiled a terrorist attack on Alcatraz, hunted down a fifty-billion-dollar Ponzi scheme a bunch of venture capitalists were running out of Cupertino, and been instrumental in convincing the largest airplane manufacturer in the world to move to California. So really, who were they kidding with all this hush-hush around announcing his gubernatorial plans? If the people of the great state of California hadn't guessed his intent by now, they were too idiotic to be worth governing.

Nonetheless, Nisha—the only one in the family who still discussed Yash's career with Trisha—had assured her that there was a method to these things and currently that method involved their family systematically courting California's elite to shore up Yash's path so it held steady beneath his feet as he marched toward Sacramento and the destiny he had been groomed for since the day of his birth. Nisha managed Yash's political campaigns, so she would know.

"Crazy busy right now. Need something?" Her sister's text buzzed through. Trisha imagined Nisha, her hair elegantly twisted on top of her head, a steaming cup of coffee in her hand as she wrestled down the million moving parts that seemed to make up these events. Even the word "event" gave Trisha heart palpitations. Nisha, on the other hand, was a badass deftly putting out fires as they exploded in tiny mushroom clouds around her. For their brother.

Trisha realized with a start that she was still holding Emma's painting—a painting about strength that she had inspired. The feeling of getting her skin caught in a hook tugged at her again, bringing with it a restlessness she couldn't quite contain. She thought about Emma being by herself when Trisha had broken the news. She thought about the brother who had dropped his life and moved across continents to help her through it. Setting the canvas carefully on the desk she stared at her sister's message on her phone. Then before she could stop herself, she tapped out her response. "Were you serious when you said I should come to tonight's dinner?" She hit send before she could delete the words. Then instantly regretted doing it.

Within seconds her phone rang.

"Seriously?" Her sister sounded exactly like someone charting a war from a control tower.

Trisha couldn't get herself to bring up the grant. She'd do it at the dinner. Because maybe it was time to go to one. "You've been saying I should come," she said tentatively. "I'm free to-night." The high of winning the grant had to have shrunk her brain.

The awkward beat of silence was swallowed up by a voice asking Nisha something about flowers. Nisha let off a string of instructions that sounded to Trisha like dolphins clicking, entirely indecipherable.

"Okay. That's great," Nisha said distractedly, when she came back on the line. "I'll see you at six then." That was it? Nothing about the years of campaign events Trisha had missed. Nothing about how HRH would react when he found out she was going to be there. "Do you have something to wear?"

Of course she didn't. Thankfully, it was a rhetorical question. One her sister always asked before she decided exactly what Trisha should wear.

"Okay, I'll take care of it." Something clattered ominously in the background. "Gotta go. And do not be late. I mean it."

Just that easily Nisha was done. A two-minute conversation to condense all those years of Nisha trying to mend the fences Trisha had burned down. And by "mend" Trisha meant "ignore." Nisha subscribed to the ostrich philosophy for conflict resolution—if you acted like a problem didn't exist, well, then it didn't. In that respect Nisha was every inch their mother's daughter.

HRH and Yash, on the other hand, were incapable of ever letting anything go.

It was too late to have second thoughts now. Trisha walked around her desk and sank into her chair.

Crap, who was she kidding? Second thoughts stampeded through her like a herd of wildebeests sensing a ravenous lion. She pressed her forehead into her desk, then banged it against the cool wood. She was a genius, dammit! Surely that meant she could handle a family dinner. Even one she wasn't welcome at.

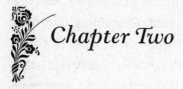

Chapter Two

It had been fifteen years. Fifteen years since Trisha had been shut out of her brother's political career, the family's most precious dream. Finding excuses to avoid Yash's rallies, and speeches, and celebrations for so long hadn't been easy but she'd managed it, and the family had long since heaved a sigh of relief and stopped involving her. For fifteen years she had existed on the fringes of her family—where all was seemingly normal, because they were the Rajes, after all, but where the fact that she had almost destroyed her brother's life hung in the air at all times, like a truth bubble ready to pop.

But Yash was finally running for governor—surely that meant things had turned out fine in the end. Maybe it was time to let the past go.

She maneuvered her Tesla up the curving, deeply forested drive that led to her parents' Woodside home. The mechanical gates recognized her car and slid open under the wrought-iron arch that spelled out the name of the house she had grown up in: The Anchorage.

A rare nod to the old country. Houses in India all had names. Not just the mansions and the estates but every little bungalow and building had a name. Looking for the often grandly ill-fitting names displayed on the houses had been one of Trisha's favorite pastimes as a child. Crumbling four-floor apartment blocks called "Royal Towers." Tiny stone cottages called "Raj Mahal." Metal placards and stenciled signs that proclaimed self-worth and told you that they were something more than just brick and concrete.

When Trisha's parents had built this house, nestled into five acres of gorgeous redwood forests, her grandmother had called it "the Anchorage." The name had been a tribute to her oldest son who had been a naval officer and the twenty-second maharaja before he died in the plane crash that had altered the family's destiny. Only the family ever called their home by the name Aji had given it. To everyone else it was just a number on a private street. The way the rest of California did it.

Trisha pulled to a stop under the white-columned porte cochere. A caravan of parked cars signaled that the dinner was in full swing inside, underscoring the fact that she was late.

Because, yes, she was late. She hadn't meant to be. Not on the day when she had recklessly decided to unfreeze herself out of banishment. Not when Nisha had probably taken the time out of her crazy day to prep their parents and Yash so this would be as easy as possible on Trisha.

Trisha hated not knowing how to handle things. Why couldn't everything be like surgery? She had just excised an adenoma on a thirteen-year-old's pituitary gland and known exactly what to do. Sure, the surgery had taken two hours longer than expected, and made her late, but a thirteen-year-old girl was going to get her life back. And sure, Trisha could have let another attending surgeon pick up the emergency surgery, but it had been the exact kind of procedure she loved. Complicated. The tumor had gone rogue and grown talons into brain tissue. Trisha had needed the sweet satisfaction of snuffing out every bit of that baby after her unexpected bout of bravado with her sister.

As if facing HRH and Yash weren't scary enough, the idea of socializing with people she barely knew made Trisha want to gnaw her limbs off. Maybe she should turn around and go back to her condo.

She groaned the kind of groan one can only groan in the privacy of one's car, loud and pathetic, and looked up at the bright white stucco facade, the marble columns, the black plantation shutters with Japanese roses and jasmine spilling from window boxes, and focused on the click of belonging that only ever happened here, in this place that mapped her life, this place where the memories of her at every age would always live.

Stepping out of the car, she handed her keys to the parking valet, a preening teen dressed like he was off to prom. One of Ma's friends' kids looking to impress her, no doubt. Ma was, after all, the Go-To Goddess for summer-internships-that-look-good-on-college-applications with her direct line to:

1. The managing director and head of general surgery at everyone's favorite hospital, HRH, Dr. Shree Raje.

2. The United States Attorney for the Northern District of California, the most illustrious Yash Raje, and . . .

3. The youngest judge on the San Francisco county court,
   Trisha's half-angel, half-saint brother-in-law, Neel Graff.

Speaking of said sainted brother-in-law, there was Neel now, smiling his sainted smile at Trisha, all dapper in what had to be an Armani jacket because her sister didn't understand why anyone would want to wear suits that weren't Armani. Although how Nisha could tell the difference between one suit and another Trisha would never understand. He tried to wave from under the assortment of garment bags and shoeboxes spilling from his hands. Only Neel could look just as comfortable buried under Nisha's fashion emergency stash as with a gavel in hand doing his best by juvenile offenders.

Trisha thanked the prom-boy valet, who seemed a little too eager to get into her Tesla, and slid a few of the garment bags off Neel's arm while dropping a kiss on his cheek. "Thanks, Neel. I'm so sorry to put you through this again."

"Of course. It makes these things kinda fun." He grinned and straightened his rimless glasses. If he was surprised that she was here, he hid it well and she loved him for it. "Nisha wants you to wear the green one." He nodded at the green garment bag Trisha had taken from him. "But she thought you should have choices."

They smiled knowingly at each other. If Nisha had decided on the green one, the green one it would be. Trisha was currently wearing standard-issue blue scrubs with a coffee stain that spanned her entire torso, which pretty much summed up her fashion expertise.

"Which shoes?" she asked.

Neel handed her a box and glanced at the stain painted across her chest. "Tough surgery?" He pointed to the cobblestone path that circled around the side of the house.

She followed him toward the pool house. "Hit the wrong artery. You wouldn't believe the force of the blood."

"You've been watching *Kill Bill* again, haven't you?"

"It's surgeon catnip. I can't stop." Smiling, she twisted around and pushed the door to the pool house open with her back. "Is Nisha going to come and help with my hair?" Because if she didn't get to tell her sister about the grant in the next two minutes, she was going to burst. Plus, she had to know how Nisha had managed to break it to their father that she was going to be here.

"Your hair looks just—" Neel's cell phone buzzed and he looked down at it. Her own phone sat dead in her pocket. She'd forgotten to charge it. "I'm not supposed to tell you your hair looks nice. Nisha's sending someone. And you've got to hurry. There's an angry emoji. She can't believe you're late." He kept his face carefully neutral as he dumped the rest of the items he was carrying on the couch.

As he headed for the door, he stopped and turned around, reading off his phone again. "She says it's okay. Don't worry. Smiley emoji." Neel did the most adorable subtle eye rolls he thought no one saw. "And she wants you to know you won't be sorry you came." He looked up from his wife's message, the slightest flush on his cheeks. "An emoji's winking at you, and fanning itself. And—oh, for heaven's sake. Just hurry up and get in there. Apparently, there's a butt in there you have to see to believe."

TRISHA PUT HER dress on in record time. Not a small achievement given how complicated it was. Admittedly, it was a gorgeous green thing, but it was made up of innumerable stretchy silken bands that wrapped around her like a full-body postsurgical dressing, and it took almost as long to put on. Nisha insisted green went well with Trisha's neither-too-dark-nor-too-light brown eyes, and her neither-too-dark-nor-too-light skin. It came down to just a little above her knees—a length Nisha insisted worked best for her five-foot-eight-inch frame that bordered on being too broad. And it was off-the-shoulder, a style her fashionista sister had undoubtedly chosen because it went well with Trisha's neither-too-curly-nor-too-straight hair that was cut to hit just above her freakishly long neck.

She slipped her feet into the precariously high wedges and left the pool house feeling somewhat equipped to prodigal her way back into the fold. And ran right into J-Auntie, their housekeeper, waiting just outside the door in her usual silent-ninja style. Trisha prided herself for not jumping in fright.

"Trisha Baby, His Highness wants to see you."

For Trisha's entire life J-Auntie had only ever called HRH that, but it still made Trisha want to giggle like a six-year-old every time she heard it in that dead-serious tone.

J-Auntie didn't crack a smile. No big surprise, she never smiled at anyone except Trisha's two brothers. "He's in his office. He wants you to use the public entrance."

With that superominous directive she strode away in measured steps, her body as severely held as her supertight jet-black bun.

So Trisha's plan to avoid HRH wasn't going to work then.

She couldn't quite remember when she and her siblings had started calling their father HRH, but it fit him perfectly. All you had to do was picture a photograph of a modern monarch of an Eastern nation in a pretentious glossy magazine—thick silver hair, proud brow, patrician nose—and there you had His Royal Highness the twenty-third maharaja of the princely state of Sripore. Even though it was a title he'd unexpectedly inherited after the death of his older brother.

The title meant nothing in America, of course, and HRH worked hard to keep it out of the family's public narrative here, where assimilation was the word. The title no longer officially meant anything in India, either. Not that the staff at the Sagar Mahal or the media put too much stock in the Indian government's stand on the matter. They were royalty, and that was a matter of blood and destiny, and Trisha's grandfather had proven it by reclaiming the family's power by throwing himself into the freedom struggle and then becoming a democratically elected member of Parliament as soon as India finally overthrew the British Raj in 1947.

Three decades after that, HRH, a second son, had migrated to America hoping for a grand adventure and a little bit of his own independence from all that royal legacy and ambition. Things hadn't turned out quite the way he had expected and now all he ever seemed to focus on was legacy and ambition.

His summoning her was entirely unexpected because there were currently at least fifty people in the house who needed to be awed and inspired, and the fact that he was spending the time on her was more than a bit disconcerting. Would he throw her out? That wasn't quite the HRH way. Silent disapproval

had so much more gravitas. They had skirted each other for fifteen years, through family gatherings and working at the same
hospital. It was amazing how easy it was to shut out problem-
atic parts of your life when your work took up the entirety of
your time and attention.

She had even forgotten when exactly she gave up bemoan-
ing the loss of her title as her father's precious little girl.

Could Dr. Entoff have told him about the grant?

Don't get excited. Do not.

He had to have heard about the grant. They never interacted
at work—they worked in different departments and it was a
big hospital. Not too big for a thriving grapevine though. The
excitement that bubbled inside her made her a certified idiot.
Her grant, no matter how groundbreaking, couldn't crack the
surface of her father's disapproval. Nothing could. Not after
what she had done.

As instructed, she used the outside entrance to his office
and took the half flight of stairs that led up to the heavy
leaded-glass doors. The night was unusually warm for March
but not warm enough to justify the sweat that gathered under
her arms. With a cursory knock she let herself into the small
mahogany-paneled waiting area. It was empty, as expected.
She made her way through the open door of his office.

There he stood, across the pristinely ordered room infused
with the smell of the leather-bound books lining the walls:
HRH, in all his HRH glory. Perfectly groomed and tailored
to highlight his tall, proud bearing. She sent a silent thank-
you to her sister for making her look halfway civilized and for
these heels that suddenly gave her a modicum of power.

He was staring out the window at the elegantly lit patio with a breathtaking view of the mountains. It was sprinkled with guests, who were no doubt contemplating the beauty of the estate and California's good fortune that Yash Raje was about to deliver them from all their woes.

"I had told you this wasn't over." He opened with that, and without bothering to turn and look at Trisha.

Whatever was in his voice, it certainly wasn't pride. Strike off Option One. This wasn't about the grant. Something told her it wasn't about the fact that she had decided to show up today either.

"What—" she began to ask, but he cut her off.

"That friend of yours is back in town." The words reached her in slow motion, one clipped syllable at a time.

The sheen of perspiration she'd acquired from the stress of seeing him picked up the chill of his office and froze against her skin.

There was only one person he could be talking about, only one person who would dredge up all his anger at Trisha and trap it in his voice. Julia.

Julia was back in town?

Trisha hadn't heard from her college roommate since their disastrous friendship ended in their sophomore year at Berkeley. Trisha's family hadn't even let her talk to Julia before they ran her out of town. She tried to breathe around the shame. All those years, and yet the kick of betrayal landed hard and swift between her ribs.

"Has she been in touch?" He still didn't turn around and look at her.

Everything inside Trisha singed at the edges and burned inward. The pride for her grant, the anticipation of trying to make amends. All of it gone as though it had never existed in the first place. All her words were gone too. She shouldn't have been surprised. There was nothing new about words failing her, especially when it came to her father. At least not since she had allowed Julia Wickham into their lives.

"Now is not the time to withdraw into your shell," her father snapped impatiently.

"Thanks, Dad, now that you've issued the order, I'll just stop with the withdrawing." That's what she wanted to say. But no one spoke to him that way. "Does Yash know?" she whispered instead, working to unlock her jaw.

Finally he turned around, his face flushed with rage. "No one is to tell Yash! Is that clear? He does not need the added stress of this. Steele is considering running against him in the primaries. Steele is a worthy adversary. A viable option for the party who could ruin everything. Our focus has to be making sure that does not happen."

Trisha had no doubt that between Dad, Yash, and their considerable armaments, they would come up with something.

"You need to make sure she stays away from him."

And how exactly was she supposed to do that? She hadn't had any contact with the woman in fifteen years. She had only found out that she was in town three seconds ago. *But sure, Dad, whatever you say.*

The disappointment in his eyes would have hurt. If she weren't so used to it. "He had a spotless record, Trisha. Spotless."

Didn't she know that? No one had stopped bludgeoning her

with that little fact. She hadn't stopped bludgeoning herself with it. She had done this, created a weak link in the chain of her brother's otherwise flawless candidacy. She could apologize again, but how many times could you apologize for the same transgression? Not that all her apologies had ever meant anything to the family.

"If she makes any contact with you, you will report it to me immediately and you will not engage."

Trisha suppressed the urge to laugh. As if she needed those orders. The last thing on earth she wanted was to have anything to do with Julia ever again. And if Julia was stupid enough to try and contact Trisha, her father's spies would make reporting anything to him redundant.

"Yash makes the official announcement next month. There's no margin for error anymore," he said, enunciating each word as though speaking to an imbecile. "Does you being here today have anything to do with her being back in town?"

"Excuse me? What exactly are you accusing me of?" That's what she wanted to say. "Of course not. I had no idea she was back." That's what she said instead, but at least she let her anger leak into her voice.

He had the gall to look taken aback at her tone.

Suddenly she wanted him to tell her to leave. Suddenly, she didn't want to be here, didn't want to face Yash.

"This dinner is important to your brother."

Really? A dinner to gather support for his campaign for governor is important to Yash? *Gee, Dad, thanks for filling me in!*

A deep frown folded between his brows. "Was it too much to expect that you be on time?"

She almost blinked. From her father's lips that sounded practically like an invitation to rejoin the Force. But she knew better. All this meant was that he wanted her where he could keep an eye on her.

That was it. They were done. He walked past her and left the office.

She may not be as infallible and brilliant as her oldest sibling, but she was pretty sure that meant she had been dismissed.

"Bye, Dad," she whispered to the empty room and followed him out.

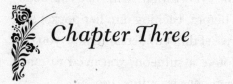

Chapter Three

"There you are, finally!" Her mother's greeting made Trisha look up from adjusting the straps on the miraculously comfortable wedges Nisha had selected knowing full well Trisha's talent for wobbling gracelessly in any other type of heels.

Ma, on the other hand, at sixty-five could pull off four-inch stilettos like no one else. To say nothing of how she rocked a hot-pink pantsuit. Not that anything she ever wore looked less than spectacular on her marathoner's body. Her ex-Bollywood-star face didn't hurt either. It was a good thing Nisha helped Trisha with clothes, because having to take fashion advice from a mother who wore everything better than you—and two sizes smaller—was just more torture than anyone should have to endure.

"You look lovely, Ma." Every bit of the sulky awe she always felt around her mother bubbled up in her voice, making her feel like she was groping for approval as though it were high-hanging fruit on the tree she had fallen woefully far from. "I'm sorry I'm late."

Her mother responded by tucking a lock of hair behind

Trisha's ear, doling out understanding—for her lateness, for the mess she had made, for everything—with her characteristic graceful nonchalance before reaching into her pocket and extracting a pair of solitaires. "I don't understand how you can stand to go bare-eared. You're a surgeon, you need to make sure your appearance doesn't get masculine, too."

Trisha took the earrings—and a calming breath—and slipped them on without bothering to answer. The list of things her mother would never understand about her was endless, especially where her appearance was concerned. Trisha would do anything to never let her mother see her in scrubs, clean or perpetually coffee stained.

"There you go, now you look like my Shasha," Ma said, using Trisha's nickname. "Regal, just like your dad." Ma paused reverently the way she always did when she mentioned HRH—a pause so perfectly pitched it did the work of clashing cymbals to herald his magnificence. "By the way, there are at least three men in that room any single girl would kill for." And there it was, the perpetual mantle of Trisha's singleness. It had taken Ma precisely three sentences to bring up her grand flaw.

Funny how Ma had suddenly developed a problem with Trisha's singleness the day she had graduated from med school. Until then Ma's only concern ever had been Trisha's grades and her career path. It was like being raised as one person and then being miraculously expected to leap across a chasm to being an entire different person. It reminded her of the chalk painting in *Mary Poppins* that magically transferred you between realities.

Trisha tried not to slouch like a gangly teen who didn't have a date for homecoming. She wanted to tell her mother about the three surgeries she had done today, about Emma, about the grant. But before she could get any of that out, her mother took her hand and led her through the crowded living room where Trisha hoped she wasn't about to introduce her to these men who supposedly turned single girls murderous.

The idea of her mother playing matchmaker for her was so mortifying she briefly considered telling her about Harry, her maybe-boyfriend-but-more-likely-casual-acquaintance-with-benefits. But the only thing Ma might find worse than her daughter's inability to form relationships in her thirties was her daughter's inability to know if she was actually in the relationship she might be in.

Suppressing another groan, she followed Ma into the dining room where the twenty-seater cherrywood table had been moved against one mahogany-paneled wall. Some fifty-odd people were scattered in groups around the room, their elegantly pitched voices creating nothing more than a harmonious din. The sixteenth-century Belgian crystal chandelier that usually lit up the table when it was just the family gathered around had been raised and dimmed. What the guests didn't know was that the king of Belgium had presented it to her great-great-grandfather after they had become friends at Oxford.

The chandelier had hung for over a century in the Sagar Mahal. Her oldest uncle had shipped it to California as a housewarming gift when HRH built the Anchorage. There was a story there, involving a cricket ball and three young princes, and emergency superglue repairs to keep their father from finding out. HRH never talked about his brothers anymore, but Trisha remembered him laughing about it with Ma long ago.

As Ma stopped to let someone gush over her pantsuit, Trisha did a quick sweep of the room for HRH, but she didn't spot him, thank God. She forced herself not to think about the expression on his face when he had informed her that the worst mistake of her life was back to haunt her.

Her sister wasn't here either, which was frustrating. As soon as she told Nisha about the grant, she would feel less like pond scum. All she needed was for just one person to know and be excited for her. Telling Ma could wait until later, when she was less preoccupied.

Someone else waved Ma over and she gave Trisha's hair another pat and tuck. "I'm glad you're here." The pain she let slip into her eyes proved the ostrich theory wasn't failproof. How had Trisha never thought about how hard it had to be for Ma to deal with Trisha's issues with Dad and Yash? "Make sure you find Yash and congratulate him before you go hide behind your sister, okay?" With that she clicked away toward a group of political wives who opened up their tight circle at her approach.

"Of course," Trisha mumbled—because Ma was gone and couldn't lecture her about how it was uncultured to mumble— and scanned the heads in suits to find her brother's halo.

There he was. The soon-to-be governor of California. He looked as serene as ever, reminding her of the mythological Prince Karna from the stories Aji loved to tell. Born encased in armor and glowing from within, eternally protected by his father the Sun God himself. *Yup, that would be our Yash.*

Trisha watched as he did his practiced politician hug thing

with the suit he was talking to. One hand on the shoulder, the other in a handshake, grip firm yet friendly. *I'm here for you,* that gesture said; *I can fix everything.*

She knew her brother meant it, believed it with every cell of his being, but the ease of the gesture made her despondent. It swallowed up the brother he had been, her Yash. And even after all these years of being shut out, she missed that brother every single day. That was the thing about Yash; even perfect strangers found it impossible to forget him after having met him once. Charisma, the media called it. Imagine being loved by him, she wanted to tell them. And then losing him.

Not that he had ever said an angry word to her after Julia had violated him in every way possible because Trisha had let her. There had been no confrontation, just a slow-bleeding falling-out, aided by the monstrous demands of their work and the constant presence of a plethora of people to hide behind at family gatherings. He didn't even seem to notice, but standing here watching him like this brought back the full force of how very much the loss still hurt.

As if he could hear her thoughts, Yash's eyes met Trisha's over the bald patch of the man who had practically melted into an awestruck puddle beneath his touch. Yash was the only one of Trisha's siblings and cousins who had inherited their grand-father's gray eyes. A gray so unique *Cosmo* had felt the need to coin a term for it—Yash-Raje-Gray—in last month's issue, the one that had featured him on a list of the country's hottest politicians. What they didn't know was that it was a genetic marking of their blue-blooded family, always inherited only by one child in every generation. It had skipped a generation for the first time with her father and his siblings, but it had returned with Yash. Of course it had.

When he first spotted her, those eyes lit up, and his smile flashed wide and carefree for a full instant before disappearing again behind the memories that had built a wall between them. He pulled on his public servant's I'm-your-man mask that Trisha hated to admit wasn't a mask anymore, but who her brother had now become. They had both come so far from being two kids who loved sneaking out the attic window to sit up on the roof where all they could see were the hills and all they could be was who they were.

He walked up to her and leaned in as if to give her a hug, but then she moved in the wrong direction and it all turned terribly awkward and he shook her hand instead.

"Congratulations, Yash," she said, fighting to channel her mother's graceful nonchalance instead of the stiffness that gripped her.

"How's my favorite skull-based neurosurgeon?" Only Yash would use the exact right terminology to describe his sister's surgical specialty.

"Super. Destroying rogue cells across the world one skull at a time. How's my favorite messiah of the masses?"

He frowned at that, hurt flashing in his eyes. His mouth twitched as though he had something to say, as though he almost cared enough to say it. But then someone across the room caught his eye, someone more important than her, and he gave her an apologetic smile so practiced she wanted to punch him.

But then he raised a finger at the person, asking for a minute, and looked at her again. "I'm glad you decided to come today, Trisha," he said sincerely, striking her speechless with surprise. "Is everything okay?" His eyes flicked briefly to the person who was waiting for him.

Trisha was tempted to grab his arm and apologize for missing years' worth of his events, apologize for everything, again. She wanted to puke out all the mad highs and lows of her day at his feet the way she used to do back in school. She wanted to tell him that Julia was in town and HRH was hiding it from him. She wanted to do it so badly, she had to press a fist into her belly to hold it inside. In the end all she could say was, "Of course everything's okay. Go."

He did his pat and pass-over thing and moved on with a promise to catch up soon.

It was more than she had gotten from him in a very long time. Instead of feeling better, guilt grew spikes inside her. Before the full wallop of it overwhelmed her, she was saved by her sister's voice.

"Don't you look lovely!" Nisha said as she strolled over. Finally, a family member who knew exactly what she needed to hear.

Trisha grabbed her sister in a too-tight, too-long hug, then realized how ridiculous she was being and let her go.

Nisha cupped her cheek—always the big sister—and studied her handiwork. "The forest green is great on you. And the ankle straps on those wedges make your legs look endless. How is it fair that you can look this hot without even trying?"

Trisha grinned, because it was a fact universally acknowledged that she was an approval slut when it came to her family. She was about to burst forth with the story of her brilliant funding coup and Emma's surgery when the wide doors that led to the tiered wooden deck opened and the guests started to pour out into the night for the fireworks display that was about to start. Unlike her, Nisha felt the need to greet every single person who passed by.

"My two favorite Rajes," a warm and familiar voice said, and both Trisha and Nisha leaned over to give Dorna Matunge a hug. Dorna was one of the first female neurosurgeons in the country and also one of the first African American physician scientists. She had retired years before Trisha joined the neurosurgery department, but she was a dear friend of HRH and Ma's, and an early supporter of Yash Raje for Governor.

More recently she had also become Trisha's patient. She was wearing a black-and-gold sari and carrying it off with poise that belied her eighty-five years and the fact that she'd been fighting cancer for the past five of those. "I don't understand why you Raje women don't wear these beautiful saris more. Mina bought me this one from India, but if she's not going to wear hers, I might as well steal all of them!"

Trisha smiled. "I'd wear one if I could carry it as well as you do, Dr. Matunge," she said worshipfully. But she couldn't imagine wearing a sari at a dinner like this. It would feel too much like a costume outside of an Indian wedding or a Diwali celebration.

Dorna patted her shoulder. "I'll see you at my appointment next week." Then she turned to Nisha. "The food was exquisite. I'm going to need the number of the chef!" And with that she followed the crowd to the patio.

As Trisha watched her walk away, she realized with horror that being this late meant she had arrived *after* the caterers had cleared out the food.

Her stomach let out a long, incredibly inelegant groan. Nisha's eyes widened before she broke into giggles exactly the way her daughter, Mishka, did.

It wasn't funny. Trisha had yet to eat today. "Please tell me the food isn't entirely gone. I think I'll die if I don't eat right now."

Nisha shook her head. "Not again. How can you wait until you're dying of hunger before realizing you're hungry?"

It was annoying as hell, but Nisha was right. Trisha found it impossible to remember to eat—or do anything else—when she got lost in her work. Then when she did remember, her hunger kicked in with such force that she could scarf down an entire pizza without stopping to breathe.

More laughter came from her sister, and no understanding whatsoever of her predicament. "Mishka is exactly like you. But she's eight, for heaven's sake!"

Her niece was the world's most perfect human, so Trisha had no problem with the comparison.

"Did you go upstairs and see her?" her sister asked walking with her toward the kitchen.

"Of course I did." Trisha had made a quick detour to the upper floor after her disastrous heart-to-heart with HRH. It was a matter of habit; the first thing she always did when she came to the Anchorage was go see their oldest cousin, Esha, and their grandmother. Both Esha and Aji lived here but they never left the upper floor when outsiders were in the house because Esha couldn't handle the stimulation. Since this was a grown-ups' party, Mishka got to stay up there with them while the rest of the family did what it did best: awe the good citizens of California.

When Trisha had gone up to their suite, Aji, Esha, and Mishka had been completely absorbed in their game of rummy. So Trisha had done no more than drop quick kisses on all three heads before coming back down to join the party. For years she had come and gone to the house and blocked out what had grown into the soul of the family—Yash's political career. Being here today she wondered how she'd done it.

"Mishka is having fun with Esha and Aji up there. Good luck taking her home tonight."

"I wasn't planning on taking her home tonight." Nisha's eyes danced. "Neel has the day off tomorrow and I've been plying the good judge with fine wine all evening." Her smile turned so suggestive that Trisha blushed, and she remembered that her sister had promised her something!

"Hey, I believe I was promised a butt that has to be seen to be believed!"

DJ CAINE STOPPED short at the kitchen door. His hand stilled on the heavy, tastefully antiqued brass handle. Something about the voice on the other side locked him in place and made him smile. DJ hadn't smiled all day.

"I'd rather hear about the promised butt than your . . . your plans for later tonight," the voice said. "And if you tell me he's gone because the dress you chose for me took half an hour to put on, I'm going to kill you with my bare hands!"

DJ couldn't help but laugh at that. There was something

about that voice, husky and sultry with an underlying lilt of sweetness. It hit him exactly the way the blast of sunshine had hit him when he'd stepped out of San Francisco airport last month. And it made the tension that had clamped his shoulders all day ease in a quick rush. He leaned his forehead into the door and listened, enjoying how completely comfortable the person was laughing at herself.

DJ was almost afraid to push the door open and see what she looked like. A strange kind of anticipation bubbled inside him. It had been so long since he'd felt anything but a gnawing sadness that he indulged himself by standing there and soaking it in. Just for a few seconds before he got his arse back to work.

"There you are, boss," Rajesh said behind him and DJ spun around with a little prayer that his assistant didn't come bearing bad news. "The timer on the soufflés just went off and I'm not risking my job by—"

DJ sprinted past Rajesh and was at the ovens before the kid could finish that thought.

A chef never runs in the kitchen, Andre had taught him. *Never ever.* The soft scrape of Andre's French *r*'s sounded in DJ's head as he skidded to a stop in front of the ovens. He took a moment to allow his hands to steady before pulling the water bath lined with soufflé ramekins out. Plump and perfect. He held his breath, counting the seconds to see if they'd hold. He had yet to sink a soufflé. But every single time he made them, the experience shaved a bloody month off his life.

Leaning over the tray he inhaled deeply, letting the steam-laden aroma flood all the way through him. The soft green clouds edged with the most delicate golden crusts smelled as perfect as they looked. Pistachio with a hint of saffron. Was there even such a thing as a hint of saffron? It was the loudest understated spice, like a soft-spoken person you couldn't stop listening to. Like the hidden lilts inside a well-held aria. Like the beauty within making what someone looked like on the outside meaningless, slowly, one encounter at a time. No matter how subtle you tried to make it, saffron always shone through, it became the soul of your preparation.

He nodded at Rajesh, who stood at the ready with the cashews DJ had candied to perfection with butter and brown sugar. He started to arrange three at the center of each ramekin in a clover of paisleys, then tucked a sugarwork swirl next to it to top things off just so.

"Have you seen the *maal* here, boss?" Rajesh said, pulling DJ out of his plating reverie.

Based on the glint in his assistant's kohl-lined eyes, DJ was quite certain he wasn't talking about the soufflé. Not that Rajesh talked about much other than women. DJ just wished he would stop calling them things like "packages" and "freight." He'd asked him not to often enough, but Rajesh was twenty-one and blessed with the thick skin of the truly obnoxious. He was determinedly impervious to criticism.

"Have you ever seen Indian chicks so fancy? Strutting about as if they're *goris*? Soft like rasgullas, hot like halwa!" He wiggled his eyebrows lecherously.

Good thing that plating the soufflés required the lightest touch and all his focus, because that meant DJ could block Rajesh out.

That didn't stop Rajesh from blathering on. "Usually, I keep away from Indian chicks. Too much emotional drama. But doing these would be like drinking *desi* booze from fancy English crystal." He made a sipping sound. "What say, boss?"

DJ straightened up. "How about we stay out of our client's guests' knickers and focus on work, what say you, *boss*?" he snapped and Rajesh looked appalled at the idea of staying out of anyone's knickers.

DJ reminded himself that he needed an assistant and he could only afford this one because he worked for room and board. Add to that the whole moral obligation to Rajesh's grandmother for her saving-his-life thing and DJ was well and truly stuck with him. The man was competent enough. And uncouth as he was, DJ couldn't exactly set every wanker straight, now could he?

However, DJ could not afford to have Rajesh go anywhere near the client's guests.

The fact that DJ had this job was nothing short of a miracle. A miracle called Ashna Raje. Ashna was one of the few friends DJ had in this world, and she'd proven that when it came to friends, quality mattered vastly more than quantity. Man, had she come through for him. First by getting his little sister in to see her cousin, who was some sort of genius surgeon at Stanford. That would have been above and beyond on its own, but then she had gotten him this gig with her aunt, Mina Raje.

He pulled out his phone and quickly checked to make sure he didn't have any new messages from Emma. She had seen her surgeon today, but she was refusing to tell him what had happened over the phone. He felt horrible about not being at the hospital when she got the scan results, but without this job, there would be no money to pay for the scans or the surgery that was his little sister's only hope.

Hope was something that hadn't exactly been abundant these past few months. Not until this surgeon he'd never met had come along. It had been three months since Emma had collapsed while teaching at the nursing home where she worked as the resident art therapist. The monster headaches had turned out to be a tumor in her brain that was so unfortunately located that the doctors had labelled it inoperable and given her six months to live.

Emma being Emma, she had only told him after the doctors had declared that she was terminal. Up until then she'd faced everything alone. The day she had called him, DJ had quit his job at Andre's. Two days later he had subleased his Paris flat and flown to San Francisco to find his little sister shrunken to half her size, one of her eyes a strange new light brown, unable to walk in a straight line.

She had learned how to walk holding his hand. He had taught her how to ride a bike, bought her her first sketchbook and box of paints. He had painted her little hand with a rainbow of colors and shown her how to stamp it on the paper, to transform it into peacocks and Christmas trees and daisies.

And she was alone right now in a hospital with information that would decide the course of their lives.

He looked at the time. It would be a few hours before he could get to the hospital. Until then he couldn't let himself think about anything but dessert, which was all he had left to do. He quickly squeezed his fingers into his eyes and scrubbed them on his smock. He could not lose Emma. She was all he had.

"I mean it, Rajesh. Clients and their guests are strictly off-limits."

The tosser winked at him. "Our client is that ancient Bollywood star. I'm most certainly not bonking that. Although have you seen the baps on the ol—"

"All right! I think these look about ready to go into the cooler for a bit. Do the honors, won't you? I need to get my caramel started." He turned away briskly, and luckily the man got to work. A world-class wanker he may be, but he understood how crucial it was for them to make a success out of this dinner. Without DJ's help Rajesh would have to return to London, where, by all accounts, a number of boots were waiting to connect with his dangly bits.

As for DJ, he didn't have the option to fail. Not with Emma's treatment hanging in the balance. He had saved every penny he could while working with Andre. Paris was not a cheap place to live, but he didn't have to live on avenue Montaigne like the other chefs in Andre's crew. Growing up the way they had in London, in an attic flat in Rajesh's grandmother's Southall house, meant a Porte de La Villette studio had felt almost luxurious. As for being ridiculed by his peers, so long as they couldn't ridicule his work, nothing else mattered.

Turned out it was a good thing he hadn't picked up expensive habits, because after paying Emma's astronomical medical bills and the deposit on his Palo Alto flat, all his savings were gone. He was as dead broke as he had been the day their mother died leaving them orphaned.

The good news was that he wasn't sixteen anymore and he had this, his art. His food. And if this dinner continued to go the way it was going, if Mrs. Raje stood by her word and gave DJ the contract for her son's fund-raising dinner next month based on tonight's success . . . well, then they'd be fine.

Mrs. Raje had been more than impressed thus far. Everything from the steamed momos to the dum biryani had turned out just so. The mayor of San Francisco had even asked to speak to DJ after tasting the California blue crab with bitter coconut cream and tucked DJ's card into his wallet.

Only dessert remained, and dessert was DJ's crowning glory, his true love. With sugar he could make love to taste buds, make adult humans sob.

The reason Mina Raje had given him, a foreigner and a newbie, a shot at tonight was his Arabica bean gelato with dark caramel. DJ had created the dessert for her after spending a week researching her. Not just her favorite restaurants, but where she shopped, how she wore her clothes, what made her laugh, even the perfume she wore and how much. The taste buds drew from who you were. How you reacted to taste as a sense was a culmination of how you processed the world, the most primal form of how you interacted with your environment.

It was DJ's greatest strength and weakness, needing to know what exact note of flavor unfurled a person. His need to find that chord and strum it was bone deep. It was why he had dreamed of being a private chef from the day he had walked into culinary school. After ten years of working at Andre's, unable to cut the cord of financial security a paycheck provided, here he was, pushed—no, tossed out on his bum—into his dream by the threat of losing the only person in the world who meant anything.

Granted, he'd only had the chance to pitch for the job because Mrs. Raje was Ashna's aunt, but turning the meeting into a gig had been all him. During the tasting, Mrs. Raje had done what most health-conscious women do, taken a small nibble of his gelato, meaning to simply taste it. After scraping the bottom of the bowl less than five minutes later, she had told him that she couldn't remember the last time she had finished an entire serving of dessert. Then she had offered him the job.

Now he needed to make sure he got all her jobs going forward. He placed the heavy-bottomed pan on the stove. All that remained for him to do tonight was turn out a perfect salted caramel, and nothing had ever stopped DJ from doing that before.

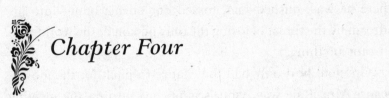

Chapter Four

When the choice was between a spectacular butt and food, Trisha, naturally, chose food. If she stood around waiting for Nisha to finish being the perfect daughter and sister and chat up every single guest who so much as looked in her direction, Trisha might starve to death. Now that her brain had acknowledged her hunger, it was starting to feel a distinct dearth of oxygen from lack of nutrition.

How much of an irony would it be to die of starvation the day she had made history? Not that anyone in her family would know that she had made history if she did die. Not one!

Hell if she cared! She was thirty-two years old, and perfectly capable of understanding that her work was its own validation. A spasm cramped her heart at the memory of the hours she had spent mapping Emma's tumor to feed the calculations into the robot, and that moment of absolute exhilaration when she had known exactly how she was going to remove an astrocytoma wrapped around the optic nerves that no other surgeon would even think of touching. This was true love, how she felt about her work. And she needed nothing more.

She wandered through the main kitchen, which was as pristine as it always was, made her way down the long corridor to the working kitchen in the back of the house, and pushed through the heavy swing door. If this had been just a family gathering and her grandma had been down here running the show, Aji would have put a plate of food aside for Trisha, knowing how hungry she would be.

Maybe she should go back up and tell Aji about the grant. She would care.

Her stomach groaned again, and seriously, she was this close to fainting. The fact that she hated kitchens made things worse. Especially when the kitchen looked like this—a million ingredients and dishes strewn about the endless granite surfaces. Nonetheless, she soldiered on.

On the stove sat a huge pot with a clear lid that looked promising, but it was too close to another pot on an open flame. She looked around for help.

For all the cooking paraphernalia lying in wait of something, there wasn't a soul here tending to it all. Who left something thick and molten bubbling on a stove unattended? Carefully reaching past it, she lifted the lid of the other dish and found pure white, long-grained rice mixed with green peas and bright orange carrots. The intoxicating smell jabbed her straight in the olfactory cortex. Drool gushed into her mouth.

"May I help you?"

She jumped. And dropped the lid.

It slammed into the bubbling pot, making the thing teeter on its side.

Trisha stumbled back, trying to get away from the splash of molten liquid.

The man in a white chef's jacket who had just scared the living crap out of her dived at the careening pot and saved it from crashing to the ground.

"Bloody hell!" he snapped, completely ignoring the fact that she had almost just had her toes burned off. "What do you think you're doing? Who the hell let you into my kitchen?"

Her heart slammed in her chest. "Excuse me?" Was he actually yelling at her? As though she were some sort of deviant child? And since when was this *his* kitchen? This was her damn home!

"You almost tipped over my caramel. My caramel! It's my pièce de résistance," he said in a tone no one had ever taken with her.

Who the hell said things like "pièce de résistance," that too in perfect French? But his voice was so enraged she almost took a step back.

Almost, because, it was her damn home! "Maybe you should not have left it unattended then," she said icily.

His skin flushed red. He swallowed and ground his jaw. "You're right. I shouldn't have. I apologize." Anger flashed in his eyes, and not a trace of apology. "To be fair, I wasn't exactly expecting anyone to be snooping around my food and tipping over my pots the moment I stepped away for one bloody second."

"I was not *snooping*." Were they really having this conversation? "You startled me and almost burned me."

He had started to turn away, but he spun back around at that. "All you had to do was set the pot straight and no one would have been burned." He enunciated each word with exaggerated calm.

If one more person spoke to her today like she was an imbecile, she was going to wring someone's neck! "Set it straight? You wanted me to touch a boiling pot? Do you have any idea what these hands are worth?"

His eyebrows rose in disbelief, as though the words she had said were somehow incomprehensible. He raised both hands, done with this conversation. Then he turned off the stove with more of that exaggerated calm, walked to the sink, and stuck his hands under running water.

Shit.

He had just set the pot straight with his bare hands.

"Are you okay?" Trisha asked, her annoyance slipping a bit.

"Do I look okay, miss?" She registered for the first time that he had an accent. A very British accent. And those tightly clipped notes gave his words the exact impact of a slap.

God help her, she had just tried to be nice! He just stood there taking deep breaths, his very stiff—very broad—back expanding and then releasing with deliberation. Between those football player shoulders and that ridiculous chef's hat he looked so large, so tall that she did take a step back this time, so she didn't have to lean her head back to take him in.

He turned the water off and inspected his hands. They had to be hurting like a bitch.

"Do you want me to take a look?" she asked his back, feeling just the tiniest bit sorry for him.

He threw a look at the ceiling as though praying for patience and turned around with unmissable reluctance.

She made a beckoning gesture with her fingers. "Let me."

He kept his hands by his sides. "As I said, I'm fine. Thank you all the same." With nothing more than that, he gave her his back again and started spooning the caramel into a bowl.

When she didn't run off the way he evidently expected her to, he half turned back toward her again. "If you don't mind, I'd rather do my job than stand around calculating the value of your hands."

Her confusion must have shown on her face because he drew another annoyingly exaggerated breath. "You asked me if I had any idea what your hands were worth." He was doing that overenunciating thing again and, news flash: it sounded even more condescending in a British accent.

She'd had enough. "I'm a sur-geon," she said, mirroring his enunciation and feeling like a prized fool for doing it. "Our hands are important to the work we do."

This only made the scowl return to his face. "Good information. Congratulations. And I'm the chef and I still have dessert to serve. Before someone else comes by and tries to destroy it."

"I was not trying to destroy your dessert." She tried to sound dignified, but this was the most juvenile conversation she had ever had. "It's just food. And your sauce seems just fine."

He went utterly still. "It's caramel. Not"—he paused as though the word tasted bitter in his mouth—"sauce." Then he continued with whatever it was he was doing with his precious *caramel*—which, Trisha realized, smelled like someone had melted heaven and slathered it in butter.

She felt light-headed. "Listen, I'm sorry. I'm just not comfortable in kitchens, okay? I was burned as a child."

Nothing. Here she was trying to be the bigger person and he wasn't even listening to her. She flipped him off in her head and without letting herself think about the trauma of the memory of being burned, or how much fun her siblings made of her because of the incident, she yanked open a drawer and pulled out the biggest bowl she could find.

Then, against her better judgment, and because she was hungry enough to commit murder, she spoke to him again. "Excuse me." She pointed her spoon at the rice when what she really wanted to do was shove him out of her way and stab her spoon into the pot and start eating right out of it.

He stepped aside, taking his precious *caramel* with him all the way to the other end of the kitchen without helping her with the rice. Weren't her parents paying him to feed people? But she said nothing. Because who wanted to unleash all that enunciating again? Instead, she served herself, piling the rice high. She had just brought a giant spoonful to her mouth when her sister sashayed into the kitchen.

"There you are," Nisha said, smiling widely. Her eyes found the sulky man at the other end of the room. His back was to them and he was so focused on his caramel, one would think he were performing lifesaving surgery. He certainly seemed to think he was.

Nisha's smile turned into a grin. She wiggled her brows, completely missing Trisha's current mood.

What? Trisha mouthed, seriously considering sororicide if her sister didn't let her eat in peace.

Nisha's eyes danced in the man's direction and dropped to his behind.

Really? Trisha narrowed her eyes, then without looking where her sister was looking, she stormed out of the kitchen, bowl in hand.

"What's got you all grumpy?" Nisha asked, catching up with her in the corridor.

"Seriously, I have the best day of my professional life and all you and Ma can think of is how to throw me at men!"

"I thought you wanted to be thrown at men. Weren't you biting my head off earlier about withholding good butt from you? Seriously, what's wrong? Didn't you see him and his . . . oh!—" Her eyes went round, and she let out a squeak of delight. "You got the grant!" She threw her arms around Trisha.

There, was that so hard? That's all Trisha had wanted. She let Nisha squeeze her tight, the irritation inside her melting away. Then again maybe it was this pulav. She shoved another spoonful into her mouth. It was seriously the best thing she had ever tasted. She thought she knew rice. She'd grown up eating rice. But this . . . this was like an explosion of familiar flavors doing an entirely unexpected dance in her mouth.

"I'm so sorry. It should have been the first thing I asked," her sister said with enough remorse that the remnants of Trisha's annoyance fizzled.

"That's okay. I know how important today was to you."

"To all of us." Reprimand flashed in Nisha's eyes. "It's happening, Shasha. After all his hard work. After all he's been through. Yash is running. He's going to be governor."

Nisha was right. It was happening. And it was important. To all of them. This was her family. If they shut her out, she could at least bang on the door. She should be part of Yash's campaign. "This rice is turning my world upside down," she said, chewing with reverence.

Her sister smiled again. "So did Entoff totally fall at your feet?"

Trisha grinned and pinched her finger over the spoon. "A teeny bit. Who am I kidding, he practically kissed them!"

Her sister's eyes brightened in a way that proved exactly why she was Trisha's favorite person in the whole world.

"And how about that artist patient of yours, is she going to be okay?"

Emma's fierce eyes, her bottle-cap-popping vagina, it all did a slo-mo flash inside Trisha's head. "She's going to lose her sight," she said softly.

Her sister stroked her hair and rolled a curl around her finger. It was such a Raje gesture. Their mother used to twirl her fingers in their hair when they were babies to put them to sleep and all the kids had picked up the habit. Even Ashna and Esha did it. It was their way of giving comfort, showing affection.

"But you're saving her life. Trisha, you're saving her life," Nisha repeated gently. "It's not like there's anything more you can do."

The rice stuck in Trisha's throat as she swallowed. She had to get a grip and stop letting this bother her so much. It was one case and she had done all she could. "Yes, and the surgery will give us a chance to use the new robot!" Thinking about the surgery brought the enthusiasm back to her voice.

"My badass baby sister!" Nisha squeezed her shoulder and Trisha pushed the memory of the despair in Emma's eyes out of her head and focused on the joy warming her insides at Nisha's praise.

She put another spoonful of the magic rice in her mouth and moaned, the satisfaction of filling her empty belly making all the tension of the day melt away. She was home. Her brother was about to make the family's dreams come true. And she wasn't going to watch from the outside anymore. Even the fact that she had been yelled at in her parents' home by some cook who seemed to think he was on the set of *Iron Chef* seemed funny in retrospect.

"You're right. I am totally badass!"

FOR THE SECOND time that day, DJ stood at the kitchen door listening to the sound of that voice. Only this time he knew exactly whom it was coming from. It was coming from someone who had almost cost him this job.

What flooded through him now was certainly not warmth.

Watching his caramel almost splatter on the floor had damn near given him a heart attack. To say nothing of his hands, which stung like the fires of hell. He could feel the blisters forming on his thumb and fingers under the platter he was carrying.

"Not just badass but also, ahem, a genius," the woman was saying, and it brought to mind an image of her staring at her hands, contemplating their worth. She tried to inject a note of self-mocking into her tone, but this time he knew better than to buy it. He'd seen the truth in her eyes back there.

Do you have any idea what these hands are worth?

He almost laughed at that. Who the hell talked like that?

"Well, you did walk away from that beautiful creature in the kitchen without so much as a glance, so I don't know about the genius part," the other woman said, and DJ felt his face warm. "You want to go back in there? I'll introduce you. You can celebrate for real."

Both women broke into giggles. DJ almost smiled; maybe he'd overreacted in there a bit.

"No thank you," the good doctor said in that voice of hers. "But thanks for thinking I'm desperate enough to be set up with the hired help."

DJ stepped away from the door, the warmth on his face turning into an angry burn.

The hired help? He had worked at a Michelin-starred restaurant, for crying out loud. For years. People across Paris knew his name.

Who the bloody hell did this woman think she was? Sometimes he really, truly hated rich people.

"This rice is like an orgasm in every bite," she said as though she hadn't just called the person who had created that rice a servant.

Suddenly, the thought of her eating his food felt like a violation. He wanted to yank it from her hands. His blistering fingers stung as his grip on the platter tightened.

Curry sweep. Smelly. Little. Curry. Sweep.

"DJ got called curry sweep at school," Emma had sobbed to Mum the moment Mum had walked in the door. She had cried all the way back from school when DJ and she had taken the bus home.

"I blame William Blake," DJ had said, getting out of the chair he was sprawled on. He'd worked in Ammaji's kitchen for six hours and he was tired, but Mum had to be even more tired. "It's a play on chimney sweep." Not even a good word-play at that. But the gits in his school weren't exactly literary geniuses.

Mum had smiled. A literary reference never failed to get a smile out of Mum. And distract her.

"You didn't get in a fight, did you?" she said, sinking into the chair DJ had just vacated, the only one they had in the rooms they rented. No fighting back—it was Mum's number one rule.

"He was wet on the bus," Emma said, wasting the hour he had spent coaching her to shut up so she wouldn't ruin Mum's evening.

Some boys in his grade had dragged him into the locker rooms and pushed him under a shower in an attempt "to teach the curry sweep how to wash off the curry" so they didn't have to hold their breath around him all day.

He didn't care. Being wet didn't hurt. At least no one had punched him that day.

Thankfully Emma hadn't mentioned the curry smells.

Because to Mum a nasty wordplay on chimney sweep was just words, but mentioning the smells of their landlady's cooking—DJ's cooking—was sticks and stones. It drew blood.

The first time Emma had let slip that the boys liked to spray DJ with cheap deodorant while passing him in the hallways, Mum had packed up DJ's clothes in a laundry bag and taken them to the local dry cleaner's instead of washing them in the ancient washer in the attic.

"Those things cost too much, Mum." He had tried to get her to see sense. "We can use that twenty quid to buy Emma paints."

She had smacked him upside his head, albeit affectionately. "Emma doesn't need any more stupid paints. You need to develop some self-respect. No one can have self-respect while smelling like curry."

"How am I supposed to develop self-respect if you still smack me around when I'm fourteen?" he'd said because he knew it would make her smile.

She'd ruffled his hair. "Why don't you care when those boys treat you like that?"

"Just because some spoiled gits say something, that doesn't make it true." He'd wanted so badly for her to believe that he didn't care. Truth was, dry-cleaning the clothes once would do nothing to get rid of the smell of frying onions for six hours in a little kitchen, every day. The smell was in his pores. An even bigger truth was that he loved it. Those six hours were the best hours of DJ's day and he would not let anyone take them away from him. Not even his mother.

"You were never supposed to cook for her. You aren't her servant, DJ!"

"I know that, Mum." It tore a tiny hole inside him every time Mum said that. Ammaji said cooking was the most noble of all service. He believed her with all his heart. But he also knew that all Mum wanted was for him to make it out of these attic rooms.

"Your father wanted you to be an engineer. What will I say to him when I meet him in heaven?"

What DJ had wanted to say was, "Maybe start with asking him why he left us penniless if he cared so much about my future?"

He never said it though. Because Ammaji had once told him that anger tears up your insides. And that only he could choose who he let tear him up.

Years later he had forgotten her words and it had ended up tearing not just him but everything he cared for apart. Emma had been the one to bring him back from the brink then. And now she was lying in a hospital bed. He needed to get back to work so he could get back to her, and not let some insufferable snob level him by bringing up nasty memories.

The two women were still talking. Instead of going through the door, he stepped away from it. He'd heard enough.

Sod all if he cared what they thought of him anyway.

Rajesh appeared next to him and pushed the door open a crack to peer at the women. "Told you the *maal* here was fit," he whispered. "They're something else, innit?"

Yup, definitely something else.

DJ took a deep breath. "We're working, Rajesh. Let's try to keep it clean." Walking back into the kitchen, he put the platter down. Then he scooped some ice out of the freezer and pressed his burning hands into it.

"In that case you take the short one and keep it clean. I'll take the tall one. She looks like she could use something dirty."

Somewhere in the distance "the tall one" let out a laugh, an unencumbered laugh, as though life in her ivory tower was just too splendid for her little heart to bear. Where *the hired help* just wouldn't stop doing things to make her titter with amusement.

"Don't waste your time, mate," he said, signaling his assistant to start taking the ramekins to the serving area. "Your tall one has no interest in cavorting with the hired help."

Chapter Five

Some people felt things in their heads, others felt them in their hearts; DJ felt things in his stomach, which was fitting for a chef. He watched as Emma dabbed and smudged oil pastels across her sketchbook. The waxy smell of the colors made it almost easy to forget that she was perched on a hospital bed. His Big Brother senses had been tingling all day. Now they mingled with that smell and made his belly cramp in discomfort.

Last night it had been past midnight when he finally got to the hospital after the Raje dinner, which had gone off flawlessly despite the caramel almost-disaster. He looked at his hands. The blisters weren't as awful as they could have been because he'd had the good sense to keep on icing them through the night. Emma had been fast asleep when he slipped into the chair next to her bed. He'd been too wired to fall asleep, so he'd watched over her and nursed his stinging palms.

She looked so peaceful when she slept, always had. Like a cherub with those ebony curls framing her face and those soft cheeks sprinkled with freckles. Unlike him she had inherited their Anglo-Indian father's coloring. His own skin was all Rwandan-Tutsi like their mother, dark and luminous. He'd taken Dad's hazel eyes. They'd cherry-picked completely different features from their parents—her dark-eyed and light-skinned, him light-eyed and dark-skinned, as though they'd known that their parents would be gone too soon and they'd wanted to keep as much of them as possible in the memory boxes that were their bodies.

Right now, Emma was trying hard to look peaceful. But there was a difference between when she actually was serene, and when she had to make the effort to appear so. As her only living relative—or at least as her only living relative who knew her—DJ had no problem identifying which it was.

"Quit studying me like I'm a recipe you're trying to reverse-engineer, Darcy!" she said, slamming the sketchbook shut. Again, it was an attempt at little-sisterly petulance, not the real deal.

She knew he hated his given name rather vehemently, and using it meant that she was pissed off and trying to needle him.

"What's wrong?" he wanted to say. But asking your sister what was wrong when she'd been told she was going to have to lose her sight if she wanted to live was just . . . stupid. So, instead, he said, "It's going to be fine, love."

She shoved the sketchbook off her lap. Then picked it up again and hugged it to her chest. "No, it's not going to be bloody fine!" Finally, she raised her voice.

Good, he wished she could scream. He wished he could take her to a mountain, into a forest, to the rooftop of the hospital and let her scream until she had no breath left. They could both use that. Some good full-chested lung-wringing yelling. Everything let out, nothing held in.

She had barely been able to whisper the words out this morning after she'd woken up. "The tumor is operable, but they'll have to slice up both my optic nerves. I'm going to go completely blind." Her voice had broken on that last word, but she hadn't cried.

He hadn't either. He'd wanted to. He'd also wanted to ask questions, respond in some way, but he had nothing. No questions to ask, no consolation to give. Nothing except an overwhelming wave of relief. In the end, all he'd been able to manage was to take her hand and hold it in silence for a long, long time. The Caine siblings had always been good at silence.

Then another flurry of tests had taken her away and he'd gone home to make her some chicken noodle soup, because some of the drugs made her nauseated. Then he'd made his daily trip to the farmers' market for this evening's job. One part of him looked forward to his work, to the soothing satisfaction of it. The other part of him was so soul sick, all he wanted was to not leave her side. Not that it mattered what he wanted. He needed every job he could get to pay for this surgery. He'd been praying for this—a cure, a solution, a way to save her life—from the moment she'd called him and used that word. *Terminal.*

The look she gave him left no doubt in his mind that she didn't share his relief. Not only did she not share it, but she wanted to shake him for feeling it until his bones rattled. "In which world is it going to be fine that I won't be able to see?"

"In a world where you'll be alive."

She locked gazes with him. When her eyes had started changing color, he had noticed. Six months ago when she had visited him in Paris, he'd seen it. The color difference had been much subtler then than it was now, but he'd caught it. Why hadn't he pushed harder for her to see a doctor about it then? *Why?*

"I can't do it, DJ."

Everything in the room went quiet. The ceaseless buzzing and beeping of the machines, the murmur and grind of conversations and rolling carts from the corridor outside—it all stopped, swallowed up by her words.

What the hell was she talking about? But he couldn't disturb the silence. He waited, staring down the answer in her eyes.

She put the sketchbook on the side table and reached for his hand. Her fingers were stained with thick oily color. Blue and yellow. Darkness and light. She squeezed his hand. "I can't go blind. I can't do it." It was the calmness with which she said it that made him spring out of his chair.

Without letting her hand go, he sat down on the bed next to her, the springs jumping, his heartbeat rising fast. "Emma, love, I get that this is hard. Hell, it's impossible. I understand. I do. But I'm here. I'll be here. We'll sort it out."

"What will you be sorting out exactly? How to live your life in darkness? How to never see colors?" She yanked her hand out of his, leaving stains on his skin. "Colors are my life, DJ! I can't live without them. When Dad died, when Mum died, when you left, they were all I had. I don't need anything else. But I need them. I need to see. I need to paint to make sense of the world." There were no tears in her eyes, her back stayed erect, but he felt her folding inward, dissolving in pain, and anger, and helplessness.

That's what this was. It was shock. It was natural, her being in denial. He just needed to be patient while she worked it out. Because he couldn't imagine how angry she was. He was furious too. He wanted to break things. Burn everything down. On his way to his flat yesterday, when he'd stopped at the railway crossing and watched the Caltrain race past, he'd imagined his car getting stuck on the tracks unable to get out of the way soon enough. That shattering slam of the train flattening the metal, crushing everything inside to pulp, that's what this felt like.

"No, don't try the silence thing with me," she said too calmly. "This is not about letting me work through this. This is not a meltdown. I've made up my mind. I'm not going to have the surgery. Dr. Entoff said there were other treatments that would give me some time, the kind of time I want."

His hands were shaking. Hers had gone back around herself, but they were still.

"Have you lost your fecking mind?" he finally managed. "Has the tumor addled your loaf, Emma Jane? This is not an option. I'm not going to let you do this."

She grabbed his sleeve, tightening her fist as though she wanted to yank his arm off. "You're not going to *let* me?" Oh no, she wasn't calm anymore. "I am twenty-four fecking years old, DJ Caine! I'm not twelve. You don't get to make decisions for me. You don't get to dump me in a boarding school and sod off."

He got off the bed, her words knocking the wind out of him. "I never dumped you."

"I know that's not what you think you did. Because you were thinking only about yourself. When you ran off with those boys, when you let those coppers drag you away. When you let Mum—"

"Emma!" He was breathing hard. She was breathing harder. *She's not herself*, he chanted to himself. *She is not herself.*

For a long moment they said nothing more. They just glared—at each other, at their own helpless hands, at the useless gray walls. The hospital sounds became audible again, coming back into focus one by one. The beep of one machine, the hiss of another, the buzz of the lights overhead. Someone laughed as they walked by. DJ picked each one out, calming himself the hell down. Because, she wasn't herself. This wasn't her. This was her trying to wrap her head around everything.

"Listen, Em—"

"I want you to leave. Go."

"Love, please, I'm sorry. Let's talk about this."

Her eyes shone with anger. *Chocolate eyes*—their father had called their mum that. Emma's eyes were the exact color as Mum's and the exact shape as Dad's, so wide they usually looked like they were filled with wonder. His parents lived on in those eyes.

"There's nothing to talk about, DJ." The finality in her voice drove a nail through his heart. "I'm not changing my mind."

He softened his tone, trying not to overdo it, trying to find balance as the earth beneath his feet crumbled. "Let's talk to your doctor. Ashna says she can do anything. Let's run this by her."

"You're not listening to me. Damn it, DJ, why won't you

listen to me?" She shook her head. "I want you to leave. Go home. Think about this there. Think about how I'm a bloody adult who gets to make up her own mind about how she wants to live. I don't want you to come back, not until you're ready to listen to me. Go!" This time she did scream, that last word, loud enough for it to reverberate inside him.

A nurse rapped on the door and strode right in. "Everything okay here?" She started examining the tubes coming out of electrodes stuck to Emma and the machines that surrounded her, but her attention was on DJ.

"My brother was just leaving." Emma's voice was a blade of ice. Who was this person? Where was his little sister? He needed her to be here. He needed her.

The nurse placed a hand on his arm. He met her eyes, begging her to let him stay, begging for something.

"You should leave," she said, gentle but firm. She sounded exactly like their mother. *This is what we have, Darcy. This is all I can give you.*

God, he was losing his mind.

"Give her some time," the gentle-firm nurse, who wasn't Mum, said.

He threw another look at Emma. "Emma, please, can we at least talk?"

She didn't even look at him and the nurse's arm nudged him, more firm now than gentle.

"I'll be back. We're going to talk then." His voice sounded stronger than his legs felt as he forced himself to leave her room.

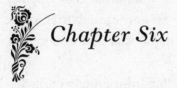

Chapter Six

For years Trisha had patiently listened to Nisha go on and on about the meetings their mother insisted on holding after every one of Yash's campaign events. Ma liked to call them "family tea." But that was factually wrong on three levels. First, they were all, except Ma, coffee drinkers—a habit they had picked up from HRH, who prized his coffee addiction as yet another all-American badge.

Second, based on Nisha's description, Trisha knew exactly what they were: postmortems. Where the family dissected every aspect of the event and analyzed every conversation in excruciating detail, then turned it all into action items, and then analyzed the ROI for those. Analyzing return on investment was a favorite Raje pastime.

Third, Trisha was part of the family and she had never been invited to one of these. For obvious reasons.

After last night's dinner, Trisha's resolve to change all that kept seesawing madly. She couldn't stop thinking about how right it had felt seeing up close all the support Yash had garnered, seeing him be within touching distance of his dream.

To keep herself from thinking about it too much or sliding back into the banishment zone, when a few hours had opened up at work, she had gotten into the car and started driving. As she neared the Anchorage, she called Nisha and announced that she was almost there.

"Where?" her sister asked, sounding infuriatingly baffled.

"At the Anchorage, of course. For the *tea*."

"I'm not going to the tea today." Only Nisha could drop a bombshell like that in such a gentle voice.

"What do you mean you're not going?" Trisha snapped, rather less gently. "Aren't you the one who's been lecturing me about how important these things are?"

"Well, I didn't expect you to go nuts and start coming to everything all of a sudden!" This time she didn't sound quite so gentle.

Maybe Nisha was right. Why was she even here?

"One of my surgeries was rescheduled," she said, contemplating a U-turn on the narrow, sloping private street. "The free afternoon seemed like a sign."

Predictably, Nisha harrumphed, albeit daintily, and responded with, "A sign? What? Are you Esha now?"

No, she was not their clairvoyant cousin, thank you very much.

She pulled through the Anchorage gates and watched them slide shut behind her in the rearview mirror with a growing sense of dread. "I'm here now and I need you to be here too. I can't do this without you, Nisha!"

"Stop being silly. The rest of the Animal Farm is there," her sister said in the exact kind of tone her family used when they thought Trisha was having what they referred to as "one of her overreactions." "Also, sweetie, you're two hours late."

"What? But . . . but . . . you told me it was at two!" Her wail had to have echoed around the woods she was driving through. This could not be happening.

"Nope, twelve," her sister said absently. She was probably juggling five other things while speaking with Trisha on her Bluetooth. "Ma rescheduled."

"Ma didn't say anything to me. You didn't say anything! And I texted both of you that I was planning to come." It had been an act of courage to put herself out there like that.

Her sister remained ominously silent.

"Nisha, what?"

"Well, we didn't really think you'd come!"

"I came to the dinner yesterday! Admit it, you say you want me to be there, but you don't really!"

"Are you seriously accusing me of that?" Nisha didn't sound angry, just hurt. Which was worse.

"No," Trisha said sulkily. "After yesterday, I thought Ma might be okay with including me." Ma had said she was glad Trisha had come. She should have known that their mother would never go up against their father. And Trisha would not be surprised if HRH had decided that things were better off without Trisha's involvement.

"You're being unfair," her sister said. "You also showed up two hours late last evening. Ma probably stood up for you to HRH, and she probably got the 'I told you so' treatment from him."

"So she punishes me by telling me the wrong time for the tea? And you go along with it?"

"Stop being so dramatic." She sounded tired. "It wasn't like that. When Ma told you the time, she had postponed it to two, then she moved it back to noon. And, well . . ."

"And what?"

"And you aren't on the campaign family group chat. She probably just forgot to text you separately."

Right. "Wait, there's a campaign family group chat?" The thought was a bit horrifying. Trisha hated that she wasn't on it, but she couldn't imagine the torture of being on it either.

She could almost see Nisha rolling her eyes at the other end. "Listen, I have to go. If you've decided to make amends, you have to be patient. You can't barrel through this like you barrel through things at work."

She did not barrel through things at work! Microneurosurgery was not something you could barrel through. And she was the one who had been shut out—why was she the only one responsible for making amends? And why was Nisha suddenly sounding so tired?

"I really have to go. Take a deep breath. I have to pack for Neel and Mishka's trip. Call you later?" And just like that, she disconnected the phone.

This was totally not like her sister. But what was really scary was her sister missing a postmortem tea. Sure, it didn't seem like a big deal on the surface. Unless you knew Nisha. The only person as batshit serious about Yash's political career as their parents was Nisha. She had quit her job two years ago to start doing the groundwork for his gubernatorial run. Now she was the one officially running his campaign.

So, yes, this was completely out of character. Even more out of character was how exhausted Nisha had sounded when she hung up. Nisha's default mode was perpetual motion. Trisha redialed her number to make sure she was okay as she pulled under the columned porte cochere. Her sister didn't answer.

Yash's Tesla was parked in front of her, which meant she wasn't so late that everyone had already left. Ugh, weren't there supposed to be silver linings to family fiascoes? Her attempt at *barreling* herself back into the fold might have crashed and burned, but did the entire family need to witness it?

Backing her car right out and leaving sounded tempting, but she was here and she could really use one of her grandmother's hugs right now, and maybe some advice on how to keep herself from becoming too emotionally invested in Emma's case. Last night had gone by in such a blur, she'd barely gotten to see Aji.

She got out of the car, and then idiot that she was, she peeked into the garage to see if HRH was still here too. Yup, there was no silver lining in sight. HRH's black Tesla, one of the test models from the first batch to leave the Fremont plant, gleamed in its spot under the rest of his cars stacked up on the hydraulic platforms of his garage. Maybe she could just hide until he left. He had to be going back to the hospital soon—he had consulting hours this afternoon.

As she made her way through the house she considered calling her sister again and screaming. Mostly because she had the urge to scream, but also because she wanted to make sure that an alien hadn't abducted Nisha and left behind a cyborg in her place. A cyborg who didn't know just how important Animal Farm debriefings were to Nisha.

The Animal Farm was the family's nickname for itself. It had all started with this picture book called *The Animal Farm* that some auntie visiting from India had brought the Raje children. HRH, a fan of the novel by George Orwell, had been horrified when he saw the book and ordered Yash to throw it away. But Yash, like any older sibling, had delegated the task to Trisha, and she had been so intrigued by the brightly colored, haphazardly printed book that she had read it. And laughed so hard that the rest of them had taken it from her and also read it.

It was the story of wild and domestic animals living together in harmony in a hamletlike forest. The animals walked on two legs, lived in houses that ranged from hutments to palaces, and wore puffy bow ties if they were male and frilly aprons if they were female. But the thing that had made the Raje children guffaw until they had tears in their eyes was the very random morals each story ended with. These animal-humans who got into all sorts of messes always made everything better with a group hug and with throwing out lines like "One step at a time. That's how you change the world!" or "A person is only as good as his word!" or "United we stand, divided we fall!"

The Raje cousins had all grown up in the same house. Trisha and her three siblings; Yash the scion of the dynasty, Nisha the perfect big sister, and Vansh the free-spirited brat who did as he pleased. He was currently in Uganda trying to dig wells and set up filtration systems, working toward his plan to save the world one clean water drop at a time. And their two cousins: Esha, HRH's older brother's daughter and the oldest of the cousins, whom Trisha's parents had raised since her parents had died in the air crash she had miraculously survived. And Ashna, HRH's younger brother's daughter, who technically hadn't lived with them, but who for all practical purposes had while her father battled alcoholism and her mother took long breaks from him and ran off to India every chance she got.

Growing up with her cousins and siblings had been fun, but also something of a whirlwind. Ma had made sure they were all too busy upholding the Raje academic and extracurricular standards to have any free time at all. But it was a whirlwind you never had to navigate by yourself. Loneliness was a feeling Trisha hadn't experienced until she left for college.

While at home, every night before bed they had all gathered in their grandmother's room to wish her good night and tell her about their day. Trisha had loved that hour they got to be together and to be kids. Raje kids, but kids nonetheless. At these nightly gatherings, they had loved reading *The Animal Farm* aloud and hamming up those moralistic concluding lines from the stories, and the strange book had become a family heirloom. When it had fallen to tatters, Aji had tucked it into a plastic sleeve and put it in the storage room where it had disappeared along with their childhood.

The book had also given birth to an entire family of nicknames. That's where "Shasha" came from. Between being the tallest and gangliest of the girls, and between it somewhat rhyming with Trisha, she had forever become Shasha, the clumsy giraffe who always missed out on things because she did not fit into places.

Yash, of course, was Shambhu, the lion who was a domineering control freak who didn't always know best. But they had all long lost their ability to poke fun at Yash. He had turned into someone you couldn't mock for any reason. Nisha was Rimbo, the hippo who kept the peace. Ashna was Tombo, the elephant who was always trying to be someone she wasn't. Esha was Siya, the detached swan, although she was never in the thick of their shenanigans so the nickname had barely stuck. Vansh had been too young to be deemed worthy of a nickname.

Trisha's was the only nickname that had stayed firmly in place.

Today the Animal Farm was all gathered on the upper floor, where Esha and Aji had their private suite of rooms. It was Trisha's favorite part of the house. Even more beloved than her own childhood room with its canopy bed and ceiling painted to resemble the Simpsons' sky from her favorite TV show growing up.

Trisha had always believed that every place had a pulse, a native texture to its air as it sank into your lungs. The air here in America vibrated at an entirely different frequency than the air in India. It was one of Trisha's earliest memories: the change when they landed in Mumbai on their trips. Then they would take their family's private jet to Sripore, and the air there would feel entirely different from Mumbai. Sometimes when Trisha found herself alone, which was almost never given how many of them there were, she would stick out her tongue to see if the air tasted different. It did. The air in the Sagar Mahal tasted clean and sweet, like rosewater.

The air in Aji's room tasted just like that. And the comfort of it alleviated some of Trisha's nerves. Still, she peeked around the corner of the sitting room. Sure, it was silly to slink around as though she were some sort of thief but she needed to know where everyone was positioned so she could strategize which corner to disappear into. But the walnut-paneled sitting room was empty.

Two life-size portraits of Sita and Parvati by Raja Ravi Varma, arguably India's most renowned classical artist, hung on two sides of a life-size dancing Ganesha statue carved from a single piece of sandalwood. All three of the deities gave her their benevolent smiles, and Trisha felt forgiven for all the sins she might ever have committed, which she suspected was the purpose of the pieces in the first place.

The door to Aji's room cracked open and sounds spilled out. Trisha heard her father's voice say, "We can discuss the rest later. I have to be at the hospital."

She dived behind the leather sectional.

Holy shit, why had she done that?

HRH strode across the sitting room in his signature trample-little-animals-in-his-way style and Trisha scrambled around the couch on all fours as silently as she could. If he heard her, she would die of mortification. Die.

He stopped. *Shit shit shit.* Ma followed him out of Aji's room. Trisha drew herself around the corner of the couch where she begged the paintings of the goddesses to keep her hidden.

"It's not like the girl is stupid," HRH said with enough disdain that Trisha had no doubt who the "girl" in question was. "We all know her brain is not the problem. It's just utter selfishness."

"She's busy," Ma said placatingly. "You know how brutal hospital hours are. And she's trying now."

He huffed—well, not really, he was HRH—but his tone was huffing as hell. "I'm here. Yash is here. Nisha called even though she couldn't make it. Ashna has a restaurant to run and she made it. What she's trying to do is make some sort of point. She's just being vindictive. We were better off with her out of things. She's hurt him enough already. You and Masaheb have to stop coddling her."

Ma made a sound that Trisha didn't hear because her ears were ringing. The elevator slid open and her parents disappeared into it.

"Shasha?"

Great. Just great! The last person she needed to see right now.

"Hi, Yash." She blinked up at him, trying to push the tears back.

"Can I help you find something?" He squatted down next to her.

"I thought I had lost a contact lens. But I think it just moved around." More blinking ensued.

"Contacts trouble again, ha?" he said, giving her a smile that commemorated every incident of her stupid lenses popping out at inopportune moments. It was a kind smile. And it set off a horrid sense of loss inside her. She would never be *vindictive* with Yash.

"I thought the meeting was at two. I'm so sorry I missed it."

The kind smile disappeared. "Ma always does these at noon." His look turned sad, as though he'd just realized that there was no reason for her to know that.

"You're the one who never wanted me to be here," she wanted to say. But it wasn't true. He had never asked her not to come. He had never asked her to come, either.

"Is Rob really running against you in the primaries?" Rob Steele had been Yash's best friend since law school. Trisha couldn't imagine how betrayed Yash must feel right now. The two of them had the same political platform. Only Steele was white.

Yash's eyes widened, clearly surprised that she knew anything about his political career. He stood and offered her his hand.

She let him pull her up. That look of surprise made her feel like a piece of shit. The only reason she knew about Steele was because HRH had slapped her head with the information.

"I really wanted to be here today, Yash," she said tiredly.

"Or you've picked this time to stick it to HRH. He's under a lot of stress, Shasha. Give the man a break." That was pure Yash, worried about every person on earth . . . except, of course, the sister who had almost ruined him.

Did it strike any of them that she had a life, that her decisions were not based on sticking it to anyone or being *vindictive*? Why had she thought this was a good idea again?

Getting sucked into this conversation was a bad idea. It would only end with her feeling even more guilty than she already did, or with Yash running out the door toward something more important. "My afternoon opened up, and after yesterday . . . I, well . . . I wanted to be here. But I can't always get away from work."

Again, he looked surprised that she had explained herself.

"Everything okay at work?" His concern seemed genuine. It was his best expression, also his favorite one. All you had to do was google him and you'd see this face telling you *Yes, I care.*

He looked at his watch, their oldest uncle's Rolex, the Raje equivalent of the Crown. Any caring she might have imagined in his eyes got buried under the need to get to the next place he needed to be.

"Peachy!" she said breezily. "Good luck with your meeting."

He stopped halfway to the stairs. He never took the elevator. It had been installed after the accident that had put him in a wheelchair for two years in high school, but he'd never stepped in there once after he had gotten out of that wheelchair.

"You don't have to come to these, you know," he said.

It was like being slapped in the face. "I'm sorry. I thought maybe we could try to . . . I thought you wouldn't mind me being there." Despite every effort not to, her voice quivered.

He squeezed his temples over those crystal gray eyes. "Come on, Shasha. All I meant was that I know how much you hate these shindigs. If you really want to be involved"—he didn't say "suddenly" but she heard it all the same—"you can help in other ways."

She had the strange urge to laugh. "Do you want to run that by HRH and have your head bitten off, or should I?"

He smiled at that. Then suddenly understanding lit his eyes and she kicked herself for not keeping her mouth shut. He glanced at the spot behind the couch where she'd been hiding. "What did Dad do now?"

"Nothing."

He looked at his watch again. "I can't be late for this meeting." Then he looked at her again, really looked at her, the way he used to years ago. "Call me, please? Let's talk, okay?"

Right. Except it was probably fifteen years too late to talk, and it might take another fifteen for him to find the time. "Sure. Go to your meeting. I'm fine."

And in true Yash Raje fashion he got right down to it and flew down the stairs.

Trisha headed toward Aji's door and ran right into Ashna. "Shasha! I didn't know you were going to be here."

"I got the time wrong," Trisha said, too tired to explain further.

Ashna laughed. But there was no judgment in it. Trisha gave her cousin a tight hug. Ashi never judged her. She was the only one in the entire family who accepted Trisha for exactly who she was. She didn't care what Trisha wore, whether or not she was single, or what she had done fifteen years ago. For all her somber bearing, she was the most stress-free, zero-expectation presence in Trisha's life.

"Good news is HRH and Mina Kaki left," she said, with a commiserating smile. "Yash, too. So your timing is actually perfect."

"You mean I missed the Avalanche of Disappointment?" Trisha said. But of course she hadn't missed it at all.

Ashi twirled one of Trisha's curls around her finger and tucked it behind her ear. Her too-perceptive jet-black eyes glittered. "Nisha told us about the grant when she called in to the meeting. That's amazing! Totally expected, but amazing!" If Ashi thought that this particular change of topic would cheer Trisha up, she was right on the money.

Trisha beamed.

Her cousin matched her beaming smile. "Listen, I've got to go, but you're stopping by later for the food, right? You can tell me about it then." She adjusted that huge bag on her shoulder—why she and Nisha needed bags this big was a complete mystery to Trisha; she only ever carried her wallet. Halfway to the stairs Ashi stopped and came back. "Oh, and thanks for taking care of Emma Caine. Is she going to be okay? I didn't get a chance to speak to DJ about it yesterday."

Trisha remembered the look in Emma's eyes when she had left her yesterday. The disappointment—the damn emotion just wouldn't stop plaguing her.

"Well, the other doctors were wrong. Her tumor isn't inoperable. I'm going to be able to remove it."

Ashna squeezed Trisha's arm. "Oh, Shasha! You are magic. I knew it! Thank you!"

It was exactly what Trisha needed to hear. Her parents' disappointment didn't matter. What anyone thought of her didn't matter. What mattered was that she got to do this. To save lives.

An alarm rang on Ashna's phone and she gave Trisha another quick hug and made her way to the stairs. "Really have to go. Can't wait to hear all about the surgery," she threw over her shoulder. Were those tears in her eyes?

Trisha hadn't realized that Ashna was so close to Emma Caine. Unless of course this was about the noble, and elusive, brother. Aha!

As she pushed the door to Aji's room open she felt a bit like one of Sripore's show horses after completing a particularly fraught obstacle course. She took a deep breath, soaking in the smell. It was beautiful. There was just no other word for it. It was sweet and decadent and calming. A perfect representation of her grandmother, in all her Queen Mother glory. Only, her grandmother wasn't there. The connecting door to Esha's room was slightly ajar. Trisha tiptoed to the door and pushed at it the slightest bit.

Esha's room was all white walls, white floors, and white linen. Completely bare except for the large circular bed, and thick shades that plunged the room into absolute darkness. The only light came from the silver oil lamp that had burned without pause for over thirty years in front of a life-size painting of Esha's parents, framed with carved marble so intricate it looked like one of Aji's lace creations. Aji sat in a white wing chair by the bed, her fingers flying on a crochet needle.

Esha lay belly down on the bed, her white comforter pulled up to her shoulders and her hip-length hair gathered in a voluminous bun at her nape. She looked like she was floating on water, ethereal.

Aji caught sight of Trisha and her eyes lit up. Trisha loved her grandmother's eyes. She had heard on more than one occasion that she had inherited them, but she didn't think it was true. Aji's eyes were a deep brown with flecks of fiery amber and gold, but the magic was in the intensity of the kindness they held. Trisha could only hope that someday, maybe fifty years from now, she could emulate even a fraction of her grandmother's poise.

Aji placed a finger on her lips, a signal that it wasn't okay to go inside. Trisha nodded and tried to smile, but her stupid lower lip protruded in a pout all on its own. She pulled it back in, but she stood there watching. She wouldn't get a hug from her grandmother today, but she could soak up some of the peace from the scene in front of her.

Disobeying Aji was out of the question. If Esha was having an episode, disturbing her would only lead to her having a seizure. Esha never left the Anchorage grounds. Not since Trisha's father had brought her to California when she was six. Aji and J-Auntie had homeschooled her. Anytime she needed medical attention, HRH took care of it. After Trisha had earned her medical degree, she had slowly started to share that job with him.

Attending any of the public Raje shindigs was out of the question. Her nerves couldn't take the overstimulation and it brought on seizures. Ambition was too violent an emotion for the eldest of the Rajes of this generation. If that wasn't an irony, Trisha didn't know what was.

Trisha had never met His Royal Highness Maheshwar Rao Raje, Esha's father, but from everything she'd heard he had been a version of HRH on steroids. A barrister, and India's youngest ever and most charismatic member of parliament, he'd been earmarked for prime ministership and leading India out of the chaos that colonization had left behind. All it had taken to derail that plan had been a failed airplane engine.

Esha's episodes had started after the airplane crash had killed her parents along with thirty other passengers, leaving Esha the miraculous sole survivor. The seizures caused her to go catatonic and were followed by debilitating migraines. All the medical scans in the world had not been able to come up with an explanation for why they came on—or for her visions.

A week after the accident, six-year-old Esha had dreamed of their Sripore estate manager, J-Auntie's husband, being crushed under a tractor. They had found his body that same day, mangled by the machine. A spate of visions about everyone who worked at the Sripore palace had followed, turning her into a shaking terrified mess.

Just the rumors of her clairvoyance had brought throngs of people seeking their futures to the palace gates. No amount of refuting the rumors had dissuaded the crowds. They took to leaving offerings for the *little goddess* outside the palace. Before the news spread further, HRH had whisked his dead brother's daughter off to California where Trisha's mother had been pregnant with Trisha.

In California they had found that not leaving the home kept her seizures under control, and it kept the visions restricted to the people Esha was connected to. She had seen Yash in a wheelchair before his accident. She'd seen other things about Yash too. Things that fueled the family's dreams.

Aji had moved to California when they had brought Esha here. She never left her side. She guarded Esha's periods of meditation and her trances with her signature soft fierceness. Trisha believed it was her way of paying for the death of her oldest child. Atonement, because she had insisted he get on that plane and take his family on vacation, because he worked too much. Everyone had tried to convince her that it wasn't her fault. But guilt had tenacious tentacles. It burrowed under your skin and possessed your entire being until you couldn't exorcise it without losing yourself.

Trisha blew Aji a kiss and was about to turn around when Esha raised her head, skewing her heavy bun to one side. "I'm sorry about your patient," she whispered, her eyes still shut as though opening them would hurt. "Good thing you never give up." Then she laid her head down and went back into her trance.

Chapter Seven

Gathering up the oversize canvas bags of groceries from his trip to the farmers' market, DJ let himself out of the Palo Alto flat that was costing him a kidney to rent. He made his way across the eight blocks that led to Curried Dreams, his friend Ashna's restaurant.

As he took High Street, every cell in his body seemed to want to turn toward University Avenue and go back to Emma. But he had promised Ashna that he would help her work on new recipes for the upcoming summer season. Plus, he had no idea how he was going to face his sister. Now that she had lost her blooming mind.

Her words still stung like oil burns on his skin, but he deserved them. She was right about all of it. It was too late to change their history, too late to change the choices he'd made. He couldn't bring their mother back, couldn't change the fact that he was responsible for her death. But he could keep Emma from taking her own life.

It was suicide. There was just no other word for it. And it was not going to happen, not while he still breathed.

He forced himself to turn toward Forest Avenue. The homes

in this part of Palo Alto were unlike the mansions a few miles away. This was where the scale still felt somewhat urban. Not quite like the tightly packed flats of avenue de Flandres but a little like the town houses in Richmond, old money so insouciant it needed to make no effort at all to be shown off.

Sunshine filtered in and out from behind the jacarandas lining the street and made him squint. There was something about California sunshine that kept him standing, kept him moving, and he hooked into it. How the sun touched you here was different from anything he'd experienced before. It carried a little more heat than Paris and definitely more light than London.

The Clapham flat they had lived in before his father died had windows that somehow trapped what little sunshine fell upon London and streamed it into their lives. DJ barely ever thought about that home anymore, or of his strapping, hazel-eyed father sitting in his threadbare tweed chair with the *Times* open in front of him, throwing headlines at the family as though he couldn't keep his newfound knowledge about their world to himself. DJ couldn't remember the last time he had thought about the car that had jumped a red light and run his father over on his walk home from the factory. DJ had been twelve.

After Dad died and his family threw Mum, Emma, and DJ out of their home and onto the street, they'd moved to the attic rooms of Ammaji's Southall house. There had been one dormer window in the attic that overlooked a tiny patch of backyard where Ammaji hung her clothes on clotheslines. No light ever seemed to reach that little square of yard but the smell of freshly washed fabric had still infused it with warmth.

He turned into the back alley that led to the deliveries entrance of Curried Dreams. Ashna stood at the top of the half flight of stairs, leaning against the service door, beaming at him in jeans and a T-shirt that proclaimed the name of her restaurant. It had been over a decade since they had attended Le Cordon Bleu in Paris together before starting their careers under Andre Renoir, but time hadn't touched Ashna.

They had barely kept in touch after she had moved back to the States. Fortunately, another thing time hadn't touched was the easy friendship they'd developed as Andre's fresh and eager assistants. When DJ had moved here a month ago, lost and unable to come to terms with the prospect of losing Emma, Ashna had taken him under her wing and made everything fall into place.

"Hullo there, love!" he said, then laughed as Ashna tried to take the bags from his hands. When he refused to release them, she kissed him on the cheek. "Hello yourself, Chef!"

Ashna had to be one of the dearest people DJ knew. Andre had tried hard to play matchmaker between them, but it had only made them laugh. There was a melancholy air about Ashna, as if tragedy fluttered like a cape behind her. She took herself a tad too seriously, something DJ too was accused of often enough. For all their shared somberness and the comfort of their connection, their friendship had never been touched by attraction.

DJ had always believed that when he met the person he was meant to be with, he'd know. It would be the way it was with food, a moment of truth when he tasted a dish and knew it was perfectly as it should be. It would just feel right. He couldn't imagine getting into a relationship until that happened. Without that connection, he was just wasting his time and he certainly hadn't been born with the privilege of time to waste on playing the field.

He followed Ashna into the sunny kitchen and put the bags on her spotless stainless-steel countertop.

"These mangoes look great." Picking one plump orange-gold fruit out of a bag, she gave it a sniff. And scrunched up her nose. "You should smell the mangoes in India. They smell like sugar melting in the summer heat. How do these have no aroma at all?" Then she smiled. "Yikes, I sound just like my aunt."

They started emptying out the bags, laying out the okra, spinach, and cilantro in little heaps across the countertop, each shade of green as distinct as each vegetable's identity.

"Oh, and speaking of my aunt"—her eyes turned positively smug—"I think you have a fan. Everyone's been asking who catered the dinner last night and she called to let me know that I was not to give anyone your contact information unless she personally okayed it, which, by the way, is the highest praise you can receive from her. You are now one of Mina Raje's favors to be handed out."

He touched his heart and beamed at her. "I'm flattered. And grateful." Mina Raje's contacts had meant his phone hadn't stopped buzzing with bookings. He removed the colander hanging from a hook over the sink and started rinsing things one by one.

Ashna's kitchen was perfect, well designed and spacious

enough to make up for the equipment from two decades ago. She spread a towel on the countertop and nudged him playfully with her elbow. "So, I believe Mina Kaki offered you 'the job' last night! How are you feeling about catering the event of the year—our future governor's first official fund-raiser?"

His smile widened until his cheeks hurt. If his hands weren't wet, he'd have hugged her. "You have no idea! I've already started working on the menu. There's some new recipes I'm thinking of." He'd woken up at four this morning in Emma's hospital room to write down an eggplant roulade with tandoori paneer. The magic was in the Indian thyme and garlic chive foam infused into the paneer.

"It's funny how excited you get," she teased fondly, and having this, an old friend in a new and foreign place, nudged some of the despondence out of him.

"Are you still okay with me doing the prep work for the dinner here?" He started patting dry the okra so it wouldn't string when they cooked it.

"Of course. Quit acting like you're taking advantage of me. You're already helping me with the Curried Dreams menu in return. You know I suck at that sort of thing. You can use my kitchen during off-hours for as long as you need it." Suddenly exhaustion flashed in her eyes. He almost asked what was wrong. But she put it away fast enough that it was obvious she didn't want him to see it.

"Are you sure?" Even though she'd said repeatedly that he wasn't taking advantage of their friendship, it felt a little bit like he was. But not too many gift horses had been smiling at him lately and he also was just exhausted enough to not inspect this one's mouth too closely. Renting a kitchen in this town would mean burying himself in debt.

Ashna nodded and her worried gaze swept the room. She had left Paris after just a couple of years with Andre and returned to California to run the restaurant that was her dead father's legacy. She'd never said it in so many words, but DJ had gathered that all these years later she was struggling to save that legacy. Although how financial troubles could touch someone with a family as influential as hers, he had no idea.

"We'll come up with a spectacular menu for you. I swear. We'll pack them in." He'd repay her in every which way he could.

The smile reached her eyes again. "I'm counting on it."

He picked up a finger of okra and pointed it at the fryer. "I was thinking, let's fry it with a light batter and then try a hot yogurt kadhi sauce with it." Extracting his smock from one of the bags, he tied it on.

"What kind of crust?" She turned on the fryer and adjusted the temperature.

"We could try a rice flour batter? We want it papery—thin and crisp." He started to mix spices into the flour, a spoonful of powdered cumin, a pinch of powdered cloves.

"I heard the good news about Emma," she said, watching him, and his hands froze for a moment.

"And I think just a dash of gram flour like a pakora batter?" He forced himself to walk to the pantry shelves and grabbed the box of besan.

He couldn't discuss Emma right now. Silence stretched between them as he added splashes of buttermilk to the dry ingredients, working the batter with his hands, feeling it turn silky between his fingers.

He couldn't let the silence get awkward. "Seriously, Ashna, thank you. For everything. For the referral to your cousin, and to your aunt. Thanks to her, I'm booked up solid for a month."

She didn't call out the awkward topic change or push about Emma and he loved her for it. Instead, she simply dipped a teaspoon into the batter for a taste and made an approving sound. "All those bookings have nothing to do with me or with Mina Kaki. It has to do with what you do in the kitchen, DJ." She raised the spoon and offered him a taste. "You more than deserve it. You know that, right?"

Deserve was such a strange word, throwing out both blame and accolades with equal mercilessness. Society's skewed scale for assigning a value to human beings. How many times had he been judged and found lacking? Was there ever a way to measure what anyone deserved? Or was it just another way to pretend that the randomness of the universe made sense?

"Uh-oh, did I turn DJ Caine all brooding?" Ashna laughed, patting his arm with one hand while using the spoon in her other to signal him to open his mouth.

Her unguardedness felt like a gift. Getting her to overcome her usual reserve and trust him lifted some of the worthlessness he'd been carrying around since Emma threw him out.

He took a taste from the spoon she was holding up. "It's a good start. Let's try it this way, then we can tweak it."

"Got it, Chef." A drop of batter dribbled from the spoon onto his chin making her giggle. "Sorry," she said and quickly used her thumb to wipe it off.

A loud gasp sounded across the kitchen. "Holy shit! I'm so sorry! I didn't know you had company."

DJ looked over Ashna's head at a woman with her hand slapped across her mouth, her eyes so round one might think she had just walked in on them shagging on the kitchen floor.

Ashna stepped away from him. "Hey, Trisha! Come on in."

"I didn't mean to interrupt, I swear." Her flushed cheeks were so high they practically swallowed up her eyes as her gaze flicked here and there as though trying to avoid looking at Ashna and him.

Where had he seen those eyes before?

Bollocks! It was that woman who had almost destroyed his caramel. Those flame-colored eyes, glinting with all those uppish airs, were burned into his brain.

"Seriously, I'm sorry," she said again. And that voice, it made a million feelings run up and down his spine. Every one of them uncomfortable.

"You're not interrupting anything," Ashna said with her trademark patience. But there was an edge of reprimand in there as well. "DJ and I were just working on some recipes." It was clear from Ashna's tone that overreacting was nothing new with this one.

Her mortification morphed into suspicion. She looked as though she smelled something dodgy in the air, and threw DJ the most reluctant smile he'd ever been at the receiving end of.

"This is DJ Caine, Trisha. Emma Caine's brother. Haven't you two met? DJ, this is my cousin Trisha Raje, Emma's doctor."

What on earth was Ashna talking about?

This was Dr. Raje?

Bloody sodding bollocks on toast. The luck he'd been having recently, of course she'd be Emma's doctor.

"Oh." She swallowed a few times, highlighting the fact that she had the longest neck he'd ever seen. "No, we've never actually met," she said finally. "But I've been looking forward to meeting you." She dropped a handful of Tupperware containers on the countertop, then stuck out her hand. There wasn't a flicker of recognition on her face.

So the hired help wasn't worth remembering then. His heartbeat elevated in that way it did when anger rose inside him too fast. He tamped it down.

"I thought you guys had met," Ashna said, looking thoroughly puzzled. "DJ's the chef who cooked that fabulous dinner at Yash's party last night." There was pride in Ashna's voice and it seemed to totally befuddle her cousin.

"The hired help with the nonsurgeon hands, remember?" he wanted to say, but of course he stayed silent and moved to rinse the batter off his hands in the sink.

"Oh my God, I'm so sorry." Her gaze slid across his shoulders, lingered there for a bit, then came back to his eyes. Now she remembered. "I had no idea who you were. Nice to meet you." She extended her hand again, and if she was embarrassed by her behavior the other evening, she hid it well.

He took his time wiping his hands on his smock and obliged her. Her precious surgeon's hand was unexpectedly delicate in his, but her grip was entirely self-assured, and yet again he pictured her staring at her palms lovingly for hours. His were still smarting from the burns.

"Are your hands okay?" she asked, as if reading his mind.

At least she remembered burning him. He feigned ignorance. "What's wrong with my hands?" She didn't need to know that he remembered, too. Or that anything she'd said had meant anything to him.

She cocked her head, confused. "Seemed like you might have burned them at my parents' house."

Parents? Great. This just got better and better. She was Ashna's cousin. Of course that made her Mina Raje's daughter. Of course he had yelled at his most important client's daughter in her own home. And she just happened to be the person who could save his sister's life.

Could everything go any more tits up than that?

"DJ, you burned your hands? Why didn't you say something?" Ashna took his hands and inspected them.

"They're fine. No harm done." That was British for *I want to sob like a baby every time I touch something.* But Ashna didn't need to know that. Dr. Raje most certainly didn't.

"May I take a look?" Trisha Raje said, her expression pinched. *Do you have any idea what these hands are worth?*

Yeah, no, she was still not taking a look. Not when she had been okay with his hands being burned because they didn't do important enough work. Not if he had anything to do with it.

God, he sounded like a petty knobhead. Evidently, something about being called the hired help had stung enough to induce pettiness.

"DJ, let Trisha look. She's really good at this doctor thing," Ashna said and Trisha Raje grinned at her as though she had just dropped the deepest curtsy in front of her.

DJ picked up the colander filled with okra and moved to the

fryer. "As I've already mentioned, my hands are fine. I hope yours are still worth as much as they were last evening." Definitely a petty bastard.

That made her tilt her head in confusion again. Apparently, you needed no memory at all to get through medical school. Or maybe it was he who needed to have his head examined for remembering every word that had come out of her mouth like some fragile, egotistical half-wit.

Instead of getting stuck in a power struggle over his hands, he should talk to the woman about how to handle Emma. Had Emma spoken to her yet about her asinine plan?

"So what all do you need?" Ashna asked, pulling an aluminum tray out of the oven, effectively distracting Trisha Raje from his attempts at making a giant arse of himself. Holding his tongue was not a problem he usually faced.

She looked at the tray with so much mortification he wondered what she was up to. "Some butter chicken," she muttered, studying the foil instead of him, much to his relief. "And you said you have saag paneer and black dal?"

"Of course," Ashna said.

"You're an angel, Ashi!" She gave Ashna a grateful smile that reminded him of how very wrongly he had judged the humor in her voice before he had met her. Then she looked at him and got all uptight again before clearing her throat and giving Ashna a pointed look she seemed to think the hired help may not be able to interpret. "May I talk to you for a moment? Privately."

"Sure." Ashna threw an apologetic smile at DJ. "Do you mind giving us a minute?"

"By all means." He turned back to the okra, the fresh crispness of the vegetable taking up his attention as he dipped it in batter and gauged how thin a coating would work best. He'd have to do a double fry, of course. He dunked a bunch of lightly battered pieces in the fryer and inhaled. The tang of fresh spices hitting hot oil set things to rights for a few seconds before the pain and worry he'd been suppressing came bubbling up like the oil around the frying vegetables.

He turned around and stared at the door Ashna and Trisha had gone through. He could hear muffled sounds of conversation in the dining room beyond.

He had to speak to Trisha Raje about Emma's surgery. Surely no doctor would let a patient throw their life away the way Emma seemed to want to. But the idea of speaking to her again made distaste prickle across his skin.

He sighed. His discomfort didn't matter. Right now, Trisha Raje was Emma's lifeline, and the fact that she made him feel smaller than he had felt in a very long time was entirely irrelevant.

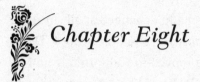

Chapter Eight

Trisha didn't know why her cheeks were flaming as she followed Ashna out of the kitchen and into the empty restaurant seating area. Her knees felt oddly wobbly. *That* was Emma Caine's supernoble brother? Also, dear God, superhot! And had he just dissed the living hell out of her?

Granted, she hadn't recognized him immediately. But there had been a chef's hat on his clean-shaven head last night, and the chef's robes were not the same as the white T-shirt stretched across his shoulders right now. She shook her head to clear it. Granted, he'd burned himself because of her, but he was at least half to blame for that. And then he'd proceeded to be incredibly rude. What kind of chef was rude to people when they were dying of hunger? Also, didn't being the person who was going to save his sister's life count for something?

Ashna turned to her with a raised eyebrow as if to say, *What was that about?*

She could ask Ashi the same question.

Meeting her cousin's curious gaze with a shrug, Trisha leaned on a chair and her pinkie finger found a little rip in the faded upholstery. Ashna's eyes caught the action and her shoulders did the tiniest slump.

The decor of Curried Dreams hadn't changed at all since her uncle had opened it when Trisha was in middle school. That's when Ashna and her father had moved to California from Sripore. Or rather, that's when HRH had forced his brother to move and open the restaurant to keep him from making more trouble in India.

Brahmanand "Bram" Raje had by all accounts been the quintessential wild young prince. A stereotype of royal debauchery and entitlement with a glamorous public lifestyle, and the debts and arrest warrants to match. What Trisha remembered about her uncle was his larger-than-life personality. His hugs big and tight, his jokes loud and bawdy, his love for food and drink such that you never left his presence without being fed to within an inch of your life.

Unlike his older brothers, Bram had barely made it through high school and had no skills other than knowing how to live large. HRH, in an attempt to fix his brother's life, had deemed a luxurious fine dining restaurant the most viable enterprise to finally help him grow up. As it often turned out, HRH had been right.

For the five years that Bram had run it, Curried Dreams had been Palo Alto's hot spot. The original decor of the restaurant had been a replica of the grand durbar hall at the Sagar Mahal. The chairs were hand-carved teakwood. The brocaded cushions and the tapestries hanging from the walls were custom woven and hand embroidered in the local Kashida tradition by artisans in Sripore and then shipped over. Everything had been vibrant shades of turquoise and magenta stippled with coppery gold. Ashna's father had loved to tell the stories detailing the history of each chair, table, and light fixture. The spirit of this place had once been as large and gregarious as Bram Raje himself.

"I remember when it used to be beautiful," Ashna said sadly.

Trisha linked arms with her. "It's still beautiful." And filled with treasured memories. "Ma wanted me to tell you that there's a buyer interested," she said softly.

"No, Shasha!" Ashna stepped away from her. "I know Mina Kaki is only trying to help, but I won't sell. I can't sell. Can't you see that?"

It was such a pain, being unable to separate yourself from your work. As Entoff had tried hard to teach Trisha, keeping your emotions out of your job was so much smarter. "This buyer is willing to keep the name and keep you on to run things. It's the perfect solution."

Ashna was about to respond, but Trisha cut her off. "No, it's not HRH trying to sneakily help you." At least that's what Ma had assured her when she had asked Trisha to speak to Ashna. But with HRH there were no guarantees when it came to limiting his meddling. "He knows you won't forgive him if he tries that again. But listen, if you default on the loan, the bank is going to take this place away, and then you'll have no say in who gets it."

"It's not going to come to that. I have a plan for a revamp. DJ is a master at menus and he's helping me. We're going to turn the place around."

The place had been steadily sinking for ten years. "How is a new menu going to fix the upholstery and the carpet?" Trisha pointed out, feeling like a jerk when she saw Ashna's eyes dim with worry. Trisha loved the restaurant, too, but even all her nostalgia wasn't keeping the dank feeling away.

"That's what brings people in," Ashna said stubbornly. "This is Palo Alto; everyone loves a little character."

Only when "character" cost millions of dollars to create. The Disneyland version of character was what had value here. Torn fabric and peeling paint didn't count unless it was executed by a designer and not by time. But Trisha couldn't say that to Ashi. Not about Curried Dreams. "Where are you going to find the money to pay this master of menus?"

Ashna sank into a chair. "I'm not paying him. We're bartering. Like the old days. He gets to use my kitchen during downtime for his private chef business."

"That's actually brilliant! Why didn't we think of that before?" Trisha sat down across from her, grinning.

Ashi grinned back. "I'm glad you think so."

"No, I mean, renting the kitchen during downtime. With the rent prices here, you could totally make enough to redecorate and pay for revamping the menu!"

"I'm not charging a friend to use my kitchen." Ashi stuck out her chin. It was her immovable face.

"I'm sure your boyfriend will understand that you're going to lose Curried Dreams if you don't charge him, or charge somebody, rent."

"He's not my boyfriend, Shasha. He's just a friend. A colleague. We've known each other for years."

Right. And that whole "feed each other with a spoon and then wipe his chin" thing was what everyone did with their "just a friend." But Ashna was always so damn serious, Trisha wanted nothing more than for her to have someone who could draw her out. Even better if that someone looked the way her chef friend did.

Trisha had the odd urge to fan herself.

"At least consider it. It's your only choice. I'll tell Ma to say no to the buyer, but let's look at renting, okay? You're going to need this. If he's a friend, he'll understand."

Ashna narrowed her eyes stubbornly, but entirely predictably she backed away from the confrontation. "You need food for this date or what?" she asked, her mood switching easily to amusement. "Come on, let's get it packed up." She stood.

Trisha pulled her back into the chair. "Shhh. I don't need your boyfriend—" Ashna glared and Trisha raised her hands. "Fine, I don't need your just-good-friend to know that I mooch off you when I'm pretending to cook for my date."

Trisha had met Harry last month, when he'd been the plastic surgeon on one of her surgeries. He had walked into her office for a consult and seen her eating some of Ashna's pakoras. She'd offered him one and he'd assumed that she had made them herself. He'd been so impressed that she hadn't corrected him. The man was cuteish and recently divorced. He'd asked her out after tasting those pakoras. No one had asked Trisha out in a really long time.

After their first date, he'd thrown caution to the wind and asked if she would cook more of that delicious Indian food for him. There had been something vulnerable about him asking, plus he kissed halfway decently and she hadn't been kissed in an embarrassingly long time, so she'd said yes.

Enter the chef cousin.

Once she'd fed him Ashna's food, Harry had practically worshiped Trisha in bed. So, here she was. This was only the third time—two surgeons trying to hook up was a scheduling nightmare—and she refused to feel guilty about the food.

"You deserve better than to have to pretend to be someone you're not." Ashna's hand went to her hip. It was her protective sister pose.

"I thought you guys said my problem was that I don't care enough about the men I go out with, and that I needed to try harder."

Ashna gave a giant sigh. "We didn't mean that you should lie! We just meant . . . never mind. When the right person comes along, you'll know what we mean."

Like that was ever going to happen.

This is how Trisha's dating life had worked since college: every now and again some guy came along and they confused the heck out of each other until he disappeared, leaving her more relieved than sad, and embarrassed as hell about her inability to know what was going on when it came to men.

Why were men such complicated beasts anyway? Relationships felt like full-time babysitting jobs crossed with high-level code cracking.

"Hey, I'm here stealing your food and pretending to be a domestic goddess just to get some. I think that qualifies as actively working on it. You don't even have to steal food, you can literally have them eating out of your hands once they taste your cooking. And you've got someone who looks like *that* in your kitchen and you're calling 'just good friends' on him? Come on, Ashi!"

"Aw, Trisha thinks DJ is cute," Ashi singsonged as though they were still in middle school.

He wasn't cute. No, most certainly nothing as mild as cute. Whatever he was, he hit you on the head with it. "Um . . . not the point. Come on, one of us has to figure out how this entire long-term relationship thing is done without selling out."

"You're such a romantic, Trisha."

"What I am is a surgeon."

"And how could anyone ever forget it?" Ashi pursed her lips, half amused, half reprimanding.

"Very funny. My point is that with neurosurgery there are always fifty things that could go wrong and often you have to choose the least damaging damage. So analyzing risk is what I do best."

Ashi relaxed into her chair, grinning like a loon. "Trisha Raje giving relationship advice. I should totally record this."

Trisha ignored her and went on. "He's a chef, you're a chef, you've known him for years. So the psychopath possibility is minimal. I say the odds of him being someone you can seriously consider are pretty high."

"Wow! Those poor men you date."

"Gah, let's please not talk about the men I date." How she hated that term. "What does dating even mean? What are the requirements?" Harry was nice enough. Maybe. They hadn't ever really talked about anything but surgery. In that department, he was fabulous. As long as she didn't compare him to herself.

He'd just gotten out of a bad marriage and all he wanted was to make up for lost time in the sack and be fed some good food. Fill the two big holes his marriage had left in his life. So she was lying to him about where the food was coming from. But at least she was helping him heal from his marriage, and wasn't she a healer?

Dear God, she was a terrible person.

Ashi was laughing now and looking at Trisha as though she were the most adorable thing since Minnie Mouse. This was the other problem. When you had so much love in your life, why would you waste your time on decoding men?

"Look at what we're working with here. Look at the men in our family. Yash, Neel, Vansh." Her little brother was an annoying know-it-all, like the youngest of any brood, but probably the best human being she knew. "How on earth do we have any chance at all of finding men who match up? You have to take your chances on the ones that aren't half bad."

At this point Ashi's laugh got so loud she let out one of her little midlaugh hyena screams. "I'm sure DJ would love to know that he passes your not-half-bad test."

"No, seriously. We've been ruined—"

"Are you okay, Ashna? I heard screaming." The man in question walked in. At first he looked a little freaked out, like someone contemplating needing to perform CPR on a dear friend. But then he saw Ashna guffawing and a smile lit up his face.

And by lit up Trisha meant: fireworks! His crystalline eyes sparkled, his skin glowed, the dimple in his chin deepened.

"We are totally fine," Ashi said. "Except I need to get Trisha to give relationship advice on YouTube. We could make a killing. And she thinks you're—"

"Ashi! I really need my stuff now. I have to go." Trisha pulled Ashna off the chair. Was there anything more annoying in the world than cousins? Trisha dragged her still-laughing cousin into her kitchen and started putting Tupperware boxes Ashi had packed for her into a cardboard box and then picked it up to take to the car.

"Let me help," the chef said, going all stiff again, and gallantly took the box from her.

"Thank you." She held the door open, pointed the remote at her car, and popped the trunk. Then she watched him walk down the steps of the service entrance under the blast of sunshine that made her squint.

"When you're done admiring the view, come in and tell me what else you want," Ashi said behind her.

Trisha scowled, hoping it would hide the flush on her skin.

As Ashi filled a few more containers, still grinning annoyingly, Trisha wondered if she should feel worse than she did about passing off her cousin's food as her own.

Nah. The fact that having her cook for him made Harry so ecstatic was sexist enough that it helped with the conscience easing. She also had a niggling feeling that his assumption that she could cook was based on the fact that she was Indian. That definitely helped with the conscience easing and if that made her messed up, well, that made two of them.

Ashi placed the remaining Tupperware containers filled with her date-bounty into a cloth bag and handed it to Trisha. "How is Emma doing?" She threw a look at the door to make sure DJ wasn't back.

"Didn't he tell you? It's a good news/bad news situation. I didn't have a chance to tell you at the Anchorage. I can operate on her tumor and it will save her life." Trisha swallowed and looked at the door. "But I can't save her optic nerves. That means she's going to go blind."

"Dear God." Ashi pressed a fist to her mouth. "Poor Emma. Poor DJ."

DJ appeared in the doorway and the light framing him from behind made the pain in his eyes stark. The drama of those thickly lashed hazel eyes against that looming physique and dark skin made Trisha blink. She hadn't registered quite how sad his eyes were. Maybe because of all the glowering he'd been doing at her. How had she forgotten a face like this even for an instant?

"I have to go," she said to Ashi, giving her a quick hug. "It was nice meeting you, Mr. Caine. I'll see you at the hospital later today, maybe?"

He nodded and held the door open as she stepped out into the sun-drenched afternoon. Passing so close to his big body made the doorway shrink around her. His scent, something citrus and masculine, stroked at her senses and nudged her slightly off-balance in that way that a first sip of wine always did. Her feet stumbled on the top step and she grabbed the metal railing, throwing a look over her shoulder, hoping he hadn't seen that.

Naturally, he had. His expression didn't alter as he watched her, the impassive look on his face only unsettling her more. She could swear he was trying to cover something else with that look. Something intense that vibrated beneath the sudden flatness in his eyes. Something that felt an awful lot like dislike.

DJ LEANED AGAINST the heavy deliveries door and watched Trisha Raje walk to her car and tried to ignore the restlessness the woman kindled inside him. Reaching for every memory of warmth that he could dig up from the slim pickings of his thirty-year-long life, he called out, "Dr. Raje!" He pushed off the door and followed her down the steps. It thunked shut behind him just as she turned around to face him. "I was wondering if I could perhaps have a word."

She looked so shocked he might as well have asked her to jump in the car with him and elope.

"We've been missing each other at Emma's appointments," he said.

"Actually, *I've* never missed an appointment with Emma." She attempted a smile.

He was fully aware that he'd not been able to make his sister's appointments with her. If there was any way he could have been there, he would have. Maybe if he had been there when Emma got the news about her eyes . . .

When he didn't smile back, her smile twisted awkwardly into a frown. "I've actually never missed an appointment with any patient ever," she declared stiffly.

Okay. Good to know. Medals all around! "I've been here

only a month and I'm trying to set up a new business, so it's been hard to coordinate schedules." Why was he explaining himself to her?

She shrugged, then stood there opening and closing her mouth. Well, not literally, but she looked completely tongue-tied and he wondered if she truly was not used to the hired help speaking to her.

"I wanted to talk to you about Emma and the treatment you're proposing."

"Of course. I'm headed to the hospital right now." She looked down at her phone and tapped her thumb on the screen. "Yup, she's the first one on my rounds this evening. I'll just see you there?" She pulled open the car door.

So she didn't know yet that Emma was planning to fire her. Thinking about Emma, about the immovable decision in her eyes, set off another storm of panic in his gut. "Is there really no way to remove the tumor without damaging her optic nerves?"

She froze in the act of getting into her car and stayed suspended like that for a beat before straightening up and turning back to him. "I'm sorry, Mr. Caine. I know this isn't the solution any of us were hoping for. But it's—"

"You know my sister is an artist, right?" he said a tad bit too desperately.

"Yes. And she's incredibly talented." A blush suffused her cheeks and DJ knew she was thinking about his sister's Sam Adams–loving vagina. He'd seen the painting Emma had done for her.

Out of nowhere he had the urge to smile. Emma's art no longer embarrassed him. She had beaten that out of him with her Penile Dysfunction series. It was more a phase than a series, really. A long phase that had lasted years, during which she had found every way to deconstruct—which was artspeak for destroy—all forms of phallic symbols—which was artspeak for penises.

Love for his sister, in all her infuriating glory, clogged up his throat, filled his chest, until he could barely breathe around it. "Then you have to understand that she can't lose her sight." His voice came out a little too forceful because he could barely get the words out. "Art is Emma's life. There has to be another way. There has to be. You just have to find it!"

She stiffened, blinked incredulously, and actually stuck her nose up in the air. "Are you aware, Mr. Caine, that your sister saw several other surgeons before she came to me?" The amber flecks in her golden eyes sparked with indignation. Obviously, she was not used to anyone challenging her opinion. "I'm the only one who was able to come up with a solution. The only one. Do you know why that is?"

He refused to nod. Something about the sheer volume of her arrogance held him in thrall.

"It's because I've worked my ass off on developing technology that can navigate through brain tissue without damaging it." There was a flash of almost crazed glee in her eyes. It reminded him of mad scientists in movies cackling over smoking test tubes. "Brain tissue is the most delicate, most vital tissue in the body. I've helped create a machine that nudges it apart instead of slicing through it. Do you have any idea how groundbreaking that is? I don't find solutions for inoperable cases by accident. I find them because I'm exceptional at what I do. And I do not leave any solution unexplored."

He raised both hands in that ridiculous universal gesture that said *calm down, there's no need to get your knickers in a twist,* but it was he who needed to calm himself down. "I didn't mean to suggest that your work isn't brilliant," he said as evenly as he could manage. "If the technology can nudge through brain tissue, why can't it remove the tumor without damaging the nerves?"

She pressed her hand into her forehead, as though she couldn't quite plumb the depths of the stupidity of that question. "You cook for a living, right? So I can understand why this sounds simple to you. But this is live tissue we're talking about, not meat. You can't just scrape the tumor off a nerve without leaving remnants of tumor behind."

For the second time in two days this woman had made what he did sound like wiping shit off the sole of your shoe, not just unskilled but unsavory. It was only the second time he'd met her, but she'd already made his heart slam with anger far too many times. He hadn't felt this kind of anger since he was a teenager with no control and far too much to be angry about.

"My sister is not live tissue, Dr. Raje, she's an artist who lives for her art. This will change her life forever." If she even agreed to let it.

"I realize that. But a changed life is still life. It's all I can do. And it's more than anyone else has been able to do."

In that she was right. The realization jabbed a hole in his anger, letting out some of its steam. "I can only hope that you can convince Emma of that." This time his bloody voice did crack, and he turned away because he couldn't let her see him fall apart.

"Excuse me?" she said behind him.

With a quick swipe of his eyes on his sleeve, he turned around and met her gaze again. "Emma's decided not to have the surgery."

"What? What is that supposed to mean?"

"Just that. She won't agree to a surgery that will cause her to go blind. She wants to look into alternative treatments."

"She can't do that!" Trisha snapped with the same finality Emma had used when declaring that she would do exactly that.

He laughed. A dark sound, coming from a dark place inside him. If Emma did this, there would be nothing left. His mind couldn't even form the thought, couldn't imagine a world without her in it. "She plans to do exactly that."

For a long beat she just stood there, then she got in her car and pulled her door shut. Her tinted windows slid down, revealing her livid face. "And you plan to stand by and watch her? What kind of brother are you?"

"The kind of brother who hopes you can change her mind."

"You better believe I will." And with that she was gone.

He couldn't believe he was thinking this, but he had never hoped for anything as much as he hoped that all her ugly arrogance was justified.

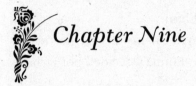

Chapter Nine

There was no frickin' way that Emma Caine could do this to her. Trisha was about to storm into Emma's room when her boss caught her at the check-in desk and dragged her into his office. Well, not dragged literally, but it felt that way.

Trisha and Entoff often disagreed about treatments and courses of action. It was one of her favorite things about her job. The fact that the two of them approached cases so differently was what made them such a formidable team.

But this was different. "You knew that Emma Caine is refusing treatment and you didn't tell me?" she said, spreading her hands on his desk and staring him down as he sank into his chair.

"How did you find out? Never mind. Sit down for a moment." He pointed to the hypermodern leather-clad chairs that always looked strangely unbalanced to her. His desk, no surprise, was spotless except for a veritable forest of frames with his children's pictures.

Entoff was one of those older men who looked like a plastic surgeon's model, with thick gray hair, perfect capped teeth, and a runner's lanky build. But his personality was more reminiscent of Santa Claus's elves. Every time Trisha disagreed with him, he became so excited and proud, she imagined him going "Ho ho ho" while clicking his heels. She couldn't tell if that's what was going on right now.

"There is no other feasible course of action, Dr. Entoff. You know that." No matter how many ways they sliced that argument, they both knew that the only way to save Emma's life was this surgery Trisha had proposed.

Instead of his usual cheeriness he gave her a sad smile. "There is such a thing as a patient's rights, Dr. Raje. Not only is it our legal obligation but it's also our moral duty to let patients decide what they want."

That was the most asinine thing Trisha had ever heard. Moral duty, her ass! Patients weren't doctors. They were entirely unequipped to make decisions about treatments. This was why she had spent ten years busting her balls, or ovaries, or whatever the gender-accurate phrase was, trying to equip herself to be able to make decisions about treatments on their behalf.

"Either way, it was wrong to meet with my patient without consulting me first."

Not many people in this building could say something like that to their boss and get away with it, but she wasn't many people when it came to her work and Entoff looked apologetic instead of insulted.

"I did text you. And I did try to calm Emma down and convinced her to wait to speak with you before making any decisions."

Good. Trisha wasn't coldhearted enough to think that

Emma shouldn't be having a panicked reaction. She just needed to be the one to talk her down from that ledge without putting counterproductive ideas in her head. "Thank you for that. I'll take care of it," she said, turning to leave.

"Trisha, remember there's only so much we can do, okay?" She knew what he was going to say next even before he said it. "We're not God."

She tamped down on the urge to stick a finger into her mouth and gag. Why did people say that? No one knew for sure that God existed. You know who existed beyond any shadow of a doubt? Doctors, that's who. And their job was to save lives.

As she walked down the corridor lined on both sides with paintings, she couldn't help but think about Emma's art. The girl was crazy gifted. The canvas Emma had given her had such power, every time Trisha was in its vicinity she found it hard to look away from the depth and impact of the strokes. Yesterday she had googled Emma and found a bunch of her pieces at various online galleries.

Her work had a stormy quality to it, like she wanted to shake things so hard she made them break apart. Most of it used some form of genitalia-based symbolism, which took some getting used to, but the fastidiously detailed complexity was what appealed to Trisha. Almost Dali-esque, but with hoo-haas and feminism.

Something about Emma's brother's face when he had talked about his sister's art made her heart twist. But letting her heart twist was stupid.

If she started thinking about what it would feel like if any of the Animal Farm needed to have this same surgery, she wouldn't be able to do what she needed to do. Which was slice the tumor out of Emma's brain with steady hands.

My sister is not live tissue.

But DJ Caine was wrong. That's precisely what Emma had to be to her, because Trisha knew exactly what to do with misbehaving live tissue.

When she entered Emma's room, she was curled into a ball, her face pressed into her knees. Silent tremors shook her shoulders.

In all the times that Trisha had met her, she'd never seen Emma be anything but aggressively upbeat. Trisha saw illness test people often enough to recognize an indomitable spirit when she saw one. Another thing that had struck Trisha about Emma's art was how intent she as an artist was on bending the universe to her will, while still acknowledging it for what it was. Those two abilities had a deeper connection than most people understood. If only Trisha could get Emma to see that connection when it came to her treatment.

The moment she realized Trisha was in the room, Emma straightened up, yanked a tissue from the box next to her, and blew her nose as though it were a cold she was struggling with, not tears.

"Why hullo there, Dr. Raje," she said as though Trisha was the last person on earth she expected to see. "I'm sorry, didn't they tell you? I changed doctors."

A stool sat in front of the wall-mounted computer. Trisha grabbed it, pushed it closer to the bed, and sat down.

"I understand how you're feeling, Emma."

Emma scowled. "Will everyone just bloody stop saying that! You have no bloody idea how this feels."

"You're right. I didn't phrase that right. I meant, I understand that this is impossibly hard."

Her patient's scowl grew furious. "Seriously, is there a bible of 'knobhead bollocks to say to the terminally ill'? Is that where you people get your lines from?"

"Actually, you're no longer classified as terminally ill. Given that your life isn't going to terminate."

Emma shook her head and looked up at the ceiling. She was praying for patience. Evidently those prayers were not being answered. She looked so livid, Trisha could practically see her fingers flying on her next piece, *Strangulation by Fallopian Tubes*. "I'm not a lab rat, Dr. Raje. And I'm not a video game that you're going to get to your next level on."

"I'm aware. I've sliced through enough lab rats to know that you look nothing like one." She attempted a smile. "And I never did get into video games. All the female avatars look too much like Barbie. Relatability was an issue."

"How can you think this is funny? Are you so jaded that someone's life ending means nothing to you?"

"Your life will not be ending if I have anything to do with it." That was the damn point of all this, wasn't it?

Emma threw another tormented glance at the ceiling. "See, this is just a notch in your belt."

Trisha thought about telling her that she didn't own belts, that if she ever needed one for notches she'd have to borrow one from Nisha's extensive collection.

"Why did you come to me, Emma?"

Instead of answering, Emma gave her a look that stood in nicely for a raised middle finger.

"If you do believe that earning notches in my belt is what I'm trying to do here, then aren't those very notches why you came to me?"

This girl wasn't stupid, just angry. Her mouth pressed into a thin line; she hated that Trisha was right, but she also understood that Trisha was indeed right.

"I came to you because my brother's friend believed that you could cure me, not play chess with my body parts." Trisha could see another painting, a chessboard with scrotums and vaginas, and in place of the king: eyeballs. Well, this was checkmate.

"All I can do is assure you that that's not true. What we're dealing with here is the exact opposite of chess, in fact. Tumors, clots, hematomas, they don't follow rules—there's no two squares forward, one square sideways move. But, yes, if it helps you understand this, we have to sacrifice your optic nerves for your life, because when that's gone, the game's over."

"See. I don't want to be treated by a doctor who treats my life like it's a game."

Trisha stood. Anger was all good and dandy, but she drew the line when someone started calling her professional integrity into question.

"I think you're being unfair," she said evenly, because she wasn't self-centered enough to be upset with a patient who was struggling with a diagnosis like this. But this wasn't the time for lies, either. "More importantly, you're misguided. The alternate treatments, the ones that you think will give you more time to live the way you're used to living, are unpredictable at best. You already know this. There was a reason why your diagnosis was considered terminal without this surgery. We can't predict the speed with which things will progress. Sure, an oncologist might be able to slow the tumor growth and give you more time, but you'd be counting on a miracle to get more than the six months they gave you before."

Every one of those words seemed to hollow Emma out, like a scalpel was eviscerating little pieces of her. "That is just your opinion. Dr. Entoff said I had options." Emma struck back like a boxer who was on her back but wasn't ready for a knockout to be called.

She looked immovable.

Trisha took a breath. Entoff might be wrong about the options, but he was right about the other part after all. There was only so much Trisha could do. At least right now when Emma was in the throes of a panic attack. She had to work through that herself. Pushing her would only make her feel even more cornered.

My sister is not live tissue. She's an artist.

But before she was an artist, Emma was human. And when it came down to it, humans were animals. Being cornered made them wild, it made them throw caution to the wind, sent them into a crouch of instinctual attack that often went with forgetting to protect themselves.

"None of the options will save your life," Trisha said softly, unable to give up.

"But it is *my* life, Dr. Raje."

That was it! Emma felt powerless right now. That's where

her decision was coming from: this was her trying to regain some control.

All Trisha had to do was find something to make Emma stop feeling so out of control. Something to give her patient a little more time to consider her life, to maybe even find her power somewhere other than in her art.

"What if I discharge you today? There is one more scan result we're waiting for. That won't come in for a week. You'll need that for a second opinion, anyway. Let's wait for that before we rush into decisions. How does that sound?"

Emma sat up. "Are you serious?" A mix of tentative excitement and suspicion leaked into her voice.

Trisha nodded. "All I ask is that you monitor your temperature and your blood pressure, and if anything changes—any blurring of vision, any severe pain—you come straight to the ER and call me. Once your results come in, we'll lay all your options out and if you still want to switch to an oncologist for treatment, then . . ."—Trisha had to swallow to get the rest out—"then I'll refer you to one myself."

"Did you say today?" For all the fierceness from a minute ago, Emma looked suddenly scared.

But the sooner they got past this, the better. "As long as you have someone making sure you're watched twenty-four seven, you'll be fine." For some reason, Trisha felt sure DJ Caine would be up to the task.

That seemed to relieve Emma. "And I can paint?"

"Of course." Trisha thought about what would happen if someone told her she could never operate again. She couldn't imagine it. Not even for a moment.

Emma studied her wordlessly for a few seconds, some of that lost respect returning. "Okay. But there's something you should know. I never change my mind once I make a decision. I don't plan to start now. I won't have the surgery. So if this is some sort of strategic maneuver, it won't work."

Trisha nodded and made the effort not to show her relief. One step at a time. That's how you changed the world.

Chapter Ten

DJ was six years old when Emma was born, but he remembered everything about the day he went to see her at the hospital for the first time. He especially remembered how that day had felt. It was the same feeling that sparkled to life at the edges of his consciousness every time something good happened to him. It was the magnet that the homing device for happiness inside him hungrily sought.

Dad had cooked him breakfast—bacon, eggs, and porridge. It was what his father always made when he wanted a day to feel special. Then he had helped DJ get dressed in his best sweater vest and checkered shirt.

"You have to look your spiffiest and eat well on important days," Dad had said, "and this is the most important day of our life."

Dad had also worn his sweater vest, the one he wore to play cricket at the neighborhood pitch every Sunday. They had gone to the hospital like that, all matched up. The reason DJ remembered it in such stark detail was that when they reached the hospital one of the nurses had pinned an "I'm a big brother" button on DJ's vest, and then taken a Polaroid shot of him in his dad's arms as he leaned down to look at Emma, a little cloth-wrapped sausage that smelled like Dad's milky porridge, pressed into Mum's chest.

Funny how photographs become the form your memories take. Of all his worldly possessions, that faded Polaroid was possibly DJ's most cherished one. Everything that meant anything to him, everything he wanted out of life, it all seemed to be trapped in that picture.

Leaning back in the ergonomic chair in the hospital waiting area, he stared at the happy faces tucked into the plastic sleeve of his wallet.

It had been eighteen years since Dad died, twelve since Mum had followed him. There had been some dark lonely times in there. But the reason he'd pushed past them was the person sitting on a bed somewhere above him with a mass growing in her brain. After Mum died, Emma had been his reason to survive, to wake up in the morning.

At twelve, she should have been the one lost, but it had been he who had fallen to bits. His guilt had felled him, paralyzed him. It had felt humongous, uncontainable inside him, unforgivable. But Emma's unhesitating forgiveness had gathered him back up, strapped him back in place. Her faith in his being worthy of redemption was what had forced him to accept Ammaji's help that last time.

Emma and Ammaji, those two had punched holes into the darkness he'd been drowning in until he could see again. Ammaji had died just a year after Mum. The idea of Emma not being around made his future seem like a road disappearing into that same darkness again.

He'd been sitting here in the waiting area for a half hour. He knew he had to go back to Emma's room. He'd left her alone all day, mostly because she was being an idiot and he needed to figure out a way to screw her head on straight. But also because he couldn't face her. He didn't know how.

Truth was, he understood exactly why she was acting the way she was. Whenever life made his sister feel powerless, she got doubly powerful. After Dad died, they'd been homeless for two days, sleeping on park benches. Emma was the one who had dragged Mum and DJ to the church. At six, she'd known to do that and not cared that the nuns would judge them. It's how Father Batista had gotten Mum her job at Heathrow, and from there everything had fallen into place.

When Emma had forced him to apply to culinary school after Mum died, she hadn't expected him to leave her behind in England. But she'd dealt with that by challenging every teacher at her art school by being more and more preposterous with art until she'd broken down every expectation they'd had of her.

Now she was doing this. It made her feel in control. But it was stupid. *Suicide.*

The word made acid rise up his gullet, made his skin feel too tight.

In one thing she was right: he had to listen to her. If she needed to feel powerful, he couldn't steamroll her. No matter what else happened, they had always listened to each other. That's why they felt heard no matter who else shut them out.

Dr. Raje had probably already seen her. Maybe she had convinced Emma that her life was worth saving. The indignation on Trisha Raje's face, infuriating as it was, might be exactly what Emma needed. The woman obviously had no experience backing down from a fight in her overindulged life. The clash of two immovable forces was his best hope.

He threw another look at the photograph that time had faded into sepia tones before folding his wallet and pressing it to his chest and caught the eye of a woman who was watching him from two seats away. She had golden dreadlocks and the most stunning blue eyes that twinkled gently when she smiled at him. He smiled back, hooking into a stranger's kindness and seeking comfort in it for a moment.

The woman got up and moved to the chair next to him. She threw a pointed look at the wallet he was clutching as though his life depended on it. "A parent?" she asked softly.

"My sister." He opened the wallet and gave her a glimpse of his almost lost family.

"Beautiful."

"Thanks." He touched the picture one more time before tucking it back into his pocket, because he was having just the kind of day where kindness from a stranger might cause him to burst into public sobs, which was a bit too horrifying for his English heart.

"Is she going to be okay?"

He hoped so, but he couldn't say it, so he shrugged. "Do you have family here too?" They were in the Neurosciences Institute. Nobody would be here if they could avoid it.

Something horribly sad flashed in her eyes. "Orphan," she said, raising her hand as though in a roll call. "Don't have a family." She tried to cover up the sadness with a breezy smile.

"I'm a journalist. I'm working on a series of films on end-of-life treatments and terminally ill patients."

"Cheery," he said.

"Someone's got to tell the stories of the people medical science can't save." She said it with the kind of sincerity only someone who had found purpose in their work would recognize.

"Until a week ago we thought no doctor could save my sister."

"And now?"

Now she didn't want to be saved. "And now it's complicated." He stood. He needed to find his complicated sister and get her to see how uncomplicated this really was.

She stood, too. "I'm Julia Wickham." She stuck out her hand and he took it. What the handshake lacked in firmness, her smile made up for in kindness.

"DJ Caine."

"Do you mind my asking who's treating your sister?"

"Dr. Trisha Raje," he said absently, eager to get to Emma and find out how her meeting with her doctor had gone. "I have to go. It was nice meeting you."

"Nice meeting you too." She gave him another stunning smile. "Is it okay if I call you? I'd be very interested in speaking with your sister."

He almost laughed; Emma would strangle him with her bare hands.

"I know it's a difficult time. But research has shown that laying out your thoughts on camera can aid in processing traumatic events and help deal with them. This might be exactly what your sister needs to uncomplicate things."

What Emma needed was her tumor to be in a different part of

her brain. Just the way she needed their mum to be here to talk her through this, and not a brother who had no idea what to do.

"Think about it. We don't pay but we set up a funding campaign and our reach on social media is so good that donations from viewers can really add up. I know what the bills can be like. And we usually raise enough to pay them off and have money left over."

"Thank you but, no, we aren't interested."

She looked disappointed, but she smiled kindly, extracted a business card from her bag, and pressed it into his hand. "Let's at least exchange cards. Who knows what might come up."

He took her card and retrieved one for her from his wallet. "I'm a private chef. In case you know anyone who needs a party catered. But, sorry, won't be able to help you with anything else."

With another bright smile she slipped his card into her bag. "Good luck with your sister."

That he could use. He thanked her and made his way to Emma, hoping she wouldn't throw him out.

SHE DIDN'T. INSTEAD, when he opened with, "I'm sorry. I should have heard you out. I'm going to listen now," Emma's skeptical brow quirked up. It didn't seem to believe him any more than she did.

But when he handed her the box of pralines he'd made her, she snatched it up and popped one in her mouth. For a while there were no words. Just satisfied sounds as she closed her eyes and soaked up the taste of her favorite candy.

Finally, she spoke around the last bits of it. She always let it melt in her mouth instead of chewing it like a normal person. "Good. Because the doctor discharged me. I need to go home with you."

Sod it all! What? All his resolve to stay calm exploded inside him. "Go home? What the bloody bollocks is that supposed to mean?"

She gave the praline in her mouth a thoughtful suck. "It means you get to take me to the flat you currently reside in."

"Quit being a cheeky cow! How the hell could she discharge you?" His voice was steadily rising.

Instead of matching his anger, Emma channeled the Dalai Lama and went utterly calm. Ever since she'd told him about the tumor, all she'd been was a crackling ball of contrariness. Even when her body had been tired, she'd ceaselessly fought the finality of the test results and diagnoses being thrown at her. Her resolve had been a bit scary, but having her act like she was making peace with something she couldn't fight, that was downright terrifying.

He opened his mouth, only to have her palm go up in his face. "Even Dr. Raje saw that this is my decision and not hers. And most certainly not yours!"

"You have a tumor in your brain!" he wanted to shout. "How am I supposed to keep you safe at home?" But he couldn't bring himself to say the word *tumor* out loud.

What kind of doctor let someone with tumors wrapped around major nerves go out into the world?

"I need to speak with her before we go anywhere." His desperation must have shown, because his sister leaned forward and took his hand.

"Get your knickers out of your arse crack. She's only letting me go home for a bit, a week maybe. We have to come back and see her in a few days. You can conspire about how to change my mind with her then." She pointed to a file folder on the nightstand. "All the instructions are in here. All my prescriptions are in my bag. There's some test results Dr. Raje's waiting on. Until then she thinks I'll be fine."

"Define fine."

"Let me see . . . Well, I get to go to work and slap some paint on a bloody canvas. I get to do what I love for a little bit longer before I die. How's that for a definition?" She poked him with a finger, right in the middle of his chest.

Warmth prickled at his eyelids and he turned away and pressed his face into his elbow.

A nurse walked in and asked if she could remove the IV. Emma nodded and held out her hand.

"I'm not asking for your permission. I'm doing this my way." Emma glared at him, not flinching as the nurse tugged out the plastic needle and pressed a wad of cotton into the blood that seeped out with it.

As a child, Emma had burst into tears at every little thing. Then Mum had died and she had turned into someone else overnight. Someone who constantly fought to become and not become their mother. Their mother's funeral was the last time she had shed tears around him; it was the first time he had shed tears around her. They had switched places that day. Her softness had calcified and gone tough, all his hot bluster had

fizzled. She had grown an armor, he had realized the uselessness of his.

Of course she wasn't asking for permission. Emma Caine
believed choice was the cornerstone of existence. Her art, everything she stood for was about tirelessly exploring the relationship between choice and power. Now for all her fierceness she
looked vulnerable, and it made her seem like the little girl who
had curled up in a ball in their mother's chair and waited up for
her when she worked the late shift.

"Okay," he said. "Tell me what you want to do."

For a second all her walls collapsed. Just fell to the ground
around her. This was what she had needed all along.

"I want to get out of here. And I want to go to work tomorrow."

The nursing home that housed the art residency she worked
at was her life. She had left London in search of something
and when she'd found the residency, she had found purpose,
found herself. It was a therapeutic residency where they used
art to treat everything from dementia to depression and anxiety and other struggles aging residents faced. Emma had once
explained it to him as helping them access their lost inner
child so they could heal that loss.

"Done. I'll drive you there and back. What else?"

She smiled a tremulous smile, which for her was like all-out
bawling. "That's good for now. Can't take up too much of a
fancy chef's time. Who will feed all those rich people if you're
babysitting me?"

"I've been babysitting you all my life, sister mine. I got it
sorted."

That, she didn't argue with.

They only realized the nurse had left when she came back with a wheelchair and insisted on taking Emma down to the car in it. Which didn't make DJ feel any better about them letting her go home. Panic started to rise again, but he pushed it away. He had to let her breathe. Even if it meant he couldn't until she changed her mind.

Grabbing her bag and sketchbook, he followed her out. She smiled up at him, and for a moment she was the little sister who'd made him feel like a bloody hero. *My Big Brother* was the first picture she'd done for him. He'd worn a cape and had six arms, a cross between a superhero and the statue of the Hindu god Vishnu who sat in the altar tucked into the corner of Ammaji's kitchen.

They waited at the curb for the valet to show up with Emma's car. The sun had slipped away for the evening, but the bright porch lights tried to play substitute and made Emma's jet-black curls glisten like a halo around her small face. Hair she had hated as a young child because it had been different from everyone else's. But then she'd grown up and turned it into a canvas. Unlike him she had gone through all the phases of embracing her African heritage: she had nurtured an Afro, had it braided, shaved it off, grown it long. Pride swelled inside him for her ability to make beauty out of everything, even her struggle to find herself.

He, on the other hand, had inherited hair genes from their father's side. His curls were more relaxed than Emma's. Indian hair, Mum always called it. It was the only thing he had inherited from his father other than his hazel eyes. He had started shaving it off when he got to Paris and had never grown it out again. Unlike his sister, he had neither the talent nor the stomach for identity struggles. The only time he had tried to find himself, he'd ended up on the wrong side of the law.

Emma stuck her nose up in the air and inhaled like a hungry dog, then laughed at herself. "Fresh air, DJ! Isn't it beautiful?"

He dropped a kiss on her head.

She looked up at the hospital building. "Thanks for taking me away from here."

"I'll take you wherever you want to go, Em. Just promise you'll tell me immediately if you don't feel good. That you won't try to be a hero."

"Try?"

"Yeah yeah, but heroes must take care of themselves, too, love."

"So they do. I will be a good girl. If the room starts to spin, I will try not to hit my head on something sharp when I fall. Good?"

"You are not doing a great job of putting me at ease," he muttered as he helped her into her Volkswagen Beetle. She wasn't allowed to drive anymore, but her eyes lit up when she saw the car. She loved the bloody thing at least as much as she loved him.

He slid behind the wheel and felt immediately like he had slipped on too-tight shoes. Did he mention it was hot pink? Which was probably why his little sister was grinning like a loon right now.

She waved bye to the nurse and settled into the puffy seats that seemed to have been created for her. The yellow halter dress and six-inch heels she was wearing made her look like one of those celebrities caught on camera while stepping out for ice cream instead of a patient leaving the hospital after a heartbreaking diagnosis.

The nurse stood there watching them drive away with a look DJ had seen far too many times. Emma saw DJ shaking his head at the rearview mirror and elbowed him in the ribs.

"Another broken heart left in your wake," he said. "Poor gits. They have no idea that Emma Caine's heart belongs to her art."

"You better believe it," she said. "Don't look so smug, brah'. It runs in the family, innit?"

So it did. When homelessness was where your life started, you fell in love with the thing that gave you hope, that fit you right, that gave you power.

They drove down Palm Drive, soaking in the posh campus, and the posh town it was nestled in. Emma's forehead puckered with worry. "Who would've thought losing your health would be so expensive? I have some money saved up. You don't have to take this entire thing on yourself."

When he didn't answer for a while, she sank deeper into the seat and closed her eyes. "Okay, so I don't. But I'll come up with something."

He reached out and patted the arm folded across her belly. Mum used to wrap her arms around herself exactly this way. "You don't need to worry," he said. "I'm a fancy chef, remember? I've got enough stashed up. You were right all along about me being miserly and insecure. Good news is it's going to get us through this."

"But I don't want it all gone. You've worked your entire life for—"

"For us."

She dismissed that with an impatient flick of her head. "You shouldn't have to start from scratch."

Truth was he'd never not felt like he was starting from scratch. Maybe it was because of those homeless days, but it didn't matter how well he did, it had never been enough to feel secure.

"Maybe I'll start blogging about this. That should take my art sales through the roof. Maybe I'll become an internet sensation and they'll make a movie: artist lives out her last days trying to make sense of death through her art. We can call it *Going Down in a Blaze of Glory!*" She made jazz hands. "Surely everyone will throw money at that!"

He stiffened, but she smiled at him. "Relax, I'm pulling your leg. Maybe." She leaned back into the headrest.

"We'll sort it all out. I've got a gig catering a fund-raiser for a bloke running for governor. Long as I get that right we'll be okay. Let's just go home now." It was strange to use that word here. He'd long stopped trying to figure out what *home* even meant. When was the last time he had thought of any place as home? Certainly not England. He had no desire to go back there. Had he ever thought of Paris as home? He'd felt established there if not exactly rooted. Like his feet held up even if the land beneath them wasn't familiar. Did he even want to feel rooted? Or did being rooted just mean you could be uprooted?

But Emma seemed to have found home here, and that meant this was where he needed to be right now.

"When has Chef Caine ever had trouble getting a dinner right?" she asked, smiling, her eyes closed.

Never. For all the things that were going tits up around them, Yash Raje's fund-raiser was one thing he would not allow anyone or anything to mess up.

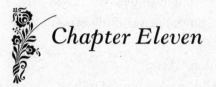

Chapter Eleven

They said shitstorms were like dominoes. Okay, so no one actually said that, but recently Trisha's personal shit-storms were falling so hard and fast they were knocking each other down.

First, Emma had completely thrown her off by refusing surgery yesterday. Then, Nisha wasn't answering her texts or calls. Then, Trisha had spent five hours in an emergency sur-gery operating on Dorna Matunge. And lost her.

She pressed a hand to her chest. She had known Dorna all her life, and she was going to miss her. All that wisdom, all that experience she had shared so generously, gone.

They had known there was no hope going in, her brain stem glioma had progressed. But Dorna had been insistent on the surgery and Trisha had thought there was a chance—albeit a tiny one—to make it work, so she had taken a stand on her behalf. Before going into the OR, Dorna had made Trisha tell her all about the technology. Unfortunately, the technology hadn't been able to help given how far her cancer had advanced.

Now, just as she was contemplating texting the Animal Farm

with the news about Dorna, she had texts from Ma and HRH, both saying the last thing she wanted to deal with right now.

She read HRH's text first. "She's been sniffing around your patients."

Gee, I wonder who he's talking about!

Then Ma: "Can you swing by the Anchorage today? It's important."

Gee, I wonder what she wants to talk about!

Trisha absolutely did not have time for her parents' Julia paranoia today. Julia hadn't contacted her. Yash was fine. End of story.

Please please let it be the end of story.

"Is there a particular patient you're worried about?" she replied to HRH's text first.

"How is that relevant?" Translation: *No particular patient.*

"What is it you want me to do exactly?" That's what she wanted to text. Instead, she went with, "I'll be careful."

"Look over your patient list for the past two months and let me know if you have any terminal cases."

"Overkill, Dad?" Of course that's not what she sent. "Sure."

"Go home and check on Esha." Translation: *Your mother needs to play good cop and knock some sense into your head.*

Trisha was annoyed enough that she almost didn't tell him. "Dorna didn't make it."

She could practically feel the sadness in the silence that preceded his words. "I know. Sorry."

Seriously? He'd known she'd lost a patient on the table an hour ago. A patient who was a close family friend. A patient she had hero-worshiped her whole life. And he'd got straight down to his badgering nonetheless?

"You okay?"

She would have been better if he had opened with that. "I'm fine. You?"

"She had a good life. We have to remember that." She felt the pain in those words. Who would have thought a bunch of electronic characters on a screen could trap as much emotion as the sounds our vocal cords made? Dorna had been one of his closest friends and his tireless partner as they'd worked on advocating for inclusion in their workplace in particular, and their world in general.

"I'll go see Esha."

He didn't respond. Not that she had expected him to.

"Bye! I love you too, Dad! TTYL!!" She tapped out the words, then deleted them with flourish as she grabbed her wallet and left for the Anchorage. She'd just come off a five-hour surgery, but energy was coursing through her. Of course HRH had known her schedule when he'd issued the order.

On her way out she stopped at the nurse's desk. Anne, the clinic nurse and general admin chieftain, had a lump of surgical steel where others kept their hearts. Her bright smile died the moment she saw Trisha approaching. "I'll call you back," she said into the phone, "one of the *surgeons* needs something." Yup, she dragged the word *surgeon* out like a piece of gum stuck stubbornly to her shoe.

Anne and her posse of clinic staff loved to use terms like "arrogant" and "brash" when it came to describing Trisha on those annoying staff surveys the department loved to do every year. Usually, Trisha didn't disagree with criticisms lobbed at her. She didn't care. She didn't have time to babysit incompetence, and the competent staff liked her well enough. They'd even said so on the stupid survey.

"Do we have Emma Caine's MRI results yet?"

"Hello to you, too, Dr. Raje," Anne said before punching some keys on her keyboard, which was so curvy and padded that it could qualify as a prosthetic. Anne was wearing her usual carpal tunnel wrist braces that sat perfectly on the padded wrist support of the keyboard. Maybe it was the pain that made her so grouchy all the time. "The MRI's done but Dr. Patel hasn't read it yet. We should have them by tomorrow afternoon."

"Good. Text me as soon as they come in and if the patient or her family calls to ask about them, tell them they're not in yet. Say it will be a few days."

"You want me to lie?"

Good God, could one damn person just take her word for something! How much harder did she have to work for people to stop acting like she didn't know what she was doing?

"No, what I want is for you to help me save a patient's life. If you don't want to *lie*, tell the patient you'll have to check with her surgeon. But do not tell her that the reports are in. Please."

Anne's usually bitter-medicine face turned even more bitter.

"Thank you. And, Anne, raise the seat on your chair; it will take the pressure off the nerves at your wrist." She had told Anne this a few times before, but she stubbornly refused to listen.

"Thank you, Dr. Raje." She turned to her spaceship controls and went back to plotting world domination. Her chair stayed as it was.

On her way to the car Trisha tried calling Nisha again. Usually Nisha texted her twenty times a day, but it had been two days since she'd responded to Trisha.

"I'm coming over!" Trisha sent when yet again Nisha didn't answer her phone.

"DO NOT COME OVER, I'M FINE!"

Was an all-caps response supposed to help her?

A lowercase message followed immediately. "Busy with Neel and Mishka's trip. Relax."

This was getting annoying. Nisha was acting like Mishka was leaving for college. On Mars! Neel and Mishka's trip to England for Neel's Oxford reunion had been planned for a year. Her hyperorganized sister had probably had Mishka's bags packed for a month. And she knew Trisha knew that.

There was only one possibility Trisha could think of that would explain her sister's bizarre behavior. It was almost too idiotic to contemplate, and yet . . . Nisha couldn't possibly be freaking out about Neel going back to England because his ex still lived there, could she? Surely her sister knew that was a nonissue.

"K. But you'd better tell me if something's wrong," she sent and got a very unconvincing smiley emoji back. She'd have to go over later.

WHEN TRISHA GOT to the Anchorage, she found her mother on the uppermost floor in the storage room, which was basically the attic that covered one-half of the mansion's footprint. The sloping roof used to have fifteen skylights when the house had first been built but those had been closed up and covered with solar panels that powered the entire estate.

On the inside, the walls of the commodious room were lined with climate-controlled storage cabinets. Their grandmother insisted on not throwing away a single thing she deemed meaningful. Everything, from each one of their first shoes, rattles, chew toys, clothes worn for various ceremonies, report cards, was wrapped in tissue and naphthalene balls and packed in trunks and then stacked in the storage cabinets.

Someday all this would be shipped back to Sripore for record keeping the way it had always been done for all the royal children. However, between HRH and Ma, there wasn't consensus on when that would be. Trisha suspected that HRH wanted the keepsakes—at least the ones that belonged to Yash—to stay stateside, where he fully expected museums to be interested in them not too far in the future.

Trisha found Ma in the special room where Yash's things were kept. Ma was wearing a linen summer dress and Trisha thanked her stars that she had changed out of her scrubs and into shorts and a blouse. She always kept a change at the office and in her car because she often came to the Anchorage directly from the hospital.

Percussion beats of Zakir Hussain's tabla lilted in from the speaker system. Ma was sitting cross-legged on a low, tufted stool cleaning Yash's wheelchair, her movements keeping time to the four-beat cycles. Her mother never did any cleaning in the house. A cleaning service under J-Auntie's hawkeyed supervision made sure the Anchorage glistened at all times. But this room, none of the help were allowed to touch.

Trisha's stomach cramped at the sight of the wheelchair. She hated that thing, had hated seeing her brother in it. The accident had happened when she was ten years old. A drunk driver had hit Yash biking home from volunteering at a pet shelter. At the time, the wheelchair had been the answer to their prayers. When Yash had gone into the OR, they hadn't known if he would come out alive.

Nisha and Ashna had dragged her into the nondenominational chapel in the hospital. There Trisha had promised whichever nondenominational gods were listening that if they helped Yash that day she would always help anyone who asked her for help. Always. All she wanted in return was for Yash to live. And she'd meant it. That child's prayer had made her keep Julia's secret years later and ruined everything.

Being taken in by Julia's words would never stop haunting her. *You have to help me, Trisha, you know how badly I want this! I have no one else!*

Ma patted the tufted stool next to her. Crossing her legs, Trisha sank onto the stool and watched her mother spray and wipe.

"Is Nisha okay?" Trisha should have known that would be Ma's first question. Ma's radar when it came to her children was a scary thing.

"Busy with sending Mishka off with Neel. I think it's the fact that it's Mishka's first trip without her. She's taking it hard." Spinning crap for Ma for the benefit of her siblings came easily. They'd all done it all their lives, covered one another's asses with Ma—a movie instead of a study date, the rare return home intoxicated. Because to call Ma protective was the wildest of understatements.

Through school they were never allowed sleepovers at friends' houses. They had only ever hung out with friends who were also Ma and HRH's friends' children. It was something no one could budge Ma on. Trisha believed it had something to do with Ma's own untraditional childhood as a child star. She treated their safety as though it were a fragile bauble in her keeping. Even a hint of a threat to their well-being sent her into a tizzy of trying to manage their lives for them and they were all united in their quest to avoid that at all costs.

Between Ma's overprotectiveness and how packed she'd kept their schedules, Trisha had never learned to make friends. The only time she had tried her hand at it was in college with Julia and that had ended badly enough that fifteen years later her mother was still pulling her into "meetings" like these. After Julia left, the rest of Trisha's time at Berkeley had been spent being gun-shy of any attempts at friendship. By the time she got to medical school at Stanford, not having time for friends had become a way of life. Every once in a while she went out for a drink with her colleagues, but otherwise the Rajes were it. And despite the tension with HRH and Yash, they had been all she'd needed.

Ma gave a delicate nod, making the sharp edges of her auburn-highlighted bob swish around her jaw, and gave the wheelchair another wipe with her gloved hands. It was a rare thing for Trisha to have Ma all to herself. As a little girl one of Trisha's favorite things had been to watch her mother. Just watch her as she talked on the phone, listened to her favorite Indian classical music, or worked on her charities and events from her office. For all her fierce protectiveness, Ma had this dignified acceptance of the world. It was a dichotomy Trisha had never understood nor been capable of emulating.

Ma smiled—it was the smile that had captivated a nation of a billion people since she had been five years old. Mina Raje, or Baby Minu as she'd been called in the child-star years, had been India's answer to Shirley Temple, jet-black curls framing large twinkling eyes, and a smile bracketed by two dimples that made every woman want to be a mother, and every father want to be a better man.

She had also been one of those rare creatures who had seamlessly made the transition from cherubic child star to beautiful leading lady with a neat leap over any hint of adolescent awkwardness.

But Ma's story did have an ugly part. Her father had forced her into acting at the age of five, and by the age of twenty she hated everything about being a film star. So, once while shooting in Amsterdam, she had decided to execute a *Roman Holiday*–style escape. She had jumped over the wall of her hotel and landed right on top of His Royal Highness, Shree Hari Raje, knocking the young prince off his feet literally and figuratively.

Shree, who had been stranded in Amsterdam thanks to a winter storm on his way from Mumbai to San Francisco, never did anything in half measures. He had fallen hard. The drama that ensued had put all of Ma's rather ridiculously over-the-top films to shame. He'd hidden her from the furious manhunt, missed his flight again, and risked his job to take her on a romp across Western Europe. Because Mina had never traveled without a film crew. Because she had never been on a vacation. Because he hadn't been able to let her go.

And he hadn't let her go, not when faced with Mina's father's wrath and very Bollywoodsy gangster connections—they'd broken his arm, and he was a surgeon! Not when faced with his own mother's utter horror at having a Bollywood actress with a history like *that* defile their royal lineage.

Mina had matched his stubbornness. She, for her part, had ignored gangster threats—that included threats of acid attacks, withstood a virulent smear campaign in the media—that included pregnancy rumors, and faced down her mother-in-law's disdain. But she had refused to let Shree go, either.

When she married him, Shree had been the very definition of a young blue blood. The world had been his playground, his job his passion. His only ambition had been to "live life king-size"—the motto behind the motto of all royalty across the world.

Then his brother—the maharaja and the bearer of the family's politics—had died, and Shree had changed. In taking on the guardianship of his niece and his title, Shree Raje had also taken on all the ambition that had driven his brother. Maheshwar had been a public servant born and bred, obsessed with helping his people and also with the political power it took to make things happen in democracies.

Shree had taken on his belief systems with the zeal of a convert. But by the time the transformation happened Shree had already fallen in love with America.

Mina dealt with her husband's transformation like she dealt with everything else. She acted as though that's how things had always been. She stood by this new Shree wholeheartedly, became his perfect partner. In all things except his obsession with assimilation. In that one thing Trisha felt like Ma wished she had pushed harder and been less accommodating.

Neel's mother, Sunita Auntie, who was Ma's best friend, had once told Trisha that Mina had ruined the lives of many an Indian man and woman by setting up entirely unrealistic standards by playing the idealized dream of the perfect wife, daughter, and daughter-in-law.

When HRH had dug in his heels about marrying Ma, Aji knew her son too well to push her reservations too hard. But she'd held on to them until that plane had gone down and Aji and Esha had moved to the Anchorage three decades ago. It was Ma's love for Esha, all the nights she stayed up holding her as she trembled with her visions and seizures, all the adjustments she made to the upper floors so Aji and Esha's lives would not be disrupted any more than they had already been. And then there was their joint love for Indian classical music. That had sealed the deal and now Ma and Aji were as much a unit as Dad and she were.

"I was so proud of you for coming to the dinner the other night." Ma didn't mention her lateness or the fact that she had missed the postmortem tea.

In return Trisha didn't mention the fact that Ma had forgotten to update her about rescheduling the tea.

"Ma-saheb told me that Esha thinks there's going to be some trouble with you," Ma said, giving the wheelchair a soulful pat.

Okay. And trouble with her automatically meant that Yash would be under threat? Really, sometimes her family was so infuriating Trisha wanted to shake them. "Ma, Julia has not contacted me. Think about it, why would she ever contact me? I made it very clear that I wanted to have nothing to do with her. I would never hurt Yash. Why is it so hard for Dad to believe that?"

"Don't take your father's name in anger, beta! He said she's been seen around the hospital speaking with your patients."

"Why does he even know these things?" Trisha said, when she really should not have, because she knew only too well why he had to know.

Ma glared. "Do you really not see what's at stake here? You've heard Steele's poking around. You know he has that whole 'working man's candidate' advantage. You know Yash has to overcome the 'West Coast elite' thing. You know what the party's looking for right now."

"They're looking for Yash, if they have any sense."

That made Ma smile. And sigh. "Oh, Shasha, haven't you learned that the world doesn't see things as simply as your brain does?"

Trisha almost gasped. Yes, she was aware of how simply, and wrongly, she had seen Julia. She should not have let HRH bully her into coming here. Her mother took her rubber gloves off. Good. Trisha was done with this entire wheelchair-cleaning drama. It was nothing but emotional blackmail. Entirely unnecessary emotional blackmail.

"I know what she did to him, Ma. I am aware."

"It's not what she did to him that matters. It's what she can do to him now. If we don't make sure she doesn't."

Trisha stood. A sick churn in her stomach. "Would I not have come to you if she had contacted me?"

"Well, one isn't always sure why you hold your silence when you do."

Wow, Ma was not pulling any punches today. Trisha definitely preferred the ostrich theory. But Ma was right. If Trisha had said something, spoken up, Julia wouldn't have been able to violate Yash the way she had. And there wouldn't be a video that could destroy everything he had worked for floating around. It wasn't like Trisha didn't know this. Didn't carry it with her constantly. If she let it, the guilt would crush her under its weight, make it impossible to crawl out from under. The way it had for months after it happened. She pressed a fist into her belly. "I'll let you know if I hear anything. I have to get back to the hospital."

Ma stood, too, with one last sad stroke of the chair's wheel. "You know what Yash has been through to get here. This is Yash we're talking about, Shasha. Your brother loves no one more than he loves you."

Trisha almost snorted at that. This was not true. Or at least it was no longer true. And it shouldn't matter. They were all grown adults and no one should be measuring who loved whom most.

"Okay, never mind all that now. At least I got to see you, baby girl," Ma said much more softly, hooking a finger around a curl that had popped out of Trisha's ponytail and tucking it back.

Trisha gave her mother a quick kiss on her cheek and was almost across the attic when Ma stopped her again. "Well, if it isn't that Wickham girl, then what's bothering you?"

"Nothing."

Ma walked up to her and took her hand. "Shasha?"

"I had to tell a patient that the surgery to save her life is going to make her blind."

Her mother waited as though it was the most obvious thing in the world that there was more.

"She's an artist. She's refusing the surgery."

The stark sense of failure that jabbed at her was embarrassing. The pain in DJ's eyes when he'd told her about Emma's decision that wouldn't stop flashing in Trisha's head was downright baffling. She tucked her chin and turned away from her mother.

Ma pulled the door to Yash's special storage room shut and punched in a code to lock it and made one of her sounds, sadness combined with disapproval that said, *such is life.*

She led Trisha down the corridor to the stairs that led to Aji's floor. "Will it affect the grant? Was this surgery key to that?"

Trisha didn't know whether to laugh or cry at her mother's pragmatism. "No, Ma, the grant won't be affected." Not unless Trisha botched the surgery, and she wouldn't. "But I can't just let a patient die when I can save her." She let her mother's hand go and made her way down the stairs.

"Beta," her mother said following her. "You know the best thing your father ever did?" Trisha rolled her eyes, since Ma couldn't see. "Somehow, he cultivated this decency, this goodness in all of you."

Trisha spun around. "Dad did not do that by himself."

Her mother flicked Trisha's words away. She was but a satellite to the greatness that was Shree Raje. "My job was to instill street smarts in all of you." She wrapped her arm around Trisha and nudged her down the last few steps. "How to present yourself to the world, how to give the world something they couldn't get enough of, but to also get what you needed in return. With the rest of them, I managed it. Some would even say I managed too well." Her smile was self-deprecating, as though raising children who were too successful wasn't a huge accomplishment. "But you . . ." She shook her head dolefully as though she didn't know where they had gone wrong with Trisha. "I think you might be the first simpleton in the Raje family."

Simpleton? "I just won my hospital a multimillion-dollar grant!" Not one of her siblings had achieved such a thing.

"True. No one said you aren't good at what you do. But the smart thing to do would be to focus on the grant and to not get hung up on one case."

She wasn't hung up on the case. This wasn't about being hung up on a case. "I can save her life, Ma. How can I let her choose not to let me?"

Her mother threw a meaningful look up the stairs. "You remember Yash in the chair?"

Well, say by some miracle she had forgotten, wasn't Ma's little performance just now aimed at jogging her memory?

"Yash didn't get out of it because any of us pushed him. He did that because it was what he wanted. You provide the solutions. In the end, the patient's decision is not on you."

Trisha let out a deep sigh. Her mother was right. She couldn't force Emma Caine into the OR.

She followed Ma into the sitting room and found Esha and Aji on the sofa. Esha gave them one of her beatific smiles. Which meant she was having a good day today. Ma stroked Esha's head. There was a way her mother softened around her nieces. Her love for them seemed not to come with the same taint of expectation. It had driven Trisha crazy when she was younger, but she understood it now. It was quintessential Ma logic, to be just a tiny bit softer on her nieces than on her own children to make sure they knew that they were just as valued.

Trisha gave her grandmother a tight squeeze from behind and soaked up all the lovely Aji smell from her thick silver hair gathered into a bun.

"It's been two days!" her grandmother said in Marathi. She spoke impeccable English, but it had been her rule to always speak to the children in Marathi. This was how she always started all her conversations. Whether it was a day or ten, she always started with how long they'd been apart. To let them know she had been counting.

Ma sank into the couch next to Aji and a look passed between them. Trisha didn't bother to pretend she didn't know what it was. *Mission accomplished*, it said.

Esha got up. "You're a gift to your patients, Shasha. But you're needed by more than just them," she said with classic Esha crypticness. Then she gave Trisha one of her rare hugs, her slight frame pressing tightly into Trisha, her head resting under Trisha's chin. Esha being physical meant she was having an exceptionally good day. This lifted Trisha's mood. She blew kisses to everyone, hamming it up, then bowed to her grandma with a salaam in a perfect imitation of the staff in Sripore and backed out of the room, making all three of them laugh.

When she pulled out of the Anchorage gates, she felt a little bit worse and a little bit better than she had when she got here. Maybe that was the true meaning of going home.

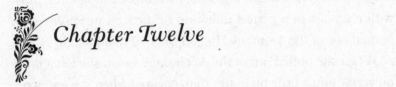

Chapter Twelve

In her entire life Trisha had never heard the words *I need you* from her big sister. Let alone *I need you right now, and if you don't get here this minute I will never speak with you again.* Let alone all this left on a voice-mail message while in tears.

Forgetting her phone in the car had been a really bad idea.

Nisha sniffling on the phone was not a pretty sound. It was, in fact, such a terrifying sound that Trisha turned the car toward Nisha and Neel's house in Los Altos Hills while desperately dialing her sister's number.

Trust Nisha to have an emergency (she had spelled the word out for Trisha, "E M E R G E N C Y, can you hear me?") and now when Trisha was calling back, incessantly, Nisha wasn't answering her phone. Calling Neel was out of the question, because Nisha had used her mad big sister voice to warn Trisha not to call anyone else.

"This is private. P R I V A T E."

Her sister spelling one word was bad enough, but her spelling out multiple words in multiple voice messages—that just made Trisha's mind ricochet in all sorts of dark directions. She restrained herself, using every focus technique she knew, and concentrated on getting to Neel and Nisha's house without running red lights.

Not bothering with the doorbell, she punched in the garage code, entered the house, and kicked off her shoes. There were no signs of anything untoward. Everything was exactly as it always was: picture perfect. Books and artifacts strewn around just so. Signs of Mishka everywhere, sketches on the fridge, walls covered with family pictures. Trisha ran past it all.

"Nisha? Hello?"

No answer. She ran into the bedroom and saw her sister on the bed. Curled up in fetal position.

No.

"Nisha?" Trisha laid a tentative hand on her sister's shoulder and heard a soft exhale in response. Relief whooshed out of her. She climbed on the bed and moved the hair off Nisha's face.

Nisha opened one wet-lashed, swollen eyelid. "You're here," she said and burst into sobs.

Trisha pulled her close but she'd seen this before. Too many times. Somewhere deep inside her the memory of what this was rose like water filling her lungs. How had Nisha not mentioned that Neel and she were trying to have a baby again?

"It's not what you think," Nisha said between sniffs. "I haven't . . . I haven't lost it."

Another wave of relief swept over Trisha. "Then why are you crying?"

"Why do you think?" Nisha reached for the box of tissues lying on its side next to her, pulled out a fistful, and blew into them with none of her usual grace. "I've lost six." Her sob trapped so much pain it didn't even sound human. "I can't . . . I can't lose another one."

"You won't." That would have been the right thing to say.

But Trisha had seen her sister break six times and pick herself up. Six times she had watched her pretend that this time, this one time would be the time it worked. She had watched her sister's marriage—without question the best marriage Trisha had ever witnessed—stretch at its seams as Neel struggled to understand why Nisha needed this so badly, why she would not see reason.

But Nisha wasn't someone you argued with once she'd made up her mind. Being a mother was what she loved best and she had wanted another baby.

"Congratulations." That would also have been the right thing to say, but they didn't say that in their family anymore when someone got pregnant. Not until the baby was born.

"I didn't know you and Neel were still trying." That's what Trisha settled on saying.

"We weren't. This one, Trisha . . . this one is like Mishka." Hope spilled from her eyes, making its way past the tears. "No meds, no treatments. Just us. Just Neel and me."

The hope in those words scared Trisha much more than the tears. How could Nisha do this to herself? She lay down next to her sister and curled around her.

"It has to be a sign, right? Please tell me you believe it's a sign," Nisha whispered.

Trisha gathered her favorite person in the world even closer. "Yes." God, please let it be a sign.

They held each other like that for a while, sniffling together. Smiling every time their sniffs matched up. Those stupid smiles made hope bubble inside Trisha too.

"How did Neel take it?"

Nisha pulled away, leaving Trisha cold, and afraid. "He doesn't know," she said quietly. "No one knows except you. No one can know. Especially not Neel. Not yet."

That's what Trisha had been afraid of.

All Nisha's failed pregnancies had terminated within the first trimester. A time when you can do almost nothing medically to save a pregnancy. Three months. Six months. Nine months. That was a long time to sustain hope, and keep a secret.

How on earth was Nisha going to keep this from the family, from Neel? From Esha!

One day at a time. It's what Esha always said when asked how she handled not leaving the house in over thirty years. One moment. Then the next.

"How are you feeling?" First things first. "How far along are you?"

"I've been queasy as hell every morning for weeks now. And exhausted. But I was so busy with Yash's dinner that I ignored it. Then this week it totally crashed on me. You know Mishka had the stomach flu last month. I thought I had picked that up. Finally I went to Sarita this morning." Sarita was their family physician. She was also someone they had grown up with.

Nisha gave her nose a dab. "I couldn't remember the last time I had my period. Sarita made me pee in a cup. Before I got home she had left me a message asking me to call her. She wanted me to call you over first. She didn't want me to be alone when she told me. But I made her." Nisha's eyes turned fierce. "I'm twelve and a half weeks."

Trisha sat up, her heart racing.

"I know! I'm almost at the end of the first trimester. One and a half more weeks. Just twelve days and it's going to be safe."

"Nisha . . ."

"No. I know it. In my heart I know it. If I can carry this baby for twelve more days." She looked down at her flat belly. Her fingers twitched but Trisha knew she was too afraid to touch it. "I know we'll have a chance. I'll tell Neel after that. I'll tell Ma, Dad, everyone else. But until then you have to help me."

"You want me to lie to everyone?" Little lies for Ma were one thing, but this? There was no way.

"Neel's leaving for his reunion tomorrow. Then he's taking Mishka all over England. They'll be gone for two weeks."

"Come on, Nisha, you have to tell him before he goes."

"No!" She almost shouted it. "I'm not putting him through this again. I can't."

"Nisha—"

"No! Do you know why I stopped trying?"

Trisha opened her mouth, then shut it. She had no idea—she'd never wondered why. What was to wonder? It had been incomprehensible to Trisha why they had gone on trying for as long as they had.

"Neel said he'd leave me if I tried again. He said he didn't have the strength to go through it one more time. He was done."

"Neel would never leave you. He didn't mean that."

"You're right," Nisha said too weakly. "Of course I know he

would never do that. That doesn't mean I get to push him to a point where he breaks."

Having known her brother-in-law her entire life, Trisha knew how solid he was. She also knew how serious his relationship with his high school sweetheart, Barbara, had been. They had started dating in their senior year and he had followed her to the University of Michigan, although Harvard and Stanford had both accepted him. His parents had been livid, but "Neel does what Neel does"—as his mother loved to say. He had proposed at the graduation ceremony in Ann Arbor. Then they had headed off to Oxford for grad school and planned to get married after they came back.

Of course, everyone also knew that Nisha had carried a rather bright torch for Neel since they were children and the two mothers had done everything they could to encourage that match starting young. But once Barbara came along everyone seemed to forget about it. Everyone except Nisha. Because the day they had heard the news about the engagement, the look that had crossed her sister's face had made Trisha want to hunt Barbara down and kill her. Or at least tell her to get out of the way because she was in the middle of someone else's love story.

But the universe had a way of setting things straight. Barbara, who had never left California until she went to Ann Arbor, had fallen in love with England and refused to return home after they graduated. Neel, being Neel, had changed his plans and stayed back even though he had wanted to come home.

Then something had gone wrong between them. Six months after earning his master's in international law at Oxford, Neel had returned home without a fiancée and one diamond lighter. "Three carats at that!" his mother loved to point out.

Who didn't return rings when they broke off engagements?

Who let a person like Neel go?

Not that Trisha wasn't immensely grateful that it had happened.

In the end Neel had left the three carats behind in London along with whatever dreams he had taken there. After coming home, he started working for a law firm in San Francisco, attended all the family parties, and hung out with the old gang. Everyone followed his lead and went on like nothing happened. Everyone except Nisha.

Nisha had refused to meet him. Not in any overt sort of way. But if she knew he was going to be somewhere, she simply didn't show up. When Ma tried to rekindle her matchmaking, Nisha told her that she would rather kill herself than have anything to do with Neel. When it came down to it, Nisha was definitely the more dramatic of the sisters no matter what anyone said. When Ma didn't take her seriously, Nisha played her ace—she went on a date with a divorced-with-children colleague who'd been pursuing her and swore that if Ma ever mentioned Neel again, she'd elope with the colleague. Not surprisingly, that second threat had worked where the first one had not.

Trisha understood Nisha's hurt. All her life, Nisha had believed that Neel was hers, until Barbara. She and Neel had been best friends. Even as kids they had been perfect together.

He hadn't seen it. Or he had seen it and he'd rejected it and wanted something else.

Almost a year after coming back, when Nisha didn't show up for the Diwali party at the Anchorage, Neel drove to her apartment. She was in her pajamas drinking wine, eating mint chocolate chip ice cream, and watching reruns of *Full House*. She'd pretended not to be home and refused to let him in. He climbed the tree outside her second-floor apartment and jumped onto her balcony. Before going up, he'd shouted out to Nisha and told her he was going to do it if she didn't tell him to go away. If that very upstanding-Neel-like gesture wasn't the most romantic thing Trisha had ever heard, the fact that he had hurt his knee while doing it was.

Then he'd asked a sobbing Nisha why she was avoiding him. Why she hadn't seen him in the year he'd been back.

Nisha had said quite simply, "Because I can't bear to see you in pain."

There was a wedding six months later, and Trisha, for one, had never doubted Neel's devotion to her sister.

Nisha sat up and scooted back to lean on the stack of white eyelet and cutwork pillows resting against the leather tufted headboard. "He meant it when he said he was done with us trying to have more children. I know I had pushed him as far as he could go, would go." She swiped her red, swollen nose. There was a veritable blanket of scrunched-up tissues on the bed. "No matter how we started out, after our babies, after what he went through with me for every one of our babies, we've been everything to each other. I can't live without him."

That Trisha knew. She took the wadded-up tissue from her

sister and tossed it clean across the room and straight into the trash can near the desk. "Did you plan this?"

Her sister glared at her. "It wasn't just that I knew he was done, it was that I knew *why* he was done. It wasn't just that he couldn't see me go through that one more time. It was him. I saw what it did to him, how much it took out of him to go from hope to loss without being able to show either because he had to be strong for me. It tore him up. Each time. The real reason I stopped was that *I* couldn't put *him* through that one more time." She plucked the last tissue from the box and pressed it into her nose. "You have to help me, Shasha."

Trisha picked up the wadded-up tissues one by one and started tossing them into the trash can. "You have a plan, I assume."

"The plan is to have you find a way to get me two weeks of staying in bed without Neel knowing. Without anyone knowing." She handed Trisha the tissue in her hand and Trisha tossed it into the trash with the others.

"Did Sarita say you had to stay in bed?" How had that not been the first question Trisha asked?

"No. She wants me to come in so she can run all the tests and do a referral to Vinay." Vinay was Sarita's husband and he specialized in high-risk pregnancies. "But no matter what Sarita and Vinay say, I'm not moving off a bed. Not until the first trimester is over. So put all that genius gray matter to use and come up with a way to help me do that without the Farm catching on."

Trisha slumped next to her sister. How? And what if something happened to Nisha—how would she explain that to

Neel? The problem with her gray matter was that it didn't work in situations like this. Everyone knew she had absolutely no emotional intelligence. She had to think of this the way she would think about one of her cases, logically.

"What about Sarita and Vinay? Sarita has probably already called Neel." Sarita was Neel's cousin a few times removed. Theirs was a crazy incestuous world.

"I've told her not to tell anyone, and she won't. Anyway she's bound by doctor-patient confidentiality." Nisha settled her head on Trisha's lap.

Doctor-patient confidentiality meant nothing around here. Sarita and Vinay were close family friends. Their parents, Sarita's parents, Vinay's parents, and Neel's parents had belonged to the same tight circle when they had first moved to America from India and all the kids had grown up together as one large extended family. Sarita had gone to school with Yash and all of them had spent more weekend nights than Trisha could count holed up in the attic, playing video games and Ping-Pong while their parents socialized and tried to re-create the old country with food, movies, music, and raucous political debate.

If Neel or anyone else decided to question Sarita, she was not going to be able to keep the secret.

"Neel leaves tomorrow. So first you have to help me find a way to stay in bed until then without him canceling his trip."

"You could pretend to have the stomach flu. He already thinks you might have it."

"Yes, but if I'm sick, he might not leave."

"It's his ten-year reunion, and you know how important that

whole Rhodes scholar thing is to him. No way would he miss it. Especially if I stay with you and promise to use vacation days and not leave your side."

"No. Too much. You know the lawyer brain. You have to sell it subtly, otherwise he'll get suspicious."

Great. And as if lying to Neel wasn't hard enough. What were they going to do about the rest of the Animal Farm? "Do we have to not tell the Farm? What about Esha?" Crap! Esha probably already knew.

"Especially not Esha. I don't want visions. No matter what happens, this baby is not going anywhere. I don't want anyone telling me otherwise," she said fiercely.

Message received.

"It would be so much easier if you could just tell Neel that you were going to DC or LA for campaign work. But then you'd have to take Yash, Ma, and HRH into confidence."

Nisha grabbed Trisha's arm, with surprising strength. "Can you not hear me? I cannot. Can. Not. Do this in public view again. I cannot watch everyone get invested, I can't manage everyone's pain. Can't manage Ma's overprotectiveness. Please. I need to focus on this on my own. I can't be brave for anyone else right now. My baby needs me. Please."

Trisha's eyes stung. She stroked the hand that was cutting off her circulation and swallowed the painful tightness in her throat. "Okay. No one finds out. That's not an option. Got it."

"And," Nisha said, "there's another problem."

"Of course there is." The look on Nisha's face did not bode well for whatever this next problem was.

"Yash's fund-raiser," Nisha said with all the gravitas of a

person who believed that their brother's campaign was her life's work. "The dinner is in San Francisco in a month. For the most part it's all planned—so do not freak out"—which was the last thing to say to someone when you did not want them to freak out—"but I need you to take care of things."

Trisha jumped off the bed. Take care of things? What things? Fund-raiser things? What? How? Oh, freaking out was building inside Trisha with the force of a pressurized hose.

She could find a way to lie to their family—although every one of them had a lie meter like a stealth missile detector. She could deceive her utterly brilliant brother-in-law—who was a blasted judge! But to expect her to take care of an event like this? An event. An *Event*. With food and guests and food-and-guests together. Was Nisha crazy? Did her sister not know her at all?

Trisha could barely plan her own meals. She lied about cooking to get men to date her. Which reminded her, she needed to cancel her dinner with Harry again tonight. The food she'd mooched off Ashna was sitting in her freezer mocking her inability to do anything with food except scarf it down. She was the last person to take care of something like a f . . . f . . . fundraising d . . . d . . . dinner. She didn't even know what something like that involved! Oh my God, what did something like that even involve?

"I said don't freak out, Shasha." Her sister glared at her as though the full blast of panic in her chest was something she could control by how much she widened her eyes.

"Too late. I'm freaking out. And I'm not doing it. I can't!" She started pacing.

Her sister intensified that glare. "I thought you wanted to be included in Yash's campaign? Or is HRH right, that you don't really care if Yash gets elected."

Did Dad actually say that? It was her turn to glare. What the hell was it with all this emotional blackmail? Nisha had always been Ma's little mini-me. But this was going too far. "Of course I want to be included. That doesn't mean throwing me straight into the snake pit. I meant start with involving me in . . . things and stuff—small things!" *And stop treating me like the Evil Witch of the East whose very presence will destroy Yash's dreams.* "Actually, I was wrong. Forget everything I've said until now. The banishment is A-okay. Really." She plopped down on the bed.

Her sister sighed. "Trisha, you realize you don't actually have to cook for this event, right?" Her sister switched strategies and, instead of glaring, tried a calm, amused look. "You work with a caterer and with an event coordinator at the ballroom."

Trisha's hands turned cold. She rubbed them on her shorts. "You are not helping. The only thing I know how to do with a c . . . caterer or an e . . . event coordinator is to remove tumors from their brains." Panic was rising again, hard and fast.

Her sister smacked her arm. "Stop it. If you put your mind to it, you can do this better than me and you know it. This is for me and for Yash. What is wrong with you?"

Trisha felt her cheeks warm with shame. "Make me walk through fire, I'll do that. Please can I do that instead?"

Her sister rolled her eyes. "No. So, the chef who's catering the dinner—"

Trisha groaned. It made her sound like an ill animal.

"Shut up and listen to me. The chef"—she paused dramatically—"will be here any moment and he's pretty good at what he does, so this will take minimum effort on your part."

Trisha jumped off the bed again and gawked at her sister. If she had been drinking something, she would have choked on it and died. Why hadn't she gotten herself something to drink? "What do you mean he'll be here any moment?"

The doorbell rang. *Horseshit!* Nisha had timed her assault perfectly. "What the hell, Nisha?" The shrillness of her shriek possibly cracked some of Nisha's windows.

"Give yourself some credit. You'll be fine."

"Credit? There's no credit to give. I have no credit in this. None. Why can't Ashi do this? Ashi does this for a living!"

The doorbell rang again.

Nisha glared at her again.

Trisha stomped to the front door. "I'm coming," she snapped and opened it to find DJ Caine standing there.

Of course it was him. Gah!

She leaned back her head and stared up at the surprised scowl on his face. How tall was this man?

He was carrying a huge padded box. One that needed both hands to be carried, which made Trisha wonder how he had managed to press the bell. Because she had the kind of brain that started analyzing random things when it was imploding.

Every single time she'd met this man, it had been a disaster. But this one was a disaster of epic proportions.

"Before you snap at me again, I'd like to mention that this weighs a ton." It really wasn't fair how a British accent made

everything sound ridiculously hot. That shrug thing he did
with one shoulder didn't help matters, either, because that
shoulder . . .

She was sweating. Sweat trickled down between her breasts,
where her heart had decided to start up a percussion band.

Channeling Nisha, she glared at him. "Literally or figuratively?"

He matched her glare with an impressive counterglare and
she stepped back to let him in.

One would think all those huge muscles weren't purely for
show. She followed him to the kitchen. He seemed to know
exactly where it was.

"They're sewn into my shirt, actually. Like a superhero
costume."

Holy crappers, had she said that out loud? What the hell
was wrong with her? *Brain, work. You're a genius. I have paperwork to prove it.*

She was about to apologize, but when he put the box down
and turned to her, she found herself frowning at him again
unable to actually form words. How pathetic was she? So he
was an attractive man. That's all. There was no reason to turn
into a complete bumbling idiot.

He craned his neck and searched the room. "I think you're
the wrong sister. I'm supposed to meet Nisha here?" He came
out from behind the island and turned around, still searching.

As if on cue Nisha walked in and caught her ogling his butt.

"Why are you up?" she said to Nisha more angrily than
she'd meant to. Because really, the whole point of this was for

Nisha to not get up. And also because she hated to be caught staring at men's butts.

"I'm being an *ass*, am I not?" Nisha said, and then grinned at her own joke as though she'd suddenly turned into Jerry Seinfeld.

The guy went completely still like a possum sensing danger, and Trisha learned that intense mortification feels exactly like motion sickness in the pit of your stomach.

"Hi, DJ! I believe you've met my sister, Trisha." Nisha went up on her toes to air-kiss his cheek and he very obligingly bent in half to let her.

"Yes, we've been introduced several times," he said in a tone that suggested being introduced to her even once was one too many times.

"Actually, we've been introduced just the once by Ashna," she snapped. "We were never actually introduced at Yash's dinner."

"How's it going with Ashna?" Nisha widened her eyes only the slightest bit at Trisha in what was Nisha's signature *Glare of Elegance* that you would only know was a glare if you shared genes with her. She saved it especially for public glarings. Then she led Bicep-chef to a barstool by his biceps.

"So you *are* with Ashna?" Trisha said. When she really, really should not have. What was it about this guy that was making every word out of her mouth stupider than stupid? She had been admitted into the nation's most prestigious schools for all that was sacred. She could operate machinery that delivered microscopic ammunition to tiny little cell clusters and saved people's lives.

He started to answer Nisha. "Things are going . . . actually . . ."—then realized what Trisha had said and turned to her. "I beg your pardon?"

Who actually said, "I beg your pardon"? Especially in a British accent. It just made you seem like a show-off.

"When Nisha asked how things were going with Ashna, I thought she meant you two were together," she babbled, her explanation only proving why she shouldn't have said what she'd said in the first place.

Nisha cleared her throat and decided to finally act like a big sister and step up to save Trisha from herself. "I was actually asking about how Ashi's new menu is coming along." Another Glare of Elegance was lobbed in Trisha's direction. *What the hell is wrong with you?*

Trisha shrugged. Hell if she knew.

"DJ is helping Ashi with her menu. His specialty is creating dishes that fuse traditional north Indian flavors with classical French technique. Right, DJ?" Nisha said kindly.

The guy smiled. A smile so grateful, so bright, Trisha blinked. His chin had a deep dimple, not one of those Ken doll chin-divide clefts, but an indentation that pierced the center of his chin, and it did a thing to his face when he smiled that caused a buzzing sensation behind Trisha's knees. She took a step away from him.

"I think we've come up with some pretty decent options for Curried Dreams." He was ignoring her entirely now and talking directly to Nisha, who was beaming at him as though he were her best friend. That job was already taken, thank you very much! How was everyone buddy-buddies with this guy anyway?

"You ready to sample what I have for you?" He strode back to the island and unzipped the hot box and all at once the most insanely delicious aroma suffused the kitchen.

Nisha's face went ashen. "I'm sorry," she sputtered before dashing to the powder room.

DJ followed her and hovered at the open door for a second as Nisha doubled over and emptied her guts into the commode. Before Trisha could push him out of the way and go to Nisha, he went in and sank down on his knees next to her, carefully gathering her hair and holding it out of the way as she brought up her insides in heaves. When she was done, he helped her up, his palm supporting her elbow with a mix of such gentleness, steadiness, and plain old-fashioned decency that the instinct to push him out of the way and go to her sister fizzled inside Trisha.

She leaned against the door and watched as he filled a glass of water from the faucet and handed it over. "Are you all right, love?"

Nisha nodded. Trisha caught herself nodding too. Fortunately, neither one of them was paying any attention to her, or the annoying reactions her body was having to his gallantry.

"Let's get you to a doctor."

Excuse him? Could those thickly lashed, hazel-flecked eyes not see her standing right here? That snapped her out of her swooning.

"Let's get her to her room. She'll be fine." This time she didn't care how harsh she sounded.

"Why don't we let a doctor decide that?" he said, so coolly he couldn't possibly be messing with her . . . could he?

"A doctor *is* deciding that. So if you don't mind." She pushed him out of the way and grabbed her sister's arm. The action made her feel like she was six and playing at being doctor instead of actually being one, and that shot her rioting emotions right into intense annoyance.

"I'm sorry," he said utterly unapologetically. "How could I forget?" And then she could swear he muttered, "The worth of your hands and all that," under his breath.

She couldn't remember the last time her ears had heated with embarrassment. What was it with him getting so hung up on that? Her hands *were* worth too much to burn on saving a pot of caramel. Why was that so hard to understand? He should be glad—she was going to save his sister's life, for shit's sake.

"That's okay," she said, then she matched his mumble with, "It's not like you need a photographic memory to cook food."

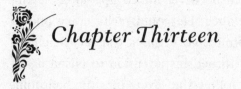

Chapter Thirteen

Trisha Raje was without a doubt the most insufferable snob DJ had ever come across in his entire bloody life. He'd been the poor boy at a Richmond private school. He'd worked at a Michelin-starred place des Vosges restaurant for ten years. He'd seen far more than his fair share of self-important, overprivileged gits. But it had never bothered him. Not like this. Her snootiness didn't just get under his skin, it chopped up every bit of pride he'd ever managed to gather up and flung it all over the place like a blender you forgot to put the lid on.

People were usually arrogant and snobby because they wanted to show you that they were superior to you. Trisha Raje's sense of superiority was so inherent, so absolute that she couldn't even seem to process why the oceans of other people's approval may not automatically part for her. She actually had the gall to be impatient with the world for not getting how amazing she thought she was.

It's not like you need a photographic memory to cook food? Really?

He'd been known to remember everything from allergies

and pet peeves and wine preferences to the names of girl-friends and wives—which he never mixed up—after having cooked for a client just once. He could recite every one of Wordsworth's poems from memory, thank you very much.

Gritting his teeth, he turned his attention to Nisha again as she beckoned him to follow the sisters into the bedroom. Getting into tussles with Trisha Raje was the last thing he needed. The woman literally held Emma's life in her hands, and her family currently held his career in their hands. Why was he having such a hard time with this? The thing he prided himself most on was his even temper.

His mother had insisted on him keeping his head down and being nonconfrontational no matter what the provoca-tion. Through his childhood he'd complied because he didn't want to be one more thing that didn't go her way. At seven-teen he'd had enough of being a pushover, though, and had let his anger out. And it had tangled him up with a bunch of boys who thought nothing of setting things on fire when something made them angry. That had been the end of it. After that he'd never had to struggle with his temper. Until of course Trisha Raje had walked into his kitchen and knocked over his caramel.

Now here he was, struggling to curb this urge to damn all good sense and unseat her from her pedestal.

Unlike her, the rest of her family was terrific. Even so, it was clear that the Raje blood wasn't just thicker than water—it was thicker than glue. They seemed to share this bond, as though they were their own galaxy, an eternal, perfectly stable system no outside force could ever breach or unbalance.

It's how families were supposed to be.

He tried not to think of his grandmother, who, after her son died, had thrown his widow and her two grandchildren out of their home.

Trisha Raje tucked the fluffy, pure white quilt around her sister and pushed her hair off her face, ignoring his presence in the room entirely.

"I'm sorry, I should have warned you not to unzip the food bag in front of me," Nisha said with the sweet grace that seemed to characterize everyone in the family except the one glaring exception. "It has nothing to do with your cooking, of course. I seem to have caught this awful stomach bug and food smells are making me sick."

Great. All that effort working on his preparations for days down the drain. "Please don't apologize. It's not your fault that you got sick. Rest now. We'll figure the tasting out later."

Nisha sank back into the cloud of pillows. Trisha took her wrist as if to check her pulse. No doubt to prove to him that he must never again forget about her being a doctor and whatnot.

He kicked himself for needling her. Because of course he'd offered to take Nisha to the doctor to get a rise out of her. Ah, sod it all, the satisfaction of seeing her turn shades was totally worth it.

With any luck, she was only here to check up on her sick sister and it was time for her to leave.

She settled in next to Nisha.

Well then, it was time for him to leave. "Just text me when you're better, and I'll be back with the sampling."

The fund-raiser was a month away and he needed that much

time for refinement and prep. Plus he had engagements on all the interim weekends so he had to work around those, too. Not that any of them mattered in the face of the fund-raising dinner, which was a two-hundred-person dinner at five thousand dollars a plate and was going to put a goodly dent in his financial troubles.

He hated being poor. Given how much experience he'd had with it early in life, he should be better at dealing with it. But ease spoiled you fast. You forgot how to deal with all the little compromises of poverty the moment you made any money at all. Andre had called this morning asking if he was interested in the position of executive chef that had just opened up at one of his Vegas restaurants. But even if leaving Emma right now were an option, the idea of working in a restaurant again made DJ sick.

He threw a despondent look at the door. In the kitchen sat the food he had spent days on. Being able to do this, to create food to fit an exact situation and an exacting audience—he wasn't ready to give up on that dream yet.

"Oh, we are doing the tasting today," Nisha said, sinking deeper into her bed. "Trisha will work on the menu with you."

"No!" he said before he could stop himself. The urge to run for his life was overwhelming. "I mean that's not necessary. Truly."

He couldn't bring himself to look at the woman in question, but something told him she was glowering at him. This was that pound of flesh thing happening to him again. "I'll wait until you're better. Really, I don't mind cooking all the food again next week when you're better."

"You'd rather cook everything over again than have me taste it?" The haughty offense in Trisha's tone wrapped up all the reasons why she was absolutely right. He would definitely rather cook the entire sampling menu ten times over than deal with her.

"I'm sorry, that's not what I meant at all." He met her gaze, reaching for all the politeness that had been drilled into him since birth and failing wholeheartedly. "I got the impression you'd rather not do this either."

All her uppish airs intensified into a glare. He imagined her eyes turning into red lasers—and burning him down in one shot. "You're right; I'd rather not. But I will if I must."

Dear Lord, please, why? Why? He'd spent hours, no, weeks trying to get these recipes just right. No way was this . . . this . . . self-aggrandizing snob getting at his food with that attitude.

Nisha cleared her throat. "DJ, I'm sorry but I'm not going to be leaving the house for the next few weeks. I'm going to need you to help me out. Trisha is also going to have to go to San Francisco next week with you to review the arrangements at the ballroom."

God, he hoped the groan that ripped through him hadn't escaped. But the pissiness on Trisha Raje's face told him it had.

Nisha turned to her sister. "Could you wait outside so I can talk to DJ for a moment?"

"Really? He's the one who needs convincing?" Her whine befitted the brat she was. "You know what? Whatever. I'll be outside digging into his precious food. I'm starving."

"Please don't touch my food." The distress in his voice was pathetic, but he didn't care.

She looked at him as though she wanted to flip him off. However, being Ms. Fancy Pants, she restrained herself.

Something he needed to start doing, too, and fast. "I mean, I'll be out in a minute and we can do this right."

"Yes, the Checklist Manifesto as it applies to the fine art of putting food in your mouth," she said grandly, to the exact effect of flipping him off. Then she flounced away and he imagined her devil's tail swishing behind her.

He almost followed her. There was no doubt in his mind that she had every intention of helping herself to his food.

"She won't touch the food," Nisha said to him. Then more loudly: "Trisha, don't touch the food, please." Then back to him, "She's usually really nice."

He grunted without meaning to and then tried to turn it into a cough. But all that accomplished was to make him look stupid.

"I think she's hungry. Have you heard the term 'hangry'? That would be her. Seriously, she's usually the most easygoing and lovable of all of us, and we're all rather adorable." Nisha smiled a tad desperately, mirroring everything he was feeling. "Okay, so we're not; but Trisha is only like this when she's hungry and I've never seen her be like this with anyone outside the family."

"I'm honored," he wanted to say. But for all of Nisha's kindness she was still the one with all the power here, and they were the Raje Galaxy after all. He didn't quite feel brave enough to risk a missed step. "It's fine. I didn't think Dr. Raje wasn't being nice." *Just do not make me work with her, please.* He buried that last part under his best smile.

Nisha responded with a grateful, albeit unconvinced, smile of her own. The woman really was lovely. "I promise Trisha will be easy to work with." The woman was also a dreamer.

But she looked exhausted and ill. "Of course. I'll be happy to work with whomever you want me to work with. Your sister seems like a perfectly nice person."

Being a pathological pleaser had always been a great asset in the service industry. It was called the service industry for a reason. Yes, he loved the spark of joy his food brought, but people were often idiots, and a professional didn't treat the idiots differently from the good ones. Nisha was certainly one of the good ones.

To her credit she laughed. Even as her eyelids drooped. For a moment she seemed so frail he was tempted to ask if she was okay again. But she had made it abundantly clear she'd told him all he needed to know. With a deferential nod he left her, trying to ignore the feeling of being forced to walk the plank.

When he reached the bedroom door, he heard some scrambling. Really? The good doctor had been eavesdropping on them?

He found her perched on a barstool at the breakfast bar.

Perched and . . . munching on one of his crunchy corn-and-lentil papads.

Red. His vision actually turned red. It had taken him three attempts to get the crunch exactly right, to get the corn and lentil to balance out, to get the wafer-thin chip to curl just so.

"This is really delicious," she said and he imagined her smacking her lips and wiping her mouth with the back of her hand like a vampire who had just fed.

Reminding her that he had asked her not to touch his food would be useless, because evidently she didn't put much value on processing simple requests from lesser beings.

He tried to paste on his most amicable smile. And failed. "Glad you like it. Would you like to taste it the way it's actually meant to be eaten?"

Her shrug was followed by a suppressed smile. She was humoring him.

The smile he forced out fought him hard. Whatever it was about her that made his civility crumble, he would not let it win. He started to plate the food the way it was meant to be presented and tried to keep his focus on the dinner he was going to blow into the stratosphere in a month.

Her gaze settled on him. The strangely discomfited feeling he always got from unwanted attention crawled along his skin. He knew women found him attractive. Everyone seemed to expect him to be all cocky about it, as though it made him somehow a bigger man and being uncomfortable with unwanted female attention made him somehow less of a man. He had never been able to bring himself to give a rat's arse.

He put a pan on the stove and roasted the rumali roti quarters for half a minute on each side just until the butter in the dough sizzled, then placed them on a plate and trickled them with truffle oil. Then he placed a paper-thin slice of heart of fennel dusted with roasted cumin over them. In a bowl next to that, he laid out chicken in the simplest Mughlai sauce of steamed onion in cream with the slightest hint of saffron. Finally, he tucked a perfectly curled papad into the bowl.

He slid the platter toward her, a ridiculous nervousness

making him want to pull it back. It felt like exposing a piece of his heart to a mythical monster from one of Ammaji's stories.

That amused smile still danced around her too-wide mouth, but when he looked into her eyes, she stiffened, unsettled enough to sit up a little bit taller. Or maybe it was disdain for this incredible love he had for something as rudimentary as food. No surgeon's hands here. He removed his plain old chef's fingers from the edge of the plate and tried to loosen the giant knot lodged between his shoulders. Her opinion was nothing. If she didn't like it, there were a thousand adjustments he could make. She was a client. Pleasing clients just so was what he did best.

"Is there a particular way to eat it?" she asked, taking him completely by surprise.

He narrowed his eyes, taking the mockery on the chin. "You put it in your mouth and chew."

"Thanks." She cocked her head just a little bit, dislodging a lock of curls from behind her ear, and turned her attention to the plate. "But just dip it? Layer it? Or one bit of this, then another of that." She pointed to things as though words were not enough.

Something stirred inside him. It was the feeling of being faced with his own stupidity.

You're a chef? she was saying. *And I have to explain these things to you?*

"The chicken first, because saffron is a lazier flavor in terms of how long it takes to surface and register. Then the roti, because truffle oil and fennel both can overwhelm, unless tempered by a palate already coated with a softer spice."

Her eyes were huge, slightly upturned at the corners, and soft—completely at odds with her personality. She blinked and looked away from him and back at his food. Then she did exactly as he had asked.

Her neck was the first thing he'd noticed about her. She had the longest neck he'd ever seen, with delicate tendons bracketing the hollow that dipped at the base of her throat where all the luminescence of her skin seemed to gather. Sitting at the kitchen island on those tall, elegant stools that seemed like an extension of her body, her neck stretched as though she were reaching into his flavors with her entire being. He stood over her unable to look away as she chewed and swallowed and closed her eyes on a sigh.

"Oh my God," she said, her eyes fluttering open. Her pupils were dilated, that finely boned jaw moving in slow savoring beats, those long, sensible surgeon's fingers dancing in front of her lips as though she wanted to lick the taste of his food off them. "You cannot possibly feed this to people."

He swallowed.

"What about it bothers you?" he asked, knowing full well that he was fishing. Like a pathetic little boy trying to please his mother. All the bloody time.

"The fact that you made me only one." She was an entirely different person in her moment of wonder. "Won't we bankrupt ourselves if people ate this, because how would they stop?" Her lush mouth parted in the center.

"I can always try to make it less delicious." He bit his lip, because he would not smile.

"You have to at least try," she said breathlessly as he put

another one together and she ate it exactly the way he loved his food to be eaten. With reverence. Slowly. As though every bit meant something. Sparkles of warmth started in his chest, rippled across his skin, and traveled down his arms to the tips of his fingers.

She ate like that for a while. No words for his stuffed peppers. None for his mint cucumber relish. None for his smoked pomfret rolls. Just eyes suffused with pleasure, the brown melting into amber with each swallow. The disdain in them smoked out of their depths, gone without a trace.

Gone temporarily, he reminded himself, rubbing the warming sensation off his arms.

"What do you think?" Nisha shouted from the bedroom after the silence had wrapped around them too long.

It took a beat for either of them to register Nisha's voice. A beat in which their gazes caught and held and then acknowledged the breaking of a spell. A spell he had woven with his food.

He imagined himself dusting off his hands, and blowing on them, his job done.

Hired help, my arse.

"I think I'll help you with Yash's fund-raiser," she shouted in response. Then she went back to eating.

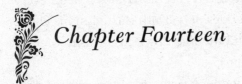 *Chapter Fourteen*

*D*o *not change your mind about her. Do not change your mind about her just because of how she ate your food.* DJ was fully aware that letting his guard down because Trisha Raje finally seemed impressed with him made him a complete and utter knobhead.

"Nice car," she said when she walked him to Emma's hot-pink Beetle after the food he had brought with him had been thoroughly sampled and approved. And by approved he meant cleaned out, every last morsel of it. The woman could eat. Who would have guessed it?

The delighted amusement that flashed across her face at the sight of the car was enough that he got a fleeting glimpse of why her family seemed to like her so much. Maybe Nisha was right and she was only insufferable when she was hungry.

"I've dreamed of a hot-pink Beetle since I was a little boy." He inserted the key in the door lock—yes, the car was that old—and unlocked it, causing Trisha Raje to smile as though he were the quaintest thing since the Queen's shoes.

"It does look like every little boy's dream."

He was about to smile at that but she seemed to realize

that she was being nice and her smile faltered. "Thank you for being flexible today. But I have to warn you that I know absolutely nothing about food or feeding people."

Shocker that. "Maybe you can ask someone else to do it. Mrs. Raje or Ashna perhaps?"

Her smile fell off her face so fast it was like a magic trick. "Listen, we weren't kidding about not letting anyone find out that Nisha isn't feeling well. It's absolutely crucial that no one finds out. Most certainly not our mother. But not even Ashna. If you can't keep this to yourself, we're going to have to find someone else to do it."

Did she just threaten to fire him? For trying to be helpful? "I didn't say I was going to tell anyone. You seemed uncomfortable with having to step in. I was trying to help." He had to work hard to keep his voice even, to not tell her to stuff her job. Maybe it wasn't a threat.

"I am uncomfortable, but Nisha assured me that you were competent enough for the both of us. Keeping this under wraps is not negotiable. If you would rather not help us keep this secret, tell me now and we can find someone who can."

There it was again. Definitely a bloody threat. He opened the boot of Emma's Beetle and placed his hot bag in there. His jaw was so tight it was going to snap out of its joint if he didn't calm down.

Actually . . . to hell with calming down. He slammed the trunk shut. "I'm sorry, but am I missing something? I wasn't aware that I was still auditioning for the job. I try to help you and you threaten to fire me?"

She met his eyes. The harshness in his tone seemed to surprise her. Not that he gave a shit. Anger rose in her gaze and matched his, their five minutes of peace gone like water drops on an overheated pan.

Just as quickly her shoulders slumped and she squeezed her temples. "Look, I'm sorry. I wasn't threatening you."

"Whatever it was you were doing, I need to know if the job is mine or not. We have the menu almost pinned down. I've spent days on prep work. I've booked assistants. I really cannot afford to go through all that if you're still considering other people. I need to talk to Nisha." He walked past her and headed for the front door to go back inside. This had to be straightened out now. He needed this job, but no matter how disposable Trisha Raje thought he was, he wasn't desperate enough to be treated like a common cook in constant fear of being thrown out of the kitchen.

She jogged after him and held his arm. "You don't have to talk to Nisha. I said I'm sorry. I shouldn't have said that. It's just really hard to explain how important it is that no one in the family finds out about Nisha."

"I thought your family was close."

She let his arm go and pressed her hand into her belly. On anyone else the gesture would've been vulnerable, but on her . . . on her he would be stupid to imagine vulnerability. "We are close. That's why. It's not serious and we don't want to alarm anyone." She worried her lip with her teeth, looking awfully anxious. "Actually, that's not true. It is serious, but not the way you would think. We aren't sure how things are going to . . . to turn out. But it . . . it impacts the entire family. I know it's not easy to understand. But I can't let Nisha be hurt. Imagine if this were your sister, imagine if it were Emma."

Was she bloody joking? "You want me to *imagine* how it feels to let Emma be hurt?" He pressed his jaw into his hand in the Thinker's pose. "That's not going to be easy now, is it?" He couldn't help but laugh. She had just sent his gravely sick sister home where anything could happen to her. Did she have absolutely no empathy at all?

Her face softened. "I'm sorry. That's not what I meant. How is Emma holding up?"

That question just made everything worse. "Holding up what? She's home and wants to act like everything is normal. But it's not." He hadn't slept one wink since she'd come home. At least not without waking up in a panic every few minutes. "She should be in a hospital being treated, not at home left to her own devices."

She blinked in surprise. A car passed behind her on the shaded street and she turned around and threw it a glance over her shoulder. For a few moments she seemed unsure of how to respond. The conversation had veered off in a direction she hadn't expected. He hadn't either. "It wasn't my decision," she said finally.

"I beg your pardon? Emma didn't discharge herself. No other doctor did either. You did." Their voices had gone quiet, but suddenly they felt louder than when they'd been nearly fighting a few minutes ago.

"No other doctor gave her a solution, either."

Didn't he know it. "But if she doesn't want your solution, isn't it your job to convince her to do what's right for her?"

She touched her fingers to her temples again, then met his eyes again. "No, actually that's her job. Your job. You're her brother. You should be able to talk sense into her. Millions of people live in the world with disabilities." Her voice gathered steam as she spoke. "My job was to analyze what was wrong with her and to find a way to save her life. And now my job is to execute that surgery—and there's no one else in the world who can execute it with as much skill as I can. *That* is my job. And I always do it well."

As opposed to him. Who was failing at his part by not talking sense into his sister.

She didn't say it. But it was there in her eyes. Right there with that uncontainable arrogance when it came to her work. This was only about the surgery to her.

He thought about backing away, but he was sick of backing away from fights. So sick of it. "And doing your job well is sending her home where she can't be monitored, where she can't be treated? For what? To teach her a lesson? Put her in a corner until she comes around to where you need her to be? So you can prove your *skill*?"

She took a step back, but she didn't look away. "I don't need to prove my skill. But you seem to need to find someone to blame. Maybe you should try stepping up instead, and try finding a solution?"

Once again, was she bloody joking? He'd been stepping up and finding solutions for problems since he was twelve years old. Feeding his family, putting a roof over their heads. Real problems, not challenges he sought out to prove his skill.

"I'm not blaming you for what's happened to Emma. Hell, I couldn't appreciate your *skill* more. But pardon me for wondering if this is about Emma at all for you, or if it's only about what you can accomplish."

A combination of emotions flashed in her strangely colored eyes; in the end, disbelief at being contradicted shone brightest. "Do you always judge people without knowing one damn thing about them? Or is it just me?"

He almost laughed. The woman had called him the hired help without giving it one thought and she thought he judged people? He turned around and looked at the idyllic white stucco home nestled into a row of other idyllic homes, at the Tesla parked in the driveway, at the ease with which she had worn those rumpled scrubs at Ashna's and still looked like a bombshell. He wanted to ask her what the hardest thing she'd ever been through was, but he couldn't bring himself to. "I guess that would make two of us judging each other then, wouldn't it?"

Her cheeks colored. But this back-and-forth was useless. He wasn't here to bring down mighty egos. He walked back to the Beetle, then abruptly turned to her again.

"I quit my job . . ." He almost didn't say the next part, because accusing her of arrogance and then showing his own was too bloody ironic, but he couldn't stop himself. ". . . at a Michelin-starred restaurant in place des Vosges, so I could be here for my sister. And I will do anything to make sure that the only family I have left on this earth does not leave me. Does that sound like me not stepping up to you?"

She swallowed, her neck stretching with the effort. For a moment he thought she wouldn't respond. "The only reason I discharged Emma was that I thought she needed some time to find her footing. From everything I've seen, your sister needs badly to feel in control—her art, everything about her, thrives on power. Pushing her into a corner will have the opposite effect of what we want. Right now she's making choices from a place of anger. Our best bet is to get her to see that. Let her do the things she loves, that she lives for, so she remembers why she loves them and bases her choice on that. My opinion is that you find a way to show her how worth living her life really is."

DJ had been kneed in the ball bag once. This is exactly what that had felt like. He slumped back into Emma's Beetle, his ears ringing. Every word she'd just said was true. It had taken him some time but he'd figured out where his sister was coming from. The fact that this woman saw it so easily, the fact that she could lay out a solution with such calm, when he had been too mired in feeling sorry for himself to do the same, made him want to kick himself, kick something. "What about her safety? Is she safe at home?"

"I would not have discharged her if I didn't believe that she was." Some of her sharpness returned and it was a ridiculous relief. "From the growth trajectory of the tumor thus far, she has at least a few more weeks before anything changes. It's still a brain tumor, so she has to be around someone who can watch her twenty-four seven. I told her that."

He nodded. "I . . . I can do that. I'm making sure." He wanted to thank her, but instead he said, "I'll keep the fact that Nisha isn't feeling well to myself."

Her shoulders slumped visibly. "And you understand that I have absolutely no idea what this fund-raiser thing involves?"

"Good thing I do." He fitted himself into the driver's seat. "Looks like we're stuck together for the sake of our sisters." He pulled the door shut, put the car in gear, and shot off around the looping driveway, watching her disappear in his rearview mirror. She didn't look any happier at the prospect than he was.

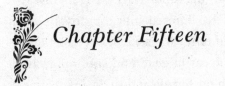

Chapter Fifteen

It was normal for Trisha to get just a few hours of sleep a night. But it was usually because she didn't make it into bed in time to get a full night. Once she hit her pillow, however, she was usually dead to the world until her alarm jolted her awake like a defibrillator.

For the tenth time that night she threw a desperate glance at her clock. It was two A.M. but she just hadn't been able to turn off the noise in her head and fall asleep.

Nisha lay next to her, so wiped from the day's events that she was emitting soft snores.

Trisha squeezed her eyes shut, but another set of fathomless eyes came alive in her head—a ring of crystalline brown rimmed around intense dark centers flecked with soft green and gold, watching her as she ate, giving nothing away, yet giving everything away from under those thick arched brows.

That food. Magic melting on her tongue. Pleasure flooded through her senses at the memory.

He'd seduced her. She couldn't remember the last time she'd felt this satisfied, this filled up, this boneless. As though a masseuse had gone at the knots in her muscles for hours. The intense explosion of flavor in each bite had consumed her in one quick beat and then stretched out slowly sliding down each cell in her body. By the time she had eaten every single morsel of every single thing he placed before her, even wiping at the plate with her fingers after it was gone in a way that would have caused Ma to faint, she'd been done for.

Is this what an addict felt like after their first hit?

That rice at the Anchorage should've been a clue. Ever since she had put that first spoonful in her mouth, the memory of those flavors had surfaced at unexpected moments and set off cravings. Ever since he'd driven away from her in that bright pink car after telling her he'd do anything for his sister, the craving for his food had been rolling in waves across her taste buds, tangling her thoughts up inside her.

It reminded her of the time when her mother had dragged her to a Kishori Amonkar concert when she was eight years old. HRH had canceled on Ma because of a surgery—which Ma had said was code for *please don't make me listen to classical music for four hours.*

Trisha was the only one of the children who seemed drawn to the ethereal presence of the long-held Indian classical notes that were a constant in their home. One of the maestros was constantly playing around Ma and Aji. Tabla, sitar, sarangi, the flute—some combination of vocals with these instruments followed the two women everywhere they went.

To this day Trisha remembered the sound of Amonkar's voice that evening. Even more clearly, she remembered how the music had felt inside her, how it had bloomed outward until it wrapped her in its folds. The near-acrobatic ragas had spun tales and gathered into emotions Trisha had no names for. It had felt as though she were unraveling into the air around her.

A sold-out audience at the Orpheum Theatre had become tied into one consciousness by the magic of that voice and the emotions it harnessed. It had continued to vibrate inside Trisha and called her back to it again and again for months after. Now that magical pull was alive inside her again.

The yearning for those flavors she had tasted yesterday was constant. Constant.

After DJ had left, Trisha had brought Nisha to her condo. Miraculously enough, they had managed to get around the Neel problem. Nisha had called him apologetically with a story about how she couldn't take him to the airport because Trisha was having "one of her meltdowns" over being kicked off a surgery team, which by the way had never ever happened in Trisha's life. Neel being Neel had insisted that Nisha stay with Trisha until she was better. Then Nisha had topped it off with a dramatically whispered "And Trisha absolutely does not want anyone in the family to know." This was a stroke of genius, because if "some drama with the sisters" wasn't enough to keep Neel off their case then a "Raje family secret" certainly was. He and Mishka were on their way to London now.

Once she'd settled Nisha in, Trisha had walked to her favorite bakery around the corner and bought their favorite blueberry and chocolate chip muffins—the combination was a specialty the bakery was renowned for and it had been Trisha's staple pick-me-up for years. The pathetic substitute for her cravings had tasted like cardboard in her mouth.

When Nisha had asked her about the tasting, she had blathered like an idiot for an hour, trying to describe each flavor.

"He is a pretty amazing chef, isn't he?" her sister had said, a little too smugly. "Yay Ashna for bringing him to us!"

A sharp twinge of something panicky hit Trisha at the thought of him and Ashna together. But she remembered how insistent Ashna had been that they were just friends, and it settled the feeling a little. Then the fact that she needed to settle the feeling in the first place made fresh panic spring up again.

For a moment there she had almost lost him. Nisha, Ashna, and Ma would have taken turns killing her if DJ had walked off the job. The man's ability to endear himself to her family was astonishing.

A violent sob snapped Trisha out of her reverie. Nisha sprang up to sitting and started gasping for air. Her face was flushed and glistening with tears. Trisha sat up, her own heart beating hard.

Nisha started patting the mattress, her hands feeling for something, gouging desperately at the sheets beneath her, all of her trembling, a horrid sniffling hiccuping out of her.

"Nisha, sweetheart. It's okay." Trisha grabbed her sister's hands, trying to still the panic in them, trying to be gentle, trying to be firm. "Nisha, stop. Look at me."

Nisha's wild eyes met hers.

Holding her gaze, she secured her sister's hands with one hand, then ran her other hand over the sheets under Nisha. They weren't wet. Looking away from Nisha's terrified eyes she threw a glance at her own hand. No blood. Without letting her relief show, she met Nisha's eyes again. "Everything is all right."

Nisha's breath slowed. She nodded and squeezed her eyes shut. A sheen of sweat glistened across her brow and upper lip.

Trisha pulled her close and reached for the remote on the nightstand. "*Chopped*?" she asked, leaning back into the headboard and tucking her sister into her side.

The TV buzzed to life across from them.

Nisha snuggled into her, still trembling a little, and wiped her cheeks as discreetly as she could.

No one would ever see Nisha like this again. Trisha wouldn't let anyone. Her sister was the strongest, most put-together person Trisha knew and for years she had let herself be a mess for everyone to see because she had wanted those babies so much. If Nisha believed keeping her pregnancy secret gave her a better chance, Trisha would do anything to make it so. If she needed to go through this horror of hoping and waiting again privately, then Trisha would make that happen. She would do anything to give her sister that.

I will do anything to make sure that the only family I have left on this earth does not leave me.

Not for the first time, the idea of Emma refusing surgery made Trisha sick to her stomach. The pain in DJ's eyes had been so immediate, so uncontainable, she had the unbearable urge to know why Emma was all he had left on this earth. Never in her life had she had such a raging need to know what her patient's life outside of her illness was like. It was usually something she avoided thinking about at all costs.

Looks like we're stuck together for the sake of our sisters.

That wasn't what the chef on *Chopped* was saying, but that's what she heard him say. The chef on *Chopped* looked nothing like DJ—no smoothly shaved head, no undulating biceps, no deep dimple in his stubborn chin, no innate gentleness when he interacted with people, no fierce purpose for the sister he loved, and most certainly no ruthless provocation in his eyes for Trisha.

Still, her mind projected him on the screen. And it annoyed her so much she pictured herself shaking him until his bones rattled and all those infuriatingly distracting parts flew off him.

"I think the guy from Kansas will be chopped first," Nisha said, her voice soft but steady.

Trisha didn't agree, so they laid wagers on who would get chopped in which round. Nisha was bang on target. Trisha, as usual, got it all wrong. But Nisha went back to sleep with a smile on her face, and that made everything all right.

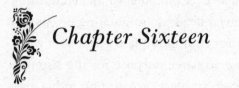 *Chapter Sixteen*

DJ shook his head in utter disbelief as he finished moving the last of Emma's things to his flat from Green Acres. Emma had lived in America for all of five years. After over a decade in Paris, the entirety of DJ's possessions had fit in two suitcases. It had taken DJ seven trips to Green Acres to retrieve all of Emma's belongings. Seven!

In Paris, the flat he had rented had come furnished and, truth be told, he had barely ever been there except to sleep and shower. His time had been spent almost entirely at Andre's. His sister had spent half that time in America and Emma's clothes, bags, and shoes were taking up one entire room in his flat right now. And hats—who even wore hats anymore? What was this, Regency England?

The rest of her stuff took up the rest of the flat. Canvases— only a few, she had left most of those in storage at Green Acres. Easels—apparently one needed three different sizes and styles. Art supplies—scores of them. He would never have pegged his sister for a hoarder.

He had to admit the smell of paint suddenly made these rooms feel like the Southhall ones they had grown up in: ramshackle yet somehow safe. He'd loved how her paints mingled with the fresh paper she liked to make by hand. The mix smelled lush and earthy, almost like the dirt on vegetables before you washed it off. Like something life-giving and alive.

And there were books, two boxes of books. Absently, DJ picked up the one that lay on top of the nearest box. *Persuasion*—their mother's copy. Through all her years of hard labor as a baggage handler at Heathrow airport he never remembered seeing Mum without a book on her person.

"If I didn't read," she had told him once, "I wouldn't know how to believe that there was more to the world than this."

Patti Bamina Caine was written in impeccable penmanship at the top of the first page that had yellowed with age. The "Caine" was written in a slightly different shade of blue ink. It had been added after she'd married Dad.

DJ stroked those careful letters that looked almost as perfect as a typeset font. Mum had come to England from Rwanda when she was twelve, but she had credited her mother for her perfect penmanship.

After her parents had been killed in the Rwandan revolution when the country made a violent transition from a Belgian colony to a republic, Patti's aunt had sewn a pocket to the thigh of her pants and placed Patti's mother's single silver chain in there, along with some Rwandan francs, and put her on a plane with an Indian family fleeing to England. The francs had become completely useless once they had landed at Heathrow, but DJ knew Emma still had those currency notes tucked away in a music box in one of these boxes strewn around his floor. Emma had become the keeper of their few family heirlooms. DJ had done all he could to distance himself from them.

The less baggage you carried, the lighter you landed when you got thrown out on your arse.

The Indian family had kept Patti with them for a year and then they had decided to move on to America, and she had been left behind at St. Joan's Home for Young Women, an orphanage for girls like her who had nowhere to go. There Patti had dreamed of going to university, maybe becoming a nurse and returning home. She had even received a scholarship to go to Queen Mary's but it only covered a part of her university fees and she had no way of making up the rest. That was how, when she outgrew the orphanage at eighteen, she found herself working at the Rounder's Rubber Plunger factory.

On her first day at the factory, James Caine had stepped on her toe and broken it. The man had immense feet, Mum always said. Over the nursing of her toe he had lost his heart—another immense appendage. He'd also lost his mind, if his family were to be believed.

James's Anglo-Indian ancestors had migrated to England from India in the forties to get away from what Churchill was rumored to have called "rascals, rogues, and freebooters." Once they had arrived in England, they had immediately gone to work on wiping away their brown half with the cleaning cloth of their lightish skin and the very British last name they had acquired from the cavalryman who had either fallen in love with or abducted—DJ had heard both stories—an Indian woman, DJ's great-grandmother.

DJ's grandfather had then married an Englishwoman (probably without telling her about his Indian lineage). The Caines had believed that they had removed the visible stain of brownness from the family line and been folded back into the bosom of their rightful heritage.

That was until James Caine, their pride and joy, with his very British factory job and his hazel eyes, had lost his mind and become mixed up with a refugee girl.

James's father, who had diligently kept out of the sun for fifty years to prevent his Indian genes from making themselves shown, had been heartbroken enough to threaten to disown his only son if he married an "African gold digger"— not that there was any gold in sight in their Clapham neighborhood. It was a threat he and his wife had more than made good on.

Despite James's disinterest in reconciling with his relatives, Patti had always craved a family. She had tried hard to coax James into winning his back. But when they had rejected her children, she'd decided James knew what he was doing and she'd given up on them too.

Had the accident not happened, she would never have regretted that decision. Had James lived past thirty-five, maybe he would have made up with his parents, or maybe he would have moved his wife and children out of the flat that, unknown to Patti, still belonged to James's father on paper although James had paid it off and cared for it for years. If that had happened, the fact that James's father deeded the flat to his daughter wouldn't have mattered, and James's sister would never have been able to throw her brother's widow and children out into the street after his death.

As it turned out, Patti was forced to regret her decision when, for the second time in her life, she had found herself without a roof over her head, and in need of charity. Then Emma had forced her to swallow her pride, and after a few days of sleeping under the London sky, she had gone to St. Joan's and sought help. With the help of their pastor, she had found herself a job lifting bags off belts at Heathrow and turned into the kind of mother who said to her children: "Your mum's a baggage handler, but she'll be damned if you don't end up doctors and engineers."

For all her efforts, it was yet another thing that had not gone Patti Bamina Caine's way.

One of the other baggage handlers at Heathrow, Charan Singh, had a few rooms to let in his house in Southall. Southall was a suburb of London just east of the airport that felt like it was a few thousand miles east of London, all the way in the middle of the Indian state of Punjab with its open street bazaars and the smell of spiced meat cooking in clay tandoor ovens scenting the air.

The rent was low enough that Patti could just about afford it. But he had offered her an even better deal: if DJ, who had been twelve at the time, spent the afternoons and evenings watching Charan Singh's epileptic mother, he would forgo the rent altogether. That meant DJ and Emma could go to a private school in Richmond.

So Patti had worked sixteen-hour days, eight at the airport and eight at a bookstore in Hounslow, and given her children the kind of education she believed would break them out of the cycle of poverty. DJ had hardly seen his mum during those years at Charan's. He was aware of how much guilt she carried about not having been there for her children. Not that DJ had ever had the time to miss her presence. He had come home from school every day, started Emma off on her homework, and then taken care of Charan's Ammaji.

Ammaji had seizures a few times a month. It was only alarming that first time he'd witnessed it. She'd collapsed as if in slow motion, the white cotton of her loose kameez and salwar pants billowing around her before settling in a cotton cloud around her spasming body.

With nothing more than the slightest deepening of his always furrowed brow, Charan Singh had shown DJ how to push a piece of rubber into her open mouth as her limbs stiffened and shook without pause and her eyes turned up in her head. When she was done, Charan had placed a hand behind her back, propped her up, and led her to the bathroom where she could clean up.

Aside from the seizures, Ammaji was the most energetic person DJ had ever met. Every day she cooked enough to feed fifty people. Together they packed all the food in small plastic containers that Charan took to the corner store to be sold. No matter how much she made, they always sold out. No one in the neighborhood knew where the Khalsa General Store sourced their saag paneer, chicken makhani, and aloo gobi. Even Mr. Khalsa, the owner, didn't know where Charan got the food from.

Ammaji was never allowed to leave the house. It was absolutely crucial that no one ever saw her have a seizure because Charan's two brothers and two sisters had children they needed to get married off. Ammaji had explained to DJ in her at once patient and impatient way that no one in their community would marry her grandchildren if they knew of her ailment.

So she never left the house.

Charan, who was single, was tasked with the sick mother. The other children only visited on weekends every once in a while when DJ and Emma sat by the attic door and giggled at the spirited fights between the people from Ammaji's stories. On weekdays Charan worked the evening and night shift, which meant he slept during the day. The only way he thought to accomplish this was to string small brass bells to a bracelet on his mother's wrists. That way, when she had a seizure she woke him up, her convulsions rattling the bells like an alarm.

When DJ first started watching Ammaji, Charan had assured him that he could go about his schoolwork so long as he kept an ear out for the bells. But Ammaji hated those bells. "They give me a headache," she said. "All day *chun-chun-chun* like a nautch girl in some brothel."

She'd said all this to him in Punjabi, her bright brown eyes dancing with amusement instead of sadness. DJ had never heard Punjabi spoken before that, but she had a way of talking with her hands and her eyes and it had been remarkably easy to understand her. When he came home from school, the first thing DJ did was remove the bell bracelet. She always reminded him to clasp it back on before he left at the end of the day. Her children had made sure the metal band needed two hands to remove and put on.

In the years that he spent with her, DJ had learned to speak

Punjabi like a Punjabi munda. But it wasn't the only thing she taught him. Before he was thirteen he could outshine the most skilled cooks in all Southall. He could smell the readiness of onion in every one of its stages of cooking and knew exactly what stage worked best for each dish. He could identify the exact rapidity with which milk had to boil before adding the lemon to make the cheese curd separate into paneer. He could sense exactly when to add the tomatoes to tie together the onion, garlic, and ginger so that the curry came together perfectly with the oil separating from it in syrupy rivulets.

Ammaji's love for sharing her gift, for teaching and instructing, found its perfect match in DJ's enthusiasm. She tested him, quizzed him, inculcated in him the thing that even Europe's finest culinary school could not teach: how to harness the spirit of food to beguile those who ate it.

His best memories from those years were of Mum coming home, exhausted, to his food. Her happy sighs as she ate. Being able to erase even her nastiest day. Knowing how to blend what Ammaji taught him about spices with maize Ugali porridge and steamed plantains. Coaxing the milder African flavors of Mum's own cooking into his food so he could take her back home with it, and loosen those smiles out of her weary face. Emma, for her part, had devoured everything he cooked with equal fervor. Her palate never judged him, and the ease of that gave him courage to fly.

DJ LOOKED UP from his mother's book to see his sister watching him. She was showered and ready to go. Her hair was pulled back in a tight ponytail, and she wore white jeans and a bright red ruffled blouse, with huge hoops dangling from her ears.

"It's mood dressing," she said and sniffed the air. "Are those brownies?" She headed into his kitchen and was about to start searching for goodies, but he pulled her back and pushed her into a chair.

"Would I make you just brownies? What am I, a teenager?"

The mood dressing was certainly working on him. For all his worry, not seeing her lying in a hospital bed in that awful gown was nice. Now that he had decided what he needed to do—remind her how very precious her life was—he didn't feel quite as pushed into a corner himself.

Getting to see her like this, living under the same roof as him, made him feel oddly young. As though he should be tugging at her pigtails while Mum grumbled at him to stop bothering his sister without pausing in her housework. It was a memory from when dad had been around, before they had been forced into all the other shapes their lives had taken, but it was still a stronger memory than all the ones that had followed.

"Aw, I love when you go all Skinner from *Ratatouille* on me!" Emma teased, but she sank into the chair and waited, her eagerness shining in her eyes, her wet ponytail a riot of curls framing her too-drawn face.

It was a good thing she had slept in. It had given him time to finish up his trip to the farmers' market and of course to whip up her favorite dessert.

DJ placed the sundae on the plastic folding picnic table in front of her. It had taken him an hour to get the flavors exactly right. But instead of digging into it, she leaned back, the plastic chair creaking at the movement. Plastic Chic, that was his current style profile. Big Lots clearance aided by Craigslist beanbags. Good thing she wasn't the only artist in the family, because it was perfect ethos for a starving artist. He definitely preferred the ethos of a healthy bank account, but what good was money if you couldn't use it when your family needed it?

Bankruptcy was a temporary condition; family was the only permanent thing in this life. Nonetheless, right about now he wanted Emma to have even the modest comfort of his Paris flat so badly it was an actual physical ache. "I'm sorry," she said softly.

He hated when she looked sad. It was a knife twisting in his chest.

When he didn't respond, she looked at the boxes and at all her stuff piled high against the walls. "I've totally disrupted everything for you." She'd given notice at her art therapist's job. But they were going to let her continue to work there for two weeks, or until they found someone new, or until she could no longer do the job. It all depended on which came first.

He grinned. "Story of my life, baby girl. Totally used to it." He slid into the chair across from her and she punched his arm. Then he watched as she dunked the tall spoon into the ice cream.

The anticipation in her eyes was all the reasons why he cooked. It turned her right back into his baby sister, no sickness, no unforgivable mistakes. She'd been such a happy child, his Emma. Joy hadn't fit inside her. It was what made her art magic. Amid all the relentless dark dinginess of their Southall attic, her art had exploded with light.

Back before adulthood wrapped her art in things like conscious exploration of identity, it had been just her diving into herself and, despite the world around her, finding brightness there. Her art had almost been enough to make the gray moroseness of their childhood bearable.

"Dear Lord in heaven, Darcy James Caine!" she managed around a mouthful, her eyes sparkling, her head tipping back, her entire body sinking into itself as it absorbed the taste in her mouth.

He grinned like an idiot.

He'd made the double chocolate brownies with a hint of cherry liqueur just the way she liked them, and almond praline. Of course almond praline.

Almond praline was their thing. In all the years they had spent apart, every time they met he had found a new way to surprise her with it. It was one of the ways he had compensated for the distance, a way to keep her from feeling abandoned. He reached across the table and clasped the tall glass in both hands. They no longer hurt from the burn, but the chill of the glass felt good against his peeling skin.

He pulled the glass to himself. Or tried, because she grabbed it and scooped up a gigantic bite before she let him steal it.

He took a bite. Oh yeah, that look on Emma's face: it was the Truth.

He gave it back to her and watched the joy explode on her face again and again, soaking it up.

How could she even think about not getting the surgery? How could she not see that she was all he had?

"So about those test results . . ." he said, wishing he could just watch her eat in silence. But he had to breach the topic somehow.

She pointed her spoon at the glass. "Really? Are you going to ruin this for me with serious talk? Can we at least wait until I'm done rolling around in this for a bit?"

She grabbed a spoon from the spoon holder on the table and handed it to him. "I'll even share."

He wasn't a terribly hopeful person by nature. Hope was a terrifying thing. Taking things as they came was more his style. But right now, try as he might, he couldn't quite bring himself to believe that this girl who spread light, who saw things in ways that could change the world, had chosen to give up so easily.

It just wasn't going to happen. He would not let it happen.

"Stop looking so serious. It makes me feel like all the things you want to talk about are waiting at the bottom of this glass."

He let his pursed lips curve into a smile. "Then hurry up and get through the brownie . . . and the gelato . . . and the praline . . . and the sea salt caramel first," he said, stretching his words out playfully.

"Oh, the things you demand of me, brother," she responded, hamming it up.

It wasn't easy but he let her eat in silence, taking a bite every now and again. "If only all the waiting in life were this easy," she said finally.

"Listen, Emma." There was only an inch of melting sundae to go, so he wasn't exactly breaking his word. "How can you not fight this?"

She jabbed the brownie so hard the spoon sliced through

it and hit the bottom of the glass with a clink. "Fight what? The tumors in my brain? Fight them how exactly? By yelling at them to get lost?"

"No. Your doctor is going to take care of that for you. You just have to let her."

"Sod it all, Darcy! What she's going to do isn't taking care of things. Not for me." She slammed her hand on the table and the glass jumped and tipped over. The few drops of syrupy chocolate left in the glass splattered on the stack of mail sitting nearby.

"Sorry." She straightened the glass, then grabbed the envelope and wiped it with her thumb. Her eyes darkened when she noticed that it was a bill from the hospital.

Bugger him sideways! He should have put the damn thing away. Without another word she tore it open.

The color drained from her face. "What the bloody hell is wrong with this country? How can tests cost thirty thousand dollars?" Emma did have health insurance, but it most certainly didn't cover treatment at Stanford. The places where treatment was covered had already deemed her tumor inoperable.

"I told you, I don't want you to worry about that."

"How can I not worry about it?" she hissed in frustration. "You've already dropped your entire bloody life for me. And I love you for it. But you're not bankrupting yourself. You're just not."

Too late, baby girl. "This one bill is not going to bankrupt me."

Wrong thing to say, because he knew exactly the thought that went through her head at that. "Paying for the surgery isn't going to bankrupt me either," he added quickly.

If it did, he had a solid enough career that he'd make it all back.

Emma met his eyes. The difference in color was particularly noticeable in the light streaming through the window; he kicked himself again, for not forcing her to see a doctor when he'd first noticed it. "I want to sell the bug."

"We're not selling your car."

She got up and started searching the kitchen. "It's not like I'm going to be able to drive it ever again, and it isn't exactly your style."

He opened a cabinet and handed her the box of pralines she was searching for. "We can afford the car for now and we need it. We're okay with the bills."

Both were lies.

The bug had belonged to Emma's friend Sabah, a girl who had gone back to Dubai after finishing her master's degree. Emma had never admitted as much, but DJ suspected there was more to that friendship than friendship. Who left a car behind for their roommate after knowing them for only two years?

"Sabah's family is wealthy. She didn't really care about selling it before she left." That was all Emma had said to him. But DJ studied people all day long and just the way Emma said Sabah's name said much.

He would not be letting anyone sell that car.

Emma popped a piece of praline into her mouth and turned weary eyes on DJ. "Maybe I should write that blog after all. Sell my story to get people to buy my art. Except I'm bollocks at writing. I think I single-handedly turned Mrs. Brendish's hair silver when I took her composition class."

DJ sat up.

Julia Wickham. The journalist had called him that morning and tried to convince him again to let her meet Emma. The woman had such a gentle way about her, speaking to her had actually made him feel better.

"What?" Emma said, studying him as she sucked on the candy in her mouth.

"Nothing." Emma was in a strange mood and he wasn't sure how she'd react.

She jabbed him in the arm. "Darcy James, that's your trying-to-manage-me face. Tell me. I really need something to distract me right now."

He had turned Julia Wickham down again, but this smacked of a window opening when doors had been slamming repeatedly in their faces. And more than the money, the idea that unburdening herself on camera might help Emma move forward kept nudging at him. "Funny you say that, because . . . because I met a journalist in the waiting room when I came to see you the other day. She wanted to talk to you."

Emma bit into her candy, something she usually never did. The crunch was loud, satisfying. There was a gleam in her eyes, and it burned through the exhaustion. A flash of the old Emma. His warrior sister. "What are you on about?"

"She's doing a web series about patients with difficult diagnoses." He refused to say the word *terminal*.

"Really? So it's one of those American air-your-laundry-in-public and sob-for-all-to-see things? Then everyone with a bleeding heart feels sorry enough for you and throws money at you on a fund-raising link?"

"That's not exactly how she described it, but yeah, something like that."

DJ had never understood the need to see the lives of others destruct on-screen. Divorce court, cops arresting drunks and batterers, all those shows where you watched people confront cheating spouses, abandoning parents, killers of loved ones felt voyeuristic to him. Even if Julia was right and it was cathartic to those involved, the pull to then view that catharsis as entertainment seemed barbaric. And if the people suffering felt forced to do it for the money, well, that just took the pathos to another level.

Emma put another piece of praline in her mouth, crunched this one, too. "Last month a woman who cut off her husband's knob because he was thrashing the shit out of her got two mil for her lawyer fees."

"You're joking."

Her eyes were flat-out glittering now. She put out her hand and wiggled her fingers. "Let's have her number then. This could be a blast, innit?" she said with a laugh. Maybe this catharsis thing was worth a shot.

"You're a crazy old cow, Emma Caine." But he laughed, too, and retrieved Julia's card from his wallet.

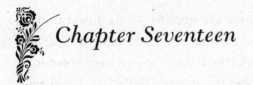 **Chapter Seventeen**

Trisha had to admit it was nice to have Nisha in her condo. For years now, Nisha, Ashna, and Trisha had met every few weeks for dinner and wine. But thanks to the demands of their work, by the time they got together, they were often wiped out. This morning Nisha and she had woken up and chatted in bed the way they had done as girls on their visits to Sripore, as though time was not snapping at their heels.

They discussed Dorna, wiping each other's tears as they laughed and cried about a woman they had both loved.

"Did anyone call Rita?" Nisha asked, sniffling.

Rita was Dorna's partner of thirty years. Dorna had watched her slowly lose her poet's mind to Alzheimer's over the last decade. Finally, last year when her own cancer had made it impossible to be a caregiver, she had moved Rita into a nursing home.

"The hospital called Green Acres, but I'll go see her this week." Trisha placed a blueberry chocolate muffin and a glass of milk on a tray across Nisha's lap.

Her sister squeezed her shoulder. "You're a good person, Shasha." She took a bite. "These are great!"

Trisha tried not to snarl at that. It wasn't Nisha's fault that the muffins tasted like mud to her. *Gee, I wonder whose fault it is.*

She pulled the blinds open with a little more force than was necessary and sat down next to her sister with her cup of coffee, watching her eat in silence.

Nisha's phone chirped, and she looked down at it and smiled. "Neel and Mishka just landed. Making up that story about you having a meltdown was genius, wasn't it?"

Trisha took a sip of the coffee, which also annoyingly tasted like bitter dishwater this morning, and put her cup down on the tray. "I'm surprised he bought it, actually. When was the last time I had a meltdown?" she asked, adjusting the pillows under Nisha's head. "Because really, I'm like the least meltdowny person I know."

"Trisha," Nisha said with all the patience of a saint—and by the way, saints only had so much patience because they really had nowhere to go and nothing to do, it was untested patience and not worth all the credit it got them—"the point was to let Neel know that the person to worry about was you, not me."

"Gee, thank you!"

More patience was lobbed at her. "Marriages are complicated creatures. He doesn't want the details. All he wants is to know that this has nothing to do with him and me. If this is about you, his mind, preoccupied as it is, doesn't go on high alert. That's what I didn't want, high alert, okay?"

Well then, mission accomplished. Keeping a secret in the Raje family could scare anyone. It was akin to burning superstrong incense and then hoping everyone's overactive sense of smell quit functioning. They were all curious and suspicious by nature and that was a deadly combination when placed in the vicinity of a secret. No wonder Neel had raised his hands and quickly backed away.

Nisha looked down at her phone again. "Ma and HRH also made it to LA." Trisha checked her own phone. Of course, Ma had only texted Nisha about her whereabouts. Typical.

After Ma's wheelchair-cleaning episode, HRH and she had both said nothing more to Trisha about Julia's baffling return. Trisha had found herself searching the waiting areas and hallways of the hospital every time she was there. But naturally, she had not caught Julia lurking around. No matter what nefarious purpose Julia had come back for, the woman was too smart to be obvious about it.

As for Ma and HRH, it was a stroke of luck that they had left for LA this morning to hobnob with Hollywood's Most Influential and raise money for Yash's campaign. At least they didn't need to deal with the overactive Ma-dar.

"Ew," Nisha said, grinning at her phone. "Ma says she's excited about their *repeat honeymoon*."

Ma loved to call any time she spent alone with HRH that.

"Ew!" Trisha echoed her sister and they both wiggled their shoulders to shake off the particularly unwelcome thought of their parents being romantic.

They both giggled.

As for the illustrious Yash Raje, he was in Washington, DC, gathering the other half of the capital required for a political campaign: endorsements. Ashna was far too stressed out about revamping the menu and saving Curried Dreams. Plus, she was the only one who wouldn't dig for answers someone didn't want to give, no matter how suspicious she got.

That left their grandmother and Esha. The good news was that those two never left the house, never used a cell phone. If the pregnancy came to Esha in one of her visions, Nisha was insistent that they didn't need to know about it.

Aji and Esha were used to seeing Nisha, like Trisha, stop by every few days, but they also knew that the announcement and the fund-raiser were keeping Nisha busy. They'd complain about it, but in the end Nisha could do no wrong in their eyes.

The biggest advantage, truly, was that none of the family ever visited Trisha's condo.

It was a miracle Ma had even agreed to let her kids get their own places. Yash had been the first person to do it and it had broken her heart a million times over. HRH, naturally, had considered it perfectly normal because it was the American way.

Their views on assimilation and owning their heritage were the one thing Ma and HRH always disagreed on. Ma believed their heritage was their greatest strength, and the more they stayed connected to their Indian roots, the more comfortable they'd be in their skin.

HRH's take on it was this advice to his children: "This is our home. This country is yours. Take everything you need. Give everything you have. From the beginning of time, humans have migrated. We've claimed land and let it claim us. Don't ever fulfill anybody else's definition of your relationship with your country. How many generations ago their forefathers got here may be how some people stake their claim, but I stake mine with how much I give. How wholly I love. This place called to me, I'm here, it's mine. And now, it's yours."

As in most things, Ma had deferred to HRH and accepted that her unmarried children would live outside of their home even though they lived in the same area. But despite her usually madly overactive protective instinct, she never could bring herself to visit their individual homes.

Nisha was the only exception. Since it was her married home, Neel and Nisha's house was okay. Even then, Ma's visits were restricted to when Nisha hosted one of her family dinners every few months, and there would be none of that until this fund-raiser was done. The idyllic and impeccable Los Altos Hills house would remain locked up until Neel and Mishka came back.

Trisha picked up the tray that Nisha had cleaned out nicely. She let out a silent sigh of relief. A good appetite meant all was well with the baby.

Nisha lay back down on Trisha's bed. "In all this confusion of trying to hide the pregnancy, I forgot that Neel's ex is going to be at the reunion." Trisha had never heard her sister utter Barbara's name.

"And?" Trisha asked, looking her straight in the eye.

"And . . . nothing. It must be the hormones that I even mentioned it."

"Hmm," Trisha said skeptically, keeping her lecture about trusting Neel to herself as she moved to put the tray in the sink.

Nonetheless, she heard Nisha pick up her phone and call Neel as she began to get dressed for the day. The underpinning of desperate sweetness that laced her sister's voice when she said, "Hi, honey, missing me yet?" Trisha hoped was just her imagination.

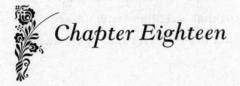

Chapter Eighteen

It had been four days since Emma had been discharged and had returned to work. Usually DJ dropped her off and picked her up outside, but today they were going to meet Julia Wickham here. The receptionist at Green Acres threw DJ a look that he tried not to interpret as suspicious. "That's not an *American* license, sir," she said in a tone that suggested that she couldn't comprehend that people from other countries actually possessed driver's licenses.

"It's a London license," he said, giving her his most charming smile. "I'm Emma Caine's brother. Emma has worked here for five years. I'm just here to pick her up."

"I'm sorry, you're going to have to wait while I find Ms. Caine. She didn't sign you in, so I can't just let you in." She fixed him with a stare that was meant to be assertive, but there was enough of a nervous undertone in it that he could plainly see all the things she thought him capable of.

They see us as outsiders, mate, we're fucking aliens to them. Look at their faces, Gulshan had loved to say while pointing at every white face on the Tube as they rode into Kingsgate.

Gulshan's anger had felt raw and freeing to seventeen-year-old DJ for those few ill-fated weeks when he'd befriended Gulshan and his gang. But even back then he had known that Gulshan's obnoxiousness had been a pathetic attempt at asserting their right to be there, to be in London, which was the only home they knew. *This is our home too, innit? But fuck if they think so.* He had jabbed a thumb in the direction of an old white woman in a floral dress and she had burst into tears.

DJ remembered waiting for the boys to get off the train before quickly handing her the packet of tissues Mum always tucked into his bag. Instead of saying thank you she had let out a terrified shriek and looked like she was about to have a stroke right there as though he'd handed her a bomb not tissue paper.

When he got off the train, his new friends had been doubling over laughing at him.

They had been quite the motley crew. All these Punjabi, Sikh, and Muslim boys in their ganji shirts and baggy jeans. None of them were black like he was. But they let him tag along. *You're one of us, mate. You got enough Desi blood for us. Them aunties-uncles don't know shit. Racist buggers.* Gulshan's large-hearted acceptance had made DJ feel like he'd somehow finally found a place where he belonged.

But no amount of wanting to belong had meant anything when Gulshan had thrown that match on the newsstand in Chelsea. The flames had come so fast. The owner, an old man in an even older tweed jacket, had gone down on his knees and broken into tears. His begging for mercy had looked an awful lot like praying.

Gulshan's words had a way of flashing back to DJ every

now and again. *We're fucking aliens to them.* Like now, with
this lovely lady looking at him as though he were here to set
fire to things. He was wearing a baby-pink button-down, for
shit's sake. He looked like he was off to church.

He pulled all of himself inward, curving his shoulders, softening his brow. It was second nature to make himself smaller
so he could pass by unnoticed and get on with things, not easy
given that he was six feet four inches tall. He reminded himself
that the woman was only doing her job. With his most non-
threatening smile in place he leaned against the granite counter. "If you can't find my sister, maybe you could call security
and have them verify that my London license is legitimate?"
He clipped his words in a way that would have made his elo-
cution teachers proud, and usually made Americans lose their
loaves.

It worked. She half smiled and did as he asked. Then apologized sheepishly when Dan, the security guard, gave him
a hug on a "'Sup brother! You must be Emma's DJ," before
proceeding to quiz him on the way to win Emma's heart. Not
exactly in those words, but DJ recognized a goner when he
saw one.

"She okay?" Dan asked.

"Yeah." She had seemed more okay today than she had
in a very long time. She'd bounced out of the car when he'd
dropped her off a few hours ago and gone to Curried Dreams
to work on some recipes with Ashna. Now he was back to pick
her up and Julia Wickham was supposed to meet them here.

Naturally, Dan knew exactly where Emma was. In the large
studio that had been Emma's office for the past five years,

working with Betsy Reyes, who used to be her boss and was now her patient.

Betsy had developed the art therapy program at Green Acres, and everything Emma knew about using art to help people with emotional challenges, she had learned from Betsy. Then dementia had come knocking two years ago and taken over fast. Ever since then Emma had worked tirelessly to develop her therapies to also treat dementia.

Emma had told DJ that even though Betsy didn't remember anyone around her most of the time, she did always remember how to paint, and so Emma painted with her every day. Or she had until she herself became sick.

DJ waved to her through the studio door. She was sitting next to Betsy at an artist's bench and painting. He watched them from outside, not wanting to intrude. Betsy looked entirely at peace with herself, entirely absorbed in the work she was doing. Then suddenly she looked up and her face crumpled in fear. DJ followed her gaze. He hadn't noticed Julia Wickham standing in an obscure corner of the room with a camera on a tripod shooting his sister and Betsy as they painted.

That was fast. Emma and he were supposed to speak with Julia together. But, of course, he was crazy to believe that his sister was going to let him make any decisions for her.

Emma placed a comforting hand on Betsy's shoulder and threw Julia a look that said it was time to leave the room. With impressive agility, Julia picked up her camera and slipped away.

DJ stepped aside to let her through the door.

Deftly maneuvering the camera and the tripod she was carrying, she stuck out her hand. "Hi again, DJ." The woman had the widest, warmest smile and for a moment the ease with which she shared it made all the turmoil of the day still inside him. "Or should I say Darcy."

DJ's surprise had to have shown on his face because her smile transformed into a giggle. The startling blue of her eyes combined with the silver stud pierced through one of her eyebrows made her seem somehow wild and in control all at once and DJ found himself smiling back.

"Your sister can't stop talking about you."

He groaned imagining his sister telling this perfect—rather attractive—stranger mortifying stories about him.

"All good things. Don't worry," she said while he continued to stare like a tongue-tied idiot. "She was telling me how your mother was an Austen fan and that's where your names come from."

He was *definitely* going to have to have a conversation with Emma. It had been years since they'd lived on the same continent and she still seemed to think it was all right to use his name to amuse herself. Mum had unfailingly called him Darcy, but Emma only did it when she was mad or when she thought it was funny. He thanked Ms. Austen yet again for having done that to him. Oh, the torture he had suffered because of his name. Grade-schoolers didn't care that Darcy was your mother's favorite literary character's last name. To them, Darcy was a girl's name and if you were named a girl's name, then that, naturally, made you a girl.

He had come home upset from school one day because his classmates had been relentless with their teasing. Ammaji had patted his head as he chopped onions with far too much force.

"My brother's name was Daljeet but when he came to England he became DJ. Just like an Englishman. You can also become DJ, no, Darcy James?" It had been that simple. Pretty much like Ammaji's approach to all of life's problems.

Mum, naturally, had not been pleased with his decision to be called DJ. The only reason she'd let it go was that she had no idea that Ammaji had suggested it. He had learned early to mention Ammaji as little as possible to Mum. It had been the only way to keep her struggle between not being there for him and not being needed from flashing in her eyes. Or to keep her from going off on one of her rants. *You're smelling of onions again. When are you supposed to do your homework? You're supposed to watch over her not work for her.* DJ had never figured out if Mum's dislike of Ammaji had to do purely with the fact that she spent so much time mothering her children, or if it had been because she had inculcated the love for cooking in DJ and derailed the dreams his mum had for him.

He finally took the hand Julia was holding out. "It's a pleasure to see you again. And I prefer DJ if you don't mind."

She grinned again as though she wasn't used to his brand of formality. Shockingly, he wasn't embarrassed by her amusement; there was something wonderfully friendly about it.

"I imagine having a name like Darcy wasn't fun growing up," she said, as though reading his mind. "But it is kind of hot."

DJ felt his face warm. "So did Emma and you have a chance to talk about anything other than my name?" He looked at the tripod and camera she had set down next to her.

"Barely. I was telling her how you and I met and she told me a little bit about what the past few months have been like.

Then she had to work with a patient and I asked if I could take some test footage of her working, just to show her how unobtrusive the camera can be."

"Hey there, bruh'." Emma strode out of the room pushing Betsy in a wheelchair, bringing with her the loamy smell of pigments and turpentine.

He gave her a quick hug. "All well?" He threw a look at Betsy in the wheelchair, with her head leaning back and her eyes closed.

"She just needs some rest. Nothing to worry about." Emma smiled fondly at her mentor.

Betsy wasn't the only one DJ was worried about. Emma's eyes had sunk deep into her face, to say nothing of how sunken her cheeks were. She turned to Julia. "Hullo again."

"So, what did you think?" Julia asked.

"Felt a bit like being a reality star!" Emma said, smiling her irreverent smile. "We could totally have some fun with it. Have any of your shows been about someone who had fun with dying?"

Julia didn't react except to give Emma an expression that mingled just the right amount of understanding with amusement. DJ wished he could mirror that expression. His own face probably looked like someone had slashed him with a meat cleaver. Julia reached out and gave his arm a gentle pat. So pathetic was he that the comfort of the contact made him want to take her hand and cling to it.

"Each subject I work with is a little different. But it's your story and you can make it anything you want."

A laugh spurted out of Emma. Her rude and angry laugh.

"You want me to make the story about how I can no longer make my life anything I want, whatever I want to make it! That's pretty bloody ironic." More of that ugly laugh. "My brother here loves some good irony, innit, Darcy?"

She seemed to have decided against going through with the interview. Which was a relief, he decided, since he really wasn't a fan of this public-airing-of-laundry thing.

Julia's demeanor remained entirely empathetic. She looked at Betsy and threw a glance at the studio door. "You've done some pretty good work here, Emma. How many people have you had go through the art residency program in the past five years? More than a hundred, based on my research. That's important work. Your art is also so unique. You have a lot to share and talk about. When I said you could make what you want of it, I meant you can use it to call attention to all the good you've done."

"So I have to be dying for people to be interested in my work? Where were you until now?"

"That's hardly fair, Emma. I'm sure Ms. Wickham will understand that you're not interested in doing the interview, but—"

"Why would I not want to do the interview?"

Because I can't bear to let the world see you like this.

"It's perfect. It might be shitty for people to be interested in me and my work only because it's such a delicious fecking tragedy. But I'm not a total knobhead. I'll tell my story for them to weep their sodding arses off at. So long as they pay me for it. What's the most you've received from the online fund-raising?"

Julia looked as embarrassed as he felt, but she stayed determinedly nonjudgmental. "My highest was close to half a million."

"See, I've got no life insurance and shit, but I can leave you a rich man, Darcy James!"

He was about to respond, but Julia met his eyes and shook her head. "We can't predict what we'll raise. But telling your story can be empowering," she said with impressive calm, while his own heart was a restless mess.

Emma offered up another scoffing, awful laugh. "Right. Fine then, let's try and beat your half-mil record."

Again, Julia smiled kindly, as though she understood fully why his sister was being so provocative. "There's somewhere I have to be, so I'll leave you two alone to discuss this. DJ, it was a pleasure. Please know that this story means everything to me and I will do everything in my power to tell it the way it deserves to be told. Emma, I'll text you about schedules. It will take a few days of shadowing you to get enough footage. We can talk more as we go."

As soon as she had left, Emma held up a hand in DJ's face. "Save it. I'm doing this. Trying to talk me out of it is a waste of your breath."

"How refreshingly different!" he said, making her grin.

But for all her bluster she looked so bloody weary, so frustrated, his chest hurt. It struck him suddenly, that at least her placid phase seemed to have passed. And this was a good thing. Maybe Julia was right, maybe venting on camera, talking about the work she loved so much, would help her work through this.

He uncrossed his arms. "Why don't we get going? We can discuss it in the car. It's been a long day, love."

She looked grateful. "I have one more student to look in on. I promised her, so don't argue."

"What are you arguing about?" Betsy woke up and looked between Emma and DJ.

"Hullo there." Emma squatted down in front of Betsy. "Your head still hurting?"

Betsy looked at her as though she had no idea what Emma was talking about, then she turned to DJ. "Charles! So lovely of you to come."

DJ met Emma's worried eyes and squatted down next to her in front of the wheelchair. "Of course, love," he said to Betsy. "Where else would I be?"

His sister grinned—her little girl grin from a different lifetime—and suddenly nothing else mattered but what she wanted. DJ stood back up and gave Emma a hand. "Is doing the interview really what you want?" It seemed like the exact kind of thing she would hate to do.

She rubbed the paint on her fingers, scraped it with her thumbnails until it wiped off in spots. "It would be great exposure for Green Acres and the program. And you have to admit, the money would be sweet."

"I don't want you to worry about the money."

"I know. I know you'll take care of it. But why not get help if it's there. What do we have to lose?"

"Charles takes care of everything, don't you, Charles?" Betsy said, looking at him as though he were some kind of god.

"Thanks," DJ said awkwardly.

"I'll see you around," Betsy said to Emma. "Charles and I need to go now."

DJ raised his brows at Emma, who shrugged rather unhelpfully.

"You promised to take me to the garden and show me the roses, remember?" Betsy said to DJ, or more accurately, to Charles.

"Do you mind taking Betsy for a spin around the park in the back?" Emma said in a softer voice. "I'll quickly look in on Sherry and gather my things and then we can go home."

At this point he'd do anything to get his sister off her feet. "Sure." It seemed like the only response he was capable of giving her anymore.

BETSY TURNED AROUND and looked at DJ as he pushed her wheelchair back in through the back entrance of Green Acres after their walk through the garden, where he'd found that Betsy, for everything she did not remember, still knew a great many things about roses and their many varieties.

"Who on earth are you?" she asked. It was the slightest change, but her eyes were suddenly a little more alert.

DJ wondered if he needed to let someone know. "I'm Emma Caine's brother. We were just walking in the garden."

She smiled widely at the mention of Emma and turned back around. "Ah! I know, you're Darcy. Emma's told me all about you."

He'd better hurry up and have that word with his sister. "Actually, I prefer to go by DJ."

"Is that Indian food I smell?" she said, sniffing the air as they passed what looked like a large cafeteria. "It must be Indian night for dinner." She sat up in her chair. "Emma tells me you're a chef. Doesn't that smell great?"

The one thing DJ had a hard time lying about was food. "Are you hungry?" he asked. "When's dinnertime?"

Her stomach growled and she placed a hand on it. "It seems like now's dinnertime, doesn't it?" She pointed imperiously at the doors that led to the cafeteria and he pushed the chair into the dining hall. It was a huge room with three sets of double doors that had all been thrown open. Some fifty-odd round tables were arranged in a perfect grid and they were currently almost all occupied. He had no idea that Green Acres had such a large resident population.

What they were smelling had to be chicken makhani, with the usual hints of cardamom, clove, and bay leaf mingling with fresh cream. But it smelled like something that came off an assembly line at a manufacturing facility for makhani sauce supplied to grocery stores. He tried not to scrunch up his nose. It wasn't easy. Chicken makhani was one of his signature dishes. His still didn't taste quite the way Ammaji's had, but he loved to play with it. It was going to be a main course for the Raje dinner. Apparently, it was one of Yash Raje's favorite dishes and it had been the first thing Mina Raje had put on the menu.

The crowd here seemed happy enough with the food, because there was a virtual riot near the buffet table. It seemed like the smell had brought every single resident to the dining hall all at once.

They joined the queue waiting to get at the food.

"It's Indian curry Thursday!" the older man standing in front of them said.

DJ cringed at the use of the word, but the man who was

dressed in a crisp dress shirt and trousers and reeked of after-shave was too busy checking Betsy out to notice. "Oh, there you are, Miss Betsy! How pretty you look this afternoon!"

She smiled and, God help him, batted her eyelashes.

DJ listened as they flirted—rather deftly he might add. He could learn a thing or two. Finally, they reached the buffet table. "Let's get you something to eat." He plated some chicken and rice for Betsy, swirled some raita on top and placed a naan quarter at just the right angle, then scanned the room for a table and found a head of golden dreadlocks all the way across the crowded room.

What was Julia doing back here? He tried to catch her eye, but she seemed to be searching for someone. Surely she wasn't looking for him. The tiny kick of anticipation in his gut made him feel thirteen years old.

He settled Betsy at a table and brought her a glass of water. "I'll be right back," he said but Betsy was busy beckoning her new boyfriend over. "I need to say hello to a friend."

Betsy followed his gaze, just as Julia's clear blue eyes met his.

"Well well well," Betsy said. "She's a looker, isn't she?"

DJ shrugged in agreement. Julia waved to him and he made a gesture letting her know he was coming over.

"But what does a white girl need dreads for?"

Luckily, Mr. Casanova joined her and DJ didn't have to respond.

He made his way across the crowded dining hall toward the corridor where Julia had headed and crashed straight into someone.

He looked down, an apology on his lips, and found himself

staring right into the flashing amber eyes of Trisha Raje, of all people.

"Hey! Watch where you're going," she snapped with her usual sunniness, pressing a hand into his chest to push him away. His skin heated under her hand, the awareness of it spreading through him. In the moment that it took for her to recognize him, her eyes went round, her mouth rounder. It was as though she had no idea what to do with the fact that he existed at all. "Oh," she followed up articulately.

"Dr. Raje," he said. Her palm was still pressed against his chest.

"What are you doing here?" they both said together and the embarrassment he saw in her eyes spread all across him.

For a few seconds, neither one of them said anything.

Then she pulled her hand away and found her voice as color rampaged across her face. "I was here to see a friend."

Something so sad flashed in her eyes that he almost wanted to ask her what was wrong. Instead what came out was, "Emma works here, so I brought her in."

Mentioning Emma seemed to bring their last conversation to life between them, accusations and hopelessness and all. She opened and closed her mouth, and yet again he had a sense that she was so uncomfortable around him that she could barely keep things straight. Well, she wasn't alone.

"How is Emma doing?" she asked.

He couldn't answer. Not without thinking about how he hadn't found a way to change Emma's mind yet.

The long column of her throat strained as she swallowed and he had a sense that she'd seen his thoughts, his feeling of uselessness, his guilt. This time sympathy flashed in her eyes and it ramped up his restlessness.

"So Emma is working today?" she said when he didn't respond, and all he could think of was how tired Emma had looked and how letting Emma work right now proved that he was failing at taking care of her.

"I thought you wanted her to experience how worth living her life is." Even to his own ears he sounded defensive. "Well, she considers this place the best part of her life."

Instead of biting his head off in return, she nodded. "I imagine she does." Her hand reached out and hovered over his forearm. "Mr. Caine . . ."

Every time she called him Mr. Caine he wanted to ask her to call him DJ, but it never seemed to come out.

She pulled her hand back without touching him. "What you're doing . . . it's really wonderful." Was she attempting pleasantness? Her face was all pinched, certainly not the right accompaniment to pleasantness. He couldn't quite reconcile pleasantness on her at all. Couldn't make it fit with what he knew of her. She pressed her hand into her belly and his own hand went to his chest where her hand had pressed into his skin.

"Should we go find Emma? I'd love to say hi." The only time her face seemed to relax was when she mentioned Emma. And somehow that made the hope that Emma would be all right nudge at him.

"DJ?" Julia said behind Trisha and she froze.

Her entire demeanor changed. She spun around as though someone had stabbed her between the shoulder blades. Her eyes scanned Julia from head to toe, the tattered jeans, the blond dreadlocks gathered over one shoulder, the Ganesha tattooed up the side of her neck, and rested in horror on her raised, pierced brow.

Julia in turn took in the doctor in her pristine pantsuit, her expensive shoes, her glossy well-cut hair that bobbed around a perfectly boned jaw, then gave her the warmest smile.

Instead of smiling back, Trisha Raje scowled. Actually it was more a sneer, dripping with all the disgust of someone who had stepped in fresh turd. She followed it up by stepping back, as though she were physically repulsed.

"Dr. Raje, this is Julia," he said sharply, offended on Julia's behalf. "Julia, this is Dr. Raje."

"Hi, Dr. Raje." Julia extended a hand, her smile turning mildly amused.

"It was nice seeing you again, Mr. Caine," Trisha said in a slicing tone that reminded him of the first time they'd met and she'd asked him if he knew the worth of her hands. That was it. That's all she threw at DJ before spinning around, her proud head held high. Then without even looking in Julia's direction she strode away.

Julia looked as though someone had slapped her. He barely knew her, but he could swear she was holding back tears.

"Sorry about that." He touched her shoulder even as his eyes followed Trisha Raje walking away. "You all right?"

Her eyes filled, but she sniffed and smiled at him, batting her lids to clear the tears. "I'm sorry you had to witness that. How well do you know Trisha?"

"Barely. Just as Emma's doctor. Do you know her?"

Her laugh at that was horridly sad. "We were best friends in college." She flicked away the tear that glided down one cheek. "Or she was mine. Apparently, I wasn't worthy of the honor. Trailer trash on scholarship at Berkeley is still trailer trash."

He knew exactly how Julia felt. Before he could respond, she scrubbed at her eyes with so much resolve it made her look years younger. "I'm sorry. I didn't mean to say that. It was a long time ago. I just came back to make sure you were okay. You looked very worried when I left. I wanted to let you know that if you have any concerns at all, all you have to do is ask and I'll address them."

She looked so earnest he had to smile at her. "You came back just to tell me that?"

Her grin went impish, every evidence of the tears she had fought gone, and he marveled at the strength that must take. "Maybe." She held up her denim jacket. "But I also left my jacket in Emma's studio."

That smile of hers made him feel lighter, as though he, too, could put things away himself. "And here I was, all flattered."

She threw him a look from beneath her lashes. "Well, I never said I didn't leave the jacket behind for a reason." With that she sashayed away, leaving him to ponder the two women who had traced that same path within the span of a few minutes, and how very different each one of them made him feel.

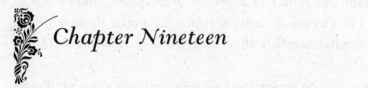

Chapter Nineteen

Trisha ran out into the shaded nursing home parking lot. Her heart was thudding in her chest. She willed herself to calm down, but she couldn't seem to bring her panic under control.

It felt like she'd seen a ghost. She had. A ghost who looked nothing like the girl who had been her roommate for a whole year. Julia had gone from looking like Disney's Cinderella to looking like someone who despised the idea of looking like Cinderella.

Had those been dreadlocks? Something about that made Trisha want to bring up her lunch, even more than the shameless amusement in Julia's eyes as she had taken Trisha in. And, oh God, had she seen Trisha drooling all over DJ Caine?

Letting herself into her car, she leaned her head back into the headrest and closed her eyes. She needed to find out how, and why, why! DJ Caine knew Julia.

And she needed to call Yash.

She sat up and tried to calm herself. Jacaranda trees cast a deep shade on the stamped concrete sidewalk. Red country tiles lined the arched porch. Cheery yellow annuals overflowed from massive ceramic planters. All the elements that attempted to mimic a homelike atmosphere jumped out at her. Everywhere there were efforts to soothe those who visited family members they couldn't keep close in their real homes.

She thought about Dorna's Rita, frail yet resilient. Trisha had come by to drop off Dorna's things and check up on her. Rita had been lucid today but not a single tear had fallen from Rita's eyes as they sat together and shared Dorna stories. "She lived," Rita had said. "Really lived. And that's nothing to shed tears over."

She had made Trisha tell her all about the ependymoma she had performed that morning the way Dorna had always done, and also all about the surgery that Dorna had insisted upon for herself. In the end they had agreed that Dorna had probably orchestrated her own death on the operating table.

When Trisha left, her heart had been so full of pain, but also joy at a life well lived. Then she'd run into DJ.

And then into the woman who should never ever be allowed anywhere near vulnerable people. *Or anywhere near where Yash was.* Her chest tightened painfully as she thought of what Julia had done to her brother.

Picking up her phone Trisha scrolled through her favorites. There were her brothers: TP—short for The Prince, not Toilet Paper—and Little TP.

The nicknames made her smile. Trisha hated that she barely ever spoke to her brothers anymore. Vansh hadn't lived in the same time zone as her in years. Plus, the boy was always in the middle of some serious shitstorm. If there wasn't shelling, or chanting, or rioting going on in the background when they spoke on the phone, Trisha might suspect someone was impersonating her little brother.

She badly wanted to call Vansh, but she knew that was just avoidance, so she took a breath and hit "TP," a part of her hoping that Yash might be too busy to answer.

He picked up immediately. "Trisha? What's wrong?" It made sense that he'd think a call from his screwup sister had to mean something was wrong.

"How are you, Yash?" she said, trying to sound breezy. "All well in DC?"

"Everything's great. Except what's not so great of course." His voice did a groaning/smiling thing. "I was actually just going to call you."

"Really?" she said without thinking, surprise far too clear in her tone.

"Yes, I wanted to know if you had seen Nisha. She's not answering her phone."

"Oh. Yes, I have. She's been a bit busy with Neel gone and your fund-raiser coming up."

"Hm. I just wanted to make sure you'd seen her and that she was okay."

"Did I tell you about my grant?" Changing topics inelegantly, yes, that was the way to go here!

"Ma did," he said, sounding alert. He'd caught the topic change but didn't point it out. He hadn't bothered to congratulate her. Not that she'd been waiting or anything. "Sorry, I should have called to congratulate you. Congratulations, Shasha. We're all so proud."

"Are you really?" she wanted to ask. But the real reason for her call meant that they couldn't possibly be.

"Thanks," she said quietly.

"You sure you're okay?" he asked.

Maybe he knew about Julia. What if this was a test? "I'm fine."

"Good. Can I call you later?" He seemed to be in a busy place with lots of voices in the background. "I need to finish this meeting and have dinner with Naina. She's only in the country for a day."

Oh. Yash's long-term girlfriend had been living all over Asia working on her postdoc on feminism and feudal Eastern cultures for almost five years. Trisha had no idea she was visiting. "Is she coming back for the fund-raiser?"

"Not sure," he said absently. Too absently. Trisha had been seeing pictures of Steele with his lovely wife and two children splashed across every California paper. At church, on vacation. Would Yash's unmarried status be a problem for his campaign? Maybe not, unless the fact that he hadn't married a woman he'd been with for close to two decades was coupled with an old video of him with an underage intern who had worked for him.

"Yash?" Sometimes her mouth did things without her permission.

"Yes?"

Other times it totally gave up on her. Seriously, why couldn't she just live in the OR? All her parts worked just fine in there.

"Shasha, what's the matter?"

"Well . . . um . . . I don't want you to worry, but I . . . I just ran into Julia." *Shit!* HRH was going to kill her for telling him. Why hadn't she thought this through?

There was a beat of silence. A very long beat. "Okay. Is that why you're sounding like this? What did she want?"

How the hell would she know what Julia Wickham wanted? Other than to destroy everything and everyone in her path. Why did her family think being her roommate for one year made Trisha an expert on a sociopath? "I don't know. I ran into her by accident. We didn't talk. She didn't seek me out. I swear."

"Sweetheart, I'm not saying she did. Listen, stop worrying so much." Easy for the gray-eyed prince to say. He had never ruined anyone's life because of his inability to judge people. "So you ran into her. It's a free country. Did HRH say something to you?"

She couldn't answer that. She wasn't a snitch. But HRH was right, Julia's timing wasn't an accident. Something was off. Actually everything about the Julia she had just seen was off. It wasn't just that she was all tattooed and pierced and dreadlocked. There was nothing wrong with being any of those things, but it reminded Trisha too much of how Julia had taken to regularly wearing Indian kurtas and bangles when they had been friends. She had even bought a book of henna and ordered henna cones off a mail-order catalog and started to wear it all the time. Trisha had only ever worn kurtas in college at the Indian Students' Association's Diwali celebrations, and she'd only ever worn bangles and henna at Nisha's wedding. The Indian ceremony, not the church one.

"Does your friend think she's desi?" Nisha had said on a

laugh, back when they had still been able to laugh at a conversation that involved Julia.

Something about Julia dressing desi all the time had made Trisha uncomfortable, but she'd said nothing. "It makes me happy! Your people's stuff is so much more beautiful," she'd said with so much longing that Trisha had told herself that her friend deserved to be happy.

And now it seemed Julia had decided that dreads made her happy. Trisha felt physically sick. More than how Julia looked, it was her eyes that terrified her. They hadn't changed at all.

"Something is off. I have a bad feeling about this," she wanted to say to Yash. But where would she even begin with explaining her bad feeling? Someone else spoke to Yash, and he asked for a minute. The brother she could pour her heart out to was long gone, she'd lost him. Julia Wickham had used her to almost destroy him and taken that from her forever. Plus, how could she dump more stress on him right now?

"Listen," he said coming back to her, "if Ma and HRH get on your case about it, you call me, okay?"

Really? Suddenly Yash was on her side? "They've been on my case about it for years. What have you ever done to help?" That's what she wanted to say. Naturally, what she did say was, "Sure. Thanks."

"Also, Trisha," he said a little more tentatively, "if she contacts you or if you think of anything else, call me, please." Then just in case she was too dense to get his meaning he added, "However small it seems. Even if it seems harmless, don't worry, just let me know. Okay?"

A pulse pounded in her temples. She had confided in him

later, when she had apologized after Julia had drugged him and violated him. *I didn't say anything because I thought she was harmless . . . I really believed she was harmless.* She had wanted him to understand. *I don't care*, he had said. *It doesn't matter.*

But of course it had mattered.

"Sure," she said once more and wished him luck with his meetings.

She just sat there in her car for a while longer, thinking of how simple it had been for her to say something back then. It had been right in front of her, the fact that Julia would do anything to get what she wanted. But Trisha had chosen not to see it. She had lied to her own brother. She had put an outsider before family, despite everything she'd ever been taught.

Her phone beeped, snapping her out of her trance.

"You here?" It was a text from Harry. Shit! She had forgotten about meeting him.

"Sorry, emergency errand."

"That's kind of shitty," he texted back. "I was looking forward to dinner." Translation: *You were supposed to be here with the food.*

What a jerk. Although she didn't think being obsessed with food was so strange anymore. Not since DJ Caine had made his annoying presence felt inside her taste buds.

"Sorry."

"I'm sorry too. I don't think this relationship is working out."

Was he breaking up with her by text? What were they, high schoolers? At least this proved that they'd been in a relationship. Then again, did it?

"I didn't realize we were in a relationship." Of course she didn't send that. She deleted those words and typed: "I agree. Things have been crazy. I'll drop the food off with your assistant tomorrow. It's frozen."

A long silence followed. "I'm sorry. I was upset. I don't really want to break up. Can we reschedule?"

She laughed, loud and so maniacal that a passing lady scowled at her.

"No thank you. I'll see you around." She hit send.

Her relief at not having that food in her fridge any longer was immense.

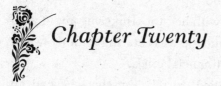

Chapter Twenty

"Maybe you should get a real job, mate, because the medical bills here will kill you," Rajesh said as he lounged on a beanbag in DJ's flat, where he was camped out on the floor of DJ's room in exchange for assisting DJ.

DJ did love irony so very much.

Good thing Rajesh only showed up a few times a week and that Emma was in the shower. The last thing she needed was another conversation about her bills. Actually, the last thing she needed was to hear Rajesh's idiotic opinions on the matter.

It had been six days since she'd been discharged. The exhaustion on her face when she had gone to bed last night had been brutal. She had spent far too much time yesterday at Green Acres. When DJ had come home last night, she'd been furiously working at her easel while Julia sat by with her camera, letting it soak up the turmoil in her frenzied strokes. Julia and he had sat together for a while, watching Emma stab at the canvas. Then Julia had left but Emma had refused to go to bed. Emma had told DJ that she had let Julia interview her about their childhood in London, which explained some of her mood. The memories of their homeless days made him want to stab at something too.

Naturally, he'd stayed up with her, too, tinkering about with some of the recipes for a dinner he was catering tomorrow and trying to make sense of his financial crisis.

Ashna had called, mortified, to tell him that she had an offer from a chef who wanted to rent her kitchen when the restaurant was closed. He had urged her to take the deal of course. "You have to save your restaurant, that has to be your priority," he'd told her.

The words she'd said after that had made anger churn inside him again.

"That's what Trisha said too."

Why was he not surprised that Dr. Raje was the one who had come up with the idea of finding a renter for Ashna when she knew DJ needed to use her kitchen? He knew she was only trying to help her cousin, but to use his own idea to screw him over when he so desperately needed money was callous if not cruel.

He'd insisted on still working with Ashna on the menu revamp. She'd tried to convince him to let her pay for it, but that was out of the question. Even if he were desperate enough to take money from a friend, he wouldn't have anywhere near enough to rent another kitchen. Not until Emma's medical bills were taken care of.

Rajesh had come in past midnight and gone straight to bed on wobbly drunken legs as usual. Now here he was sharing his unsolicited opinion on how to tackle the bills DJ had been admittedly glowering at.

When Charan Singh had called asking if DJ had a job for

Rajesh, DJ had naturally said yes. Apparently the idiot had picked the wrong married woman to start an affair with back in the old neighborhood.

Rajesh poured half a carton of cream and half a jar of sugar into his coffee and took a slurping sip. Really, it was a shame to let this guy near food. "The car seems to be your only asset, mate," he said.

DJ heard Emma open and shut the bathroom door. Rajesh dug his fingers into the slice of frittata DJ had cut for Emma. "Even if you are okay with Emma's hospital bills, what about the kitchen? We need prep work space. There's no place to do it here." He swept his eggy fingers in an arc, indicating the two-foot countertop.

DJ handed him a fork and a napkin.

"Why can't you just keep on using Ashna Raje's kitchen and keep giving her whatever she's getting in return." How a creep like Rajesh had descended from someone like Ammaji, DJ would never know.

Instead of punching Rajesh's nose, he took a deep breath. "Ashna is getting new recipes and my eternal gratitude in return. Is there any woman in this universe whom you respect?" But of course he should not have asked the question. Because now that he had asked the question, he'd have to hear the answer, and nothing good could come of that.

"Respect them? What for? They don't care about being respected anymore. Not like our mothers. They want you to be a man again. Haven't you been on Twitter lately? Hashtag-WomenAgainstFeminism. Buy them things, pay for their dinner, and they don't give a fig about respect."

"I'm so glad Twitter's not where I go to find women."

"That's because you don't go anywhere to find women, mate. Not that you would ever find the paragon you're looking for."

"I'm not looking for anything." How had he let himself get involved in this conversation?

"Of course you are. But what you're looking for doesn't exist." He stuffed his face full of frittata and leaned his hip on the table. "You're one of those blokes who wants someone he can put on a pedestal. But you also want someone who puts you on a pedestal too. That's why, my friend, you're going to be looking for a very long time. A woman is either a diva or a devi. Either you take care of her or she takes care of you. You can't have both." He wiggled his brows. "And that's true when it comes to shagging them as well."

"All right." DJ pushed himself off his plastic chair and pulled himself up to his full height. Which put him at a good six inches above Ammaji's fool grandson who straightened up but didn't look in the least bit intimidated. "I did not need to hear that."

DJ went into the kitchen and cut Emma another slice of frittata, just as Emma's door opened. Thank the good Lord she hadn't been here to hear Rajesh's depraved soliloquy.

Rajesh shrugged. "Sure. My experience is wasted on you anyway. Come to think of it, that Ashna would be perfect for you. She's just as uptight as you."

Emma raised her brows at DJ as she sank into a chair.

DJ moved the bills aside, put the frittata in front of her, and dropped a kiss on her wet head. "Morning, love." Then to Rajesh: "Thank you but I really meant I don't need to discuss relationships with you. Ever." Or anything else for that matter, truly.

"Fine, so let's talk about your bills then. How are you going to afford a kitchen and pay for these bills if you don't want to get a real job?"

Emma picked up the bills and smacked Rajesh upside the head with them. "He has a 'real job,' you wanker. If he didn't, you'd be out on your arse, now wouldn't you?" She shook the bills at him. "And he no longer has to worry about these, either. We've got it sorted." She looked at DJ. "You aren't actually taking advice from him are you? You know he's a chocolate teapot—totally fecking useless."

That made DJ smile. "I'm not looking for a *real job*, no." He nudged the frittata he'd been experimenting with toward her. "Try this. I'm trying to see if it works as a cold appetizer."

She took a bite and made a face. "I prefer my eggs hot." But when he tried to take it back, she held on to the plate and kept eating. "Julia thinks she can have the video produced and online in a week."

"You've made up your mind about this, yeah?" The plastic chair creaked as he sat down next to her.

Emma nodded, but she looked tired. "Are you going to go off on another rant about why I shouldn't do it? Or did the blue-eyed Julia doll change your mind?" she said cheekily and he felt a blush rise up his neck.

"I don't rant," he said defensively. "And what good would it do me?"

Emma was about to respond when the doorbell rang.

Rajesh sauntered over to the door licking his fingers and

opened it and did a double take so hard, he might have cracked his neck. "Oh hullo, hullo, who do we have here?" Mr. Sleaze-ball stepped too close to Julia and took both her hands in his as though he were some sort of posh bloke. Blech!

Julia smiled kindly. "Hello to you, too. I'm Julia. I'm here to interview Emma." She threw DJ an amused look over Rajesh's shoulder.

"I'm Raj. I'm a friend of the family's and the camera loves me." He threw a look at the camera hanging from Julia's neck.

"Come on in," DJ said before Rajesh embarrassed himself further.

To his surprise Julia reached up and gave him a quick hug. He returned it, albeit with all the requisite awkwardness befitting an Englishman.

"How are you, Emma dear?" she asked, setting her tripod down.

"Peachy," Emma said flatly. "Especially the part where everyone keeps asking me that. It's just bloody lovely."

Julia took it on the chin and DJ had to be impressed. She was just so even-keeled and approachable. There wasn't anything confusing about her and he found that restful.

As for his sister, dear God, let Julia be right—let getting out her feelings on camera set her head straight.

"I was just trying to convince Darcy that we're going to make a killing with this video. I'm going to leave him a rich man."

Julia walked to DJ and rubbed his arm. A comfort that failed to comfort him. "I'm sorry. But she's right. This will help, won't it? To pay the bills."

"Thanks," he said. "We're going to be fine with the bills. I have some good gigs coming up. We'll crunch the numbers somehow."

Rajesh shouldered his way between Julia and DJ. "What's to crunch? You need half a mil down to lease a running kitchen and then you need to pay ten grand every month to keep it going. Basically, you are going to need an investor or a loan or you're going to have to marry rich in a hurry."

If he had a penny for every time he wanted to tell Rajesh to shut up, this entire financial crisis might be averted.

"I'm telling you that fancy Raje chick is perfect for you, and she's sweet on you and everything."

"Shut up, Rajesh. Do you have to be a wanker all the bloody time!" Emma said with so much force Rajesh drew back. "Leave DJ alone."

Rajesh raised his hands, grinning like the thick-skinned idiot he was. "Keep your knickers on. No one likes to hear the truth. I get it." He winked at Julia, who gave DJ a curious look.

"I have to go." DJ looked at his watch. "The farmers' market closes in a half hour." He handed Rajesh a list of suppliers to call and kissed Emma's cheek. "I'll be back in time to drive you to work."

"Do you mind if I walk out with you? I need to grab some coffee," Julia said, giving him another one of those bright smiles he was getting used to, and followed him out the door when he nodded.

"I didn't realize you knew Trisha Raje outside of her being Emma's doctor," she said, falling in step next to him. "Your friend in there seemed to indicate that you were . . . close?" she added when he looked confused.

"Oh, that. No, he was talking about her cousin Ashna. We're friends. We worked together in Paris for a while."

"Ah. She's the one with the restaurant, right? That's a relief." She stopped outside Philz Coffee. Mixed in with the rich coffee aroma was the smell of blueberry and chocolate chips baking together. It wasn't the most common combination, but you could do some good things with it.

"A relief, huh?" He gave her a curious smile.

She seemed a million miles away, and his lame attempts at being flirtatious totally nose-dived into the pavement. "Oh. You meant it was a relief that it wasn't Trisha Raje I was friends with. Not a relief that Ashna and I weren't involved." Great. "Now I feel like a prized arse."

This time her smile was shy, but when her eyes met his, there was a flirtatious spark there. "I have a feeling you could never be an . . ." She cleared her throat. ". . . arse?"

They both laughed. Then she looked worried again.

"Did I say something wrong?" The last thing he wanted was to make her uncomfortable with his ungainly flirting.

"No, not at all. I'm just . . . I hope you don't think I'm being too nosy, but . . ."

"Tell me," he urged.

"I just don't want you to get hurt, DJ."

She didn't have to tell him that whatever this was, it had to do with Trisha Raje. He could see it on her face. The utter disgust on Trisha's face when she'd seen Julia had been downright cruel.

"She's Emma's doctor. That's all." The idea of there being

anything more between him and Dr. Raje was preposterous. It made him want to laugh, but not in a good way.

She touched his arm and looked so anxious he put his hand over hers. "I'm sorry. I shouldn't have interfered. But these memories. I got triggered, I'm sorry."

"It's all right."

She turned her hand in his and clasped his fingers. "Just be careful. I know how easy it is to trust her. I am painfully aware." She slipped into a chair on the sidewalk and he sat down next to her, his hand still in hers. "I grew up in a trailer park. Can you imagine what it was like to have Trisha Raje as a roommate? All that working my ass off to get accepted into Berkeley had felt like it had been worth it. I have no idea how we got matched up as roommates. It was probably because we'd both graduated early and made it to college at sixteen. But it felt like I had won the lottery. She came back to the dorm every weekend with boxes full of food. She had tickets to every concert on campus. She had everything . . . a mother who called her every day. A family who called her all the damn time. One would think I'd be jealous. But I lapped it up. It changed me. I knew what I wanted. I knew life could be beautiful if I worked hard, if I tried to be just like her. And then I met her brother. Have you ever met . . ." She cleared her throat. "Have you ever met Yash Raje?"

DJ nodded. He had met him just once on the day of the party at his parents' house, for all of five minutes. In those five minutes, Yash Raje had gotten him to talk about Emma, his love for cooking, basically everything that mattered to DJ. The young candidate had this way of reaching out and making you feel like he saw you. Even though the meeting had lasted just minutes, DJ would remember it for the rest of his life.

"Then you know what I'm talking about. The world moved beneath my feet when he took a second look at me. Have you ever fallen in love, DJ? Everything they say in books, all the feelings and swooning and yearning—all of it happened at once. I never expected that he'd notice me. I never expected to know what it felt like when he returned my feelings, but he did."

She had tears running down her face now. DJ didn't know quite what to say, so he stroked his thumb across her hand. They weren't long fingered and sure, but calloused from work and weary, like his.

"I don't think I can explain to you how cold Trisha can be. And you have to see her when she gets mean and ruthless to know what that feels like. Before I knew what was happening to me, they had framed me for dealing drugs. They tied me to my mother's boyfriends. Men who were dealers. All the things I had shared with her as a friend, she used against me. I was expelled from school, my record ruined. A record I had worked hard to keep clean despite where I came from. It was gone in a day. The man I loved never looked at me again. But you know what hurt the most? Being dropped by the only friend I'd ever had.

"I ended up on the street. I was homeless for a year. Homeless. Do you know what it feels like to be homeless, DJ? Just when you thought you were done with it?"

Oh, he knew only too well.

As he plucked out some napkins from the holder on the table, he saw his hands were shaking. He dabbed her tears. Mascara ran in black lines down her cheeks. He set her to rights.

She squeezed her eyes shut. "I'm sorry. I didn't mean to dump this on you. I've never talked about this to anyone." She looked mortified.

He dragged his chair closer and pulled her against his shoulder. Sobs shuddered through her, all those awful memories making her breath stutter as she tried to calm herself. She pressed her face into his shoulder and he rubbed her back. All the things Trisha had said and done flashed in his mind.

Hired help.

Her words mixed with the slurs his father's sister had shouted at his mother as they sat on the curb outside the home she had thrown them out of, all their possessions next to them in three meager suitcases. Ammaji opening the door to take them in. Walking up the steep stairway to the attic where one single bulb hung from the ceiling. *Curry sweep. Filthy. Little. Curry. Sweep.*

He ran his hand up and down Julia's back, soothing his twelve-year-old self, soothing Mum, soothing Emma, soothing everyone who didn't have the good fortune to be born into the right circumstances. "I'm so sorry that happened to you. But look at you now." He attempted a smile. "A fancy journalist. Look at how you wield that camera. Look at all the people you help."

"I'm pretty badass, ha?"

"Totally hundred-proof badass."

She smiled through her tears. "All I want is for you to not get hurt. We—people like you and me—we're playthings to the Rajes. We're nothing to them."

He knew.

"Thank you for trusting me with that," he said, but it felt insuf-
ficient, because how did you thank someone who shared their
darkest hurt with you, especially when they barely knew you?

"You're welcome," she said softly, smiling. Then even more
softly she placed a kiss on his cheek.

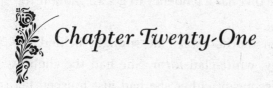

Chapter Twenty-One

Trisha really should not have decided to stop over at the Anchorage. Not when she was late to meet DJ. But Aji had called complaining about a stomachache and Trisha couldn't ignore that. She hadn't told Nisha, because Nisha would kill her for going anywhere near Esha right now. As for DJ, they were going to San Francisco, so he could just hop off 280 and pick her up. It was barely a ten-minute detour. Plus, she'd been at the hospital most of last night and she hadn't had a chance to charge her car. At least she'd stopped breaking into a panicky sweat every time she thought about the fund-raiser, thanks to DJ. Between being grateful to him for his competence and livid that she was going to have to confront him about Julia, she was dreading their meeting today.

"It's been four days!" her grandmother said as soon as Trisha entered her room.

Trisha hugged her, rubbing her cheek on her soft Chanderi sari. "See, first you don't see me for four days and then you act like this, how can I be upset with you?"

"How can you be upset with me no matter what? I thought ajis weren't allowed to be upset with their granddaughters."

"There is that," Aji said. "Have you eaten? You know you have the kind of face that has a tendency to get all gaunt if you don't eat."

Esha smiled from the doorway, the sunlight behind her outlining her wispy, white-clad form. She had the slightly disoriented look that meant either she had just finished her meditation or she'd seen something. Trisha went to her but waited for Esha to hug her. Or not. They were all trained to let Esha follow her own emotional state. She always set the tone based on how she was feeling right then.

Today was not a day for hugs. But calm embraced Trisha as Esha moved her hand to the center of her chest, pressing into Trisha's heart.

"How beautiful you look, Shasha," she said. "My soft warrior. War is a violent thing but its purpose is often to protect your own, and to ultimately bring peace. Sometimes you have to go to war to move forward and past suffering, to get closer to our natural state as humans. That of equilibrium and well-being."

Trisha simply nodded. The only time Esha ever lectured was when she'd seen something and she was trying to tell you what she'd seen.

"When it's time to fight, it's okay to fight," Esha said. "Even if sometimes your biggest enemies may be hiding inside you. Not everyone who fights you is your enemy."

Finally Esha nodded and Trisha touched the hand Esha had pressed into her chest.

"Thanks, Esha." She never asked Esha for details. She never wanted to know. Every single time Esha had warned against something it had come true. *Your loyalty is to blood*, she'd told Trisha when the thing with Yash had happened. Trisha had ignored her and look how that had ended up.

Suddenly Esha frowned. "Where is Nisha?"

Trisha stepped away from her. Keeping Nisha's secret around Esha was impossible.

"I have to go, Esha; I just came by to check Aji's stomachache because Dad's in LA."

Esha smiled at her. They both knew Aji was perfectly fine. She just hadn't seen Trisha in a few days and had wanted her to come over.

"Do you want me to write you a prescription for Zantac, Aji? Or will your pudin hara work?"

"Yes yes, I got it. But at least eat a ladoo before you go? I put a few aside for you. Here." Her grandmother handed her a box full of her delicious sweet cream-of-wheat balls. "Eat one now. You know how you get when you get hungry."

Trisha was about to open the box when her phone buzzed. A text from Bicep-chef—she'd put his name down as that in her contacts the day Nisha had stuck her with the fund-raising dinner.

"I'm almost there." How did even his texts sound pissed off? And why was he texting while driving?

Trisha frowned at the text, then frowned even harder at the ladoos. "I'll eat them in the car," she said to Aji before giving her another quick hug.

Before she got away, Esha caught her hand. "Be careful," she said, her eyes somber.

"Always am."

"Some things require more care than you're giving them, Shasha."

How she hated these nebulous prophetic declarations.

"Tell Nisha to—"

"Really, Esha, I have to go!" She practically ran from the room before Esha could finish.

She remembered the horror on Esha's face every time Nisha got pregnant. After the first two miscarriages, Nisha had refused to meet Esha, but Trisha somehow was the conduit between the cousins. She'd transferred the unease between the two and she hated it.

Tell Nisha some things can't be made through force of will.

Yeah, no. No way had Trisha been able to tell Nisha that. And when she had refused to ferry Esha's messages to Nisha like a carrier pigeon, Esha had suffered seizure after seizure from whatever it was that built up inside her.

Remembering that made Trisha stop. Reluctantly, she turned around and went back to Esha. But Esha only smiled. "I'm fine. Go on."

That was all Trisha needed to hear. She ran down the stairs, ladoo box in hand. Sometimes she hated Esha. Guilt blasted through her at that thought, hard and sharp. No. No, she didn't hate Esha. She loved her more than anything, but she hated her visions, hated that she could not keep them to herself. She also hated having to keep Nisha's secret.

As much as she loved her sister, sleeping in the same bed as her right now was nerve-racking. Every time Nisha moved, Trisha skipped a heartbeat. She'd woken up again this morning to Nisha crying in her sleep. She'd wiped her cheeks, mumbled reassurances, and fallen back to sleep feeling incredibly alone. Being the only person in the family who knew about the baby felt too heavy, a crushing weight on her chest.

The last time Esha had asked her to be careful, Trisha had learned that she couldn't trust her own judgment and she'd lost Yash, HRH, and even Ma, a little bit. A horrible exhaustion rose inside her. Suddenly three hours of sleep and two surgeries descended on her like a crumbling ceiling.

Groaning, she pulled the heavy front door open and slammed straight into the big body of DJ Caine.

His hands gripped her upper arms as he steadied her; they were warm and gentle and reminded her of the solidity of his chest when she'd pressed her hand into it at Green Acres. She could still feel his heart beating a frantic rhythm against her palm.

"Hey, you all right?" His expression was so kind, she almost let the choked-up feeling welling inside her turn into tears. It was a horrifying thought. Just as horrifying as the fact that she hadn't been able to get the feel of his chest off her hand. And now she had the feel of his fingers on her arms to deal with.

She pushed him away with both hands and swept past him down the steps. "I'm fine."

"All right then." He stretched the words out in a weirdly British way and fell in step next to her.

"Whose car is that?" A beast of a yellow Porsche stood to one side of the sweeping driveway. "You don't own that thing, do you?" Where was the adorable pink Beetle?

"No, I just stole it to drive you to the city in the style to which you're accustomed."

She turned around and glared at him. "Don't be tasteless. That's not what I meant."

DJ WONDERED WHAT else Trisha Raje could possibly have meant.

He didn't bother with asking the question. It didn't matter. He couldn't afford a Porsche right now and there was no point pretending to be offended when other people recognized that fact.

Emma's Beetle had sprung a flat when he had driven her to Green Acres that afternoon. Emma's friend Betsy had told DJ to take her car—and she could be utterly insistent when she was coherent. It was Betsy's late husband's car. She refused to sell it. Instead, she parked it at Green Acres and used it as bait to get her nieces and nephews to come see her.

When she had pressed him to take it, DJ had accepted gratefully, and hurriedly, because he hadn't wanted to be late for the meeting with Trisha. As it turned out, the good doctor had been running late herself and had ordered him to meet her at her parents' mansion.

After his conversation with Julia yesterday, he'd considered calling Nisha and begging off the job. But it was too important a job to walk away from and they were tangled up in far too many knots for him to avoid her. At least not until Emma was taken care of.

If it hadn't been for the fact that Betsy owned a Porsche Neunelfer, his mood would be complete bollocks right now. But it was a fecking 911 Carrera! Who could be in a bad mood driving that?

The beauty might not be his, but he couldn't bear to watch

Dr. High and Mighty giving her the stink eye. "It doesn't meet your approval?"

"I usually make it a point not to approve of things that guzzle gas by the ton," she said tightly.

"Ah, so that Tesla there is yours then?"

She nodded at the bright red car with so much fondness she looked almost warm and fuzzy for a moment. Of course it would be an expensive car that was softening her up. Fitting.

"But I see it's charging, so we're going to have to take the gas guzzler," he said with a touch too much delight.

He shouldn't have. She was, after all, the Client.

"How's Emma?" she asked with the kindness she saved up for his sister, and he was reminded of all the reasons why he should keep his feelings to himself.

"She's fine. She's at Green Acres. And I . . . I'm really glad she's getting to do that."

She paled, then opened her mouth and shut it again. Finally, she took a deep breath. "About Green Acres. That woman you were with. Is she . . . um . . . you two seemed um . . . actually . . ."

"You mean Julia?"

She stepped back as though he'd said something offensive again, and rage at what she'd done to Julia rose inside him.

"Please don't take this the wrong way, but my family can't work with anyone who has any relationship with her."

Sodding hell, was she threatening to fire him again? When they were on their way to check out the venue?

"I'm not threatening you," she said quickly, but her voice held none of the softness from before and her eyes held all the arrogant power that was the one thing he had no trouble associating with her. "I have to know. Because between the fund-raiser and Emma's surgery . . ."

Unbelievable. Now she was throwing Emma's surgery into her threats? "But you are threatening me," he wanted to say. Except he wasn't quite that reckless and he was not losing this gig because of her pettiness. "There's no relationship," he said flatly. "I had barely even spoken to her until that day." *But I know what you did to her.*

"Okay," she said, but there was something icy and brittle about the way she said the word, as though trusting him was not an option. "She isn't the kind of person you should be associating with."

Excuse him?

Those boys aren't the kind of people you should be associating with. It's what Ammaji had said to him when she'd seen him come home from hanging with Gulshan and the crew.

Every single time he came in contact with this woman, he ended up here, his worst memories surfacing, and all the rage he'd put away long ago dredged up with them.

And yet there was no getting away from her. Nowhere to go. There was never any bloody where to go. One of these days, he'd turn around and there would be no corner behind him. He wouldn't be trapped. He'd be able to breathe.

Today was not that day.

"Shall we?" He held the car door open for her out of habit.

"Thank you." She sank into the seat as though it was her birthright to have doors held open for her.

He took his time walking around the car and focused on the beautiful lines, stroking the glossy metal as he went. The pleasure of fitting himself behind the wheel of a machine this perfect anchored him in the present. If anything could make the journey ahead bearable, it was a ride like this.

She looked at the gold-appointed dashboard. "It's cute."

"The gas guzzler thanks you," he said, not bothering to curb his sarcasm. "She's probably never carried an outstanding surgeon before."

Her only response was a weary look. Obviously, he wasn't the only one dreading the afternoon ahead. But there was something so tired about her eyes that despite himself he felt like an arse. What was it about this woman that made him want to be a prick? Oh yeah, it was the fact that she was a callous snob and she made him feel like—what was the phrase?—ah, the hired help.

On the upside, there was something comforting about knowing that he hadn't been wrong about her after that disastrous first meeting in the Raje kitchen. No wonder all those times when she'd been endearing had felt like trying to fit a square peg in a round hole.

Her fingers rested on her temples and for a moment he wondered what was bothering her in her perfect life.

The car purred under his foot as he circled the sweeping driveway. "Nisha well?" He tried not to think about how sad she had looked when he had run into her. Before she had shoved him away as though he were disease ridden and then proceeded to threaten him again.

"She's fine. Why would you think she's not?" she said shortly and he kicked himself for not leaving her be.

"Well, she was sick the last time I saw her, and apparently

something is wrong enough that you're going through all this trouble to keep anyone from finding out what it is. So excuse me for checking to make sure she's fine."

Her hand pressed into her belly, a gesture she seemed to reach for every time something overwhelmed her or made her uncomfortable. As he evidently did every time he was near her. "I'm sorry. You're right. I shouldn't have snapped at you."

Was he hearing things? Had she just apologized? The woman was giving him whiplash and it was irritating the hell out of him. His grip on the steering wheel tightened until the leather practically squeaked beneath his fingers.

She wasn't done. "I'm also sorry that I was late and that you had to drive to Woodside to get me."

Two whole apologies? Had Christmas come early?

But of course it hadn't because when he didn't respond immediately, she went right back to her most sunny demeanor. "The least you can do is acknowledge my apology!" she snapped, and it set the world straight again.

They passed under the arch that spelled out the words *The Anchorage.* What kind of people lived in a house with a name, with sliding gates? The indignant frown on her face made him imagine her as a little girl, driving down the thickly wooded street, knowing nothing of the world outside it where there was no anchorage for those cast out in storms, no easy acknowledgment of meaningless apologies.

"What good will my acknowledging your apology do?" he said, despite every instinct telling him to shut up.

"It will make me feel better, for one."

"Ah, that most pressing reason." He pulled out of the private street and just like that they were in city traffic.

"What is that supposed to mean?" Apparently she wasn't in the mood to let things go either.

"It means I accept. There, you should feel all better now."

"Thanks, but I think you have to actually mean it for me to feel better."

He had to laugh at that. "Well, maybe if you'd meant the apology, you wouldn't need my acknowledgment for it to matter."

Her brows drew together, the flame-colored flecks in her eyes sparking with indignation. "It's not like I meant to be late."

"I'm sure you didn't."

For a few minutes she didn't say more. But she glanced at him several times before saying, "What?"

"Nothing."

"You're thinking it, you might as well say it. It's too long a drive for awkward silences."

He very much doubted any drive with her would be too short for awkward silences. "Fine. Being late is a form of selfishness. It shows that you value your own time above others'."

She made an appalled sound. "That's the most ridiculous accusation I've ever heard. I'm a neurosurgeon, my life literally revolves around being selfless."

How could he not laugh at that? Had no one ever bothered to tell her that being a neurosurgeon did not absolve her of practicing common decency? Her entire family was incredibly gracious and kind. For all their poshness, Mrs. Raje, Nisha, and Ashna had always treated him with consideration and respect. Not one of them had ever said a single obnoxious thing around him. And this one had rarely said anything that wasn't obnoxious.

Naturally, she didn't like that he laughed. "I'll have you know that I've never been late to a single surgery or consult ever." She scowled, but in her eyes was genuine hurt.

"So someone has to be dying for you to value their time? Normal old healthy blokes don't deserve your consideration?"

"I was all of fifteen minutes late. I can't believe that you don't have the grace to pretend to be okay with that. How much *consideration* are you showing me?"

"I was trying to do just that. You're the one who insisted on having me share what I was thinking."

She emitted a grunting sound. Good. There was no reason why he should be the only one exasperated. For a while neither one of them spoke. And yes, the silence was awkward as hell.

Until her stomach let out a long low growl and she sat up, cheeks flushed. With a sheepish smile that transformed her into someone else entirely, she looked at the plastic box on her lap. "I might be a little hungry. Do you mind if I eat in the car?"

"By all means." God, if eating would improve her demeanor, he'd feed her himself.

The thought brought to mind the way she had eaten his food at the tasting, and he struggled to push the memory away.

Lifting a smooth round ladoo out of the box, she held it up. "It's a ladoo. An Indian dessert."

She held the box out to him and as soon as he took one she popped one whole in her mouth with near desperation.

"I know what a ladoo is. Are these rava or besan?"

The way she blinked at him he might as well have unexpectedly spouted Enochian. The ladoo poked into her cheek and her surprise seemed to make it hard for her to chew and swallow at the same time. "Right," she said on a gulp. "Your specialty is fusing traditional north Indian flavors with classical French technique." She took a second ladoo out of the box. "This is rava. You probably know how to make these and everything. But my aji—that's my grandma—makes the best ones." A worshipful smile danced around her lush mouth, which was glossy from the ghee. A few grains of semolina clung to her full lips. With a delicate and slightly self-conscious flick of her tongue she licked them off.

He took a bite. "They're pretty good." They were great, actually. The kind of great that came from internalizing recipes from prolonged and organic repetition. The kind of great that trained chefs found the hardest to achieve.

"How did you get interested in Indian food anyway?" Another sweet round ball went into her mouth whole. She was going through them so fast he was having a hard time keeping his eyes on the road.

The way she had eaten his food in Nisha's kitchen flashed in his mind once again. Eyes suffused with pleasure, body limp with satisfaction. Artless, with nothing held back. This time he had a harder time pushing the memory away. It settled in his gut and sent the strangest buzz coursing through him. "Well, it is the official cuisine of London, didn't you know?" he said finally.

That made her smile and relax into her seat. Or maybe it was all that sugar and ghee.

"My father was Indian." He had no idea why he added that. He had hardly learned how to cook Indian food from Dad. "Anglo-Indian, actually. Or at least that's what my father liked to call being half British and half Indian."

"You're Indian?" This time her shock wasn't a surprise. Both Emma and he favored their Rwandan mother.

"My dad was born in England, but his family migrated from India a few years before Indian independence. I'm not sure, but I think my grandfather was born there. He married an English-woman."

"You're not sure?" she said with the puzzlement of someone who couldn't imagine families who didn't know each other, didn't know their own history. For a moment he wanted what she had so badly, he couldn't speak.

"My father's family threw him out when he married my mum. She was a refugee from Rwanda. We never really knew his family." All DJ knew of his family history was what he'd pieced together from overhearing his parents' conversations before his father died.

He had never talked about his parents to anyone, but some-thing about how much his words seemed to horrify her made him go on. "It had taken my father's family a few generations to wash the brown out of them, so by marrying Mum, my father basically nullified half a century's worth of effort for whitening up the Caine line." He tried to sound nonchalant but ended up sounding more bitter than he actually felt about the entire sordid business.

"That's terrible." She twisted in her seat as though what he'd just told her was so disturbing it made it impossible for her to sit still.

It struck him suddenly, the realization that he'd never met a brown person more comfortable in her own skin than Trisha Raje. He wondered if it had always been this way. If she'd ever struggled with her identity.

"My mother quit her movie career in India and ran away with my father against her father's wishes. He never spoke to her after that and died soon after their wedding. Ma never talks about him—but there's this distinct pain in her that surfaces if he ever comes up."

DJ couldn't imagine anything cracking Mrs. Raje's pleasant demeanor. For all their shared beauty, how very different the two women were. He wondered what their relationship was like. His own mother's softness had been snuffed out by hardship. The world never saw her warmth. But the love in her eyes had always shone strong and open for him and Emma. And saved them.

"Did your dad ever reconcile with his family?" Trisha asked, studying him, her voice catching a tiny bit on the word *reconcile*. "They must've been heartbroken when he died."

He gave her the ugly laugh he saved especially for his Caine relatives. "Not in the least bit." One would require a heart to be heartbroken. "They threw us out on the street after Dad died, took our home, and never spared a second look on us."

Another stretch of that neck followed by another deep swallow. "So your mother raised you by herself?"

The pain in her eyes made him mirror her swallow. "Yes.

She died when I was eighteen." Somehow it felt important to say that. To highlight the differences between their lives.

"Emma and you really only have each other." Her voice fell to a gentle whisper.

He nodded. Emma was all he'd had for a very long time.

"I'm sorry." Her eyes blazed and dimmed at once, and it felt like the old pain in his own heart finding fresh release.

He reminded himself that the tale of one's orphaning usually made even the most hard-hearted sorry.

"I'm glad she's getting to spend this time with her work and with her art," she added in the same gentle whisper, as though his pain actually meant something.

He noticed she didn't include him in the list.

"She'll still have you after the surgery," she said and he hated being transparent to her.

There were just two ladoos left in the box. She put the one in her hand back. Apparently sympathy made her lose her appetite. Or maybe after eating eight, she was finally full. He had no idea where she put it all.

"I hadn't eaten all day," she said, reading him again. Not that any normal human would not be thinking what he was thinking after seeing her devour upwards of a day's worth of calories at one go.

He shrugged and they fell silent. The next time he looked over she had fallen asleep. He couldn't decide if it was relief he was feeling at not having to continue their conversation or regret. There was a slight sheen of sweat on her upper lip and he lowered the temperature and adjusted the golden vents in the borrowed dream. The redirected air lifted the loosened wisps of hair off her forehead and she relaxed deeper into sleep.

She was a whole different person in sleep, beautiful in a way that was so guileless and real that for one unguarded second he craved knowing this person—the woman beneath all that arrogance and prickliness. The one who sparkled with anger and hurt at the thought of a family casting out its own. The one who read her patients' innermost demons with so little effort.

When he pulled into a parking spot on a street just a block from the ballroom, she was still asleep.

"Dr. Raje," he said softly.

When she didn't so much as budge, he gave her shoulder a gentle nudge.

Her large, heavy-lidded eyes blinked open, the soft amber limpid and sleep soaked. For a second they stared at each other, the mix of the heat from the sun radiating through the windshield and the cool from the air vents hitting their faces at once. A car honked as it drove by and she jolted to full wakefulness. Realization dawned in her eyes, like flames catching from a spark, and turned to shock and then . . . was that fear?

He pulled away and she scampered back in her seat. She pressed a hand on her heart and he imagined it slamming in her chest.

"We're here." He pushed himself farther back and away from her.

Mortification colored her cheeks. One would think he had walked in on her in the shower. Falling asleep around a virtual stranger was obviously not something she did often.

"How long have I been out?" she said, her tone harsh beneath the huskiness of her sleep-drenched voice, and dabbed tentative fingers around her mouth, checking in horror to see if she had drooled. She had.

He let himself out of the car, his own heartbeat too fast and stuttering. "It took us about an hour to get here." No stranger had ever fallen asleep around him; he most certainly had never done it. He didn't know what the protocol was either.

She flipped the visor down and started to check herself in the mirror. He turned away to give her some privacy.

"You should have woken me up," she said from inside the car, her tone accusatory.

"I just did."

"After an hour of watching me sleep?"

What the hell was that supposed to mean? "You seemed tired. And I usually watch the road when I drive." There it was again, the hard slam of his heart that went with the rage she made him feel, and now there was the added thump of feeling like a prized knob for letting his guard down. "I'll see you inside." He retrieved his briefcase from the boot of the car and strode off toward the Astoria without waiting for her.

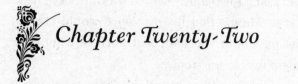

Chapter Twenty-Two

Despite how it had started out, DJ was amazed at how well their visit to the ballroom was going. The Astoria was a perfect venue. To be able to serve food on the terrace overlooking the bay with a clear view of the Golden Gate—it was an honor. DJ was already tweaking the menu in his head to suit the ambience.

Trisha was leaning over the Italian villa–style concrete railing, her long limbs at once gangly and graceful and entirely at home in this place that was designed with only one aim—to unabashedly showcase wealth and exclusivity.

They had barely spoken to each other over the past half hour as the Astoria's event manager, the very aptly named Mr. Mantis, had given them the tour. A few minutes ago some sort of emergency had cropped up and Mantis had effusively apologized before excusing himself and left them to enjoy the magnificent mosaic-tiled terrace while he took care of things.

"It's lovely, isn't it?" Trisha said, tentatively studying him over her shoulder.

DJ nodded. He still didn't know what had happened in the car, didn't know what she had accused him of. But when she had walked in on Mantis giving him the stiff treatment about being late, she had taken the blame—which was indeed hers—and made it clear to Mantis that his insolence would not be tolerated. For the past hour the man had been bowing and scraping to make up for his misstep.

"It is lovely," he said, breaking his silence because this inexplicable roller coaster of emotions she seemed to strap him into couldn't get in the way of the excitement fizzing through him about this job. The menu he had laid out was going to have Yash Raje's supporters eating out of his hands. The ballroom was DJ's playground and he was positively bursting out of his skin to conquer it.

Standing there on that terrace, she was lovely, too. The thought popped into his head out of nowhere. The no-nonsense white linen shirt she was wearing over jeans softened her usual prickly countenance. It should have made her look like any other girl, out to run an errand for her family, but nothing about her was common. Every inch of her spoke of perfection without struggle.

Maybe it was the expanse of blue sky and blue sea that framed her that did it, maybe it was the low sun that tinted her chocolate hair coppery as it flew about her face, but in that moment, he knew exactly how he felt about her, how he would feel until the day he died.

He hated her. Hated that there were people in the world who had what she had and didn't even know it. Or knew it but thought they somehow deserved it. Simply by being born.

"I have to take a picture of this view for Nisha." She felt her pocket for a few seconds. "Shoot, I left my phone in your car."

"I'll go get it," he said and then kicked himself for always being so damn accommodating. But Mum had been brutal in her expectation of manners. *Manners aren't about appearance at all*, she had loved to say, *they are about kindness. You put the other person's comfort before yours, that's good breeding.*

Ammaji had had no concept of any formal English rules of etiquette. She'd never set a table the proper way or even used a fork and knife to eat, but she'd taught DJ the exact same lesson. *No one is so special that they can't exert themselves a little for others.*

He'd never had a hard time with politeness until he had met this woman. With her he had to pull on every bit of protocol to keep from going head-to-head with her about everything. Unsuccessfully.

"No, you stay and finish the tour of the kitchen. And I . . . um . . . kitchens aren't my favorite place," Trisha said, looking faintly traumatized. "I . . . I was burned as a child. When my aji was teaching me how to cook."

Well, that explained a lot. Before he could ask her about it, the unusually tall and sullen Mr. Mantis reappeared on the terrace.

"Ready to get started again, Dr. Raje?"

She gave the manager a smile that managed to be both gracious and distant. "Mr. Caine will do the tour of the kitchens without me. I have to run to the car. Is there anything else?"

Mantis assured her there wasn't, and if she wanted him to wait, it would be his pleasure, no no, his honor, to wait until she returned. His time was hers, etc., etc.

DJ manufactured an obliging smile to match Mantis's and

made all the right sounds: He was at their disposal. Whatever they wanted, etc., etc.

She studied his face. He didn't care what she saw. All he cared about was the kitchen Mantis was about to show him, the place where he was going to make magic.

"Sorry," she said directly to DJ. "Go ahead and finish up. I'll see you in the car." She attempted a smile. "It's not like you need me."

Oh, she couldn't be more right about that. "Don't give it another thought." He dropped the keys on her palm and followed the manager into the area where the supplies would be stocked.

The amenities were perfect. The kitchen was every chef's dream brought to life in quartz and steel. Familiarizing himself with all of it took a good half hour more.

After Dr. Raje's departure, all the pleasant subservience disappeared rather quickly from Mantis's demeanor. "So this is your first time catering at the Astoria," he stated rather than asked.

"It is. And it's an honor," DJ said as pleasantly as he could. At least that wasn't a lie.

"Our own restaurant has a Michelin star and all the private chefs we allow to cater here are trained under star chefs, if not star chefs themselves."

"That's impressive," DJ said. Andre had two Michelin stars, but DJ didn't feel like mentioning that fact. Maybe because, in a perverse way, he needed to see this side of the manager. It kept DJ's view of the world firmly grounded.

"The Rajes are a very generous family. So gracious. So

open-minded," Mantis said pointedly, as though the fact that the Rajes were actually allowing him to cater for them was somehow "gracious."

"We did their older daughter's wedding here. It was in *Architectural Digest* and *People* magazine. I was the resident event manager on that, too." Evidently Nisha's wedding had been one of the highlights of Mantis's career because he spent the next five minutes waxing eloquent about all the details and pulling up the magazine articles on his phone.

DJ presented him with a sufficiently impressed smile. He really shouldn't judge. Catering a fund-raiser for Yash Raje was definitely the highlight of his own career, no point pretending like it wasn't.

"Do you know the family?" Mantis asked, encouraged into expanding their conversation into the personal realm by DJ's show of interest in his chatter.

"Somewhat," DJ said, picking out his favorite word for stopping conversations of this nature in their tracks. Of course he knew where the man was going with this. Mantis's curiosity— which was really incredulousness in disguise—had little to do with getting to know DJ, and more to do with the color of DJ's skin, which was, unlike the Rajes', not rendered irrelevant by wealth. The syntax of prejudice—threaded into conversation with the perfect pauses and facial expressions—was like ciphers and spy codes. The meaning clear to those it was meant for. To everyone else, it was harmless scribbles. Easy enough to deny.

"I'd better be getting back to Dr. Raje," DJ said finally, jotting down a last note on his tablet.

Extracting his phone out of his pocket, he tried to call her but she didn't answer. He texted her, but there was no response to that, either.

He tamped down on his usual worry reflex. She didn't need his worry. Maybe she'd fallen asleep again now that he wasn't there to watch her.

"I think I have all the information I need. I'll call you if I have questions."

"Call my assistant," Mantis said with a stiff smile. "And please let Dr. Raje know it was a pleasure meeting her."

Despite himself, DJ gave the bastard an amused look. He retrieved his briefcase and it was a good thing that he had the iPad he'd been using to take notes in the other hand, because the idea of shaking the man's hand was not an appealing one. Nonetheless, he thanked him before heading for the exit. Being angry at people like Mantis was an utter waste of his time. He could deal with them in his sleep. He was an acrobat, a ringmaster, anger his pet beast, the practice of his art so deeply ingrained that the rage barely even registered. Actually, that wasn't true. It registered well enough. He had just lost his ability to let it transfer into temper.

Unless of course he was dealing with a certain long-legged snob.

He sent up a prayer that they would get through the drive back without any more eruptions or any more heart-to-hearts. He didn't know which was worse. He was barely halfway to the car when he saw her hurrying toward him. One look at him and she jumped. He had never met anyone who acted quite so shocked every single time they saw him. One would think he arrived places by teleportation.

She held up what looked like a straightened wire hanger, her expression apologetic. "I'm really sorry, but I left your keys inside your car."

"I beg your pardon?"

She blinked as though he had said something entirely unexpected, then she shook her head. "I grabbed my phone and I thought I'd come back to the ballroom. I realized it wasn't fair to leave you to suffer Praying Mantis by yourself. I swear I thought I had the keys in my hand, but when I got there I realized that they were missing. I went back to look for them and they're in the car. It's the twenty-first century! Who makes cars that let you lock your keys inside?"

"It's a 1980 Nine Eleven," he said, feeling, among other things, the need to make a case for Betsy's beauty.

His indignation was entirely lost on her. "AAA can't get here for another hour, they're backed up. And I need to get back to take Nisha to the doctor." That last part made a panicked look cross her face, but she pulled herself together and pointed the wire at the car. "Let's hurry."

He followed her across the street, easily matching her stride. "What's the hanger for?" And why were they hurrying?

"To slide through the window to open the door," she said as though it made perfect sense. "The windows are not all the way up."

He stopped in his tracks. "You're planning to break into the car?"

She held the hanger out to him. "Actually, I was hoping you would do it."

He massaged his temples, anger collecting inside him so fast his fingers shook. "Is there a reason why you believe that I can break into cars?"

"What? No! You jump to the most absurd conclusions, you know that?"

"Not that I think I need to say this, but I've never broken into a car or stolen anything in my life."

"I know that! But you seem to know about cars. That's all I meant."

He studied her. Even if she hadn't meant to imply that he was somehow adept at breaking into cars, she had to be crazy not to see the obvious flaw with her plan. "Do you realize what it would look like if someone saw me breaking into a Porsche on these streets?" He wasn't from around here, but he did watch the bloody news. Didn't she?

She had the gall to look amused. "Come on. Seriously? You think someone would think you—dressed in that two-hundred-dollar shirt and with that choirboy face—that you would be stealing a car? You need to chill out. This is California!"

Was she for real? That out-of-control roller coaster he'd been riding all afternoon crashed right back into anger. "Has no one ever looked at you and seen nothing but the color of your skin? What the hell is wrong with you? How can you act so . . . so *white*?"

She balked at that, shock sharpening her features. "I don't act white. I don't act anything."

All he could do was throw up his hands. It was not his job to set every numbskull straight. It was definitely not his job to set some clueless, overprivileged brown girl who had no idea she was brown straight. "I'm just going to wait for the mechanic to get here, if you don't mind." He leaned against the car's bonnet and crossed his arms.

The sun was still high and hot in the sky, and the air was suffused with the smell of the bay mixed with the garlic and soy aroma from the Chinese restaurant behind them.

Her phone buzzed and she looked at the text that had just come through. "It's Nisha," she said. "I really have to get home."

He didn't care. He wasn't stupid enough to care.

"Fine." She slid the hanger through the open gap in the window. "But it's broad daylight. Nothing is going to happen." Her eyes narrowed in concentration over the gleaming yellow top of the car.

Being arrogant and feeling as entitled as the bloody Queen was all good and dandy, but he had never expected her to be ignorant, of all things. He watched as she fiddled with the hanger. This was such a bad idea. "Where did you manage to get that from?"

Her focus stayed on the task at hand but she flicked her head at the street. "There's a laundry up that hill. I saw it in a movie once. With this kind of old car, you can pop the lock right up."

An ache was starting in his temples. He threw a look up and down the street. "It's a friend's car. We can't damage it."

"I won't damage anything." There wasn't a whit of doubt in her voice. He tried not to think about how much repairing a

Porsche might cost. Well, if she damaged it, she was bloody well paying for it. "Seriously, relax."

It must be nice to be her. To live in a world where you felt this invincible. He glanced up and down the street again. A man on a bicycle was riding downhill and a woman was running uphill. She threw DJ a suspicious look as she sped by and reached for her phone.

Oblivious to the world around her, Trisha continued to twist away at the metal with remarkable strength and deftness. It was obvious that she was good at using her hands.

"Ow!" A squeak emitted from her. She grabbed one hand with the other without letting the hanger go. "Damn it, I cut myself!" The sharp end of the wire had nicked her skin.

Bloody hell. So much for being good at using her hands. He pushed off the car and walked to her.

There was a small cut at the center of her palm.

"It's nothing," she said. But it was bleeding and tiny dots of blood were sprinkled on the cuffs of her white shirt. He reached into his bag, extracted some tissues, and held them out. At least they could stop this nonsense now.

"Thanks," she said as she tried to pull the wire out. "Shit, it's stuck." She let the wire go but it stayed there jammed in the window.

He pressed the tissue to her palm as she watched him.

"It's just a surface cut." She pulled away and went back to trying to pry it out. But the thing wouldn't budge. She was going to wreck Betsy's car.

He moved her out of the way and took the end of the wire from her and started working it to wiggle it free. But it was well and truly jammed in place. He put all his strength into the next pull and heard the lock pop open.

Just as he felt the touch of a baton on his shoulder.

Her gasp reached him from a distance. Everything slowed to a stop. He closed his eyes, breathing through the hard clench of panic in his belly.

"Put your hands up and turn around."

He did as he was told and turned around to face the cop, another lanky white man who looked uncannily like Mr. Mantis. His hand was on his holster.

"My hands are in the air, mate, you don't have to reach for your gun." To one side of him he heard a movement. *God, please don't let her do something stupid.*

"Please don't tell me how to do my job, sir."

He said nothing more. Head down. Mouth shut. The blast of terror that had sparked in his belly for a moment, gone. Everything numb, cold. The flash of anger that had erupted as though it had a right to, dead. He focused his energy on not reliving the shit from years ago, on not feeling the cop's hand on his head as he pushed him into the squad car, on not seeing the metal grid separating him from the driver's seat as it blurred through tears.

Trisha walked up behind the cop. "Officer, you are making a mistake. We were just trying to get into the car because I left the keys inside. It was my fault."

The cop reached for his gun again. "You need to step back, miss."

"She's unarmed. I'm unarmed. It's cool, Officer. We're cool." There was a thread of something in his voice, something he refused to name, something that was a thousand times worse because she was here.

"It's not cool," she snapped, her voice raised and entirely fearless. "Are you actually going to draw a gun on me before you find out what is going on? His hands are on his head, for shit's sake. And mine are up in the air too; look."

"Dr. Raje, please," DJ said. "Let the officer do his job." He tried to meet the cop's eyes—just his eyes, because he wasn't about to make any sudden movements.

"Is this your car, sir?"

"No, it's a friend's car."

The cop stiffened, took his gun out of his holster, and called for backup. "I need to see your license and registration, please."

"Sure." DJ forced himself to relax. Breathe. "My license is in my wallet in my back pocket. The registration is in the car."

"Turn around, please, and keep your hands up where I can see them."

He turned around and the cop patted his bottom and pulled his wallet out of his pocket.

"Oh, for shit's sake," Trisha said behind him.

"Miss, what are you doing?"

"I'm recording this."

DJ couldn't see her but he imagined her pointing her camera at the cop and his temper rose so hard and fast he could barely breathe.

"Ma'am, please put your phone away. I'm just doing my job," the cop said, a trace of panic entering his voice.

"Dr. Raje, stop it," DJ said, every instance of phone cameras making cops panic flashing in his head along with Emma lying alone in a hospital bed.

"Your job is to draw a gun at a man trying to retrieve his keys from his car?" Trisha said, her voice dead calm yet laced with rage.

"He was trying to break into a Porsche that does not belong to him. If you don't stop, ma'am, I'm going to have to take you both in."

"Take us in for what? I suggest you put away your gun and let this gentleman show you his license and registration like the upstanding citizen he is, and I will think about not sending this video to every news outlet in the country. Or getting my brother Yash—that's Yash Raje, who you should know is the United States Attorney for the Northern District of California—on the phone right now."

There was a long silence. "You can turn around, sir," the cop said finally, his voice distinctly a few notches less assertive. He lowered his gun but didn't put it back in his holster. "License and registration, please." He handed DJ his wallet, then turned to Trisha. "I apologize, ma'am, but surely you understand that I was only doing my job."

His tone was entirely different now. He was young, just a kid, really. He looked scared.

Finally he tucked his gun back in its holster, and DJ moved enough to open his wallet. He still couldn't feel his heartbeat, and he could barely feel his fingers enough to move them.

The officer—Officer Dunn—ran the information through

his system. Fortunately, Green Acres was able to verify that Betsy had willingly let him borrow her car and they were free to go.

For the entire hour all that took, DJ had focused on trying to bring the feeling back into his limbs. Dunn had tried his best to strike up a conversation with Trisha, with absolutely no luck. Every attempt at apology from the officer had been met with a monosyllable or a grunt. She'd been in full-fledged tyrant mode, seething.

But she had nothing on the rage gathered to bursting inside him.

They wouldn't be in this situation if she weren't so stubbornly ignorant in the first place. The last thing DJ needed was to get involved in something like this. Even a whiff of negative publicity could destroy his business before it took off. If anyone dug up his record, everything would be over. There was a word for brown kids arrested for arson. Terrorist.

Emma's face flashed before him just the way it had when he'd stood there with his hands over his head and the cop had reached for his gun. One wrong move and Emma would have been entirely alone. He would never forgive Trisha Raje for putting him in that situation. Never.

Through the entire thing, he'd had a hard time looking at her. Now he threw her a glance as she sat in silence in the passenger seat as he maneuvered the car through rush hour traffic. Her usually luminous skin was ashen, her lashes lowered in shame. She looked like the world had shifted beneath her feet and it made a sick mix of sadness and vindication burn inside him.

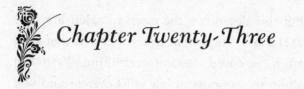

Chapter Twenty-Three

"You're not asleep, are you?" Nisha said, twirling a lock of Trisha's hair around her finger.

"Well, not anymore." Trisha smiled and opened her eyes, not that she'd been able to fall asleep. "You okay?"

Nisha smiled, but looked concerned. "I'm fine. You don't seem fine though. You haven't been sleeping lately."

Except in a car. Where she had fallen asleep and drooled in front of the one man she didn't want to be drooling around.

"It's natural to be upset about what happened with DJ. I know it was awful. But you have to let it go."

Trisha couldn't respond. After coming home last night with anger roaring inside her, she'd told Nisha what had happened. It hadn't helped.

DJ's expression as he'd stood with his hands over his head wouldn't stop playing in her mind. A horrible pang spasmed in her chest. A crater had opened up inside her at the blankness in his eyes, at everything he had banked away behind it, the anger, the shame, the pride. How had she never noticed what that combination of vulnerability and strength did to his face? To have seen it tainted like that, it made her want to hunt down the cop. To send that video out across the internet for the world to see.

Nisha had shut the idea down the moment it left her lips. "Are you crazy? The last thing we need right now is that kind of media attention. It could destroy everything. Yash has worked hard to win the support of law enforcement and you know how strongly he supports the Black Lives Matter movement. Providing a bridge across that divide is one of his biggest platforms. He won't get past the primary if he loses either one of those votes. It's out of the question." Nisha had become so fired up that for the first time since she'd found out about the baby she had seemed like herself. Trisha had immediately backed off.

Their visit to the doctor had been a relief. Everything was progressing normally, which in this case meant miraculously. The timing wasn't great for giving Nisha something to lose her shit over again. But that wasn't why Trisha would never take this public.

She had given DJ her word.

Trisha squeezed her eyes shut again, but there was no banishing the icy waves of anger that had radiated from his body as he had stared at the road, the unspent rage in his eyes completely at odds with how utterly calm he had seemed in his interactions with the cop. No, *calm* was the wrong word. He'd been completely devoid of emotion, entirely empty.

In all her interactions with him she had felt a blaze of assertiveness under his very polished veneer. An almost immovable self-possession. His ability to never back down from butting heads with her—it had made something come alive inside her for the first time in her life.

When the cop had touched his gun, all that confidence had fizzled like a candle doused with a flood. It had been snuffed out without so much as a hiss of smoke. And she had been the one to put him through that. Because she had been blind, even when he'd tried to get her to see.

She hadn't told Nisha about their conversation in the car coming back.

"Are you . . . are you okay?" she had asked, feeling incredibly stupid. Of course he wasn't, but she had needed to reach him.

"Peachy," he'd said. "You needed a demonstration of what happens when a black man tries to break into his own car and you got it. I hope that was entertaining."

He thought she was entertained? "You blame me for what happened back there."

He hadn't even taken a breath. "No, it was my fault. All the way mine. I should have walked away the moment you started that madness."

His anger returning had been a relief.

"I'm sorry." She'd say those words a million times if it would ease him. "But how could you have been so calm when that cop was treating you that way?" She hadn't been able to keep the question inside.

He had laughed then, as though she'd made the most tasteless of jokes. A sound so harsh it had gouged out everything she had been up until that moment. "Maybe because I don't have a 'U.S. Attorney brother' card to pull."

She'd deserved that. "So you just let them do what they want?"

"Yes! I'm not keen on the idea of a bullet in my head, or find-ing my arse dumped in jail. I have a sister who needs medical care and has absolutely no one to take care of her if I disap-pear. So, yes, they can do whatever the bloody hell they want."

After that she'd stayed quiet.

When he pulled up next to her Tesla, she hadn't wanted to leave him. She'd wanted to apologize again, to do some-thing to erase her unforgivable stupidity, erase the hurt she had caused. "Tell me what I can do."

All his simmering rage had darkened his eyes, tightened his muscles under the fine, laundered cotton of his shirt. But in the end all he did was let out that ugly laugh again.

"Are you laughing because you think you taught me some sort of lesson?" Because he had, he had pulled the world from beneath her feet.

"You give me too much credit, Dr. Raje. It's not my place to teach you anything." She hated when he did that, withdrew behind those clipped words. But his eyes continued to blaze, and that she couldn't hate.

"We can do something about this. I have it on video. We can file a complaint against Officer Dunn." The need to do something screamed inside her.

He had drawn up at that, fear dampening his gaze. "Abso-lutely not. Listen to me, I do not want to go down that path. I do not want this to go any further. My focus has to be Emma right now. If you feel the need to mete out justice, find a way to get my sister into the OR. Save her life." Then with every iota of his anger gone, with everything gone, he met her eyes again. No armor, nothing but the truth of who he was naked in front of her. For the first time since she'd met him, she felt like she was seeing him, all his strength, all his fear. "I mean it. Please. Let me have my privacy and let what happened today go."

Every single time Trisha came in contact with the man, she had come away feeling childish and petty. Today she had felt insubstantial, as though she were a feather held up against the wind in unsteady fingers, seconds from being blown into an endless sky.

She sat up in bed. "Go back to sleep," she said to Nisha, tucking the sheets around her. "I have some work to do. I'll be in my office if you need anything. And don't worry, I'm never going to let anyone see that video." Not when she had promised DJ.

"A person is only as good as his word." Nisha mumbled the line with a sad smile and fell back to sleep, satisfied.

Trisha poured herself a glass of milk and opened up her laptop. It was barely two A.M. and there was an email from HRH in her in-box. The email she'd sent him yesterday had completely slipped her mind. She had finally gathered the courage to let him know that she had run into Julia at Green Acres. She opened his response. It was, as usual, serialized into a neat clinical list.

Dear Trisha,

1. I have information that she has been working on interviews with terminally ill patients. (attached: PI report of cases against her for stealing funds from families of patients after claiming to help them raise funds)

2. This is the second reminder to review your terminal cases.

3. Do not take this lightly. Covering up for your errors in judgment will not be possible this time around. Think about your family when you make decisions, please.

4. Inform me of ANY and EVERY detail of your interactions with her.

Sincerely,
Dad

There are no interactions, Dad! she wanted to scream.

This explained what Julia was doing at Green Acres. It wasn't a hospice, but patients sometimes went there prior to entering hospice care.

Trisha had said nothing about DJ knowing Julia to HRH—or to anyone in the family—because even the hint of a connection would mean that DJ would not be catering Yash's dinner. Restlessness swelled inside her at the thought.

She responded to the email with "Dear Dad: Check, check, check, and check. Sincerely, Trisha."

All her conditioning to never be rude to her parents made her almost delete those words and type a more appropriate response. But something made her hit send.

Her snarkiness gave her no peace. A pathetic part of her wished she could pick up the phone and tell HRH what had happened with DJ and the cop. What if he had a different theory about reporting the incident? The cop had insisted that he'd just been doing his job, but would he have done his job differently had DJ looked different? Dad would know what to do. He never faltered when it came to knowing right from wrong.

But she knew she was kidding herself. Even if she hadn't promised DJ she would stay silent, she knew that the time when she could have a conversation with her father about something that was bothering her was long gone. She was also fully aware of the fact that Nisha was right. This could destroy Yash's campaign. If Yash found out, he would want to do something about it. He would not be able to let it go. Yash's political charm might piss the hell out of her sometimes, but that didn't change the fact that his integrity was untouchable.

Their dad had drilled that mantra into them with a sledgehammer: Do something about things that bother you.

And he'd lived by that mantra. Even though somewhere along the way his focus had shifted to making sure that a political win came before everything else because you needed power to truly bring about change.

If she was being honest, she was the one to blame for that. Had she not exposed Yash to Julia, HRH might not have become so aware of—and paranoid about—how fragile their dream to see Yash take office was. If not for her, her father would not have had to spend the past fifteen years obsessed with making sure nothing destroyed that dream before it had a chance.

That day at the orphanage for the blind, his words had changed her life forever. And even after losing him, she had always followed his words. *That compass inside that told you something wasn't right. That is your greatest gift. Do something with it.*

Until today she had never realized how easy it had been for her to follow that edict.

DJ had stood there helpless as a cop reached for his gun for no reason other than fear based in prejudice. DJ's defense had been to withdraw into himself and to let the reality unfolding around him wash over him like a wave, his eyes closed, his breath held to minimize damage.

Trisha didn't want him to be standing there in that inequitable ocean, unable to do anything about it. She wanted to live in a world where the waves hit everyone the same way, where everyone could choose how they surfed them. Where the only thing that mattered was ability.

And she had allowed herself to become oblivious to the fact that they did not live in that world.

Ma's pet peeve was how the Western world misunderstood the theory of karma. "I mean it's the *Bhagavad Gita* they're bastardizing. What is all this 'karma's a bitch' nonsense!" Ma loved to say.

The entire "what goes around comes around" thing was a backward view of karma. Karma was simply Sanskrit for *action*, and the theory was that your actions are the only thing under your control, as opposed to the fruits of your actions, which are not. And since actions always bear fruit, you were better off focusing your energy on your own actions, rather than worrying about the results you wanted them to produce.

Until now it had seemed simple enough.

Now her naiveté at thinking it simple felt irresponsible, harmful.

While it was true that you only had control over your actions, your power to choose those actions didn't exist in a vacuum. DJ was right; she had been ignorant to push him into breaking into the car, to negate his experience when he warned her. And later, she had been able to stand up to the cop because she'd had the power of Yash's name and she'd pulled it out without a second thought. Was it a metaphor for everything she had achieved in her life?

Of course she'd worked hard, but growing up in the Bay Area in a family like hers, she had never borne the weight of being seen as different. She had never had the odds stacked against her.

She stared at her computer for a while. Emma's latest test results were in. It had been eight days since she'd discharged Emma. Nothing had changed. Trisha started flipping through her images, back and forth, zooming in from the lateral view to the anterior. The tumor was wrapped snugly around the nerves, like a fist squeezing two ropes together. She clicked the crosses on the screen, mindlessly taking measurements, poking at the mass of tissue that would kill Emma if she didn't wake up soon. The clicks of her mouse punctuated the silence.

Click. *If you feel the need to mete out justice, find a way to get my sister into the OR.*

Click. *She's all I've got.*

Click. Click. *My sister is not live tissue . . .* Click *. . . she's an artist who lives for her art . . .*

Click *. . . this will change her life forever.*

Click. Click. Click. The blind girl's hands on her face. Click. *You're pretty.*

Click. Click.

What if they could find a way to not take Emma's art away?

She thought about the basket of knickknacks at the orphanage. Colorful pieces of felt and leather, stamped and glued and perfectly beautiful.

She typed "Artists and Blindness" into Google. And an entire world opened up in front of her.

Artists who were blind from birth, artists who had lost their sight and transferred their need to create to another medium: sculpture, weaving, pottery, metalwork, yarn work. There was an entire slew of associations of visually impaired artists, of books by artists who created art without sight. She downloaded as many as she could find, soaking up the words, taking them in, letting them churn. And churn. And churn.

There was also a tactile art program near Monterey.

Before Trisha could think about it, she had typed an email to Jane Liu, one of the artists at the program, asking for more information. Even before Nisha woke up, Jane responded and invited Trisha to come down for a visit to the facility.

Now all Trisha had to do was find a gap in her schedule so she could drive there.

FOR FOUR DAYS Trisha worked fourteen-hour days, only returning home to bring her sister food and collapse into restless sleep. Four days that she didn't see DJ. It felt like months, or maybe like moments. She no longer had any sense of time or place when she thought about him—which was all the damn time. He had emailed Nisha a few times regarding decisions about food for the fund-raiser and had copied Trisha on the emails: "Would it be all right to top the crab kachoris with date chutney foam, so the hors d'oeuvre could be circulated without a mess? Should the chicken be served over a bed of pulav or plated individually in bowls?"

She read his emails over and over again. His slightly formal tone, his attention to detail, his utter competence at his job, all that he was seemed to jump up from his words, and she felt like a teenager walking around school trying to catch a glimpse of her crush.

This morning she had turned on the coffee machine without filling it with water. The stink of burnt grounds had been horrid. Thankfully, Nisha wasn't throwing up anymore.

Last night Trisha had put lasagna in the oven and turned on the timer for an hour, without turning the oven on. In the end she'd had to run down to Curried Dreams and pick up dinner.

Then there was the craving. Consuming. Incessant. Brutal. The flavors from the tasting were a wild, live thing inside her. She wasn't able to taste one damn thing she put in her mouth. When she had stopped at the restaurant, Ashi had given her some chicken kababs in a mint chutney. They had tasted like coming home. Even before Ashna told her who had made them, she had known. After that she had found herself at the restaurant again this morning. Ashi had given her all the kababs she had left over and Trisha had pulled over to the side of the road and eaten them in her car, chewing at them slowly, reverently, desperately stretching out the pleasure of his flavors.

It had only intensified her craving for everything about him that the taste of his food invoked. The strength that poured from him in waves, the steadiness, the gentle humor, the merciless challenge of things she had always accepted without question.

On the extreme upside, Nisha's pregnancy was progressing without incident. Neel was scheduled to come home in four days, and Yash and their parents a day before that. DJ had kept his promise and everyone seemed entirely oblivious that Nisha had not left Trisha's condo for ten days.

"Yum." Nisha dunked a tall spoon into the bowl of mint chocolate chip Trisha had brought her and sucked it up as though it were the best thing she'd ever tasted. "So, genius sister of mine, have you come up with how you're going to keep me hidden here for one more week?"

Trisha dipped her own spoon into the ice cream and took a nibble. It tasted like toothpaste. "Maybe we'll tell everyone that you have a communicable disease, like tuberculosis, and you're quarantined by the CDC. And I've been inoculated, so I'm the only one who can take care of you."

Nisha gulped down the ice cream. "Actually, that's the best idea you've come up with thus far."

"You haven't come up with any. So quit judging." Trisha put down her spoon.

Her sister raised her usually impeccably shaped eyebrow—it

had grown out a little and didn't look quite as imperious without its perfectly threaded arch. "Speaking of tuberculosis. Are you sick?"

Trisha made a face. "I don't have TB, thank you very much."

"You have something," her sister mumbled around a mouthful of ice cream. "I think you just nibbled. I've never seen you nibble anything in your life."

"I did not nibble." She had nibbled.

What she really wanted to nibble on was a perfectly flaky papad with chicken and saffron, with someone telling her about how a lazy spice took time to surface.

"Something's definitely wrong. Is it your imaginary boyfriend? The one you used to steal food from Ashi for?"

She should've known that the sister gossip machine would be active and well. "Harry and I broke up. I think."

He had texted her thanking her for the food and she had finally told him that he could get it any time he wanted from Curried Dreams.

"You *think* you broke up?"

"I wasn't really sure if we were together or not, okay?" Trisha poked the spoon back in the ice cream and then put it back down on the tray with a clang.

"This isn't about Harry at all, is it?"

Trisha didn't answer.

"First . . ." Nisha licked her spoon before pointing it at Trisha's face. "If you don't know whether you have feelings for someone or not that means you don't have feelings for them."

Well, she knew that *now*.

She wished she didn't. Because these feelings, God, these

feelings. Why had she never seen how fortunate she'd been to never have them?

Nisha laughed. "Stop sulking. It was bound to happen. It happens to everybody. Instead of sulking, you should do something about it."

"I have no idea what you're talking about."

"You haven't been sleeping, you haven't been eating, you look like you're pacing even when you're sitting still. This is me, Trisha. Talk to me."

"There's nothing to talk about. Work just sucks right now." That was a blatant lie. Work was spectacular. The research study was giving them the exact results they had expected, which never, ever happened. The only thing at work not going well was Emma's refusal to get surgery. But Trisha hoped her trip to Monterey today would generate some solutions on how to fix that.

Nisha set her spoon into the empty ice-cream cup and sank back against the pillows. "Fine. But listen, no one can see what's going on inside you if you don't show it."

How could anyone not see what she was feeling? It felt like it was bursting out of her skin. "You saw it," she said, immensely grateful that Nisha hadn't asked for details.

"Sweetheart, of course I did. You're my Shasha. Listen, you know you're not like anyone else, right? If you want someone to see what's inside you, you have to put yourself out there. The rest of the world is not programmed to decode you. You're adorable and all, but no one can see that if you keep scaring everyone away."

What she wanted right now was to scare Nisha away. She scowled.

To no avail. "Trust yourself," her big sister said kindly. "You know how you're fearless with your work? Well, work isn't the only thing that requires you to be badass. Sometimes life does too. Letting people know you is scary. Especially for us. We don't do well with trusting outsiders." She paused, and a world of silent shared fears passed between them. "But when something feels right, you have to have the courage to let it happen, to tell people how you feel. Even when someone's broken your trust before." It was the most forgiving thing Nisha had ever said about what Trisha had allowed Julia to do.

The idea of telling anyone—least of all DJ—how she was feeling about DJ bloated the bubble of panic in her chest. But the thought also strangely relieved the pressure, just the tiniest bit.

Trisha picked up the tray and got off the bed. "You need anything else?"

Nisha shook her head and studied her like a mother hen.

When Trisha put the bowl in the dishwasher and went back into the bedroom, her sister continued to watch her, arms crossed across her still-flat belly.

"I need to go to Monterey today to check out a tactile art program for a case. I'm on call this evening. I'll be back before then. Will you be okay? I'll leave you a sandwich for lunch and I'll bring dinner from Ashi?"

"Of course." Nisha slid back under the sheets. "Is 'tactile art' a euphemism for a booty call?"

"Shut up! I'd never leave you alone for a booty call. Also, ew!"

Nisha laughed. "One of these days, Trisha, one of these days."

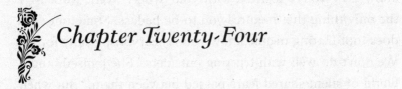

Chapter Twenty-Four

The drive to Monterey was one of Trisha's favorites. The Rajes owned a beach house in Carmel-by-the-Sea. Growing up, Ma had insisted on the family getting away for weekends at least once a month. That time spent lying on the white sand, catching the blue-gray surf, breathing the salt-laden air, and having family friends come up for house parties had been a needed respite in their madly hectic lives.

It was a place Trisha associated with everyone letting their proverbial hair down. Yash in shorts, Nisha and Ashi in T-shirts. Vansh, in . . . what he always wore. He was the only one in the family who didn't feel the need to dress as though he were ready for a TV appearance all the time.

She remembered when Ma had tried to throw one of his T-shirts away once. "It has a hole, beta!" Ma had said.

"Yes, but it also has dirt from Malawi on it and raindrops from Djibouti. Do you have any idea how rare rain in Djibouti is?"

Trisha's own sanctuary from her family's clothing issues was her scrubs.

Today, of course, with Nisha at home, Trisha was dressed

in a "buttercup" pantsuit that her sister had declared "fresh and powerful without being threatening." It was naturally a suit Nisha had picked out for her. Which could be said about pretty much all the clothing Trisha owned. Nisha was showing distinct signs of fashionista withdrawal lying in that bed. She did own the loveliest pajamas—all organic cotton cut to fit her body perfectly—and she still wore "a touch of tinted gloss" in bed. There was no way she would let Trisha leave the house in scrubs unless she was going into surgery.

"It's offensive to meet a blind person dressed sloppily," Nisha had said.

Trisha wasn't sure if saying that in itself wasn't offensive.

But Nisha knew about these things, because the suit actually made Trisha feel somewhat put together, after days of feeling like she was in pieces. As for the other thing Nisha had said—Trisha had spent the entire car ride hurtling miserably between the possibility and the preposterousness of the idea of herself with DJ Caine.

Just as Trisha got on Highway 1, her sister called. "Don't forget to pick up muffins from Tangent. I just called and Naomi said they're open for only another hour. So do it now, on your way out."

Tangent was a little café right outside Laguna Grande, just a few miles from the beach house. It was one of those cute wooden shacks that was so eclectic you forgot where you were when you entered it. It could easily have been Hawaii, South Africa, Brazil, anywhere in the world.

A stop at Tangent had always signaled being near the end of

their drive, and they were all addicted, rather pathetically, to those muffins and that coffee. The fact that Trisha had totally forgotten about it today ratcheted up all her restlessness.

She assured Nisha that she would not come home without the bounty of their favorite muffins and took the exit that led to the quaint little café. The first thing she saw when she pulled into the dirt parking lot was a hot-pink Volkswagen Beetle.

Her heart did a hard little kick start, the spasm almost painful in the charged blast it radiated through her body. She had clearly and certifiably lost her mind, because he wasn't the only person in California who drove a hot-pink bug.

She took a deep breath and walked inside.

And there he was, the first person she saw. DJ Caine. Trisha pulled her jacket tighter around herself. He was laughing at something Naomi had said. And to see him like this, relaxed, restored, after their last meeting, made relief rush through her. The white-haired model-turned-baker had owned the café for a good thirty years. She had always been a beautiful woman, but today she looked stunning in a fitted black tank top and jeans, her long lean yoga-instructor muscles standing out under her glowing skin. DJ was looking at her as though she were a goddess—which she was.

"Trisha!" she said as recognition lit up her eyes. "How's my favorite Raje girl?" She gave Trisha a quick hug.

"Nisha is great," Trisha said dryly, making Naomi grin even wider.

"And the love of my life? Is he running for president yet?"

That would be Yash all the damn time. "He's fine, too. You

know Yash, he dreams only of serving California and Californians." HRH would be so proud of her right now.

"Dr. Raje." DJ came out from behind the glass display case arranged with luscious fruit-filled pastries. He wore dark jeans and white chef's robes that made his hazel eyes look more green than brown. They reflected all the shock she was feeling at finding him here. Trisha's heart zapped another ruthless blast of electricity through her body.

"You two know each other!" Naomi said with some surprise, then smacked her forehead daintily. "Of course you do. Through Ashna. And of course you're doing work for the family, DJ. You did tell me about the fund-raiser." She seemed incredibly familiar with him.

As if Trisha's insides weren't already mired in all sorts of quivery sensations, a stab of envy sliced through her and she wrapped her arms around herself. "And you two know each other," she repeated stupidly.

"Yes! Andre—DJ's old boss—is a dear friend. DJ was my savior every time Andre broke my heart when I visited Paris. Ashna told me he was here, so I had to have him come in and help with my pop-up in Carmel today."

DJ smiled that smile he saved only for his work, and Trisha had to tighten her grip around herself.

"What can I get you? Other than two dozen blueberry muffins, that is," Naomi asked, patting Trisha's arm and pushing her into a chair.

"Thank you. I'll take whatever the special for today is."

"The special is a curried stew from the visiting chef."

Every cell in Trisha's body let out a ravenous moan. She nodded vigorously and felt like Oliver Twist holding out his bowl for more. *Please, sir . . .*

She was in so much trouble. So. Much. Trouble.

Her desperation did not improve when he brought her the stew, his big hands clasped around the white bowl.

It was magic stew. It tasted of everything. Every good thing Trisha had ever eaten, ever.

"Dear girl, when was the last time you ate?" Naomi asked, watching her inhale the stew in amused horror as she placed a bag of muffins next to her.

She mumbled something around the spoon.

DJ was watching her too. Was that a smile he was trying to suppress? A smile *and* food—was he trying to kill her?

Could she get a grip, please? All good sense was jumping out of her head and scattering about the floor with every sip of the stew. She was unraveling.

"I need to go out to the coops and check on the chickens. DJ, do you mind keeping the starving child company?" Naomi said, forcing Trisha to look up from her nearly empty bowl.

DJ opened his mouth as if to protest and threw a quick look at his watch, but in the end he smiled at Naomi. "Of course. Go tend to your chickens. I'll hold down the fort."

The way he said "fort," as though there were no "r" in the word, made the hair up and down Trisha's arms dance with awareness.

Was she drunk? Surely there was alcohol in this stew. Could she drive?

She took a sip of her iced coffee and it only made her more woozy. "Did you make this, too?" she asked without thinking.

That almost made him crack another smile. The dimple in his chin danced to life. He nodded and sank into a chair as she dived back into the Magic Stew. "I wasn't expecting to see you here. Are you on a minibreak?"

Trisha had no idea what a minibreak was but it sounded like something she wanted to do. Over and over again. With him murmuring the word. Minibreak. Mini Break. Mi Ni Break-ah in her ear.

What was wrong with her? It was like having another person inside her. A person she had no control over. This having-feelings-for-someone business was like being infected by a tapeworm.

She thought about telling him that she was on her way to visit the art institute to see how it could help Emma, but she had no idea what she would find there, and she didn't want to raise his hopes until she knew for sure. The way hope for Emma blazed in his eyes had been her constant companion for days, tapping at her mind every time she tried to sleep. "Sort of," she answered finally. "How's Emma doing?"

He stiffened, the dark centers of his eyes sharpening with worry so intense it made her want to pull him close, promise him she'd make everything okay, wipe away the pain.

"It's been twelve days." It sounded like an accusation. "She seems to have decided to ignore that she's sick. Maybe discharging her wasn't such a great idea after all."

The muscles down Trisha's back tightened. Her hospital

wasn't a prison, but she didn't have it in her to fight him today. "I think it needed to be done. I know my job." If today went as she had planned, she'd get to take that worry away from his eyes. "As do you." She looked at the Magic Stew. "This is . . . it's . . . um . . ."

"Would you like some more?" he said, with a touch of impatience.

"It might kill me," she wanted to say, but she nodded, channeling Oliver Twist again. *Please, sir . . .*

He brought her more.

"Thanks for staying," she said as she started on the second bowl. "I mean . . . not that you stayed for me. I mean, I'm sure you wanted to spend time with Naomi."

"I beg your pardon?"

Gah! Would he stop saying that? "You and Naomi—" the idiot who'd crawled inside her said; she was in a mood today.

"What is it with you wanting to pair me up with every woman you see within five feet of me?" He was in a mood today too.

"I do not!" She totally had.

"You thought Ashna and I had something. When clearly we don't." Their eyes locked and she felt things melting inside her.

"Okay, I did do that. But it doesn't mean anything. I . . . I'm not great at relationships." She laughed like someone who absolutely did not possess a brain. "My siblings call it emotional blindness." She stood. She had never in her life told that to anyone who wasn't related to her.

She took another desperate sip of her iced coffee. "I have to go."

He stood too. "Dr. Raje, are you well?"

No! No, she wasn't. She hadn't been well since she had met him, since he had left his life behind to take care of his sick sister, since he had remained unshaken when faced with a gun, since she had taken one bite of his food.

He rubbed the back of his neck, his biceps bulging. Another merciless zing zapped through her. She felt paralyzed. Unable to move away from him.

Nisha was right, she had to do something about it.

She might explode and splatter all over the café if she didn't.

"Okay, yes, I do that. I imagine everyone wanting to be with you. But do you want to know why that is?" Oh God, she had lost her mind. "No, wait, don't answer that. I don't know why I said that."

"All right." He stepped back. He'd caught on that she'd lost it.

"But you . . . you noticed it enough to say something about it."

He didn't respond. He had gone entirely still.

"What are you thinking?" she wanted to shout. "It's because . . . because . . ." she said instead. "Because I'm attracted to you."

Holy shit. She had not just said that out loud.

Instead of responding, he took another step away from her.

She pressed her hand into her belly. The coffee she was holding splashed against her suit, turning the buttercup to khaki in splotches. She put the glass down on the table and resisted the urge to slide under it.

Had she thought she was badass? Turns out she was just a straight-up ass.

He handed her a napkin and she pressed it into her jacket

as he stood there silent, unmoving, his chest rising and falling under the fabric stretched across those wide wide shoulders.

Stop staring.

It felt like time had halted. It felt like nothing she'd ever experienced. She was light-headed and queasy and unsteady on her feet. "You didn't slip something into my food, did you?" she said weakly.

His eyes went cold. Okay, maybe that had been the wrong thing to say.

"I shouldn't have said that. I was making a joke. A bad one. I . . . I can't seem to do anything right around you." *Someone help me.* "I . . . I swear this doesn't ever happen to me with anyone else. It's . . . it's just you. The way I feel around you . . ." This unbearable, hopeless pull as though the ground beneath her turned into a slope that slid toward him whenever he was near. "I can't even imagine why, or when it happened or how. I mean . . . look at us! We have absolutely nothing in common. Not one thing."

His face did not alter at all except for the slightest tightening of his chin that deepened the blasted dimple. And she knew she had said something wrong, something to freeze him even more. She wanted to take her words back, but that train had left the station. All her trains were hurtling off the tracks. They had run amok. She gave up and joined them. "Stop looking at me like that. I thought you valued honesty."

She loved that he was honest with her, that he didn't tiptoe around how differently they saw things. But they did see so much so differently. Their worlds were too far apart. "Surely you see why this would be utterly terrifying for me. I've never been with someone like you. We . . . us . . . us getting to-gether . . . it would be a total disaster."

DJ COULD NOT believe this was actually happening. Four days ago this woman had almost caused him to get shot, or at least to get arrested. And now she was propositioning him? Or do-ing something that seemed oddly like propositioning, but with none of the requisite joy of it.

If he was being honest, she looked like she was having a stroke. Her face had gone all splotchy and her neck was pitched at an awkward angle.

DJ had the strongest urge to pinch himself. "Oh, a disaster is definitely how I would describe it. But do go on."

The hand she had pressed into her belly turned into a fist. "*Do go on* . . . see, I think it's the way you talk. It's like those historical novels Nisha reads. *'Do go on,' drawled the duke* . . ." She was babbling, and also doing the worst imitation of Brit-ish English he'd ever heard.

Suddenly her face collapsed into panic as though she'd just realized she was having a mental episode. "You can't possibly not see how ridiculous this is. You . . . You . . . I've never dated anyone who isn't a physician . . . let alone someone who hasn't been to college." Just saying those words made her look like she was going to burst into tears. "You cook for a living. I'm terrified of kitchens. But I don't care. I . . . I . . . When I'm with you, I feel, I feel . . . Maybe we should just get this out of our systems."

Excuse him?

He took another two steps away from her but she followed

him. She seemed desperate to get it all out now, this awful affliction that plagued her that was somehow his fault.

"I don't know . . . I don't know how to get you out of my mind." She looked up at him with big limpid eyes that should have melted him. But all he felt was a restlessness to get the hell away from here. "What are we going to do?"

All right then, time to stop this nonsense.

He held out his hand so she wouldn't get closer to him. "We? *We* are not going to do anything." Was she addled? He'd spent the last four days wanting to hunt her down and kill her for almost getting him killed, for the humiliation that hadn't stopped burning inside him. Not for one sodding moment.

Then there was what Julia had told him—the pain in her eyes when she'd talked about being homeless, like him. Because of her.

Even if he did have feelings for her—and thank the good Lord that he wasn't that much of an arse—he wasn't quite reckless enough to put himself in the path of the kind of callous destruction Julia had experienced.

"I have absolutely no interest in you, Dr. Raje," he said, meeting the wild plea in her eyes.

Her hand went to her mouth in disbelief, and she made a sound somewhere between "Why?" and "How?"

It hadn't struck her for one moment that he might not lap up her proposition, or whatever this was.

"This might baffle you, but despite not being a *physician*, I do have some pride. Although most certainly not enough to withstand the kind of beating you're capable of dealing it. The kind of beating you've repeatedly dealt it from the first time we've met. You're right, I value honesty, so I'll tell you that I make it a practice not to find women who insult me at every opportunity attractive."

Color flooded her cheeks and traveled down her neck. Finally, she stepped away from him, too, and found the back of a chair to clutch. She looked entirely devastated. Had no one ever denied her anything? He hated the hurt in her eyes. But it was done now.

"How is telling you I'm attracted to you an insult?"

He pressed the back of his hand into his forehead. It made him feel like a drama queen in some sort of musical farce. Which this had to be. "Telling me how unworthy I am of your attraction, that's the insulting part. And, no, that's not all it is. Even if you hadn't told me at every opportunity how inferior to you I am . . . how all I do is cook . . . every assumption you've made about me is insulting. Culinary school is definitely college. And Le Cordon Bleu is one of the most competitive institutions in the world. The fact that that's so wholly incomprehensible to you . . . that's the insulting part. And it wasn't thrown in my overly privileged lap either. I had to work my bottom off to make it in."

Ammaji had sold her dowry jewels to pay for his application, something her family would have thrown her out on the street for had they found out.

Trisha squared her shoulders, the devastation draining fast from her face, leaving behind the self-possession he was so much more used to. And the speed with which she gathered herself shook something inside him. "I might not do what you see as *important work*, but I work hard at being a decent human being, and I would need anyone I'm with to be that first and foremost. Even if I didn't find snobbery in general incredibly unattractive, I would never go anywhere near a person as self-absorbed and arrogant as you, Dr. Raje. I would have to be insane to subject myself to your view of me and the world."

"Wow." She was panting, or maybe it was him. He couldn't be sure.

"You wanted honesty. I'm sorry if I hurt you."

She cleared her throat. "I'm surprised you think someone as . . . as . . . self-absorbed and arrogant as me is even capable of being hurt." With trembling hands, she picked up the bag of muffins Naomi had left on her table, but she looked too unsteady on her feet to move. He reached out to steady her, but this time she stepped away and clutched the brown paper to her stomach. "I'm the one who's sorry. Sorry that I asked for your honesty. What you just said to me wasn't just hurtful, it was judgmental. Honesty, I now realize, only has value when it goes with fairness."

He had to laugh at that. "And honesty is only *fair* when it reinforces your own high opinion of yourself?"

"Which you've made crystal clear you do not share." She turned to leave, then turned back. "I would never have imagined you as someone who came with such a truckload of preconceived notions and prejudices."

"Are you bloody joking? You did not just pull the 'reverse prejudice is real' thing on me."

"I'm not trying to pull anything on you. From what I just

heard, my greatest fault is that I dare to take pride in my work, in knowing I'm excellent at it." The brown paper crumpled tighter in her hands. "How is that snobbery?"

"Of course being excellent at your work and knowing it isn't snobbery. But believing that you are somehow unique in excelling at your work while looking down on what others do—that's the snobbish part. Especially given the life you were born into."

She paled at that. "I'm not going to apologize for the life I was born into. Which, by the way, I have never taken for granted or misused for one moment. Tell me, if I were a man, would you see my confidence in my work and my pride in where I come from as arrogance?"

"This gets better and better. As you pointed out, so disdainfully, I cook for a living. Nurturing people, nourishing them holds incredible meaning to me. You cannot pull the gender-role card on me. Plus, I have a vested interest in you being good at your work. My issue is with how you think it absolves you from treating those around you with consideration and respect. Cooking for a living is something I happen to be incredibly proud of."

"As you should be. You're amazing at it." That of all things made her voice crack. She threw a look of such longing at the two empty bowls on the table that despite his anger pride swelled inside him.

It was followed by a sense of hypocrisy that he pushed away. "Yes, I am, and I don't appreciate when someone treats me like a servant for doing it."

She looked horrified. Obviously, she didn't even remember calling him the hired help. Which made it that much worse.

"Then there's the offhanded way in which you negate everything that isn't your personal experience. Thanks to you, I had a cop pull a gun on me. Certainly not conducive to feelings of attraction. Oh, then there's the way you treat people less fortunate than you. I know what you did to your college roommate. You're not emotionally blind, Dr. Raje; you are too focused on yourself to take the time to think about anyone else. That's not an affliction, it's a choice."

She blinked. Color flooded her face again. What he had said had to be painful. But returning a blow with a blow felt so bloody good. It felt like taking off a straitjacket that was crushing his lungs, and he refused to feel guilty about it.

With another blink, she blanked out all feeling from her eyes and he hated that he saw what it cost her to do it.

"At least there's no doubt that my feelings are not reciprocated. I'm sorry I put you in this position. I don't know what came over me. I was trying to be someone I'm not." She gave an embarrassed little laugh, and it made him feel two inches tall. "I do have one question. Are you this angry with me about the cop because I'm brown and I still didn't expect it? Would you have been less angry if I had been white, instead of just 'acting white,' as you called it?"

He would not dignify that with an answer.

The breath she took made her lips tremble. "As for the lies Julia Wickham has been filling your head with, I might've wondered why you've believed them so easily, but I know only too well what a skilled liar Julia is." Grabbing her coat off the back of a chair, she slung it over her arm. The top half of the brown paper bag had been crushed beyond recognition. "If my family ever finds out that you're in any way associated with her, there will be no chance of them ever working with you. That's not a threat. It's simply the truth." With that she walked out the door, her head held high but her legs unsteady.

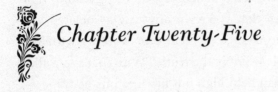

Chapter Twenty-Five

Trying to combat instant regret with instant gratification wasn't working. Trisha took another bite of Naomi's blueberry muffin straight out of the bag. She had torn off the crushed upper part of it so the muffins sat on her lap, exposed. A mangled mess of discarded muffin paper and crumbs peeked up from the carnage. When she stopped at a light, she would look down and count how many she had eaten.

Stuffing muffins into her face to keep from sobbing was just making the muffins salty. Which was tragic. They were the taste of her childhood and now all she tasted was the salt of her tears and the desperation of swallowing them down in great gulps.

I make it a practice not to find women who insult me at every opportunity attractive.

When had she insulted him? When had she looked down on what he did? When? She'd lost all her dignity over his food, salivated over it. She'd salivated over him! And shown it, which made her want to die. All her inhibitions, all her reservations, she had put them away and been honest with him. That was insulting?

I would never go anywhere near a person as self-absorbed and arrogant as you.

That . . . that was insulting.

Self-absorbed?

She had just driven eighty miles to meet with an artist on the off chance that she might help Emma choose to have the surgery. Eighty miles! She pressed a fist into her chest. Who would have thought it could hurt so damn much?

He thought she'd never worked for anything in her life? That it had all fallen in her lap? She did not remember sleeping more than four hours a night since high school. Her siblings were the ones who had made good grades effortlessly. She'd thrown up before every exam—in the school bathroom so no one at home would know. Her anxiety had been that brutal. She'd spent so much time staring at textbooks she couldn't see without her glasses—a surgeon who performed microscopic surgery and was practically blind, with weird eye curvature so that no contacts ever fit right. Not one single school dance. Not one relationship that meant anything. Because all she had done all her life was work.

He thought she didn't know what it was to want something? To work for it? She pulled a tissue from the box and blew into it. This man was not worth the mess she was letting herself become right now.

A huge crusty crumb poked at her breast. It must have fallen down her suit and into her bra when she was shoving a muffin into her mouth. She reached into her bra and grabbed it, then popped it in her mouth.

She'd had to remove her contact lenses and put on her

glasses because tears made her contacts slide out of place. But she never let anyone see her in glasses. They magnified her eyes and made her look bug-eyed. She pulled into the parking lot. Good thing she was done crying. Done. Forcing her contacts back in, she tucked her glasses away and recited both the periodic table and some of the Sanskrit shlokas Aji had taught her to center herself. She would not be walking into her meeting with Jane Liu looking like a watering can.

The building where the institute was housed was beautiful, with a glass-and-steel facade and an ambience so cozy and whimsical it lifted Trisha's distraught spirits. If her heart didn't hurt so much, it might even have sung with hope.

And when she met Jane, the singing-with-hope option no longer seemed like such an impossibility. Jane was one of those people who carried within her a deep sense of her own human perfection. She emanated peace, the kind that was born from self-assurance. Not only had she worked tirelessly for the past two decades for the rights of people with visual impairment, but she herself was an artist of amazing skill who had started painting as a child by using her hands to see objects and then transferring them onto sketchbooks with crayons and paints.

For years she had worked with oil pastels, clay, and acrylics but now she had discovered tactile art, which was a sculptural medium and allowed artists with visual impairment to interact with their work at a more intimate level.

Jane let Trisha play with her pieces, which was how they were meant to be "viewed" anyway. Trisha stroked and caressed the metal wires, knotted ropes, and blown glass all mixed up together to form a symphony of textures as they discussed the several brain studies Jane had participated in to explore how brain chemistry altered physically when a blind artist perceived objects and tried to transmit them into art.

After spending two hours with her, Trisha felt she had never before met another person whose brain functioned so similarly to her own. Methodical and analytical to a fault but also entirely too easily tired of frills and artifice.

Jane promised to speak to Emma, and Trisha had that sense she always had when something she had been trying to solve for a long time finally fell into place. The kind of relief that was all the more special because the resolution had taken so much faith and had been just out of reach for so long. Meeting Jane Liu had been just the thing she had needed today.

"Is he worth this kind of pain?" Jane asked unexpectedly as they were saying good-bye.

Trisha hadn't said one thing about what had happened with DJ, but she had talked about him in the context of Emma, whom they had discussed in detail.

Still, she'd grown up with Esha, so Jane's perception didn't faze Trisha. "It doesn't matter if he is or isn't," she answered. Except, deep inside she knew that he was.

As she began the drive home, that realization ramped up the pain again, making her heart feel like it was having an infarction. This had to be how it felt when your heart muscle died. Switching out her contacts for her magnifying-lens glasses again, she tried not to sob in tune to Kishori Amonkar belting out her agony in raga Durbari.

AN HOUR INTO the drive, Aretha Franklin's "RESPECT" ringtone cut Amonkar off. Trisha honked into a tissue to clear her voice before answering her sister's call.

"Where are you?" Nisha said, sounding as desperate as Trisha was feeling.

"I'm an hour away. What happened? Are you okay?"

"No, Trisha, I'm not okay!" Nisha let out a sob. "It's not the baby. It's Neel. He's on a plane. He's coming home early."

"What? Why?"

"I don't know. But Neel never changes his plans. Ever. What do you think it is?"

How on earth was she supposed to know? "What did he say it was?"

"For some reason his call didn't come through. He left a voice mail hours ago, but I just got it. He said he wanted to see me and that Mishka was done with the trip, so they were getting on a plane. That doesn't sound right, does it?"

"It sounds fine." Mishka was at that age. A tween, or whatever they called it. She could get bored with London. Children that age could get bored anywhere. Trisha still got bored most everywhere that wasn't the hospital. "She's probably bored and Neel doesn't know what to do with her. Maybe he's just missing you."

"Then why didn't he say that? He says things when he feels them. He's not one of those uncommunicative men."

"Sweetheart, your husband's coming home to you *earlier* than he had planned to. That's a good thing."

Except, shit, what were they going to tell Neel about Nisha not being home?

"Caught on, have you? I'm in your condo. I'm four days away from this trimester being over, and he lands in a couple hours. What are we going to do? I have a terrible feeling about all this!"

"What? Are you Esha now?" But Nisha had had a terrible feeling about everything recently. "Nothing is wrong with someone coming home early."

"Trisha, his ex lives in London!" Great, now she'd said it. And now they had to deal with it.

"Nisha, I want you to take a deep breath. Are you listening to yourself? He's coming home, not staying longer."

"Something has happened between them. I can feel it."

"Did Esha infect you or something? Neel is the most solid man I know. He worships you."

There was a long pause where Trisha could practically hear Nisha breathe through processing those words. "You have to go get them at the airport," she said finally. "He'll be expecting me. Think of something."

"I'll think of something, I promise. Do not freak out." Although that ship seemed to have left the harbor some time ago.

Nisha grunted. "Did you get my muffins?" she asked much more calmly.

Trisha looked down at the carnage of crumbs and tried to salvage—and count—the unravaged ones. "Yes. But Naomi only had a dozen."

"Everything okay with you?" her sister asked when Trisha couldn't quite stop her voice from wobbling.

It felt like she would never again be okay. It felt like she had never before truly understood that question.

She assured her sister that she was fine and let her discuss the fund-raiser for a while.

"Why didn't you tell me that Julia Wickham was back in town?" Nisha asked suddenly.

"What, you're spying on me for HRH and Ma now?"

"Shasha." Nisha used her big sister voice. The one she used when she was spying. "Has she contacted you?"

Trisha snapped. "What is wrong with you people? Julia Wickham is too damn smart to contact me. She knows that I will never let her hurt our family again. Apparently, she's the only one who knows it."

"Don't be dramatic. You know why I'm asking. Now don't sulk. And drive safely." With that Nisha hung up.

As a matter of fact, Trisha had no frickin' idea why Nisha had asked. Why they all kept asking. For a moment she wondered if she should have told Nisha that DJ and Julia knew each other. The idea that she might be repeating the worst mistake of her life jabbed at her. Was she doing it again, protecting an outsider at the risk of harm to her family? But there was no artifice in DJ. If he had meant to get close to her and harm her family, she had just presented him with the perfect opportunity to do it.

Pain scraped at her insides at how that had gone.

For all that she had got wrong about him, there was not a speck of evil in him. She wasn't seventeen anymore, and that much she knew without a doubt. When she had kept Julia's secret, Julia had already betrayed her and then used their friendship and Trisha's fear of being a bad person against her. This was not the same thing.

No, she couldn't bring herself to be the cause of her family firing DJ. Not until she had figured out what the hell Julia was up to with him.

He might think she was too self-absorbed to care about anyone but herself. But then he'd already proven that he didn't know her at all.

TRISHA'S BROTHER-IN-LAW HAD one of those boyish faces that made him look like he was still in high school. He sported a goatee and wore rimless glasses from the last century to make himself look more mature, but none of it stopped him from being regularly subjected to those "whom are you kidding with that judge thing" looks. They were his favorite stories to tell. But today Neel looked so exhausted he could have been a hundred years old. At least that's how his eyes looked.

Trisha's first thought when she saw him was that Nisha was right, something was very wrong. Neel hadn't just decided to come home early for nothing.

Naturally, he looked surprised when he saw Trisha. "Where's Nisha?" he asked, searching over her shoulder.

Yup, definitely something going on with that look.

Mishka body-tackled Trisha. "Trisha Maushi! I missed you so much!"

For the first time that day, Trisha didn't feel like she wanted to lie down and die. "I loved London. We have to go back. You and Mom and me. We'll take Aji, too, and Ashi Maushi. Everyone there talks like Aji. Did you know?"

"Come to think of it, you're sounding kinda funny too." Trish tucked a lock of wild curls—a prettier version of her own hair—behind Mishka's ear and tried not to think of DJ saying *Are you bloody joking?* in that accent of his.

"Am I now?" Mishka said, hamming up her swanky London accent. Then like Neel she, too, seemed to register that Nisha wasn't here. "Where's Mom? Dad made me come home early. I didn't want to! It was so unfair!"

Trisha's heart sank.

Their bags showed up on the baggage claim belt and Trisha pulled them off. Neel had gone to find a cart. Mishka's phone pinged and she started to furiously type something out. Then she flipped her phone over and showed Trisha her new phone case. "It's Mr. Bean . . . well, Rowan Atkinson; doesn't he look totally different? It's from the National Portrait Gallery. I loved it so much that Barbara had it printed on a phone case for me. Isn't it amazing?"

Barbara? Why the hell was ex-Barbara giving Mishka phone cases? "Totally amazing." Trisha handed the phone back to Mishka. "Did you enjoy it? The gallery?" And why the hell was ex-Barbara taking her niece to art galleries? That was something she did with Mishka. It was their auntie-niece thing.

Mishka actually bounced on her heels in excitement. "It was incredible! Barbara's friend gave us a tour. Like a backstage tour at a concert. She was really cool."

Trisha had never thought of Barbara as cool. Too pseudon-erdy for her taste. Horn-rimmed glasses, plaid—who dressed like that outside of books? "Barbara must've gotten cooler over time," she said, when she shouldn't have.

"Yipes, not Barbara!" Mishka said, and Trisha tried not to

smile. Really, she did. "I meant Reina, the curator. She's really cool. Wore the highest boots I've ever seen." She pointed to her thighs, looking completely smitten.

She did sound different. They were going to have to go to the movies, eat some In-N-Out. Do something American. "Ah, so Barbara didn't go with you?"

"No, she did. For a while, then she and Dad went off and left me with Reina. You want to see a picture?"

"Sure."

Neel came back with a cart and started to put the bags on it.

"That's Reina and that's Barbara." Mishka handed Trisha the phone.

The bag slammed Neel's fingers into the metal of the cart. Not even a whisper escaped him, but Trisha gasped. "Neel! You okay?" She pushed the bag into place and grabbed his hand.

The skin on his knuckles was all scratched up and a blue welt was starting to form across his fingers. "I'm fine." He pulled his hand away and started pushing the cart toward the parking garage.

When they got to the car, Mishka climbed in the backseat and pressed her phone to her ear. "Mom's not answering," she announced and then popped her earbuds into her ears.

Neel waited a moment to make sure her music was on, then took a deep breath. "Where's Nisha, Shasha?" he said without looking at her.

"She's got tuberculosis."

"What?" Neel spun to face her.

"What?" Trisha moved the car into traffic.

"Did you just say Nisha has tuberculosis?" He squeezed his

hurt fingers with his other hand because he'd just slammed them against the dashboard in his shock.

"No. What? Not Nisha. I thought you were asking about a patient of mine. Um . . . Nisha's in Carmel." *Someone help me.* "Mishka's phone case is really nice."

Neel turned back around still gripping his fingers, poor guy.

"Should we stop for ice? Or an x-ray?"

He shook his head. "I'm fine. What's Nisha doing in Carmel? Why didn't she tell me?"

Why did you drop you daughter off with a stranger to go off with your ex? "It was an emergency. Well, not an emergency exactly, but Naomi had some ideas for the fund-raiser and Nisha needed to go check them out."

"I thought DJ Caine was doing the fund-raiser. How is Naomi involved?"

"I'm not quite sure but DJ and Naomi were trying some . . . um . . . farm-to-table stuff. Naomi has coops. Did you know Naomi has coops? But yes, it has to do with California and farmers and everything." She took a breath. "They've been working all day. In fact, it's going to take a couple days, because while Nisha is there she was going to set up the family getaway at the beach house."

"A family getaway?" He looked like he was furiously trying to remember if he had forgotten about a family event. See, she *was* a genius.

"Did you forget? We're all going to the beach for the weekend once the fund-raiser is done. Ma wants to do a postmortem weekend this time instead of just a tea."

Neel groaned. Then covered it with a vigorous throat clearing. "Of course I didn't forget."

Trisha felt awful. "Nisha said she'd call you as soon as she gets back to the beach house and gets service."

That seemed to satisfy him.

"So why the rush to come home?" she asked, focusing hard on the road.

"We were done with the trip," he said a little softer than usual. He must have realized how cryptic that sounded, because he added, "Work was piling up and I figured being gone so close to the fund-raiser wasn't fair to Nisha. I wanted to make sure Yash didn't need something before the big announcement."

With that he moved the conversation to the fund-raiser and kept it there until Trisha dropped him and Mishka off at their house and went back home to her sister.

Before she got home, Neel had already called Nisha.

"Why did you have to come up with a place that's only two hours away? Now Neel wants to drive out and see me. It wasn't easy to hold him off." It was the first thing Nisha said when Trisha walked into her room.

Then Nisha burst into tears.

"What's wrong now?" Trisha didn't even know why she was asking. She sat down on the bed next to her sister and felt a few leftover crumbs move around under her blouse. She thought she had cleaned up, dusted herself and the car off thoroughly before going inside the airport terminal, but apparently the remnants of heartbreak-fueled muffin binges were tenacious.

"Nothing. Nothing's wrong." Nisha blew into a tissue.

Headline: The Raje sisters deplete California's tissue supply just before their brother announces his candidacy to run the state that takes its tree hugging very seriously.

"It's not nothing. Come on."

"I was worried for nothing. He came home because he thought I'd need him for the fund-raiser. He came home because he missed me. You should have heard him. He just got off a transatlantic flight and he was ready to jump into the car to come see me. I was such a bitch to be suspicious of him."

Trisha lay down next to her sister. They stared up at the ceiling for a while. Her sister did not need to see her face, and she most certainly couldn't handle seeing Nisha's. "What is it you were suspicious of, exactly?" she said before she could stop herself.

"Nothing."

"Okay."

Nisha rolled over on her side and propped herself up on her elbow. "Are you saying I'm missing something? Did he say something to you?" She shook Trisha's shoulder. "What are you not telling me?"

"Nothing. I was just asking because you're never suspicious of Neel."

Nisha fell onto her back again. "Actually," she whispered so softly Trisha barely heard her, "I'm suspicious of him all the time. All the damn time. We've been married ten years and I keep thinking he's going to figure out that he settled for me." Another tissue bit the dust.

"Nisha, come on!" It was Trisha's turn to roll over on her

side. She couldn't believe Nisha had felt this way for her entire marriage.

Nisha's response was a look that told Trisha exactly how hard it was for her to say what she said next. "Do you remember all those years ago when Neel came back from England? Do you remember how he looked?"

Trisha did remember how devastated Neel had looked despite all his forced good cheer. It wasn't like anyone had expected anything different. "How would you know how he looked? You didn't see him for a year after he came home."

"Actually, that's not true. I did see him once. Just after he came back. He was still staying with his parents. You were all in the backyard. The housekeeper told me he was in his room, so I decided to go straight up and say hi. His room door was slightly ajar. He was sitting on his bed crying. He didn't even notice me." Nisha looked like she was going to be sick again. "I left without telling anyone. That's why I didn't see him again. I couldn't. That day . . . the way he looked was exactly the way I had felt when he started seeing her."

Trisha twirled a lock of Nisha's hair and tucked it off her face. "Why did you never say anything?"

"Say what? That I'm married to a man who feels about someone else the way I feel about him?" She pressed her cheek into Trisha's hand.

"*Felt*, Nisha. Past tense. You've been married for ten years. He's stood by you through everything. He's lived and breathed for you and Mishka."

Trisha would not read anything into the hell she'd seen in

her brother-in-law's eyes today. She had no way of knowing
what that was. Someone had judged her today on the basis of
incomplete facts. She wouldn't do that to Neel.

Nisha's shoulders were shaking again and Trisha did what
she'd done so many times these past two weeks; she pulled
Nisha into her arms and settled back against her headboard.

"He threatened to leave me if I tried to get pregnant again."
Nisha sniffed. "And he just went to England to spend more
than a week with the love of his life. And I'm pregnant."

Trisha shot the blob of tissue across her room straight into
the garbage can. "Those facts are all out of context. All of
them. You did not try to get pregnant. Neel did not go there to
spend time with her. And *you* are the love of Neel's life."

Nisha exhaled. As though she'd been waiting for Trisha to
say it.

It was true.

It had to be true.

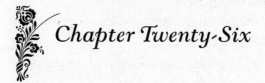

Chapter Twenty-Six

If the fact that Emma didn't want to go to Green Acres today was a sign, DJ didn't want to see it. The wretched worry inside him had been steadily growing.

Emma and he were sitting at his excuse for a dining table waiting for Julia to show up and pretending to focus on their work. Julia wanted to get some final footage of Emma painting before she finished up the film and posted it on social media. After trying to film interviews where Emma refused to do more than grunt and give monosyllabic answers, Julia had settled on having the camera capture Emma while she worked.

"I'm happy to be accommodating," she'd told DJ. "Emma's silence will be more emotionally devastating to the audience than her words anyway."

DJ wasn't particularly keen on anyone being emotionally devastated because of what his sister was going through.

With every passing day, Emma seemed to be sinking deeper and deeper into herself. Tomorrow would mark two weeks since Trisha Raje had discharged her. They were out of time. They were going to see Trisha right after Julia's visit and DJ had no doubt how that meeting was going to go. He'd made sure she would be more than happy to wash her hands of him and his sister and send her off to an oncologist. Not that she wouldn't perform the surgery if he managed by some miracle to change his hardheaded sister's mind.

And something about knowing that about Trisha with such certainty made him restless as hell.

"Are you going to get your finger out and tell me what happened?" Emma said looking up from her sketchbook.

Sure. Right after she got her finger out and took her arse to the operating table. "Absolutely nothing." Other than the fact that she was effectively trying to kill herself, and the most infuriating woman he'd ever met had propositioned him in the most insulting way possible and then acted like he had cut her off at the knees when he had pointed that out.

Emma grunted, then jabbed at the paper, her stabs getting more and more forceful, until finally she tossed the sketchbook across the table. "Hell and bollocks!" she yelled as it went flying to the floor.

He put his iPad down—he'd been calculating how many pounds of tomatoes he would need for the makhani sauce for the Raje dinner—and was about to retrieve the sketchpad, but she put out a hand to stop him and stood, her body tight with frustration. She took a deep breath and was halfway around the table when she tripped and with nothing more than a startled yelp fell facedown to the floor.

DJ jumped up and was next to her in a second, his heart slamming in his chest. "Emma! Love, are you all right?"

He gave her a hand and sat her up on the floor.

Her shoulders were shaking. "I tripped. I fecking tripped!

That wanker left his sodding shoes in the middle of the sodding floor!" She glared at Rajesh's shoes, but her shoulders wouldn't stop shaking.

"Are you laughing, you cow?" he said, a laugh starting in his own chest. "You damn near killed me just now."

"That'd be funny, innit? If you died of fright before me!" She dealt him a soft kick on his shins then slumped back into the wall and shook with laughter.

DJ reached for the shoes she had tripped over and tossed them across the room with far more force than necessary. They slammed against one of her many, many boxes covering the flat and slid to the floor. "I'm going to kill him. What the hell is wrong with him?"

"Isn't that the question to end all questions? Where would we begin?"

They were both laughing hard now, unable to stop. And none of this shit was actually funny.

"Truth is, I didn't see those," she said suddenly, throwing a pained glance at the shoes lying in a sad heap. DJ's laughter dried up inside him. "I don't see that well anymore." Her voice was small. So terribly small. "It's not all the time. But everything disappears suddenly. When I'm sketching or painting. It all just goes away."

He scooted closer to her. "I'm so sorry, love." She let him put his arm around her and pull her close. Let him hold her. For all of five seconds.

Then she shoved him away, with all her strength. "Why are you bloody sorry? Why is everyone so bloody sorry? It's not like you bloody did this!"

Rage and sadness, hot and pure, twisted in his gut, turning into acid he could taste. Who would have known you could taste your feelings? Taste the awful, acrid heat of them. "Your doctor should never have discharged you. This isn't any place for you." This stupid fecking pin-box-size flat. "You need to be in a hospital right now, not in a cupboard with some plonker's clogs tossed about."

"Shut up, DJ. This isn't Rajesh's fault. Fun as it is to blame that wanker for everything, this is not his fault. And it certainly is not Dr. Raje's fault either. Don't be an arse. It's not fair to blame her when I didn't give her a choice." She gave him another shove, but she looked a little less angry now, a little more gentle. "You have to stop trying to find someone to blame for everything, bruh'."

This was precious. "For everything?"

She looked away, done with this conversation. "Forget it."

Oh, he most certainly would love to forget it. But she'd said it and now it lay on the floor between them like an uncooked chunk of meat they couldn't just leave there. "Why did you bring it up if you wanted to forget it?"

"Listen, all I'm saying is that this is no one's fault." She pushed herself off the floor and he suppressed the urge to help, because he didn't need another dressing-down. "And other things that you can't let go of aren't anyone's fault either."

He squeezed the back of his neck where a knot the size of a fist was forming. "Like what?" Whom did he blame that didn't deserve it?

Her response was an eye roll and a whole lot of silence.

"Like our aunt?" he pushed. "Throwing us out on the street was not our darling aunt's fault then?"

She gave him a hand and pulled him to his feet. "Oh, that was most certainly her fault. But Dad dying without providing for us was not her fault."

He pulled his hand away from hers. "You're right about that. That was all him." All bloody him.

Her eyes softened. She'd been too young to know Dad, too young to have memories of him, his smiles, his silly jokes, the way he followed Mum around the house like a smitten puppy, his ability to wrap you up and make you feel safe.

"Yes. But isn't it bloody time you forgave him for it?" She whispered it, but no whisper was soft enough for those words.

"Forgive him for leaving a young wife and two children homeless, when he knew how much his family hated us? Did he think he was bloody immortal? Don't tell me to forgive Dad. I'm not even bloody angry at him anyway."

She laughed—mirthless laughter had become their language now—and sank into the plastic chair. "You're thirty years old, Darcy James!" She sounded exactly like their mother. "Isn't it time you figured out how to deal with all that anger? Or one of these days, you're going to blow up like a volcano and hurt someone entirely undeserving of it." She grabbed her pencil and started picking at it.

"Yeah, and you're one to talk."

"What the hell is that supposed to mean?"

"Aren't you blowing up right now?"

Her hand fisted around the pencil, turning her knuckles white.

"Yeah, you're bloody imploding, Emma Jane. You're so angry you don't even care who you destroy along the way."

Her eyes widened with shock. She was about to respond, but the doorbell rang and they both looked at the door.

"That's Julia," she said, calming down so fast he felt like a prized lunatic for how much anger was still lodged all the way up his gullet. "It's showtime." Despite her best effort, sadness suffused her eyes and his anger fizzled.

"You don't have to do this, Emma." The knot in his neck squeezed tight.

Her only response was a bitter laugh. "A bit late for that, innit? Open the door."

He did as she said and found Julia smiling brightly, blond dreadlocks spilling over her bare shoulders.

"Hullo there." He took the tripod from her and she followed him inside.

"Am I interrupting something?" she whispered, giving him a quick hug, as was her way.

Emma shoved her hand at Julia before she could hug her, and they shook. "Yes, but I'm glad you are," she said lightly. Had his sister always put up such a good show for everyone? She was excellent at it. No one else would see everything swirling inside her. But it was all he saw, maybe because it was inside him, too.

Julia snapped the camera on the tripod. "He's ready when you are." She gave it a little pat.

Emma threw DJ a look that told him exactly what she

thought of anyone who talked about cameras like they were pets. He almost smiled.

"Some *pain perdu*?" he asked, trying to buy his sister some time. He'd made some earlier.

Julia raised one brow.

"That's fancy speak for French toast," Emma supplied.

"Sounds fabulous," Julia said.

Emma gave a bored grunt. "It's all right." But her eyes shone.

DJ made up two plates, but took only one out and handed it to Julia.

Emma took it from her. "Very funny. You can give her the one you're hiding in the kitchen for me."

He shook his head and dropped a kiss on her idiot head.

When he brought Julia her plate, she had turned the camera on and aimed it at Emma who was sitting stiffly on a beanbag.

"So what made you decide not to have the surgery?" Julia asked.

His temper flared again. Wasn't she not supposed to do interviews anymore?

Emma stared at her toes. "What kind of question is that?" Which wasn't an answer but DJ had a feeling Emma no longer had a simple answer to that question.

"It's the kind of question our viewers are most interested in."

Emma stopped looking sad and glared at Julia. "Why are your viewers so interested in terminally ill people, anyway? Why are you? Have you ever wondered why you've chosen to tell these stories where there's no longer any help to be had?" Once again he was struck by how wrong this was, this wanting to watch someone die, this curiosity about what that pain and fear might be like. It was unarguably barbaric and he hated that he hadn't talked Emma out of it.

Julia didn't even bat an eyelid. "That's good, that's very good. So you're angry that this has happened to you. Let the anger out. It'll help."

"Oh, it'll help, will it? What if I'm not angry at all? What if I'm tickled. It's so droll that there's shit growing in my brain that's going to kill me." She kept saying it was going to kill her. But it wasn't. She threw DJ a warning glance—*don't you dare go there!*—and he stayed silent.

Julia looked at him. "Why don't we get some of you today? Since it seems like Emma might need a moment."

Emma laughed. "Several moments, actually." She bit into the *pain perdu.*

"I beg your pardon?" he said to Julia, because when had he agreed to being part of this?

"It's nothing really. Just sit down and talk and let the camera pick you up. I won't use anything that you don't want me to use."

There was no way he was getting on camera and talking about anything, let alone his sister's illness.

"Leave him be," Emma said, taking another bite. "I'm the one these people are interested in. Let's start with me trying to send myself into a food coma." She looked straight into the camera. "I just consumed a million calories of this before you got here, but I can't stop. Because my brother puts crack in his food. Write his name down, DJ Caine. Anytime you get the opportunity to eat his food, run don't walk." She took another bite and chomped with exaggerated delight. "Did you know he's catering the big fund-raiser for that hottie Yash Raje?" She waved the syrupy bread at the camera like a campaign flag. "Yash Raje for governor!"

DJ squeezed his temples. Julia threw DJ a hurt look.

Emma patted the giant beanbag she was sitting on. "Come on, bruh', you might as well get in on this."

DJ sank down next to her, shaking his head.

Julia settled herself into the other beanbag next to them. "When you heard she was sick, what went through your mind?"

He threw a glance at the camera.

"Don't worry, DJ, this is just us talking. Ignore the camera."

Her blue gaze zeroed in on him as though he were the most fascinating thing she'd ever seen, and he felt the corner behind him close in.

"He was thrilled," Emma said. "I mean what big brother wouldn't be thrilled that his annoying baby sister was going to die?" Her bugger-off grin gleamed in her eyes.

He started to stand. Enough was enough. The camera did not need to catch this.

Emma held his hand and pulled him back. "He was angry, all right?" she said to the camera. "I was angry. We both wanted to burn the world down. It had taken us years, but we were both finally fine, we'd both finally built lives we loved."

Julia lifted her chin at him. "And then you had to leave everything behind."

"Wouldn't you?" He hated that she'd made him say it with a camera watching.

Emma's grip on his hand tightened. She rested her head on

his shoulder. "He was always a great big brother." She looked up at him with her mismatched eyes, their parents' eyes fused together. "DJ was twelve when he started working to help our mother take care of us. He didn't buy new shoes if it meant I could buy paints. He never asked for a bloody thing, not once. But he made sure I had everything I ever needed. And now I've bankrupted him. All these years of working, and my medical bills, and the rent for this place have taken everything he's worked for."

He almost opened his mouth, but she stopped him again.

"You want to watch me die? Go ahead. I'll leave these cameras on at my last breath if that'll give you your kicks. But you're going to have to click that donate button. Go on. Let's see what you can cough up. Click it. Click it now. You're not dying, you bastards, look at you, sitting in your home, staring at my—"

Julia stood and turned off the camera. "This isn't a joke, Emma. You told me you wanted to do this, and now you're turning my work into some sort of mockery?"

"Actually, you're the one who told me I'd want to do this. You're the one who told me I could make this what I wanted to make it, told me to let my anger out so I'd feel better. Now you want to tell me that my feelings are a mockery?"

Something like unbanked rage flashed across Julia's face. But it was gone so fast he wasn't sure if he'd imagined it.

I know only too well what a skilled liar Julia is.

Out of nowhere Trisha's words came back to him.

Had Julia seen Emma's art? This was nothing compared to what she did with her iconoclastic humor there. He thought about the painting Emma had done for Trisha.

Julia didn't look like she would ever get that painting.

She threw him a desperate look and he sobered.

"You're not being fair, Emma," he said, evenly. "Julia's time is valuable." Then to Julia. "I'm sorry."

Emma shrugged, waved the last piece of *pain perdu* at Julia with an "Au revoir," and sauntered off into the bedroom, munching on the sweet bread as she went.

"It's fine," Julia said, her voice calm again. "I can edit around it." The blue of her eyes was bright again. She unhooked her camera from the tripod and looped it around her neck. "I'm sure she'll love it once it's done."

That made him want to laugh. All the same, Emma had behaved badly with her. "I really am sorry. As you can imagine this isn't easy. She has an appointment with her surgeon today and she's stressed about it."

Julia's smile tightened around her mouth. She folded up the tripod and headed for the door.

DJ took the tripod from her. "I'll walk you out." Once they were out on the porch of the building, he asked her the question he'd been holding inside. "Can we forget about the video, please? I'm sorry if we wasted your time, but I think this was a mistake."

Her smile didn't budge but something slipped in her eyes again, another flash of temper beneath the twinkle. Again, it was gone in the barest second. "Nothing about meeting you has been a mistake, DJ." She placed a hand on his arm. "Let's not hurry to conclusions. As you said, Emma's just in a bad place today." She laughed a little. "If I were going to go see Trisha Raje, I'd be a raging bitch too."

He attempted a smile but couldn't quite manage it.

Julia's smile lost some of its force, but she didn't remove the hand from his arm. "Why didn't you tell me you were catering Yash's fund-raiser?"

"Didn't I?"

"I don't understand why you're cozying up with the Rajes. Didn't you hear a thing I said that day?"

"I assure you there's no cozying up going on. It's just work. Which, as you can imagine, I really need right now."

She studied him for a bit, and this time he saw fatigue flash in her eyes. A tiredness he recognized only too well. "Take care, DJ. This is not a family who reacts well to people forgetting their place in the world." And with that she hooked the tripod on her shoulder and was gone.

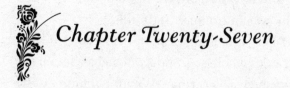

Chapter Twenty-Seven

It was instantly obvious to Trisha that something about Emma had changed. And that nothing about her brother had, or about how her own traitorous body—not to mention brain—reacted to him. But this was not the time to indulge her infatuated adolescent self. She returned his courteous nod, watched him move to a corner of the room and lean against a wall, and turned her attention to her patient.

Emma shook her hand. Her grip was tight, her color not terrible. Her vitals were stable.

She gave Trisha a careful smile. "How many surgeries this morning, Doctor?"

Her patients almost never asked about her day and Trisha's heart warmed toward this amazingly brave, albeit very angry, woman. "Just two. Light day."

That got her a full-fledged smile.

"How have you been feeling?" Before Emma could get a snarky answer out, she added, "Any change in pain levels?" She had already put her on a pain management regimen. "Your vision altering in any way?"

Emma threw a quick look at her brother, giving Trisha a

glimpse of what they must've been like growing up. It made her think of Yash, and how he'd always stood up to HRH and Ma any time Trisha was in trouble. Until Julia.

A frown folded between Emma's perfectly arched brows. "I've had a few episodes where . . ." She scratched a spot on the blue hospital gown she was wearing. "Where I couldn't quite see. Not the usual blurring I've been having for months, but just . . . well, everything just disappeared."

Trisha kept her voice even. "When was the first episode? How long do they last?" She hadn't expected this so soon.

"A few days ago, and only for a few seconds. It's happened just a few times."

"May I?" She shone an ophthalmoscope into Emma's eyes. But she already knew what it was. The tumor was squeezing the optic nerves.

"You were supposed to call me if anything changed." She heard the sternness in her own voice and Emma's frown deepened. She didn't care. It was important for patients to follow instructions. "As long as you're under my care, you have to understand that it's important that you do as I ask."

Apparently, it was just the opening Emma had been waiting for. "So, about being under your care. The last time we spoke—"

Trisha pulled a stool closer to the bed and sat down. "I've done some research since the last time we spoke. I want you to hear me out."

Her patient opened her mouth then shut it again, which with Emma meant she was listening, really listening.

"You should know that this is a first for me. I've never had a patient who has lost their sight before—"

"Aw, I'm your first! What an honor." Emma smirked, and Trisha had to smile, because, really, a person who retained their humor—however dark—in a situation like this was more badass than she'd ever be.

"Go on," Emma said with a sigh.

"Have you heard of Jane Liu? She's an artist from the area. From Monterey actually." Trisha turned on her iPad and pulled up the pictures she'd taken of Jane's work. "She's been blind since birth. Her work is remarkable. She's one of a handful of artists who're changing how scientists perceive blindness."

"That's nice. But Jane's never had her vision, so her brain is probably wired differently from mine." Nevertheless, Emma took the iPad from Trisha and started swiping through the pictures. When she came to the images of the classrooms and the tactile art, she paused.

"She's not the only blind artist in the world, and not all the ones I researched were blind from birth. There are programs around the world where blind and visually impaired artists are creating some amazing work. They claim to see the images in their head before transferring them onto paper or other material. And study after study shows that the visual cortex in the brain lights up like a Christmas tree in scans when they paint or visualize their pieces." Jane was participating in a study and Trisha had seen the scans. They were entirely unexpected, completely paradigm shifting.

Emma's fingers started shaking over the pictures. Her face

had gone so pale her freckles turned stark against her skin. DJ walked over and sat down on the bed next to her, studying the pictures as she swiped back and forth. Yet again she stopped on a picture of a classroom, children touching the metal strips swirling and projecting from a baseboard, but she couldn't form the question she wanted to ask.

"Jane runs an institute where she teaches what she calls tactile art to artists of all ages. They've been doing studies that prove we *see* with more than just our eyes, that our tactile senses can be just as responsible for creating mental images. There are many different ways to process the world. One sense isn't the be-all and end-all."

Emma shoved the tablet back at her. "Really? That easy, is it? Which sense have you ever given up? In fact, what have you ever lost? What have you ever had to live without?"

Not much. "You're right, I've been blessed with a great deal. But there are millions of people who have not. Millions of people who live with all sorts of challenges. And they live happy lives. Full lives. Meet Jane once. That is all I'm asking."

Emma shook her head. There was a violent force to the action, but the eyes that met Trisha's were filled with doubt. "I can't."

DJ rubbed his temples, but he didn't say anything, and Trisha's heart squeezed.

"Why do you paint, Emma?"

She shrugged, as though the question were too easy for her to dignify with an answer. But then she relented. "Because it's the only way I know how to survive. How to trudge through all the shit in the world. I paint because it makes me bloody happy. I am my work, Dr. Raje."

"No. No, you aren't. You aren't your art any more than I am my surgery or your brother is his food." She felt DJ's gaze on her but she couldn't look at him. "We, all three of us in this room, think we live for our work. But is it really that simple?"

Emma didn't respond, and Trisha went on. "Sure, you paint because you want to understand the world, but I think you really do it because you want to change it, by changing every person who looks at your paintings, one by one. You want to make people uncomfortable. You want to force them to think about things they've never bothered to consider . . . Your brother cooks because he wants to comfort people, to show them the pleasure their bodies are capable of experiencing, to make them pause and savor their own existence as they fly through life. You can see it in his face every time someone eats his food . . . And me? I do it because I want to save lives, take away suffering. Whatever the case, we want to change things around us. Because we want to matter, and we believe that our work makes us matter. The work isn't the end, it's the means for what we really want: to matter.

"If it were the work itself, every failure would destroy us. Instead, it makes us try harder. Because it's the changing things that makes us matter. But that's only part of it. Having someone who can see us, especially someone who can see and love that us who works so hard to matter—that's what completes it, completes us. If that went away, that's the thing that would destroy us. You're already loved. Your brother left his life for you. You already matter. All you need is to find another way to change the world. And there are other ways." She swiped through the pictures and held them up to Emma.

Emma stared at the screen, but she shook her head stubbornly. "That's a great speech, but there is only this one way I know how to process my world. I can't do it."

Trisha stood. "You know, I've been accused of being self-absorbed, of not bothering with the feelings of others." She still would not look at DJ. "But what you're doing makes me look like the empath of the year."

"This is not a tantrum, Dr. Raje. I'm—"

"Actually, it is, love." Finally DJ spoke, cutting Emma off. He threw a quick look at Trisha, and what she saw in his eyes was different from anything she'd ever seen. Then he looked back at Emma. "It is a tantrum. Do you have any idea how many terminal patients would die for a cure, for a chance to live? Do you have any idea how many people in this world live with disabilities? It's a simple Google search." He held out his hand and Trisha handed him her iPad. He typed out the search, his fingers steady, all of him filled with purpose. The way he looked back at his sister, his heart in his eyes, made Trisha want to wrap her arms around him. "One out of five people in America, according to the Census Bureau. And every one of them is as alive as you or I." He pushed the tablet into Emma's hands.

Emma didn't answer, but they looked at each other, so many unsaid things clogging the air between them.

"Brain surgery is not open-ended," Trisha said. "The bigger the tumor grows, the harder it will get to not damage healthy brain tissue. In fact, those episodes of vision loss that you've been experiencing—they most likely mean that nerve atrophy is setting in. You're risking your life for your vision, but the chances that you'll have your vision much longer aren't good."

Emma clutched the iPad.

"I know you're angry, that you've been through things no one should have to go through, but we're out of time. You have to make a decision. Think about your brother. Think about what losing you would do to him. Meet Jane once. If not for yourself, do it for him."

DJ closed his eyes and Emma looked at him like she was going to die from the pain.

Trisha opened the door and took a second to wave over the nurse who was waiting down the corridor with a wheelchair. "The nurse is going to take you in for your scan. I know that if you do it, if you meet Jane, you won't regret it. But in the end this is your life and your decision."

Emma didn't answer. But she didn't say no and that was all the answer Trisha needed for now.

The moment Emma was gone, leaving Trisha alone with DJ, the air in the room changed.

He looked at her, the intensity in his eyes from a moment ago replaced by wariness. The purpose inside her was replaced by mortification.

Seriously, what on earth had come over her when she'd blurted out her feelings? He was her patient's brother. He was working with her family. Why hadn't she thought about the fact that she'd be seeing him again? Over and over again. Now here she was standing a mere few feet from him unable to look at him without every single word they'd said rising up between them like one of those tacky bead curtains.

"Thank you," he said simply.

"Just doing my job."

Awkward silence loomed.

"I really do believe that meeting Jane will change Emma's mind."

Something shifted in his eyes, something raw and vulnerable. "I think so too. I think what you said to her back there, it . . . it really broke through. She's been struggling these last couple days." The saddest smile tugged at his lips. "She had a bit of a meltdown this morning while shooting this film about her illness that she's been working on. I was hoping it would be cathartic for her to do it, help her process her thoughts. But I think meeting Jane will do it. So thank you." He looked sincerely grateful, then suddenly he looked uncomfortable again as though he'd said something wrong. Thanking her had to be hard.

Well, that was her cue to leave. "My hopes are high. I've set up a meeting with Jane for tomorrow. I'll leave the details with the nurse."

He nodded and she left the room.

She had taken a few steps when it struck her.

No.

No, no, no.

When she turned around, he was standing outside the door watching her with those intense eyes. She walked back to him. It took her a few seconds to get the words out. "Do you mind walking with me to my office?"

Another nod before he fell in step next to her.

They were halfway to her office before she managed to speak again. "I know this isn't the best time to bring this up. But I think it's time we talked about how you know Julia Wickham."

He threw her a look, but he didn't stop walking. The full

blast of coldness was back in his eyes, and it was like a punch to her throat.

She thought about the warmth with which he treated Ashi and Nisha. The inherent gentleness with which he took care of his sister. Naomi, the nurses here, he was lovely to everyone. Everyone except her.

What was wrong with her? Why was she hurting herself this way? It didn't matter how he felt about her. Nothing else mattered if what she suspected was true.

"My asking you this has nothing to do with anything I said to you that day. I have no intention of embarrassing you by ever bringing that up again. I'm truly sorry for how I behaved. But I have to know. Did you say Emma was working on a film about her illness?"

She got another curt nod.

"She's working with Julia, isn't she?"

HRH's email had said Julia had been doing interviews with terminally ill patients. The fact that she'd picked Emma, when she wasn't terminal—there was something going on that Trisha couldn't wrap her head around.

They had stopped outside her office. She knew his livid stillness by now. The way his mouth pursed, making the dent in his chin deepen. Those eyes, hazel rings around dark centers, turned on her. "Is this leading up to another threat to fire me?"

She pushed the door to her office open. "You have to understand—"

"Hi, Trisha." What the hell was Neel doing in her office?

"Oh," all three of them said as DJ and she stared at her brother-in-law sitting on the couch.

Breath whooshed out of her in a panic. "Neel! What's wrong?"

"Nothing's wrong. I just needed to talk to you." He threw a look at DJ and stood. "I can wait outside until you're done." But he stopped and studied DJ again. "Aren't you the chef Nisha's working with for the fund-raiser?"

Great, this was just great.

With a quick glance at Trisha, DJ stuck out his hand. "DJ Caine." Despite her panic, the way he said his name made all sorts of heat zigzag inside her.

Neel shook his hand and threw a curious look at Trisha. She felt a bull's-eye burning in the center of her forehead. "Neel Graff. We met briefly at the dinner—it was great, by the way. I thought you were in Monterey, working on the event with Nisha."

DJ's expression did not alter. "I am working with your wife. My sister had an appointment with Dr. Raje, that's what I'm here for."

"I see," Neel said. "I hope your sister's okay."

"Dr. Raje assures me that she will be."

Neel squeezed DJ's shoulder. "She's in very good hands with Trisha. You couldn't ask for a more talented doctor."

DJ threw her one of those looks. The kind that undid everything she was. "So everyone keeps telling me."

Neel smiled, blissfully unaware of the storm of undertone in DJ's voice. So much for emotionally blind. Her mind had taken to zeroing in on every minute nuance when it came to him.

"I look forward to seeing you at the fund-raiser," Neel said in his typical slightly formal way.

"That remains to be seen." DJ had it, too, that old-world formality all the men in her family possessed.

"I thought you were catering it."

"I did too. But apparently, I might not have the opportunity." His eyes met hers, still deliberately flat.

She couldn't respond, not with her breath held.

He turned back to a confused-looking Neel and smiled his most stiff smile. "If my sister's health worsens, I might need to recuse myself from the job. But I'm hoping Dr. Raje will not let it come to that."

Neel gave his shoulder another supportive squeeze and left. Trisha exhaled and shut the door behind him. "Thank you for that."

"Well, I didn't not out Nisha because of your threats. I did it because I would never do anything to harm your sister."

She walked to her desk and leaned back into it. "I know that."

For a moment he said nothing, just studied Emma's painting on her wall with some surprise. She'd had it mounted the day after Emma gave it to her.

"Nisha has her reasons for keeping her secret."

"Everyone always has reasons for keeping secrets."

He was right.

Everyone always had reasons. She'd had a reason for not telling Yash that Julia had developed an unhealthy obsession with him. She'd thought Julia was her friend. And when her friend had begged her to keep her secret, she'd done what her friend needed. It had been the biggest mistake of her life. One she'd be repeating if she didn't tell her family that Julia was working with DJ and Emma. But it would mean he'd lose the job.

In her gut she knew that he didn't deserve that. She'd seen the fire in his eyes at the Astoria, during the tasting at Nisha's. She also knew in her gut that Julia's being here wasn't a coincidence. And Yash . . .

"Mr. Caine . . ." He turned to her. "Do you mind if I call you DJ? It's seems like it's time we moved past last names."

He swallowed, a strange look crossing his face. "Please."

"Julia is taking advantage of you and Emma to hurt my family. I know this for sure."

"Can you tell me how you know this?"

"No, I can't. It could hurt my family too much if I did."

Pride in who he was glittered in his eyes. "I would never break a confidence."

"I know that—you didn't just now with Neel and I appreciate that." But not everyone was like him. That was the problem, wasn't it? Ashi had told her that he was still helping with her menu, even after she'd rented the kitchen and couldn't let him use it.

Worry about how much Julia could hurt him stomped through her. But she couldn't compromise Yash.

"Why didn't you tell me that Julia was working with Emma, DJ?"

"I wasn't aware that I had to run whom I choose to associate with by you, Trisha." He pronounced it "Trish*er*" and said it deliberately, as though to emphasize how long it had taken them to get around to this basic level of intimacy, and how she had leapt right over that threshold to dumping her feelings at his feet.

And now all she wanted was for him to say her name over and over like that.

Could the floor open and swallow her up, please? "I told you my family won't work with you if you associate with her."

"Maybe that's why I didn't tell you. I didn't think it was fair for you to take another thing away from her."

She laughed. "I have no idea what Julia's been telling you, but I assure you that I've never taken anything away from anyone, most of all not her. I have always been honest with you—often to my detriment. Can you at least weigh what you've seen before deciding you want to trust her over me?"

"You want me to mistrust someone on your word?"

"You're mistrusting me on her word, aren't you?"

That gave him pause. He squeezed the back of his neck. "In the absence of it being refuted."

"I can't refute it because there are things I cannot reveal. Things that aren't mine to reveal."

"Well then, we have a problem, don't we?"

That they did. Actually they had a clusterfuck of problems. "She hurt my brother very badly. I just can't give you the details. You wouldn't let anyone hurt Emma, either."

"No, I wouldn't. But Emma wouldn't destroy anyone's life."

That made her take a step away from him. "My brother has never hurt anyone. He is the best human being I know."

"Wow! I don't think I've ever heard a sister say that. Emma's more interested in telling me how I'm a total git." He smiled, then realized he'd smiled and went stormy again.

"It's obvious Emma feels that way about you, too." She'd

never told Yash how she felt about him. "It's hard to tell your family how you feel. Have you told Emma?"

"Told her what?"

"How you're feeling right now? How important it is to you to not lose her."

"She knows."

Trisha thought about all the things Yash and she hadn't said to each other when they should have. "Or maybe it's exactly what she needs to hear."

He didn't respond.

"At least look Julia up. She's taken thousands from the FundMe campaigns she's done. This is how she makes money." Of course she'd looked over HRH's PI reports and googled the heck out of her.

He pressed his hand into the back of his head again. "She hasn't asked Emma for a penny."

He wasn't going to believe her. Not with how he saw her. Not without her side of the story, which she couldn't give him. "I can tell you that she's cost me my family. I lost their trust because of her. I got thrown out." For fifteen years.

He glanced at the door beyond which Neel was waiting. "From where I'm standing, you don't seem thrown out of your family."

"It's complicated."

That made him laugh. "In my experience, when families throw you out, it's really quite simple." He snapped his fingers. "They throw you out. You cease to exist. End of story."

The pain in his eyes made the urge to reach for him tear at

her again. But all she could do was stand there, their gazes locked.

Finally, he looked away. "I think we've kept Nisha's husband waiting long enough."

But she couldn't let him go. Not like this. "Listen, I behaved terribly. I should never have said those things. All my life I've been taught that doing the right thing gets you what you want. So I focus too much on doing things and getting what I want, maybe to a point where I become callous to everything else. I get that. And I'm sorry. But I have no reason to lie to you about Julia." She pressed a hand into her belly. "She has a talent for finding every vulnerability in you and manipulating it. She's here because she wants something and she'll hurt you to get it."

His eyes softened, the anger-tinted curtain he always kept between them lifted for a moment. "You did deal my ego some good wallops, but I haven't done any better either. So, yes, we've had a hard time getting around our judgments of each other. But if you can't trust me with the truth, you're asking me to judge someone else unfairly, too." He took a breath, that chin dimple digging deep. "I thought being on camera might help Emma get her head on straight. And maybe it did a little bit. Neither Emma nor I meant you or your family any harm when we got involved in this. If Julia does indeed mean to harm you, I'll do all I can to stop her."

If disdainful DJ had turned her into a bumbling idiot, this sincere avatar of him saying those words made something inside her fall in place and click tight. She couldn't do it, couldn't punish him for what Julia had done. Not without knowing more.

Neel coughed outside and they both looked away from each other and at the door.

"Thank you. I need time to think this through," she forced out. *Just be careful, please.*

"Emma's probably back from her scans. And Neel looked like he needed to talk." He paused, brow furrowed, lips pursed. "You seem to be holding so many secrets on so many people's behalf. I imagine it must be exhausting."

On that note he left, his words hanging in the air behind him like his clean, intoxicating scent. For a moment she was almost afraid to move, lest she step on one of the pieces of her heart that lay scattered in his wake.

He was right about Neel, though. He had looked tortured. She sent Nisha a text before asking him to come inside: "Neel's here, what do I do?"

Nisha didn't respond, so Trisha was pretty much on her own.

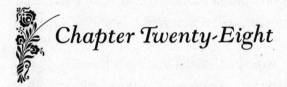

Chapter Twenty-Eight

You're hiding something from me, Trisha." Neel was most certainly not looking like himself. "And my wife's hiding something too."

Oh dear.

"What about you, are you hiding something from us?" She sounded like a complete nutjob, but all she wanted was to deflect.

Neel looked like she had ripped off his skin. He dropped into a chair. Dropped, as though his legs had given way, and pressed his face into his hands. Something about his reaction made her think about Mishka's phone case, which made her think about ex-Barbara.

His shoulders started to shake.

"Are you crying? Neel, what's wrong?" He was scaring the shit out of her.

He looked up, eyes glistening with fear and shame. And shame, did she mention shame? Fear was okay—it kept you from doing stupid things. But shame? Shame was not good. Shame meant a stupid thing had already been done.

"Did you say anything to Nisha?" he asked.

"About what?"

"About that bloody phone case." British curses were not good either. Given that ex-Barbara had refused to leave England for him.

"Do you think I would tell Nisha that right now?"

His eyes widened then narrowed. "You two tell each other everything." This was not true; she had not told Nisha about how she had humiliated herself in front of DJ under the influence of his food. "And what do you mean 'right now'? Something's wrong with Nisha, isn't it? How can you not tell me?"

How could she tell him? "How could you do what you did?" She deflected again. "How?"

He had taken her niece, Nisha's daughter, to the National Portrait Gallery with ex-Barbara. Behind Nisha's back. That felt like a betrayal on so many levels. "Actually I don't want to know." If he told her, she'd have to tell Nisha. She refused to be the person who hurt Nisha.

"Trisha, please, I need your help."

She leaned back into her desk. "Listen, I have a lot going on. I don't have time for this right now."

He stood and pushed his glasses up his nose with an unsteady finger. "Okay."

Not only was his finger unsteady, but the shadows under his eyes were dark and deep.

He was trying to tell her something, and she'd made up her mind about what it was before he'd spoken.

Less than ten minutes ago she had told DJ that she regretted her callousness. Now she was turning away her brother-in-law—a man who had never done anything but stand by her—when he'd asked her for help. That was definitely callous.

"Wait, Neel. Come back. Sit down. Can I get you something?"

He shook his head but sat. "Thanks."

"Tell me what happened in London."

He slumped into the chair. "We dated for seven years. That's a very long time."

Trisha forced herself to not groan, or strangle him with her bare hands. He was bringing up ex-Barbara? Now, when Nisha was home struggling with herself over a baby? "You and Nisha have been married for ten years, that's even longer!"

"I know. Don't you think I know that? But why do people believe that everything you ever felt for someone else before you got married disappears when you get married? Yes, you put it away and you move on. But you don't die. Your ability to feel things for other people does not die. When someone who dumped you looks at you with longing, it . . . it feels like . . . it feels like such a victory. It feels like all the pain, all the humiliation you felt was redeemed." He ran his hands through his hair. "Bloody hell, I'm a terrible person."

"Please stop saying that."

"Saying what?"

"'Bloody.' It makes you sound British and . . . never mind. Wait, she looked at you with longing?" How dare she! "You let her look at you with longing?" How dare he!

"Barb wanted to catch up, wanted to meet Mishka. Mishka

wanted to go to the National Portrait Gallery. No points for guessing who put that idea in her head."

Despite the conversation they were having, pride for her niece flooded through her. She'd told Mishka all about the gallery before she left, and she'd remembered. Best niece in the world.

"When Barb heard that Mishka wanted to go, she offered to take us. She knows one of the curators and offered to give Mishka a behind-the-scenes tour. Mishka got so excited. How could I refuse?"

Trisha squeezed her temples. "Why did you come home early?"

"Because I shouldn't have done it. I shouldn't have gone out to lunch with her. Because she told me she regretted losing me. Because she's alone and unhappy. And I'm not. Because I realized that Mishka was going to tell her mother and that Nisha wouldn't see it as a simple thing. She'll let it break her heart. And I should have thought about that before I went to lunch." His hands were still in his hair and his grip tightened. "Has she left me?"

"What? No! Why would you think that?"

"Because it's Nisha and we came home early and, well, it's Nisha and she wasn't home."

At least he knew Nisha. Apparently better than Trisha or even Nisha herself, because he was right. Under remotely normal circumstances Nisha would have had a coming-home dinner laid out, balloons and flowers for Mishka. God knows what kinds of embarrassing homecoming treats for Neel. And they had both forgotten that Neel would notice that she hadn't done it. Even if she were really traveling for work, she'd have rushed home the moment she heard they were back.

"She's working, Neel. Now that Yash is running, you know things are going to get crazy for her. She's been revving up for this for years. There might be some changes coming. The demands on her time are going to increase. You know that, right?"

He lifted his glasses and dabbed his eyes on his sleeve. His hair was standing up in spikes, making him look like the boy who'd slipped her his ladoos at parties, not because he didn't want them but because he knew how much she loved them. "Does she know?"

"No." Nisha didn't know about Barbara yet. "But Mishka telling her is only a matter of time." She squatted down in front of him. "Call Nisha. She'll tell you she's okay. She needs to take care of this, then she'll come back home."

Neel looked at his hands.

"You do want her to come home, right?"

His head snapped up. "Of course! How can you ask me that? She's the best thing that's ever happened to me. I've never doubted it, not even for a minute. I did a stupid thing. I let my ego get stupid. But when I was sitting there at lunch, all I could think about was how she was going to feel when she found out. And I haven't stopped kicking myself since."

She reached out and rubbed his arm. "It's going to be okay. But I have to go. I have patients waiting. Trust me—just call Nisha."

They both stood.

"Thanks for hearing me out, Shasha."

She smiled at him. "You know I love you like a brother, right? You and Nisha . . . I knew you two would end up together. I always knew it. Even when you were with . . . with her. Even when you were with Barbara, I knew you'd find your way back to Nisha, that the way she felt couldn't be one-sided. I've seen you two for ten years and I *know* it isn't one-sided. But if having that with someone who's so perfect for you hasn't been redemption enough for the pain you felt—" She had to take a breath here. "*Ten* years ago, then maybe I was wrong."

He took her hand and squeezed it. "You aren't wrong. I swear. Nisha is everything, you know that. She's given me everything. Never asked for anything in return. I can't even articulate how much . . . how much I love her." His voice cracked on those words and it was the most beautiful thing.

Her sister was bearing all her fear and anxiety alone. It was easy to think it was because she was scared, because she lived in fear of Neel deciding he'd settled for her, but the truth was, she was trying to protect him from the pain of hope and worry, and taking all of it on by herself.

All her life Trisha had prided herself on being someone who fought for things she wanted. And yet she had accepted Yash shutting her out, HRH writing her off. She'd believed in her own guilt so much she had never had the courage to ask for forgiveness, to forgive herself. DJ was right; they might be angry with her but she hadn't ceased to exist for them. That much she knew. Maybe it wasn't too late.

Unlike her, Nisha was brave, and she knew what to do with her love. She had loved Neel hard, and despite her insecurities, she'd given him everything she had. Fortunately, he saw that.

She threw her arms around him. "Then prove it to her, Neel. Prove it to her."

AFTER NEEL LEFT, Trisha was about to call HRH to try and figure out the Julia problem, but her fingers dialed Yash instead.

"All okay, Shasha?"

The day had been an emotional roller coaster. All her days seemed to be going that way recently. But it was that question from her brother that finally tipped her over the edge. Regret choked her throat. "No, no it's not. Can we meet? I need to talk to you."

"I've got a full day," he said, then shouted a random string of statistics to someone in the room. "How about later in the week?" He'd just come back and had to be busy.

"Yash, I need to see you today." She didn't bother to suppress the sniff that hiccuped through her. "Can't you make time for me?" Even to her own ears she sounded ten. Actually, she sounded seventeen. Her *before* voice.

There was a beat of silence. "Okay. I'll see you at the Anchorage this evening."

"Really?"

He laughed. "Why do you sound so surprised? You did want to meet, right? Please tell me this wasn't some sort of test. I think I just blew off the mayor of San Francisco."

"Did you really?" Maybe it was a test. She wasn't sure. Now she felt awful.

"No. I'm kidding. I love you, but I do want to get elected.

I needed to stop by the Anchorage anyway. Will you be done
with patients by six?"

"Yes. Thanks, Yash."

NATURALLY, JUST AS she finished with her last patient, an emergency came up. Anne told her that Dr. Entoff was happy to
take it, "But I'll let him know you're here so you'll want it."

She almost asked Anne for the case details, but then she
said, "No, thank Dr. Entoff for me. I have to leave."

Anne stopped typing at her prosthetic keyboard and almost
fell off her too-high chair. "Really?" she said, then quickly, "I
mean, okay." She was channeling the Grim Reaper, as usual.
"Also, I set an appointment up for Emma Caine with Jane Liu
tomorrow."

"Thank you, Anne." She turned to walk away, but there was
a notepad sitting on Anne's desk and she picked it up and
started to draw on it. "Actually, would you do me a favor?"

Anne blinked and looked around her to make sure Trisha
was talking to her. "Sure, what do you need?"

"Could you stand up, please?"

"Excuse me?"

Trisha turned the notepad toward her showing her the line
drawing of the chair she'd done. "See the length of your legs?
Here?" She circled the distance from the chair seat to the floor.
"See, if your feet are not resting on the floor and you're bent at
this angle and your elbow pulls here, these nerves here can get
pinched and then the pain that radiates from here can be felt
here because your nerves all connect to your spinal column."

On every "here" she circled and drew lines along the human figure she'd sketched.

Anne stood. Her mouth was hanging open.

Trisha walked around the desk. "You mind?" Anne shook her head and Trisha bent down and adjusted the chair until it was the right height so Anne's legs would rest on the floor correctly.

"Try that."

Anne sat and wiggled about in her seat. "It doesn't feel any different," she mumbled.

Trisha smiled at her. "Give it a day or two. If it doesn't help, you can always change it back."

She was barely down the hall when she heard Anne on the phone. "You're not going to flippin' believe this . . ."

TRISHA PULLED UNDER the porte cochere and parked next to Yash's car and turned the rearview mirror to look at her face. There were deep smudges under her eyes. She hadn't had a chance to get out of her scrubs. It was a good thing Ma and HRH were not back from LA yet.

After a quick stop in the kitchen, she took the stairs up to Aji's room. The portraits of Sita and Parvati gave her their usual half-compassionate, half-amused smiles. Sita, at least, had no right to be amused at Trisha. Sita had sent her husband chasing after a golden doe to make herself a blouse, for crying out loud! And then she'd left the safety of her home when he'd begged her not to. Sure, that entire story was structured to scare women from ever crossing the boundaries society and the men in their lives set for them, so Trisha did feel bad for her. But she had paid for it by being abducted by a ten-headed monster and by causing a war for the ages.

All Trisha had done was lose her heart to a man who detested her and puked out her feelings on his shoes like a drunk sorority girl. And years ago, she had trusted a friend who had betrayed her. And now she was choosing to trust someone again, but the betrayal wouldn't stop nudging at her.

"I'm sorry," she said to Sita. She understood how trusting the world to be a safe place could make you stupid.

Raja Ravi Varma's brushstrokes had a way of trapping a million emotions into the faces he painted, and Sita's expression softened in returned commiseration.

Trisha made her way to Esha's room. As usual, it instantly relaxed her. Maybe it was the smell of incense, at once light and heavy. Maybe it was all the lingering memories—Trisha and her siblings had experienced so many of life's significant moments here. Then again maybe it was the giant circular bed they had all loved to flop down on.

Yash was flopped there right now. Esha and he were on their backs, their heads almost touching, their bodies radiating at angles like two rays radiating from the sun that was Aji, who sat there, stroking their foreheads in turn. To Aji they would always be her babies, and they in turn lost all their adulting pressures when they were with her.

Trisha smiled. This was a part of Yash Raje his voters would never have. It was a selfish thought, but Trisha wasn't ashamed of it. Yash needed something of himself for himself, for them, for her. Suddenly she was so exhausted, all she wanted was to put her head on Aji's lap, too, and sleep for ten hours straight, maybe twenty. Aji waved her over and patted the spot where there was space for one more ray in the sun Esha and Yash were making.

"It's been five days," her grandmother admonished before letting Trisha lean over and kiss her cheek.

"Hey, Shasha," Yash and Esha said together without opening their eyes.

The smile on Trisha's face spread down to her heart.

"Why so sad, baby girl?" Esha asked, eyes still closed.

"What's going on?" Yash asked, also not opening his eyes.

"How was your trip?" Trisha let Aji kiss her forehead before falling into her slot between her brother and her cousin and closing her eyes.

"The trip was successful. Nothing new. Now tell us," Yash said, sounding like he might have turned toward her. "What's bothering you?"

"I have a patient who might choose not to have surgery that can save her life because she's afraid of going blind."

The silence before Yash spoke was heavy and long. "It's terrifying to suddenly be faced with a disability."

Trisha had no doubt that every single person in the room relived the moment when they'd been told he would never walk again. "Does she have time?" Aji asked.

"Not too much. I'm hoping she'll see the light soon. This new robotic technology, it's amazing." She had to clear her throat. "It can change how we remove tumors forever." God, the robot was spectacular and she wanted to snuff out that tumor so badly she could feel her adrenaline rising. "But if she waits too long, it may not have a chance to help her."

"Well, you have been putting all your time and attention into that technology for years, so it was bound to happen." This from their grandmother whose hand stroked Trisha's forehead. "When was the last time you ate?"

"J-Auntie wouldn't let her up here without food," Yash said, right as always. "I'm sure you'll find a way to change her mind. But there's something else going on, isn't there?"

All Trisha could get out was a "hmm" laced with all the sadness she was feeling.

"Secrets can get heavy." This from Esha. "Undressing a secret makes it naked and takes away its power."

But how do you undress a secret that isn't yours?

"Julia Wickham has been filming the patient. The one who's refusing surgery."

She felt Yash sit up. "Okay."

Something in his voice made her open her eyes. She sat up, too, taking in his studiedly calm expression.

"She's been doing these films and raising money for a while now." Of course Yash would know this. "It would actually be a noble thing to do, if she weren't taking half the donations."

"I have a really bad feeling about this. I'm sorry, I should have pushed for more information when I found out that she knew DJ . . . that's . . . um . . . my patient's brother. Actually . . ." She turned to Esha.

"Your feeling is valid," Esha said without opening her eyes. "But you can't stop this."

She said "this" and not "her," and Trisha wasn't sure if she meant they couldn't stop Julia, or if she meant she couldn't stop something else. Because yes, there were several things Trisha was currently trying to stop, like Emma making the wrong decision, the threat to Yash, the end of her sister's marriage, the possession of her heart by an alien spirit who had fixated on a man who wanted nothing to do with her.

"Of course we can't stop her," Yash said. "We can't stop anyone from making films on medical science, or anyone trying to make money to pay for the ridiculous medical bills in our country." He cleared his throat. "And I'm pretty certain that the film that we're really worried about was destroyed. And the NDA Julia signed was pretty watertight. She can't talk about any of it." He sounded calm and lawyerly, but there was a thread of strain in his voice.

Julia Wickham could destroy him and he knew it. No one would care that he'd been the victim, not in today's climate. The worst part was that if he did get justice, if people did believe him, it could set the progress women were making back a hundred years. He would never want that.

No, there was no justice to be had. Julia would never be punished for what she'd done to him, and he'd always have to live in fear of the story coming out. Even after he won the election, it would always be there, hanging in his past.

He had every right to be angry at Trisha, to shut her out.

"I just wanted you to know. Thanks for coming out to see me." Warmth prickled at her eyelids. "I'm so sorry, Yash."

Yash got off the bed. "Get up. Come with me."

"Where?"

Without answering, he grabbed her hand, pulled her up. And started striding across the room. "We'll be back soon," he threw at Aji and Esha. Neither one of them would question him. He was Yash.

They went through the sitting room and up the stairs, and down the passage that led to the attic playroom. Trisha didn't have to run to catch up with him, but it felt like that was exactly what she was doing. A memory of trying to keep up with HRH as he strode across the halls of the Sagar Mahal flashed in her mind. HRH had never slowed down for anyone until Yash had landed in a wheelchair. The only thing their father had ever trailed was Yash's wheelchair.

They walked through the playroom. It had gone from housing an indoor children's play set, complete with slide and climber, to a pool table and a Ping-Pong table when she got to middle school, and back to the play set for Mishka over the decades. For some reason, no one had removed the slide and climber when Mishka had outgrown it. God, please, please let them need it again.

Yash yanked the dormer window open and dislodged the screen, then climbed through it. The man was as limber as he'd been when they'd last done this. "How on earth do you find the time to run?" she asked, wondering if she could climb through a window in her current unexercised state. Fortunately, her body hadn't started to disintegrate yet and she stepped out into the sunshine on the eastern roof for the first time in over fifteen years.

It was like stepping back in time.

Yash sank down onto the ledge. They had been like the family from *3rd Rock from the Sun*. Only they weren't searching for their home planet in the sky, they were rooted in their home and surveying their life and dreams from its solid foundation.

"I really am sorry. I'll do whatever it takes to stop her. I promise."

He turned to her, and she blinked in shock.

Emotions darkened his face, anger and impatience, the calm facade of the public servant nowhere in sight. "I should have kept track." He was livid. He ran his hand through his hair, a restless childhood tic that his handlers—as in, Ma and Nisha—had almost trained out of him.

She stuck out her chin, bracing herself. She hadn't realized how badly she'd wanted to have this out. Her guilt was crushing. Her shoulders, her lungs, everything was collapsing under it. They'd danced around it too long. He hadn't been able to so much as reprimand her when she so richly deserved a good solid blast of anger. It was about damn time, and if it would end this simmering coldness she felt around him, she'd take it.

"I swear you've apologized at least a thousand times since it happened. In fact, I don't think we've had any other conversation since then. Not one. Nothing but apologies. You haven't said one damn thing to me in fifteen years, except 'sorry,' Trisha!"

"I'm pretty sure I've said other things," she mumbled, worrying one big toe with the other.

His expression did not alter, but now she wasn't sure it was anger at her she was seeing. "So you made a mistake. So what?" He drew in a breath and she had a sense he wanted to shake her. "I want you to mean what you said about doing something to stop her."

She looked up from her toes. She did mean it. She would do anything.

"Here's what you need to do: let it go. Forgive yourself. Don't you see what she's taken away from us? You've let her ruin us." He waved his arms around their view. Their mountain, with its redwoods, that he'd taught her to hike up. He'd been the first one to show her Anchor Point, the rocky ledge from where you could look straight across the clearing in the trees at their home.

"I miss you, Trisha. So you made a mistake . . . Actually, no. No, you didn't. *I* made a mistake. This was my fault; I was the one who trusted her and allowed myself to be put in that position. I was an adult. You didn't put Rohypnol in that drink. Yes, I blamed you right then, in that moment. But it was me. I needed to blame someone. I knew even then it was on me, not you. I should have stood up for you more with Dad. I should have tried harder to convince you that it was not your fault. I should have shaken you out of your goddamned guilt. God knows I know what living with guilt feels like."

"Yash, it wasn't all you. I could have stopped her. I knew. I knew that she'd hacked into my computer. I—"

"No. You were seventeen. She was your friend. This isn't on you." He tucked a lock of hair behind her ear. "Let's stop this, okay? I'm sorry. You're sorry. So, please, please, let's let it go."

Her contacts moved in her eyes and she squeezed them shut. "You know I'm blind as a bat without my glasses."

"Then don't cry, giraffe. There's nothing to cry about."

"But the people of California—"

"Voters aren't stupid. We've taken care of the video, but if by some misfortune she resurrects it, they'll understand. I was twenty-three. I was drugged."

"You know that won't matter. The visual is what will matter. The fact that she was seventeen is what will matter. We can do something." She turned to him. "We can talk to DJ . . . that's . . . that's my patient's brother. He doesn't know any of this, but . . . but . . . he said he wouldn't let her hurt us . . . he's not exactly friends with her . . . but she might . . . I mean, he's just . . . it's not his fault that . . ." *Shut up, Trisha!*

But it was too late to shut up. Yash was looking at her too carefully, one brow arched. *Kill me now, please!*

"DJ is the chef catering your event." *Stop talking about him. Talk about something else. Quick.*

"Ah."

She did not like the way he said that. She didn't like it one bit.

Her brother leaned back on his arms, prosecution settling in to cross-examine the witness. "This DJ," he said, sounding too much like HRH—possibly on purpose. "He's the chef who did Ma's last party? That was some seriously good food, ha?"

Idiot that she was she groaned. Please, please let it have been a groan and not a moan. Then she did that stupid thing she hadn't done with Yash in a very long time—she turned the groan/moan into a cough.

It only ramped up his level of intrigue. Why did she have to have a brother who was a lawyer? Why? "He looks like a bit of a male model, if I remember right." He waggled his brows in that probing way she knew well but hadn't seen in a while.

She rolled her eyes, but thinking about DJ hurt. Yash's

searching look acquired a sharp edge. "You want to tell me about this DJ?"

She all but squirmed, which just made him study her more intently.

"You have to promise not to fire him."

"Fire him for what? What did he do to you, Shasha?" Was Yash growling? The role of chest-thumping elder brother did not suit him in the least bit.

"He didn't do anything to me." She was the one, in fact, who had gone batshit drooler on him. "But you know HRH will not let him work the fund-raiser if he finds out Emma's done the film with Julia. You don't understand. He has to cater it."

More of that studying ensued. "Did you tell him that we can't work with him if he works with Julia?"

God, they sounded like they were in some sort of seedy mobster flick. "Yes, but he's not the kind of person who'd dump anyone without reason." Especially not on her word. "And I'm afraid . . . well . . ." Julia was going to hurt him. Trisha just knew it. "You can't fire him. Please. He has to do this dinner. He's here for his sister. He quit his job. The money. Have you eaten his food? But HRH. You have to talk to HRH." She looked at her toes desperately.

Her brother reached for the hand she was pressing into her belly and patted it as though it were a lost puppy. "Shasha, sweetheart, have you told him how you feel?"

The choking was instant and violent. Yash started thumping her back to save her from dying. She'd rather choke to death than answer that question.

She tucked her chin into her chest, but when Yash pulled

her into his shoulder, she snuggled into him like a little girl who wasn't a badass surgeon. Then again, she didn't feel like a badass anything.

How had this happened? How had she fallen for someone who despised her? Just thinking about him hurt, those eyes, that dimple in his chin, that voice that touched you like textured velvet rubbing against your skin.

"I'm going to kill this guy," Yash muttered and she hiccuped a sob-laugh.

It would appear she had her brother back, so there was that. "Stop it. The desi protective big brother thing doesn't suit you."

"I'm going to tear him limb from limb."

"Yuck. Is that a mobster impression?"

He laughed and his gray eyes twinkled. He rubbed her shoulder. "If you trust him, tell him. Tell him what Julia did if you need to."

Another pathetic sob escaped her. Leaning her head back, she used the sleeve of her scrubs to squeeze back the tears. "You sure?"

"Esha's right, the secret is what gives her power. She's not supposed to be talking about any of this, but she is because she knows we can't refute anything she says without acknowledging that it happened. At least in this one case we can take that power away from her."

"HRH will kill me. And fire DJ." She would never forgive herself if that happened. "You have to promise to not let HRH fire him. No matter what happens."

He didn't respond.

"Please, Yash."

"You think I can budge HRH on this?"

Was that even a question? "Come on, how long has Dad wanted this? You're giving him his dream. You can pretty much get him to do anything."

Yash laughed. "This is HRH we're talking about. None of us can ever do enough. I'll be president and he'll say, 'You know you can be more, beta!'" Yash had always done a spot-on HRH imitation.

He had a point. "Whatever happened to unconditional love?"

"His definition of love is pushing us to meet our potential. Unconditional love is an oxymoron to Ma and HRH."

It was her turn to laugh. "That explains our life, doesn't it?"

He wrapped his arm tighter around her. "It's a good life, giraffe. Because we have the Animal Farm."

"So you'll take care of it?"

He dropped a kiss on top of her head. "Oh, I'm definitely going to have to take care of it."

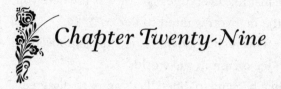

Chapter Twenty-Nine

Carmel-by-the-Sea was beautiful in a way that made DJ crave coming back to it again and again. He couldn't remember the last place he'd felt that pull from. Leaving London was tied up in too many painful mistakes and memories, and he had never had an interest in revisiting those. Paris had enchanted him, the way she did everyone. There was something about Paris that made you feel like you could forget who you were and become hers. But he was starting to realize that escaping who you were wasn't the same as becoming who you wanted to be.

Here, in Carmel, in California, in America, asking who he wanted to be finally seemed like a worthwhile pursuit. Everything and everyone here seemed free to ask that question. Even the places here felt like they still hadn't fully made up their mind about who they were. Even Carmel for all its old-world charm felt like it was aspiring to become something else from somewhere else.

"Why are you scowling at the ice cream?" His sister turned away from the sapphire-blue Pacific and mirrored his scowl.

It was stupid to let bad ice cream make you ponder the

meaning of home. What was home anyway? Was it somewhere you could be just like everyone else, or was it where you could be whoever the hell you wanted to be?

When he didn't answer, she elbowed him. "It's supposed to be some of the best ice cream in the world."

He handed it to her, begging to differ. "Let's agree to disagree."

Jane smiled from her perch on the beach chair where the sun shone off her mirrored rhinestone sunglasses. "Did you know that it was illegal to eat ice cream in public in Carmel until recently?"

"Until the late eighties when Clint Eastwood became mayor and freed the people from ice-cream jailing," DJ said.

"My brother is a food-trivia enthusiast," Emma said, when Jane looked impressed that he knew.

Naturally he'd done some research about what people ate when they came here. Didn't everyone look that kind of thing up before they visited a place? "Although Mr. Eastwood might have saved us the torture." He frowned at the cone that was fast disappearing in Emma's hands. "Let's go home and I'll make you some real ice cream that doesn't use sugar as a stand-in for flavor."

"How does one go through life only ever wanting to eat food they've cooked themselves?" his sister asked, laughing at him. The salty sea air lifted the strands of hair that had escaped her ponytail and framed her face in a cloud of curls, reminding him of a doll she had carried everywhere as a child.

"But going home sounds good. We might have to stop at the hospital first, though." Words he'd been dying to hear. He tried to hold it in, but a relieved breath still escaped him.

They had spent the morning at Jane's institute and Emma's resolve, which had already taken a severe blow after Trisha had gone full-scale philosopher on her yesterday, had crumbled within minutes of meeting Jane and seeing her work.

On their drive to Monterey that morning he'd also finally laid out what was in his heart. "You're all I have, Em, I can't lose you."

Emma being Emma had snorted. "Ship's sailed, innit, bruh'?"

"No it hasn't, you stubborn cow!" he'd said, finally losing it and yelling at his sick sister. "The ship is waiting for you back at the hospital. Don't you see? Don't you see the hole in our lives where Mum and Dad used to be? We've barely survived around that, and you want to do that to me again, because you're too bloody selfish to care? How will I get past it, you think? Yes, I could have stopped Mum from dying. Yes, I could have used my brain and stayed away from Gulshan and the boys. I'm sorry, all right? Don't punish me like this."

Her attempt to roll her eyes hadn't worked. "It's *my* life, Darcy," she'd said, sounding so very tired and terrified.

All the anger had drained from him. "Your life is never just yours, love. My life is tied to yours because I love you."

She'd snorted out a laugh, but for the first time since he got here she had tears in her eyes. "America's buggered with your head, hasn't it? I like you well enough, but don't get carried away with love and all."

He'd tugged her ponytail. "Give this a chance. Of course, I'll stand by whatever you choose, but just give it a fair shake, all right?"

Trisha had been right. Emma had needed to hear it almost

as much as he'd needed to say it. She had walked into the tactile art center with her defenses down and walked out of there with all her resolve torn up to bits.

After their visit, they'd driven Jane to Carmel for an appointment on their way back to Palo Alto, and she had insisted they try the ice cream. DJ suspected that Emma had laid a wager with her new best friend about how DJ would pitch a "Skinner from *Ratatouille* fit" after tasting any ice cream not made by him. He'd walked right into that trap, gladly. Because his ice cream was, indeed, better than this overly sweet travesty.

"I'm so glad Trisha came to see me and that I got to meet you," Jane said. "I've literally been looking for someone with art therapy experience to teach at the institute for two years now."

Emma laughed her big throaty laugh. "Are you actually cheering for my upcoming blindness?"

"I always did want to try out for the cheer team," Jane said, making sweeping movements with her arms and sending his sister into fits.

He couldn't have imagined anyone more irreverent than his sister, but now here was someone. "To Dr. Raje!" Jane held up her ice-cream cone in a toast and Emma tapped her cone against it in cheers. Both women gulped down the rest of their ice cream.

Discomfort shifted inside DJ. It did feel like Trisha had been saving the day all over the place. He sat up, a thought that had been jabbing at his conscience finally solidifying into shape. "When did Trisha come to see you, Jane?" he asked, his heart beating in a way it only seemed to beat when the good doctor was in question.

"Thursday afternoon."

Her words landed like a kick to his ball bag.

Thursday was when they'd had that disastrous encounter at Naomi's café.

"Are you sure it was the afternoon?" he asked.

"Dude, I may be blind but I'm very attached to my Braille watch." She held up her wrist. "Our appointment was for four in the afternoon. She was exactly on time."

Everything around him seemed to slow.

Jane stood. "Speaking of appointments, I've got to go. Mine is probably already here."

Emma jumped up from her beach chair. "I'll walk with you there. I need to use the loo."

DJ said good-bye to Jane, his heart still pounding. Trisha had gone to see Jane right after she'd met him? Right after he'd shredded her to pieces. He thought about her leaving the café, the paper bag clutched to her belly. And she had sat in her car and driven to meet Jane, to find his sister a solution.

Strange thing was, he could imagine her doing it. Going to see Jane for Emma after he'd been a giant git, the idea of hurting him after he'd hurt her not even striking her.

He squeezed the bridge of his nose. A headache was starting between his brows. Every single thing the woman had ever done wouldn't stop playing in his head. All the words she'd ever said wouldn't stop ringing in his ears. All she'd done to help Emma, and Nisha, and Ashna, and him, too, actually.

His phone beeped; he saw a couple of emails from Nisha— they'd been trying to sort out whether to go with ceviche or escabeche—and a missed call from Trisha. She had never called him before. She left fund-raiser business to Nisha and him. Something about working with food freaked her out. Suddenly he wanted to know how she'd been burned. And he wanted to know why she'd called him.

He watched as Jane and Emma disappeared into the ice-cream shop, chattering away, and Emma threw her head back and laughed at something Jane said. DJ found himself smiling too.

He responded to Nisha's emails first, letting her know that mango and shrimp escabeche it would be, because, yes, ceviche was becoming a bit of a cliché.

Then he tapped Trisha's number, the strangest sensation bouncing in the pit of his stomach.

For a few rings nothing happened. He almost disconnected. But then she answered, clearing her throat before getting out a breathless "Hello?"

He could see her so clearly in his head. All the anticipation on her face creating a strange kind of unguardedness, and he had to rack his brains to conjure up that arrogance he'd held on to so tightly. "I had a missed call."

"Yes. Um . . . Are you in Carmel?"

His surprise stole his voice.

"Sorry. I can hear the ocean. And I knew you had an appointment with Jane." She sounded terribly apologetic. The thought that he'd done that to her, caused her to sound like she constantly had something to defend, made discomfort stab inside him again. "How's Emma? Did she fall under Jane's spell yet?"

He had to smile at that. "It's impossible not to, isn't it? Dr. Raje . . . Trisha, thank you. I don't know how to—"

"DJ, please, before you say anything, I have something I need to tell you. About Julia . . ." His hand tightened around the phone. "You were right, you deserve to hear the other side of whatever she told you."

"I thought you couldn't talk about it." He didn't want her breaking confidences and suddenly he didn't want her sounding like this, as though she'd found herself in a corner with nowhere to go.

"I talked to Yash. He thinks you should know. But, please, this has to stay between us."

He sat up on the beach chair. "You don't have to—"

"No, please, hear me out."

"Okay."

There was a long pause; he imagined her neck stretching as she swallowed and steeled herself. "As I've mentioned before, my family is very aware of the gifts we've been given and I swear we do our best to use them to do good. It's all we were ever taught. But we were also taught that the world isn't forgiving to those who want to change things. Trusting people outside of the family is not one of our strengths." There was another pause.

Then she went on. "My greatest lesson in this came from Julia. She and I were roommates at Berkeley. Yash had just graduated from law school and was working for the then U.S. Attorney for Northern California. At the end of our freshman year, he came to Berkeley to speak at the law school. Julia went with me to listen to his speech, and she was instantly smitten.

"The first thing I remember her saying when she saw him onstage was, 'How does anyone in the U.S. Attorney's office

ever get any work done with him around?' I was used to that
reaction. I had heard some form of it all my life. Even back
then Yash was mesmerizing to listen to. If you've heard him
give a speech, you know that anytime he takes the podium—he
makes magic.

"It's his ability to let people into his mind, which happens
to be beautiful and brilliant. Listening to him even if you're in
a room full of people feels like being alone with him. It feels
like being in the presence of someone who has the power to
understand every problem, break it down, and make it disappear. He's always had it. That combination of intellect, humil-
ity, and an insatiable need to care and serve. Every time I hear
my brother speak, I believe in the world again.

"His speech was about the history of the role of the judi-
ciary in social programs and the responsibility of democratic
governments toward those in need of assistance. Naturally the
subject matter only helped mesmerize Julia. After the speech,
Yash took us out to dinner. From the way she hung on to his
every word, it was clear that she had it bad.

"Julia was the first real friend I ever made. Through school
there had hardly been any time for friends and having five
siblings and cousins in the house meant never really feeling
the need for friends. The first time in my life that I remember
being lonely was that first week at Berkeley. Then Julia showed
up with her bright smile and easy humor.

"She had grown up in the California heartland in a town
called Hesperia. I didn't find out until after the private investigators came into it that she had worked for an old people's
home through high school and that there were a few cases

against her by families of patients for theft and pressuring patients to change their wills. But charm wasn't fraud and she had never been convicted.

"She has a vulture's instinct when it comes to identifying your vulnerabilities and filling them up until you let her in. In me she saw someone who was such a part of something that there was never anything that was just mine. She became that, a friend who was just mine. I loved having a friend whose family was not friends with mine, who didn't even know who my family was. She was the first person I knew who saw me only as an individual and still acted as though I was cool and funny and enough. And I let the headiness of that put my brother at risk.

"She was so inspired by Yash's speech that she switched to prelaw. Then she started pushing me to get him to take her on as an intern. Yash has been engaged—or at least betrothed—to his childhood friend Naina for many years. I told Julia this. I had started to get uncomfortable with how obsessed she was getting. I tried to make her see sense. When she acted like she got it, I believed her.

"Then one day, without telling me, she used my computer to email Yash as me from my account, asking him to employ her.

"The awful part, the part that I will never forgive myself for, is that after I found out that she had impersonated me to my brother, instead of going to him, I confronted her, because I didn't want to lose her friendship. She apologized and begged me to let her have this opportunity, told me I was like a sister to her, that she needed my help because she had no one else and that she wanted this internship more than she had ever wanted anything in her life. And I let it go. I didn't tell my brother.

"I let him give her that internship, when I knew in my gut that something was very wrong. I put him at risk, knowingly." She stopped. Somewhere during the course of the conversation, her voice had become so choked up that DJ wanted to say something to make it better. But something told him she needed to get this out, so he stayed silent.

"No one outside of our family and Yash's most trusted political aides know this next part." Again he almost told her she didn't need to tell him. But she'd chosen to tell him, and he knew she hadn't done that lightly, given how much guilt she carried about it, and he couldn't stop her.

"I'm listening." That was all he said.

With a quiet sniff she went on. "A week into her internship she took him to a bar under the pretext of meeting me and discussing some problems I was supposedly struggling with at school. There, while they waited for me because I was 'late' she drugged Yash's drink. Then she taped them having sex. She was seventeen—both of us had graduated from high school early—and he was twenty-three and she worked for him.

"Her intent at that point had been to send the video to his girlfriend so she would break up with him. Naina isn't just Yash's girlfriend, she's the daughter of close family friends. She's family. Naina took the video to Yash. She . . . she did what I hadn't done. She did the right thing. Yash was running for San Francisco alderman then. It was his first campaign. We all knew that it wasn't going to be his last. It's a joke in our family that my dad had a road map planned out for all Yash's future campaigns since before he learned to walk. Except, it's not really a joke.

"The footage could have destroyed everything. My family hired the best private investigators. They dug up all sorts of dirt on her. They threatened her with ruin and gave her the option to transfer from Berkeley elsewhere. As long as she never came back to California and never mentioned Yash again. She signed the papers, took an insane sum of money, and disappeared for the past fifteen years.

"And now, when Yash has just announced his candidacy, she's back in town. I know that it's a free country, but she's been looking for patients in my department's waiting room. If you believe her intention is innocent, it's your prerogative. But please, please be careful."

He stood, too restless to stay in the chair. In front of him the ocean churned. "I don't know what to say." Except that, yes, Julia had found him in the waiting room. But he was too embarrassed to say it.

"I'm sorry. This is a lot to dump on you, and I know how horribly selfish what I did was. But you should also know that I regret it every day."

He paced toward the beach. *How is this your fault?* he wanted to ask her. But he understood exactly how she had convinced herself that it was. That moment when Mum had collapsed when the detectives had picked him up for questioning blazed to life in his head. Her brother was running for governor. Julia could ruin that.

Of course her family would fire him if they found out. And she'd warned him over and over again. God, what had it cost her? "What about the dinner?" he asked. As soon as he said it he realized how self-serving it sounded. He was about to clarify that he wouldn't blame her if her family decided not to let him do it when he heard a loud knocking on her side of the line.

"I'm so sorry; I have to go," she said, sounding alarmed, and before he could finish asking what the matter was, she hung up.

JUST AS TRISHA disconnected the phone her office door flew open.

"I'm having a hard time believing how your mother and I raised someone as irresponsible as you." HRH in all his HRH glory stormed into her office. For the first time in her life.

"Hi, Dad. Come on in," she mumbled as he shut the door behind him, making it feel like he'd slammed it even though he hadn't.

"Everything's a joke to you. That's the problem."

Right, that was definitely her problem, when her father had called her irresponsible loud enough that everyone up and down the hallway might have heard. *Ha ha, Dad.*

He walked straight to her desk, placed both hands on it, and leaned forward, rage and disappointment spilling from him. Trisha shrank back into her chair. She had never in her life shrunk away from her father. But then, she'd never in her life seen him like this.

"You knew that the chef catering Yash's fund-raiser is going out with that woman, and you did not bother to inform me!"

DJ was dating Julia? What the hell?

"He's not . . . I don't . . ."

"And you go running to your brother? After barely giving a damn about what he's been up to for fifteen years, you go to him and tell him to look the other way? What the hell is wrong with you? And you're letting your patients do video documentaries with her? Would you also like to invite her into our home so she can drug and screw us all?"

Trisha winced. She had seen her father angry a lot, but she'd never heard him swear and she'd certainly never heard him be crass.

"You will drop that patient. You will recuse yourself of the case and pass it on to Entoff. I've spoken to him."

Trisha stood. Her hands slammed on the desk, exactly the way HRH's had. "You spoke to my boss about my work?"

They were eye to eye. "I don't care about your work. I care that you do not mess up your brother's life yet again because you can't think about anyone but yourself. How many times did I warn you?" He gave her another incredulous glare, then finally he turned away, as though looking at her was no longer bearable. Then he spun back around. "You're not seventeen anymore. Getting involved with the wrong people and then letting the rest of the family suffer the brunt is no longer acceptable. No more, Trisha. You will not work with this patient and that's that."

"Dad! You know I can't do that. I won't do that."

He pressed his hand into his forehead, and she found herself mirroring the action. "Entoff is fully capable of doing the surgery. He has twenty years on you. And much as you don't see it, experience counts. Some of us choose to learn from it."

She met his eyes squarely. "You are right; experience does

count. I made a mistake when I was seventeen years old. I am no longer seventeen. I know what I'm doing. She is my patient. She has nothing to do with any of this. I will be the one operating on her."

His face darkened. The very room seemed to darken. "You will not work with a patient who is working with that woman. It's too dangerous, it's too close to the campaign. I won't argue this with you. This is not a choice. It's too late for that. You will listen to me or you will not set foot in my home ever again."

Her knees buckled and her hands tightened on the desk. But she couldn't move, couldn't sit back in her chair. "You don't mean that."

"Do I look like I don't mean it? The *Chronicle* is already trying to make the fact that Naina and he haven't married after being together for so long an issue; they're digging around for something sordid in his past. And now this woman is back, and her work depends on getting attention, and speaking about Yash and our family will give her all the attention she needs. Did I teach you nothing? Do the right thing, for God's sake." With that he headed for the door. "I'm not making empty threats, Trisha. The Anchorage is my home, this is my family. If you choose to continue to be callous, you can do it where I don't have to watch you do it."

And just like that he was gone, the soft click of the door behind him feeling like another slam.

She collapsed into her chair. Could any more shit possibly blow up?

The second she'd formed the thought she knew she shouldn't have because this was not the time to tempt fate.

Her phone rang and it was DJ. She had hung up on him just as he'd asked about the dinner. Naturally, that was the part he cared about. But she didn't have an answer for him, especially now. Despite all good sense telling her to let the call go to voice mail, she took it, because it was DJ and Emma was her patient.

"It's Emma," he said, his voice shaking. "She collapsed in the bathroom when we were . . . when we were talking."

"Where are you right now?" *Please be in an ambulance, please.*

"In an ambulance. She was fine, she was laughing. She . . ."

"DJ," she said as gently as she could, "is she conscious?"

"Yes, but she . . . the pain. It seems awful . . . Her head . . . They have her hooked up to an IV . . . They're giving her something."

Trisha left her office and headed for Anne's desk. "Is there a paramedic near you? Can you put them on?"

"Emma's doctor wants to speak to you," he said to someone.

Trisha got an update from the paramedic and made sure they were bringing Emma straight to Stanford. They tried to tell her that they had to take her to the closest hospital. It took her another five minutes to make sure they did no such thing. "I will get authorization from your dispatch. But this patient has an astrocytoma that I am very closely familiar with. We may not have time for another doctor to get the images and get familiarized with the case. If the patient does not come straight here, you will be responsible for the outcome and it will not be a good one." She was barking orders, but this was not open to discussion.

Anne stood when she saw Trisha approach. Trisha scribbled the name of the ambulance company on a notepad for Anne. "Call them and make sure they're routed here."

Anne nodded and was on it.

"You have to make sure they come straight to Stanford," she told DJ when he got back on the phone. "Now tell me exactly what happened."

DJ walked her through it. They had met Jane, and Emma had been in a really good mood. Then she'd gone to use the restroom while he'd been speaking to Trisha. When Trisha hung up, he went to see why it was taking so long. Someone came running out of the bathroom and said Emma had passed out in there. She had regained consciousness, but she'd woken up with an unbearable headache. Yes, she was still coherent. No, she hadn't thrown up. Yes, she knew her name. Yes, she knew what day of the week it was. She had asked to be taken to Trisha. Over and over again.

This was good news. This meant Emma was going to have the surgery. Please, please let it mean that. And please, please let it still be possible to perform the surgery.

"Hang in there," she said. "I'll be waiting for her when you get in. They'll bring you straight into the ER."

EMMA WAS CONSCIOUS when they brought her in. But there was almost certainly a bleed in her brain. The OR was already prepped and the anesthesiologist and the team were waiting.

"There's something I need to say before you put me under." Emma grabbed her hand and Trisha turned her focus to her. "I want you to save my life, to remove the tumor. And if you can't now, if it's too late, I want you to know that I'm grateful for how hard you tried."

Trisha leaned over and hugged her. "Thank you. I'm going to do everything I can. You're going to be painting vaginas destroying things for a long time. Or maybe sculpting them. Vaginas destroying things in 3-D? I cannot wait to see what you do."

Emma grinned. "You bet. I have all sorts of ideas popping in my head for pieces. I'm thinking: mixed media, wrought-iron work mixed in with my canvases. The breaking of chains around physical abilities, that sort of thing."

"Navigating limitations but not as boundaries. I like it."

"See, she gets it," Emma said to her brother. He smiled through his tears and Trisha, despite all good sense, gave his arm a squeeze.

"Seriously, Dr. Raje," Emma said. "You have no idea how grateful I am. I will literally carry your bags around for you for the rest of your life if you ask."

"That's a tempting offer. I do hate carrying bags."

Emma actually got wistful. "Really? I love my bags."

"You should meet my sister."

Emma grinned. Then she turned to her brother and took his hand. "It was not your fault. Mum would have had that stroke, anyway, at work or somewhere else. It wasn't your fault."

He nodded.

"It's not always about you, knobhead. But I do love you."

"You're the best thing in my life," he said simply before dropping a kiss on her forehead, holding on for a few seconds, and letting the nurse lead him away.

Dr. Entoff met her outside the OR. "You don't have to do the surgery. I can handle it. You can observe if you like."

To quote DJ: *Was he bloody joking?* "This is my patient, Dr. Entoff. You'll have to fire me to keep me from doing this surgery."

He squeezed her shoulder. "It's one case."

Entoff loved to tell the story of how she'd organized that mission of doctors when she was thirteen. "Do you know why I chose neurosurgery, sir? Because the mission we organized to perform those surgeries couldn't help the patients with neurogenic blindness. So this isn't one case—it's the reason I became a doctor."

And no one was going to keep her from going into that OR.

Entoff pushed the button that opened the OR doors. "After you, Dr. Raje," he said.

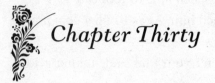

Chapter Thirty

Every hospital waiting room in the world had to have been designed by the same architect because hell if they didn't feel exactly the same. They even breathed the same way. Had the same pulse. DJ's mother had been in the ICU for four days before she had passed and Emma and he hadn't left the waiting room that entire time except when they were by her side. And now here he was again, and it felt as though he'd never left.

That probably wasn't the best train of thought right now, but he hated being here alone, sitting on the floral couches, staring at the single potted plant and the generic painting with the stone house surrounded by a profusion of flowers.

He'd been in the waiting room for four hours. Someone from the surgical team had come out every so often and filled him in. There wasn't any new information, but every time they told him that Emma was stable he felt every bit of life rush back into his limbs.

A little after the four-hour mark, Ashna came in.

"How did you know I was here?" he asked her.

"Trisha had the nurse call me," she said, pouring him a steaming cup of her legendary chai out of a flask. The woman could do things with ginger and cardamom and tea leaves that left him in awe. He had never been able to replicate it.

Thinking about work calmed him. A taste of her chai practically tranquilized him.

"You put crack in this, don't you?" he said, taking a long satisfying sip.

Someone else had said similar words to him about his curried stew. Someone who had eyes much like the woman who put her head on his shoulder and let him drink.

"I'm going to take that as a compliment, Chef Caine," she said, making something an awful lot like hypocrisy prick at his conscience.

When he was done with his chai, he filled Ashna in on how they'd ended up here after their trip to Monterey.

"It's beautiful, isn't it? My family owns a beach house there. I feel like I spent all my weekends there growing up." She studied him with her usual calm expression. Her eyes were the same shape as Trisha's, large, heavy lidded, and turned up at the ends. But Trisha's were that unique brown and amber, like the fiery licks of flames. And Ashna's were guarded. She could blank them out so you only saw what she wanted you to see. Trisha could blank nothing out. Everything she was feeling leapt out of her eyes.

"Isn't Naomi's café something else? A world in itself. The way every restaurant should be." There was the distinct burn of envy in her voice. It was the chef's burn—that particular grudging note chefs got when they praised each other's work or restaurants.

"It's beautiful," he said, the disaster with Trisha that had taken place in their friend's beautiful café doing a slow-motion replay in his head.

Ashna smiled, albeit a little despondently.

DJ couldn't understand why Ashna's own restaurant was having such a hard time. She was incredibly talented.

"How's the response to the new specials been?" he asked. Ashna was supposed to have test-driven some of his new recipes this week.

She brightened. "Fabulous! We've seen a few people come in a few times this week for the okra and the tilapia. And the Yelp ratings have jumped." Then she got somber again. "I just hope it lasts."

"It will, love. This is just the beginning." He was going to do all he could to help her turn Curried Dreams around.

They spent the next half hour discussing menus. Having Ashna here was exactly what he needed right now and he couldn't stop telling her that.

"Emma will be fine, DJ. I'm really glad you were able to convince her to have the surgery."

"Actually, I wasn't the one who convinced her. Your cousin Trisha . . . she . . . she figured out exactly what Emma was afraid of and . . ." God, what an idiot he'd been.

Ashna studied him, her usually distant gaze probing. "That sounds like Trisha. She's the solver in the family. It's that brain of hers. Sees everything in all its parts and pieces and knows how to break problems down and put them back together as solutions. Emma is in great hands with her. Truly."

For everything he had accused Trisha of, that much he'd always known. That much he'd never doubted. For all the sad-

ness and worry pressing against his chest, he smiled. Ashna
gave him another quick sideways hug.

"You really should let me pay you for the menu consulta-
tion. Especially if it's going to get these results."

"Actually, that would mean I'd have to pay you for the
kitchen." They'd decided that he would use her kitchen overnight and early in the morning, before the renter came in.
At least until he could afford to pay her rent or find another
place. That way she could still make money on it and he'd still
have a prep place.

"Barter then," she said, and they shook on it.

Ashna sat with him for the next six hours, comfortable silences interspersed with comforting conversation. Finally, ten
hours after Emma had gone into surgery, she turned to him. "I
have to run out and take care of closing up. Will you be okay?
I'll come back after."

"Of course. I'll be fine." As long as his little sister was all
right, he would be all right.

She stopped in the doorway on her way out and turned to
him. "I meant what I said about Trisha earlier, DJ. This isn't
just a job to her. I know she's hard to understand sometimes.
But she's not what she seems to be. Do you know what I'm
saying? She won't let a patient down. She won't let anyone
down. It would kill her. She is the most dependable person I
know. I just thought you should know that."

He nodded. Had Trisha told her sisters what had happened
at Naomi's? The idea that Ashna and Nisha might know how
he had behaved was more than a little embarrassing.

Something told him she hadn't told her sisters. For all the

uncertainty he was filled with right now, the only things he felt certain about seemed to have to do with her.

"Thank you," he said and he must have looked really pathetic because she came back inside and pulled him into a hug.

TRISHA LOVED HER cousin like a sister. Truly, she did. But the kick of envy in her gut at seeing DJ holding Ashna made her want to fold over.

After ten hours of destroying a tumor lodged deeply into brain tissue, one cell at a time, she was bursting with adrenaline. Surgery never exhausted her. It wiped her mind clean of everything else but her patient, and that put her in a place she couldn't describe with words. She felt hollowed out yet full. Like she carried everything, yet nothing weighed her down.

Now here she was, out of the OR, and everything she'd left outside it came crashing down on her—the way DJ felt about her, the fact that HRH had disowned her. Had that been real? A wave of panic washed over her.

Looking at DJ, she knew she had made the right decision. The way everything inside her melted into a pool of wanting when she was near him had nothing to do with her decision to go ahead with the surgery. A man getting to keep the only family he had—that had everything to do with it. It didn't matter who the man was. This was why she did what she did. This is what she had wanted with a singular obsession all her life. HRH had taught her too well. If he'd lost sight of what was important because his ambitions were under threat, that wasn't Trisha's problem.

The excitement of telling DJ that the surgery had been a

success and that his sister was stable had felt uncontainable moments ago. No, it still felt uncontainable. It wasn't going to be ruined by how badly she wanted to hold him the way Ashna was doing right now. He deserved his peace wherever he got it. Sitting by yourself in a hospital with no idea if someone you loved would survive was not something she wished upon anyone.

She remembered sitting in the waiting room while Yash underwent surgery. Nisha's tight grip on one hand and Ashna's on the other was what had gotten her through it.

DJ looked up from Ashna's shoulder. His eyes darkened with awareness, mixed in with a whole slew of other emotions she couldn't name. He pulled away from Ashna and blasted Trisha with the desperate question in his eyes.

"We got the tumor—all of it," she said, fighting hard to keep her voice professional. "Emma is stable." It was hard forcing herself to not imagine scenarios where he'd suddenly realize he was in love with her and fly into her arms. "The next twenty-four hours are critical. But everything looks good."

"That's great!" her cousin said, beaming.

She smiled back, but she couldn't look away from DJ's eyes. There was such relief there that in that moment it was just the two of them in the room.

"Can I see her?" he said, his voice hoarse with emotion.

"They're setting her up in post-op. A nurse will come and get you when she's ready. It will be a while before she wakes up, maybe even a day. I . . ." Ashna's gaze on her suddenly made her feel naked. "I can come by later and fill you in on the details and answer questions." Her voice sounded professional enough, but Ashi's eyes were getting more and more knowing.

Then again, having a nurse call Ashna in the middle of surgery to tell her that DJ was by himself in the waiting room had been akin to confessing all her feelings for him anyway.

The idea of her family seeing how she felt about him was horrifying. There was no way she could bear their sympathy. So she had no idea what came over her when she reached out as though to take his hand, and then halfway through withdrew it because suddenly she didn't want to touch him. Not with Ashna's concerned eyes watching her as though she were a puppy hit by a car with no hope of recovery.

His hand hung midair as she turned around and hurried out of the room.

God, when would she stop being such a dimwit around him?

When she'd left the OR, she had felt powerful. Then she'd seen him and the sight had hit her like a full-body blow and now all she wanted was to attach herself to him like a leech.

She pictured him plucking off the leech and flicking it into the air. Turning down the empty corridor, she thumped her head against the wall, giving in to an urge that was becoming as habitual as not being able to keep her shit together when it came to DJ *bloody* Caine! A nurse scurried past, working hard to avoid eye contact. Maybe Trisha just needed to move away. To the moon, or maybe Mars. What was the holdup with colonizing planets anyway?

She pulled herself together, got some coffee, and without waiting to think about it stepped into Entoff's office. Maybe she couldn't move to Mars, but she could talk her boss into helping her get away for a while. There was a team of surgeons traveling to Africa this week to train the surgeons there on a new technology. Even if she had to beg, she was getting on that team.

BY THE TIME she got to her patient rounds, she was feeling human again. As she spoke to patients and their families, the storm inside her stilled. Was it really obnoxious to know you were good at your job? To love it so much it actually helped soothe your broken heart?

As she strode down the hallway, she thought about DJ in Nisha's kitchen, arranging delicate, thinly sliced pieces of chicken as though they were butterfly wings. Her steps faltered.

He was right, the obnoxious part wasn't loving her own work; it was seeing other people's love for their work as somehow less important.

That first day she'd seen him he'd used his bare hands to straighten a boiling pot. It had seemed crazy to her then, but she understood it now. Had she known the magic he made with food, she might have risked her own hands for that caramel, too. Oh, what she wouldn't do to turn the clock back to that day.

Her response had been to ask him if he knew how valuable her hands were. God, what the hell was wrong with her?

I've never dated anyone who hasn't been to college.

He had gone to college with Ashi! How the hell had that slipped her mind? She knew how hard Ashi had worked to get into Le Cordon Bleu.

No wonder the man thought her self-absorbed and arrogant.

She wrapped her arms around herself. Squeezing herself tight did nothing to stem the leaky pain inside her. The truth was, he was right about many things—things she could change, like how she treated people. He was also wrong about a few—things she could not change, like who she was.

Emma's room was not on her way to her office, but her feet, stupid as they were, took the scenic route. And scenic it was, because as she approached Emma's room, she saw DJ's tall form looming over the nurses' station. Seriously, if you cooked food the way he did, you had absolutely no business looking like an athlete. *That* was what was obnoxious.

He started to turn and without thinking about it, she dived into a random room. Yes, she was hiding again, because once you lost your self-respect, you realized it was a burden in the first place.

Actually, it wasn't. She would very much like it back. But that battle was lost, because she peeped out of the thankfully empty room and watched as DJ made his way to Emma's. Maybe it was the fact that she hadn't slept in twenty-four hours, but the sight of him made her want to weep. All her exhaustion gathered inside her in one fell swoop. He looked so incredibly sad, and beautiful. All she wanted was to go sit by him, hold his hand, tell him everything was going to be okay. And maybe smell his neck.

A long, deep, incredibly pathetic sigh emanated from her. It was time to take herself home. Thinking about home made her want to weep even more. Had her father really banished her? In so many words this time. Wasn't banishment outlawed when electricity was invented? She needed to call her mother and beg. No, not beg, but yell at her for never standing up to HRH's high-handedness. She for one was done with it.

WHEN TRISHA FINALLY left the hospital, she could barely feel her extremities, from exhaustion and sleep deprivation. Fortunately, the drive home was less than one mile.

The longing for her bed, her beautiful bed, was a physical ache. Before she got to her car Aretha belted out of her phone. Nisha.

Trisha hesitated a moment—she'd be home in a few minutes—but something made her answer.

"I'm at the hospital," Nisha said, and Trisha started to jog through the parking garage.

"I'm on my way. Are you in Sarita's office?"

"Yes. But I'm fine. I thought I had contractions. I tried to call you. But you were in surgery. So I called an ambulance."

Oh God. "I'm so sorr—"

"No! Stop it! Do not say that word. I'm fine. It was just me being paranoid."

"You were being safe. Safe is good. I'm picking you up." In another five minutes, she found her sister waiting for her outside her OB's office.

Trisha was so exhausted she could barely keep her eyes open. So she gladly let Nisha take the wheel.

"Sarita says I need to stop hiding out in your condo and start to move about. She wants me to be brave." Nisha laughed while saying it but with sleep trying to wrap itself around Trisha as she fought it, the sound felt distorted.

"Are you high?" her sister asked.

"Have barely slept a few hours in the last forty. It feels like an acid trip."

"When did you do acid?"

"Well, I feel like I've done it now." She was definitely slurring, and her words tasted slurpy. "Neel came to my office. Sarita is right. You should be brave."

Nisha swerved into a parking spot across the street from Trisha's condo. Which was not a good place to swerve into given that it was a parking spot. "What the hell do you mean Neel came to your office?"

Trisha scratched her head. "I think I mean he came to see me."

Her sister was probably giving her the Glare of Elegance. She couldn't tell because her eyes wouldn't open. She lifted them with her fingers. "He wanted to know where you were. Can you carry me up to bed?"

"He already knew where I was. Or he knew where I was supposed to be. What are you not telling me?"

"Nothing. He was just concerned. He wanted to make sure you weren't gone because you were upset."

Nisha didn't respond and this was not a conversation Trisha could fall asleep in the middle of, so she sat up and tried to blink her eyes open. Her sister was crying again and trying to pretend like she wasn't. Trisha wiped her cheek clumsily.

"I spoke with Mishka. She told me that she met, you know—"

"The evil ex-Barbara," Trisha supplied.

"You knew."

Trisha was tired enough to deny it. But she couldn't.

"How could you not tell me?"

"Tell you what?"

"That my husband went out with his ex."

Trisha rubbed her eyes. "Are you listening to yourself, Nisha? She's his *ex*. E X. It's Neel. The guy worships the ground you walk on. He paints your toenails! He sits through Ma's postmortems. He massages Aji's feet when she's tired. Takes Mishka on dad evenings. Carries fashion emergency stashes for me because I can't pick my own clothes out. He hasn't ever hurt you or anyone in the family by word or action. Ever. Why isn't that enough? What more do you want him to do? You might have seen him cry over someone ten years ago, but I saw him cry over hurting you today. And if anyone ever felt that way about me, I'd be brave enough to believe it."

Great, now she'd made her pregnant sister cry even more. She reached out and touched Nisha's shoulder. "Listen, remember how you told me that sometimes you have to be brave and put yourself out there? You also have to be brave to accept what you have, even if you're terrified of losing it. Because not everyone gets what they want in the first place."

Here she was delivering a long speech even though she was tired enough to pass out, and Nisha wasn't even paying attention. She was staring openmouthed over Trisha's shoulder. "Is there someone on your balcony?"

Trisha spun around and followed her gaze. Yipes! There really was someone on her balcony. A burst of adrenaline broke through her drowsiness and she jumped out of the car.

Nisha followed her out. "Neel?" Nisha shouted up at him. "What are you doing on Trisha's balcony? And what's wrong with your arm?"

He waved with his left hand. His right hand was hugged

to his side at an awkward angle. "Can you come up and let me in? I think I've dislocated my shoulder. I climbed up the balcony to see you."

Nisha ran into the building, Trisha close on her heels.

"Slow down, Nisha. The baby."

"Shhh," Nisha shushed her and they made their way up in the elevator to the second floor. Trisha thanked the gods for the day she had decided not to wait for the fourth-floor condo to become available.

No one ever talks about how weird it is to see your siblings making out with someone. Almost as weird as watching your parents do it.

Nisha and Neel wouldn't stop kissing.

Which had to be hard to do with a dislocated shoulder. Which apparently was easy to do when you tried to climb up to a second-floor balcony when you were pushing forty. Trisha didn't say that to him, though. Or maybe she did. Also, he'd done it with two dozen roses stuck down the back of his shirt. Those things had thorns!

When Neel tried to prove a point, he really tried to prove a point.

"It's only you for me," he said to Nisha. "Please don't shut me out."

That made Nisha cry again. Trisha too sniffed into one of the last remaining tissues in her home. Then Nisha told him she was pregnant. Thank God.

"I swear I was not trying," she said sniffling into his shoulder, the one that wasn't dislocated. "It just happened."

Since they were being gross and swapping tongues again, Trisha left them in her room and threw herself onto the futon in her office.

"Nisha, sweetheart. I know. This is . . . it's great. Why didn't you just tell me? I would've come back," she heard her favorite brother-in-law in the whole wide world say from the next room.

"I didn't want you to come back. I didn't want you to even know for another few days. But it's . . . it's almost safe. In two days it will be safe."

"It's going to be okay, baby. We have each other. We have Mishka. We have the Farm. It's going to be okay."

Then silence, which meant they were tongue swapping again.

"Go get his shoulder looked at," Trisha shouted. It was the last thing she remembered doing before she fell into a boneless sleep.

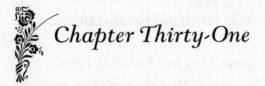

Chapter Thirty-One

When Trisha woke up the next morning, Nisha was gone. Which felt strange. Having someone stay with you for two weeks altered your routines. She automatically pulled two cups out of the cabinet before popping her pod in the coffee machine, then put one back. For the first time in her adult life the idea of being alone made her lonely.

Nisha had left a sticky note on the machine saying "Went home with a hot judge. Go back to bed, you need sleep."

She texted her sister to check if all was well and then opened her fridge and stared at its contents. Would she ever be able to think about food without thinking about DJ? Would she ever be able to do anything without thinking about DJ?

It was her day off, but of course she was going to go in to the hospital. She had to take care of things before she left for Africa—naturally she'd been able to talk Entoff into letting her go—and make sure everything with Emma was in order before she got on that plane. It wasn't the thought of seeing Emma, however, that was making her heart chirrup like the myna birds in the Sagar Mahal aviary.

Her intercom buzzed and she jumped off her barstool in fright. She wasn't expecting anyone.

"Will you let your mother in? Or do I have to call ahead like some stranger?"

Trisha's mouth fell open. What was Ma doing here?

"Depends on what you want, Ma," she said, but of course she buzzed her in immediately.

Ma walked in imperiously, handed Trisha coffee and chocolate-blueberry muffins, and surveyed the condo while patting her perfectly fitted top tucked into her perfectly fitted white linen pants. "You've done a good job with the place."

"Well, Nisha has." Nisha had helped Trisha with the furnishing, but Trisha had bought all the art herself. She, in fact, might need to stop buying art soon. Five new Emma Caines had been delivered last week. She was running out of wall space to put things up.

"What is wrong with you, Trisha?" her mother said staring at the massive canvas over the fireplace.

"You don't like it?" Trisha said dryly, knowing full well that Ma was not talking about the painting.

Ma went on as though Trisha had not spoken. "What do you mean by planning a trip to Malawi when Yash has his fund-raiser?"

So HRH had not told her about the banishment. And Vansh had told Ma about her upcoming trip, because he was the only one Trisha had told. She was going to have to box his snitch ears.

"They needed someone to run workshops on one of our procedures."

"And you're the only one who can teach this workshop?"

Actually, she'd had to beg Entoff to let her go instead of him. "Yes."

Her mother gave her the original version of the Glare of Elegance and took a sip of her coffee.

"Also, I'm not invited to the fund-raiser. His Royal Highness Shree Hari Raje disowned me. I'm not welcome at the Anchorage anymore, which I guess means I'm not welcome at family dos anymore either." She sat down on a barstool and gave the muffin her mother had put in front of her the stink eye.

Ma's hand went to her mouth. "What did you do now?"

Was Ma serious? Trisha almost didn't respond. But she was too tired of holding in things she wanted to say. "Other than treat a patient who needed my care? I'm not sure. Why don't you ask him? You'll only ever believe him anyway."

"What is that supposed to mean? Of course I'll talk to him."

"Sure. And that should set everything straight. Because he always listens to you, right?"

Ma looked outraged. As though she couldn't imagine what Trisha meant.

"Come on, Ma. Why do you have to act like you're always on the exact same page as him? Would it be so bad to admit that you differ on things? Shouldn't that be okay in a marriage?"

"Differ? Whatever on?"

"Well, for starters on things like having to raise us as though our Indian heritage was something to hide. Like always following his lead on everything."

Ma walked to the iPod dock and turned it off. The tranquil rhythms of Zakir Hussain's tabla stopped, creating a vacuum of silence. She turned around and looked at the painting over the fireplace—a circle of women doing the ghoomar in the sands of Rajasthan. "Need I open the fridge to find the stash of Ashi's kababs and bhajis?"

Trisha stared at her, feeling like a bit of an idiot.

"You spent every summer while you were growing up in Sripore. You work at Stanford. Your ancestors were maharajas. Your brother is running for governor of California. Which of those two identities is you? Only one of them? We didn't want our children to pick just one. We wanted you to own both. That's how we raised you, to honor everything, to choose what felt right for you. To not conform to stereotypes anyone else assigned to you."

Trisha took a grudging bite of her muffin, unable to respond to that.

How can you act so white?

When DJ had asked her that, she had wondered why being comfortable in your skin was "acting white." But of course she knew why. Of course she understood the norms of her country, and his, and perceptions and privilege. But Ma was right, Trisha's comfort in her identity came from the fact that Ma and HRH had consciously owned both their identities and insisted on their children owning theirs.

"Your father is the most fair man in the world."

Trisha choked on her muffin, which gave her the opportunity to spit the vile thing out into a napkin and throw it in the garbage. Ma might have had a point just now, but this was pushing it.

Her mother was not amused. "You know the stress of this

campaign is killing him. Why can't you be a little more under-standing?"

"Understanding? He disowned me, Ma! It's that easy for him. To throw me out. And, honestly, he threw me out fifteen years ago, when Julia made that video. For fifteen years he's barely tolerated me. Now finally he gets what he wants." She took another bite of the muffin because she was determined to make it taste good.

Ma placed the coffee on the breakfast bar and crossed her arms, her raised eyebrows trapping all her substantial disap-pointment. "This is your father you're talking about, beta."

"My father who wants to control everything. Who's lost his head to this campaign." Because sure, she'd made a mistake, but she'd been seventeen. Seventeen! "I was a child, Ma. A sociopath took advantage of me. How was I supposed to pre-dict what she did? Why didn't you see that? Why didn't you see what Julia did was not on me?" She had so badly needed someone to say that to her. Just once.

This time Ma's hand went to her mouth. For a moment she looked like she might cry. Trisha didn't know if it was because she saw how much she'd hurt Trisha or because none of her children ever spoke to her that way.

Trisha wanted to apologize. But she also wanted to scream!

"Was nothing more important to you and Dad than 'your dream'? Wasn't I?"

"That's unfair. You children are more important than every-thing."

"If I'm important, then why didn't you stand up for me? Why don't you ever stand up to him, Ma?"

"Stand up to him for what? What does he ever do that's not for the good of us all?"

Trisha gulped down the muffin. It wasn't easy, because really, swallowing cardboard and crap at the same time made her want to gag.

Ma watched her for a while wordlessly, then she turned and walked to the couch. "Come here. Sit with me." She sank into the couch and patted it. "I'm going to tell you why. I guess it's time."

Something about her tone made Trisha do as she said.

"You know how your dad and I met, right?"

Trisha nodded but she was seriously not in the mood for another rendition of how the perfect prince swept the perfect film star off her feet.

Ma didn't look like this was going to be a romantic story, though. She shifted in her seat until she was pressed into a corner and stared at her hands. It made her look awfully small and more unsure than Trisha had ever seen her.

Just when the silence had stretched so long that Trisha thought Ma had changed her mind, Ma spoke. "When we first got together, there were only two things people ever asked me. The press, our friends, they were only interested in knowing: one, what it was like to give up stardom, and two, how on earth had I landed a prince?

"I had to make up answers to both those questions because no one wanted the truth. Getting rid of stardom was something I had been trying to figure out how to do for years. Not because I wasn't ambitious, although I wasn't, or because I took for granted something everyone else coveted, I didn't. But because of the price I had to pay for it."

Trisha sat up. Ma's face had paled, her usually bright eyes dimmed beyond recognition. The way she was looking at Trisha, as though she were trying to soak up how Trisha was looking at her—it was as though what she was about to tell Trisha was going to change how Trisha saw her forever.

It made Trisha want to ask her to stop. But Ma's jaw was set. "All the things you hear about men in power in the entertainment industry—they were doubly true in my time. But we had none of your hashtags, no movements to give us voice, to help us. Not that all the help in the world could help a child . . . a child of five, ten, fifteen, twenty . . ." Her voice cracked. Fractured innocence from a long time ago glittered in her eyes. Trisha couldn't move, couldn't react, all she could do was hold herself motionless.

"A child does not understand power and silence, actions or reasons. She just feels dirty." Her fingers twitched as though she wanted to rub at her arms, but she held herself still. "Filthy. Grotesque. Ugly. When millions of people sob at her beauty, write poetry about it, paint pictures in bright colors she can't bear, it makes her want to slash her own face to ribbons. But she's too scared to do even that. When the person who should protect her is the person she is most terrified of, she dies. She dies. She's a corpse."

For a long time, she said no more. The hand in her lap fisted and loosened. Fisted and loosened. As though she were working an invisible stress ball.

Then suddenly her gaze fell on Trisha's hand pressed into her belly, and she took it and stroked it. A smile softened her face, brought the strength back to it, as though a memory had parted its way past the ugliness of the words she'd just spoken. "The first question your father ever asked me when I . . . when I jumped on him"—her smile turned real, her trance broken—"and landed in his lap, and told him he'd ruined my escape, was: 'But why? Why are you trying to run away?'

"It was probably my utter dismay at having been caught before I had made it out of the hotel premises, at knowing that my only chance at escape was gone, that I answered him honestly. For the first time in my life I told the truth. That if I didn't run away I would kill myself.

"You know what he said? He said: 'In that case we're going to have to make sure you escape, aren't we?'

"I remember thinking, 'He sounds so posh, like an actor playing a prince in a Hollywood film.' Isn't that funny?"

It was. It was funny as hell, because HRH did talk that way. Ma reached out and lifted Trisha's glasses and wiped her tears. Her fingers on Trisha's cheeks were so warm and steady, so *Ma*.

"He talked like a prince, but I didn't give a damn." She actually blushed at the swear and Trisha wanted to hug her. But she wasn't done. "Every man I'd ever met had made my skin crawl. Every producer, actor, all those men, they knew I didn't want to do what I was being made to do. They took it all the same. Even the ones who never touched me—there were some who believed they were decent enough for that—even they never thought to help, to remove me from my father's control, to stand up to him. They thought of me as my father's property. They had this code, like they didn't mess with another man's property.

"Your dad, he . . . he was the only person who cared about what was right and wrong. People think he fell in love with me, because people only saw the mask on the screen. But I was too ugly for anyone to fall in love with. I showed him everything right at the beginning and it was all ugly.

"It was the fact that what my father was doing was wrong, that's what made him dig his heels in. He would have died for me, but not for *me*, not at first—for what was right. He let my father's goons break his arm rather than give me up. Because he sees right and wrong as absolutes."

Trisha found her arms wrapped tightly around herself. It was a good thing she had her bugeye glasses on because her contacts would never have withstood this. "And he thinks what I did by introducing Julia to Yash was that absolutely wrong?"

Ma cupped her cheek. "No, silly girl. He thinks what Julia did was that absolutely wrong. And the fact that you don't feel that way, too, is what makes him incredibly angry. He always thought you were the most like him. That you saw things in black and white too."

"But I do! What she did disgusts me. If I could do anything to change it, I would. The guilt I felt for not stopping her, for not seeing what she was, ate me alive. It still eats at me, every single day!"

"But you've never said that. You've always acted as though we did something incredibly unfair by taking care of it the way we did. You stopped coming to family gatherings. You refused to participate in Yash's campaign."

"You stopped asking me to come!"

"When, Trisha? All you wanted to do was work and sulk

when anyone talked about Yash's career. You barely came home from college after that. You acted like you were being dragged into things, dragged away from your work. Always late. You know how you are. You're so impatient with everything that's not your work. We thought you wanted nothing to do with it."

God, Ma wasn't entirely wrong. Of course she wasn't. "I just hated myself so much for what happened. She violated him, Ma. And it was because of me." Maybe she'd wanted to be banished—because she believed she deserved it. But not anymore. Talking to Yash had changed everything. Or maybe she'd just grown up.

"You're right, though," Ma said. "I should have told you it wasn't your fault. I, of all people, should have known that you needed to hear that. But . . . Yash . . . I thought I'd done everything to keep you kids safe, and—"

Trisha crawled over to her mother and wrapped her arms around her. "No, Ma. It was a lot. It was . . ." How had Ma even borne it after what she'd been through herself?

Ma stroked her hair. And she smelled so good that somehow everything didn't seem lost. "I didn't tell you then, but I'll tell you now. The thing about human beings is that they heal," Ma said. "We're nature's creations, we regenerate like the seasons. We just need someone to let us know that we're worthy of healing. Yash knows that." Then she rolled a lock of Trisha's hair around her finger and held it tight. "And you are, too. But the healing itself, the changing, that you can only do yourself. No one else can do that for you."

How solid Ma had always seemed, how hard she must have worked to get there, to heal herself so she could be whole for them. Her ferocious protectiveness made sense now. How had she even let them out of her sight? Trisha reached out and rolled a lock of her mother's hair around her finger in turn. And the two of them sat there like that, soothing each other in that way that was all theirs.

"How are we going to get rid of her, Ma?"

"Well, we're lucky the evil Ms. Wickham is also stupid. She's gone and released the video about your patient claiming she's dying. The last time I checked people have donated over a hundred thousand dollars. If I understand correctly, Emma Caine is going to be just fine and Julia knew this. That's fraud, and our lawyers are on it. If DJ and his sister cooperate, we can send her to jail, or at least use it as leverage to make sure she stays out of our hair and out of our state."

Oh God. Did DJ know the video was out? There was no way that he would have authorized it.

Ma didn't look worried. Ruthless, badass Ma. And that made Trisha feel like everything would be okay.

"Did I just see you spit out a chocolate-blueberry muffin earlier?" her mother asked suddenly. "Are you sick?"

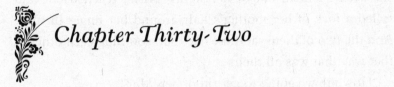

Chapter Thirty-Two

DJ had been staring at Emma's monitors like a hypnotist's victim and drifting in and out of sleep. It had been two days since Emma's surgery. She had regained consciousness a few times for only a handful of minutes at a time. For the most part, her body was too filled with drugs and painkillers for her to be coherent, but she had mumbled his name when she'd woken.

All he'd been able to do was hold her hand and tell her he was right here.

Trisha had said it might take her a few days to actually wake up, but she insisted that Emma was going to make a full recovery. Which was all the assurance DJ needed. She came by several times a day to check on Emma and each time she stopped by, his confidence rose, along with other feelings.

It had been coming on slowly, but he was plagued with the sense of having made a huge mistake, of having lost something because he was too stupid to know its value. Worse yet, he knew he had done something unforgivable. He had hurt someone unfairly. Trisha didn't deserve the things he'd said to her. Not even remotely. But how did you take words like that back?

He'd been dreaming about a strangely elongated figure stuffing her lush, wide mouth with ladoos without pause when a hand shook him awake. "DJ."

He opened his eyes to find Julia standing over him.

"Oh," he said and jumped up.

"Hi!" She leaned forward to give him a hug, but he pulled an Emma maneuver and shook her hand. Seeing that she was hauling her camera made discomfort prickle at him.

She noticed the look he threw at the camera and put it down on one of the tables. "You never told me Emma had gone into surgery. How is she? You? Can I get you something? Some coffee?"

He was a tea drinker. Had never gotten into coffee, which was a minor miracle after living in Paris, and a major miracle after working with Andre.

Come to think of it, Andre was the most arrogant man DJ knew—almost obnoxiously so—and he had never once held that against his boss.

"No, thank you. I just had chai." The taste of the chai Ashna had brought in again today was still fresh in his mouth, her words about Trisha from the other day still fresh in his mind.

She won't let anyone down. It would kill her.

What must being betrayed by a friend have done to her?

"DJ? Are you okay?" Julia studied him. It seemed like everyone had taken to studying him, possibly because he'd turned into an arse who had no idea what was going on in his own head.

"I'm fine. I'm told Emma will be fine too. Thanks to her doctor."

The look on Julia's face turned a little amused, a little hurt. "It's really endearing, isn't it? That poor little rich girl act? It has a way of finding its way under your skin really quickly."

He laughed. Quite the contrary. It had taken too bloody long. "What's endearing is the fact that she found a way to convince my sister to have surgery and then spent ten hours saving her life." Did he say endearing? It wasn't just endearing, it was enough to knock him right off his feet and onto his bum. He'd never seen anything as fierce as Trisha in that moment when the paramedics had wheeled Emma into the hospital. And she'd done it after he had hurt her more than he'd ever hurt anyone in his life.

She had called Ashna because he was in the waiting room alone. In the middle of her surgery she had thought about how to make this easier on him.

"Be careful. She's got a way of getting to you."

Yeah, no bloody joking. "She's Emma's doctor and that's what's important right now, not who's getting to me and why."

"Hey, I know. Emma's health is all that matters. I get that. That's why I'm here; despite the fact that her doctor would have me thrown out of the hospital if she knew I was here, I'm here. For Emma. For you. I thought we were friends."

He had thought they were, too, but she had lied to him. An awful, ugly lie, covering up an awful, ugly act. "Thanks so much for coming."

She stepped close to him and wrapped her arms around him. "Anything you need. Emma's like a sister to me. I'm really going to miss her."

He pulled away. What was wrong with the woman? Emma wasn't going anywhere.

Julia held on to his arm. "I meant I'm going to miss her because I won't be filming her anymore. Relax. What's happened to you? We're on the same side here. In fact, now that I'm not working with Emma, it would not be unethical for me to say yes if you asked me out."

DJ tried to be gentle as he removed her hand from his arm. "So you're fine about not releasing the film?"

She stepped back with a laugh. "Did you just change subjects on me? Are you blowing me off? After all the time I spent on your sister, you want me to get nothing in return?"

"I'm really sorry to have wasted your time." Although she'd known going in that Emma was not terminal, nor a great candidate for her film. "I'll compensate you for your time, if you'd like."

"You're not really that naive, are you? You paying me back doesn't pay for everything I've put into this. Listen, I know right now you're feeling hopeful. But Trisha's never going to go for you. Her family won't let her."

DJ threw a look at Emma. He couldn't believe they were having this conversation here, now. "Can we not talk about this here?" He stepped away from the bed and pulled the curtain around Emma.

"What's gotten into you, DJ?" She pressed her hand against his chest and stepped closer.

He was about to remove her hand again when he heard a sound by the door.

Trisha stood there looking like someone had stuck a stake through her heart. "I'm sorry, I'll come back later." Her eyes hitched on Julia's hand on his chest, and pain flared there, quick and intense.

Before he could stop her, she turned away and was gone.

He was about to follow her when Julia held his arm, her fingers digging into his flesh. "So I was right. The poor little rich girl did get to you."

"She's Emma's doctor."

"I saw how you looked at her. Are you crazy? You're a cook. She would never think of you as an equal." There was such naked hatred in her eyes, he could imagine clearly what she had done to Trisha at seventeen.

Even now, with how much she valued those she loved, those she chose to let in, Trisha's feelings were like exposed live wires. How much this woman must have destroyed in her when she'd been that young. And now he had made Trisha vulnerable to her again, because he had allowed himself to be blinded by his pride.

"I don't think she's the one who doesn't think of me as her equal." He removed her hand from his arm. Again. And took several steps away from her.

"I see." How had he thought her eyes pretty? There was a flat immobility to them, and it made a strange mix with the cold certainty on her face of someone who believed they'd been irreversibly wronged.

"And how do you think this affair is going to end up when the Rajes learn that their daughter has gotten mixed up with a terrorist?"

The screech of a cart sounded in the distance. He realized with a start that it wasn't in the distance at all; he'd slammed into the cart behind him when he'd stumbled back. "What the hell are you talking about?"

"Oh, have you not told your girlfriend that you were arrested for arson as part of a racially motivated terrorist attack?" she asked casually, reaching for her camera.

"You're entirely insane."

"What I am is a good journalist. Just because you're blinded by the Raje glow, and fickle—don't think I didn't see how you looked at me when we first met—I'm not giving up my credibility as a journalist. I've released Emma's film. I was going to share the donations with you, but now I'm not so sure." She pulled a sheaf of papers from her bag. "This is a release form for the film. Sign it and I won't go to the Rajes with your background. Oh, and if you think your girlfriend won't care—because I know she's dumb when it comes to things like that—I assure you that the family will care. And imagine the field day the press will have when I go to them with the fact that Yash Raje and his family are associating with a terrorist. You can't cook fund-raising dinners for a candidate who doesn't get to run, now, can you?"

TRISHA COULD HAVE sworn that she had made some progress with DJ over the past two days. She hadn't hoped for much, but something about the way he looked at her had changed. There was a tenderness to him that made her extremities tingle and her insides warm. He'd never been like that with her before. It had made her hope that at least he didn't dislike her anymore.

Evidently, she was wrong. The least he could have done was warn her that he was with Julia.

How could he be with her? How? It just didn't make sense. Was she drugging him too? Was she blackmailing him? Maybe he was sacrificing himself for Trisha. Maybe he was secretly in love with Trisha and bearing Julia's horrible presence to protect Trisha and her family from threat of ruin.

Trisha groaned. She shouldn't have binge-watched nineties Bollywood films on Netflix last night.

She heard a knock on her office door and sat up.

Julia walked in and without an invitation dropped into the chair across from Trisha's desk.

"What the hell are you doing here?"

"You don't own this hospital, Trisha. It's public property. You don't own everything"

Actually, the hospital was private property. But arguing with Julia would only make her crazier.

"What do you want?" Best to make this quick, because the sight of Julia in her beloved office was making her nauseated.

"I've slept with him, you know," Julia said with absolute calm.

Don't rise to her bait. Do not. "With whom?"

"Funny. You know exactly whom. You always had that face, transparent as a fishbowl. But it would figure that a princess whose family takes care of everything for her would never have to learn how to hide her feelings. Because God help anyone who would dare to hurt her." She mock trembled.

"And yet, here you are."

The original plan to not rise to her bait was much smarter, because Julia didn't like that. Her eyes went glassier with anger.

"I've had to do it all myself, Sha-Sha," she said, making the nickname sound ugly. "Someone like you would never understand that. I've had to care for *me*, my whole life. There was no one else. Excuse me for stepping on your little feelings along the way."

You didn't step on my feelings, you sick fuck. You drugged and sexually assaulted my brother and then tried to ruin him. The words almost burst from her tongue. But Trisha held them in because she wasn't going to let her anger risk Yash by turning Julia's focus on him. "How is hurting everyone who tries to be your friend taking care of yourself?" That she did say. She had to say it. But even as she said it, she knew it would make no difference. Julia didn't understand how things like love and friendship worked. "If you stopped for one moment to think about giving instead of taking, you might not be so alone."

If Trisha had thought Julia was angry before, now she came unhinged with rage. "You want me to give?" she snarled. "You selfish bitch. You know what? You know how many news channels would pay me to *give* them an interview about Yash? About what your family did to me? Maybe that's what I'll *give*."

Trish stood, blood pounding in her ears. Screw being compassionate. Holding back was not going to work. "And if you do, you'll go to jail. Your NDA is watertight, and you know it. If you so much as mention my brother in the media, our lawyers will make sure you regret ever being that stupid. You can't touch what you did to Yash back then and you know it."

Julia's jaw tightened with frustration. She didn't have a response to that. Which was both a relief and terrifying. Her being here didn't have anything to do with the video, but that just meant Julia had something else up her ugly sleeve. "Actually, why are you even back?"

That made her smile. She loved having information Trisha wanted, loved having something, anything, Trisha wanted. "Did you think you could just throw me out like garbage and then have Yash saunter into the governor's mansion without consequences? Do you have any idea what my life's been like for the past fifteen years?"

With the amount her family had paid her, Trisha guessed it couldn't have been too bad, but Julia's eyes glittered with satisfaction as though she'd been dying to tell Trisha. This was why she was back; she'd seen Yash's news as the perfect time to seek redemption from Trisha for having wronged her.

"I've been married four times. I'm trapped in what therapists call a pattern, because of the trauma you caused me. Do you have any idea how expensive divorces are?"

Trisha knew a million ways to lobotomize a human. Could she please use just one of those on this woman? "Hasn't your business of stealing from the terminally ill helped pay for them, though?"

"I don't steal. I work hard and I take my share. You think it was easy to put up with Emma Caine? But you better believe it's going to pay off."

Trisha walked around her desk and loomed over Julia, for once glad for her giraffelike body. Julia gave her a bored slow blink. "You've released Emma's video without her permission. That's illegal. You also misled the donors about her being terminal when you knew she wasn't. That's fraud."

Julia laughed. "Who said I don't have permission to release

the video?" She reached into her bag and slid out some papers. "Oh, did Big DJ betray Little Trisha?"

Trisha snatched the papers and studied them. "This has today's date."

Julia snatched them back. "So?"

Ma was right. It was such a lucky break to have a stupid adversary. The release wasn't signed by Emma. It didn't count. Trisha laughed. "DJ doesn't have power of attorney over Emma." Trisha was pretty sure Emma hadn't completed the paperwork for that before she went into surgery and she was an adult.

Julia stopped lounging in her chair and straightened up. "You're lying."

"Is that what my fishbowl face is telling you?" Trisha leaned back on her desk; two could play the bored game. Fifteen years of guilt she'd suffered at the hands of this woman. She would never hurt anyone Trisha loved again. "Listen to me very carefully. Because I'm only going to lay this out for you once. I'm no longer the easy prey I once was and if you go up against me I will make sure you end up behind bars. You've fraudulently pocketed the money from the video. Our lawyers already have a criminal suit against you ready to go. Unless you're particularly keen on jail, you will leave my family alone, and you will withdraw the video and return all that money to the people you stole it from."

Julia opened her mouth, but Trisha held up her hand and she closed it. "And if you do one thing to harm DJ"—because suddenly Trisha was sure Julia had something on DJ; her nineties-Bollywood-plot theory didn't seem so farfetched—"I will make sure that every one of the families you've preyed on to make money off their tragedies gets together and sues your ass until every penny you've ever leeched is gone. Now get out of my office. Get out of my building—which by the way *is* private property. Soliciting business here is illegal. So the next time you think of setting foot here, know that I will have security throw you out on your cowardly, pathetic ass." She walked to the door and held it open.

Julia stood; there was still a flicker of fight left in her face. "Fine. But DJ isn't what you think he is. And he doesn't even want you. Why would he have signed if he did?" And with that last swipe she slunk away like the weasel she was.

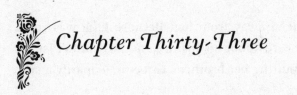

Chapter Thirty-Three

DJ enjoyed the graveyard shift. Truly he did. Four in the morning was when his brain was sharp, his senses entirely focused on work. He usually went to the farmers' market at five every morning anyway. Now he just went two hours before that and got to Curried Dreams a little before four so he could vacate the kitchen by eight for Ashna's renter.

The deliveries alley was still dark when he pulled into it and got out. Every single time he saw those steps he saw Trisha standing there, her unusually shiny hair catching the light, her unusually long neck held high, the flames in her eyes flashing all sorts of secrets at him that she didn't know how to hide.

It was all his imagination, of course, because he hadn't seen her in a couple of weeks. Two days after Emma had woken up, Trisha had handed her care over to Dr. Entoff and disappeared to somewhere in Africa. Not a word of good-bye to him. Which was expected after their last conversation.

She had stormed into Emma's room and asked him why he'd signed Julia's release. There had been such beautiful hope in her eyes. "What's she holding over your head?" she'd asked, as usual laying all her cards on the table.

Which was exactly why he'd had to say what he'd said. "We need the money."

And he'd walked away from her. Because Julia was right, Trisha wouldn't care about his history and he couldn't let her be the cause of putting her brother's career in jeopardy again. It would kill her.

He pushed away the mix of regret and yearning that lurked close to the surface all the bloody time. The fact that he had found everything about her unusual should have been a sign. The fact that he had noticed every little thing about her should have been another. But those three words, *the hired help*, those three words had destroyed his rice-paper-thin ego and he'd lost all sense of how to deal with his own awareness of her and how she brought everything inside him to the fore in big disruptive waves.

He was a bloody wanker.

Popping open the boot of the Beetle, he stared at the eighty pounds of tomatoes that sat in cardboard boxes. Today he would prep the makhani sauce for the fund-raiser. No one had fired him yet, so he was forging ahead as planned. Julia had kept her end of the deal and said nothing about the arson thing to anyone. He wasn't going to think about her lining her pockets from Emma's video. He didn't care so long as she left Trisha alone.

He grabbed the bags of cilantro, green chilies, ginger, and garlic. To move the tomato boxes he'd have to bring the trolley out. He trudged up the steps that sent another wave of yearning coursing through him and was about to punch in the security code when he realized that it wasn't armed. Someone had already disarmed the security system.

He turned the handle. It was unlocked. There had to be something wrong.

"Hullo?" He pushed the heavy metal door open. Then putting the bags down on the floor, he reached for his phone to call Ashna.

"There's no need to wake Ashna at this hour."

A man dressed as if he were off to a *GQ* photo shoot was looking at him with eyes the exact shape of Trisha's, a neck just as unusually long, and lips that quirked with just as much sardonic focus.

He extended his hand and gave DJ a firm handshake. "Yash Raje."

"I know." DJ looked around the kitchen. There was no one else there.

"You expecting someone else?" Yash leaned over and picked up one of the bags that DJ had put down and took it into the kitchen.

"Thank you." DJ followed him and put the bag he was carrying down next to the sink. "Actually, I wasn't expecting anyone at all. Ashna lets me use the kitchen for a few hours every morning. How may I help you?"

"I know. I have a slew of sisters who seem quite ready to do anything for you."

"I beg your pardon?"

Yash smiled at that and DJ was reminded of the look that crossed Trisha's face every time he said those words. "I mean they'd do anything to make sure they get to eat your food."

"I've been told I do all right. Probably why I'm cooking the food for your event."

The man didn't respond and DJ studied his face. Was he here to fire him? God knows, he had enough reason to.

Four A.M. was too early for games. "Am I cooking for your dinner?" DJ asked. Because if he wasn't, he'd rather find out before he made eighty pounds of makhani sauce.

Trisha's brother peeked into the bag he'd put down. But didn't respond.

"Do you mind if I unload my car?" DJ asked because he had only four hours to get this done. Just in case he wasn't about to be fired.

"Of course. Let me help you." Yash followed him out with the trolley and helped him haul the tomato boxes out of the trunk and onto it. He seemed focused enough on the task, but DJ had a sense he was being studied the entire time.

"My sister is the least devious person I know," he said when DJ was halfway up the ramp with the trolley, which was rather heavy. Then Yash sauntered past him and held the door open. "She's also the easiest person in the world to hurt when she lets her guard down."

"I am aware." DJ dragged the trolley into the kitchen, cut open a box, and started transferring the tomatoes into the sink. "And she doesn't let that guard down much, does she? But when she does . . ." The tomato in his hand was in danger of being crushed, so he put it down, pulled the extendable faucet, and filled a pot on the stove and set it to boil. "She's also incredibly brilliant and brave and I've never met anyone who works harder. And her focus is a scary thing. And everyone in your family seems to depend on her and she devotes all her existence into being there for you. I know."

God, what had he done? How was he ever going to make it right? He started to wash the tomatoes, rubbing at little patches of dirt, trying to scrape them off without damaging the delicate skin. Then he wiped his hands on his smock, wishing he could wipe away the words he had just said because Yash stood there, watching him with hooded eyes. "You're not one of those Indian blokes who kills anyone who looks in his sister's direction, are you?"

That earned him a laugh but the man's eyes stayed guarded. "My sisters can take care of their honor by themselves just fine, thank you very much."

"Yeah, mine too, mate. God help anyone who thinks she needs protecting."

A commiserating smile slipped past Yash's lips and he dipped his head in response. "How is Emma doing?"

"She's doing great. Thanks to Trisha. Ready to come home. You didn't answer my question—am I catering your event?"

"If you know Trisha, you should know the answer to that question."

He did. She had already told him that she would do what she could to make sure he kept his job. He started to empty out the rest of the tomatoes and wash them.

Yash helped him, slicing open the boxes and handing him the tomatoes.

They worked in silence until the boxes were empty. When the water on the stove came to a boil, DJ dumped the first batch of tomatoes into it and watched as they bobbed, ready to have their skin peeled off and their most tender flesh exposed.

"And what about Julia Wickham making a film on Emma?"

If the guy was going to play games DJ didn't have time for, it fell on him to lay things out. He prodded the tomatoes and set a timer on his phone.

"Trisha warned you about working with her. She told you we wouldn't work with you if you did. Why didn't you listen?"

DJ met the inquisition in his eyes unflinchingly. "Julia lied to me. I didn't have any reason not to believe her." The phone beeped. His half minute was up. He dunked a handled colander into the water and scooped the tomatoes into a cold-water bath. "Actually, that's not true. I wanted to believe her, because I was angry."

"With Trisha?"

"Yes, and with things she dug up from my past."

"What changed your mind?"

"How can you not change your mind if you hang around Trisha long enough?"

"Ah."

He wasn't interested in analyzing that response so he said what he'd been wanting to say from the moment he'd seen Yash. "If you're done with your questions, may I ask you one?" The skin on the tomatoes stretched and cracked. "Why did Trisha leave? The Africa thing? Was that—" But he couldn't ask if it was him she'd wanted to get away from.

"Have you met our father yet?"

"Haven't had the pleasure."

Yash let out another cryptic laugh. "He thinks it was irresponsible of Trisha to work with anyone who worked with Julia, given the history."

DJ dunked his hands in the ice bath and started to yank the

peels off the tomatoes. The coldness of the water seeped up his arms like dread.

Yash paused, as though he could tell how badly DJ wanted to know the rest of it and he was gauging whether he was worthy. "He threatened to disown Trisha if she didn't pass Emma's surgery on to another doctor."

"That's ridiculous! Did he . . . did he *send* her to Africa?" He tried to pull his hands out of the ice water, but the cold burn on his fingers held them in place. "Can he do that?"

Had he really thought Yash's eyes were anything like Trisha's? The guy was a vault. "Our father can go to some crazy lengths to get his way, and he has. But no, he can't pack Trisha off to Africa. We aren't quite that medieval. She did believe him, though, when he told her she wasn't welcome in the family anymore and ran off to Africa so she wouldn't be here for the fund-raiser. Our youngest brother lives there."

"But she still did Emma's surgery."

Yash nodded.

"She never even considered not doing it, did she?" DJ said and Yash gave him that look again. The one that said, *Ah.*

He pulled his hands out of the water and turned to Yash. "Well, Julia's not going to hurt Trisha—or any of you—ever again." Her getting to keep all of Emma's FundMe money would take care of that.

For the first time since Yash had shown up, the way he was watching DJ changed. It was the slightest change, but DJ felt like he had parted one layer of the many that the candidate so deftly kept between himself and the world. "There's really no way to take care of someone like Julia for good. I suspect she's going to be like a whack-a-mole jumping up at us at every turn. Our best bet is to know her hand, so she doesn't have any surprises she can spring on us."

DJ's hand froze in the act of setting up the ricer.

Yash was watching him again. "One of her favorite weapons to use against people is love. She's skilled at putting us in positions where we're forced to keep secrets. The threat of loved ones being hurt is great ammunition."

That's exactly how she had gotten DJ to sign the release.

DJ stared at the mound of peeled tomatoes. This was just one-third of them. A pile of rubbish unless he turned them into sauce. Which he could only do if this man didn't fire him. But he hadn't done as Julia asked to keep from being fired. He'd done it because of how he felt about Trisha.

But Yash was right. The secrets she forced you to keep were her power. The only way to beat her was to take those away.

DJ started feeding the tomatoes into the ricer. "My guess is, your real reason for being here is to find out why I signed that release." He had never told this to anyone, this secret that had chased him his entire adult life. "Julia has pulled something out of my past. Something she's misrepresenting. Something she's found a way to use to hurt you and consequently Trisha. She can have the money if that'll keep her quiet. Emma and I never wanted it anyway."

Yash's hands went to his hair, his first display of real emotion. "So you don't know."

"Don't know what?"

"Your signature on the release didn't mean anything. Emma hadn't given you power of attorney. Trisha figured it out. She made Julia withdraw the FundMe. There's almost one hundred and fifty thousand dollars that she siphoned out of the account just waiting to be turned into fraud charges if you and Emma cooperate."

"Of course. It would be our absolute pleasure." God, he would do anything to put the woman behind bars where she couldn't hurt people.

"And this thing she blackmailed you with?"

"I can't tell you what that is. Not until I've told your sister first. You can decide if you want to work with me or not. But I won't tell you before I've told Trisha."

For a long time they both stood there wordlessly, contemplating the pile of tomatoes, their gazes moving from the ones being ground up by the ricer to the ones sitting in piles on the kitchen counter.

Finally, Yash spoke. "Are these for my party?"

DJ nodded.

"That's an awful lot of tomatoes to waste." He pushed off the counter he was leaning on. "I'll see you in two days at the dinner. Trisha will be back from Malawi that morning. I suspect you two will have a lot to talk about."

He was halfway to the door when he turned around. "I believe you are well acquainted with my other sister, Nisha? Her husband makes it a habit to climb on and off balconies to impress her. It seems to me like the most ridiculous thing to do. But both my sisters seem to find it inexplicably endearing."

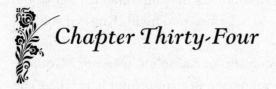

Chapter Thirty-Four

Trisha was hiding out in the bathroom of the Astoria. There were many reasons for this, but the only one that mattered was that DJ was working his magic in the kitchen and she needed to keep from making her way there and embarrassing herself. As promised, Yash had taken care of things and kept HRH from firing him. Trisha hadn't been involved in the event planning after Neel and Nisha's supermushy reunion—who would have thought ten years of a good marriage needed an ex to make it even better? But Nisha was feeling well and had taken the reins back fully.

Trisha had been relieved.

Yes, she had.

She'd spent the past two weeks in Malawi performing surgeries and training surgeons from around southern Africa. When Ma had convinced her that HRH had "forgiven her" and asked her to be at the fund-raiser, Trisha had thought about canceling her trip. But her little brother had talked her into taking the time for herself. "There's no place like Africa to set your head straight," Vansh had declared, and Trisha had been in just the mood to test out his wisdom. Plus, her head was in desperate need of being set straight. Along with her heart after DJ had looked at her the way she'd always wanted to be looked at and then walked away from her.

"Don't be a damn tourist," Vansh had said. "Don't try to see Africa. No one can 'see' Africa in ten days. Just stay put and do your work and be."

Being was good. Being had been very good.

But she was glad to be back home.

The first thing she'd done after coming back was go see Emma. She'd been by herself. She was doing remarkably well and was ready to be discharged in a few days. Her balance and orientation were slowly getting normalized. Jane had been spending a lot of time with her and there had been a veritable forest of, ahem, phallic sculptures in the hospital room that they'd been "testing some new clay on."

"How accurate are they?" Emma had asked her.

"I've never really seen one bent at quite that angle, but I'm no expert," Trisha had answered.

"Bloody hell," Emma had said. "That's exactly what DJ said."

As entirely useless information went, that had been good to know.

Trisha wiped her hands one more time, possibly setting a record for the longest time spent wiping hands in a bathroom, when J-Auntie walked in, her tight bun tighter than ever. But she was wearing a salwar kurta instead of her usual slacks and shirt and something about that tilted Trisha's world a little bit.

"You look lovely, J-Auntie," Trisha said.

"You think so?" Instead of her usual stiff nod, the older woman smiled and patted the beaded chiffon of the kurta.

"Thank you," she added when Trisha nodded. "You too, beta. As always."

Trisha had the oddest urge to cry.

"His Highness is looking for you," she said before disappearing into a stall. "He's waiting outside."

Trisha pushed out of the ladies' room and sure enough, HRH was perched in the pretty alcove outside the restrooms, in all his HRH glory, making the wing chair look like a throne.

"Join me." His tone was imperious but there was something in his eyes from a very long time ago. Trisha sank down into the chair next to him.

"I'm glad you're here," he said a bit gruffly.

Wait, were those violins wailing or was that the sound of her head exploding? "Wouldn't miss it for all the threats in the world, Dad." No, she didn't say that. Well, she did, but she left out *all the threats in.*

He grinned. Actually grinned at her for the first time in years. "Good job with the dinner."

"I'll let Nisha know."

He leaned forward and patted her cheek. She almost passed out from his display of affection. "I heard what you did. You worked with a caterer for Yash." There was genuine wonder in his voice.

"Have you *seen* the caterer?" she wanted to say. Instead she met his eyes. "You shouldn't be surprised, Dad. There's very little I wouldn't do for Yash."

He nodded. "I can see that. And I should never have doubted it." His eyes were heavy with exhaustion and Trisha's heart squeezed a little. This truly was the culmination of a lifetime of work for him.

"Yash's speech was something, wasn't it?" Her brother had completely outdone himself. He'd opened with the story about their *Animal Farm* book, making everyone laugh with the moralistic adages that had become woven into their personalities. Then he'd led into all the things that had made him who he was: growing up in the Bay Area with Ma and HRH's activism and uncompromising standards, walking again after every doctor had deemed it impossible, being with the same woman for twenty years. Then he'd gone there and talked about family values, and what that really meant to him. Was it just having a picture-perfect family that went to church? Or was it loyalty and fidelity and taking care of all the generations of your family, and loving your significant other enough that you respected her wishes to follow her own dreams? To everyone's dismay, Naina hadn't flown in for the event. Yash had shown no pain, and he'd spared no punches. What had sealed the deal and driven the crowd insane was his declaration that right and wrong were not nebulous concepts, they weren't based on political agendas. Right was right and wrong was wrong and he planned to bring that back into governance.

"Nobody who ever hears Yash speak would ever vote for anyone else," she said.

Her father smiled. "If only it were that easy. But yes, I'm very proud." The fierceness in his eyes backed up those words. Why had she resented his ambition so much? She believed what he believed, wanted for the country what he wanted. "And not just proud of Yash. I'm proud of all of you."

"Does that mean I'm not banished anymore?" No, of course, she didn't say that. She already knew she wasn't. What she did say was, "Thanks, Dad. Yash wouldn't be where he is today without you. Actually, none of us would be."

HRH leaned forward and placed a hand on hers. "Nonetheless, asking you not to do that surgery was going too far."

Could she text this conversation to all her siblings?

"It was. But you were right to be concerned about Julia being back in town, about her going after my patients. I'm sorry Yash has to pay for my error in judgment forever," she said, her voice surprisingly firm. "But my biggest mistake was in being so angry with myself, so guilty that I thought only of myself, that I withdrew from my role in the family. It didn't mean I supported her. I want to be involved now. I want to make sure Yash wins."

In all her life, Trisha didn't think she'd seen her father cry. Not even when Yash had his accident. He'd held Nisha, Ashna, and her. Kept Vansh on his lap the entire time they waited outside surgery. But he'd stayed dry-eyed, strong and immovable, the way they'd needed him to be. Now there was the slightest sheen of moisture in his eyes. "We'll find you a way to be involved that doesn't make you want to poke your—or my—eyes out."

She smiled. "Good thing you never back down from a challenge." Yes, she did say that out loud and he smiled and stood.

They walked back to the ballroom together, where Ma brightened as soon as she saw them. She'd obviously been waiting for them.

"How's my most brilliant child doing?" Ma said, linking arms with her.

"I think he's done pretty well today," Trisha said with a grin.

Her mother gave her the original Glare of Elegance.

HRH dropped a kiss on her head and walked away. Seriously, she would never be able to speak again. Ever.

"Your sisters and I are having a drink at the bar," Ma said, her eyes following HRH with the smug devotion that had been the cornerstone of Trisha's life and her heart did another needless tug in the direction of the kitchen. "We were missing our world traveler. Join us?"

She followed her mother.

Most of the guests had left. A congressman and the mayor were at a corner table talking to Yash, Neel, and Vansh—their baby brother had flown home with her. HRH joined them. It was like the old days when the men retired to their cigars and cognac, except there were no cigars or cognac, just really expensive scotch.

Every party Trisha had ever been to ended like this, with the men and the women separating out, as though there was only so much of each other's conversation they could take. This was actually her favorite part of any party, the winding down with just her sisters and her mother. Her brothers would join them soon enough.

Nisha kissed her cheek. "You look so gorgeous, Shasha!"

"You did a good job on her, Nisha," Ma said.

Nisha had "worked her like a canvas," getting someone to "define her curls," which just meant she felt like she was carrying around a bouquet of flowers atop her head. "Yes, thank you for making me gorgeous." Trisha picked up a glass of wine and lifted it at Nisha, then at Ma. "Well, both of you, I guess."

Ashna smiled from behind the bar, leaned over to take the glass from her, and handed her another. "This is the one you want."

Trisha took a sip. Woah! This was definitely the one she wanted. It was rich and filled her entire mouth then settled like warmth deep into her taste buds, reminding her of the dinner.

No, don't think about his food.

Ashi threw her the Look. "The chef recommended this one for after that saffron crème brûlée."

Her mother beckoned for the glass and took a sip, studying her.

Trisha smiled for her.

"Nisha didn't have to make you beautiful. You're already beautiful, beta, and you're my most brilliant one, too." She tried to push one curl behind Trisha's ear, but it bounced right back.

"I should go away more often," Trisha said.

Ma gave her a sad smile. "I know I should tell you the good things more. Sometimes when I try to remember your childhoods, only all the mistakes I ever made come back."

Ma was in a pensive mood, which was not good at all for the lump that seemed permanently lodged in Trisha's throat these days. HRH had already not helped with that.

"There were no mistakes, Ma," Nisha said, because she was the one who always knew what to say to Ma.

"Well, no big ones, I hope." This time Ma tucked a lock of

hair behind Nisha's ear and it responded as hair was supposed to and stayed there. Then she pulled Ashi across the bar and kissed her forehead. "Look at how you all turned out. I'm not saying that wasn't some amazing parenting."

Both Nisha and Ashi rolled their eyes without losing any of their worshipfulness. Another one of their many good-daughter skills.

Trisha sat down close to Ma and snuggled up to her. "But there were so many little slips. Like when I yelled at you when you got a bad grade in that art class instead of sympathizing with how hard it must have been. You loved art class so much."

But she had sucked at it.

Ma smiled another wistful smile and took another sip of Trisha's wine. "Or like when I asked Nisha how she could have done something as stupid as run a stop sign when I should have asked her how she was after she totaled that car her junior year. But she was calling me. Of course I knew she was okay. I can always tell from your voices, you know."

She wrapped her arm around Trisha's shoulders and rubbed. "Especially this one. Her voice gets dry and raspy as though in trying to hide her sadness she strips it of everything."

Warmth prickled beneath Trisha's eyelids and that dry raspiness scraped along her throat.

"And Ashi chatters. It's the only time the girl chatters. All that silence and then when she's afraid or lost, she tries to drown out the sound of her panic with her words." Ashi handed Trisha another glass.

"And me, Ma?" Nisha said needily, and they all laughed, because yay, Nisha being normal!

"You get mean."

"I do not!"

"You do," Ma said calmly. "You forget to be poised and patient when you're really upset. Like you're angry that your poise didn't keep the bad thing from happening. The opposite of this one, who gets poised when she's upset." Ma turned to Trisha again.

"Who knew you were such a therapist," Nisha said. "And this is me being mean, because I am upset right now."

Ashi popped the cork off another bottle of wine without any of her chef's finesse and topped everyone up, except Nisha, of course. Nisha had told the Farm about the baby, and they were all dealing with it using the ostrich theory and pretending that there was absolutely nothing to be afraid of. "To Ma!"

"To Ma," they all said and Ma downed half her wineglass just as Yash strolled over, showing not a trace of the exhaustion Trisha was feeling just thinking about him having spoken to two hundred people today.

"To my oldest baby," Ma said and took another sip.

"I think your youngest baby needs you right now to hold him back a little bit," Yash said, throwing a look over his shoulder at Vansh who was grinning at HRH and three other men who looked like they were going to have joint coronaries.

"Is Vansh being Vansh?" Ashi said.

"Yup, he's making a case for giving California back to Mexico."

They all groaned, and Ma took another long sip and then went off to save the day.

A silent something passed between Yash, Ashi, and Nisha.

They had been treating her like someone on the verge of a breakdown all evening. "I'm fine," she wanted to scream, but she just took another sip of her wine.

"I think we're all squared away," a voice said behind her, a voice she did not need to hear right now, not with this particular audience watching.

All three of them made a show of looking over her and around her at the man whose presence she could suddenly feel with every part of her being. It had been thirteen days, five hours, and some fourteen minutes since she'd laid eyes on him.

Do not close your eyes.

All three of them grinned widely at him.

"Fabulous dinner." "Exquisite." "That chicken makhani was the best thing I've ever tasted." "And those corn papad crisps. I thought I was going to die."

Trisha's ears felt like there was a tornado swirling between them. Her entire body felt like it was going to melt outward. She felt color rise across her skin. Never in her life had she experienced such mortification.

DJ cleared his throat. "Hullo, Trish*er*," his deep vibrating voice said and everyone fell silent. "May I have a word, please? Alone. If you don't mind."

Don't shake. Don't cry. Don't do anything but turn around. Turn around!

Two siblings jumped off their barstools in tandem and one cousin sprang up straight. God, could she make them disappear? Please.

Yash placed a hand on her shoulder and turned her around.

"Hi." Fabulously. Articulate.

DJ smiled and her limbs loosened. But it was a tentative smile, filled with questions.

"Can we step outside for a moment?" He gestured to the French doors that led to the terrace.

Someone pushed her from behind and she started walking.

DJ WATCHED TRISHA standing on the balcony beneath a cloudless star-sprinkled sky and a sense of déjà vu rolled over him. He'd seen her standing like this on this very terrace just about a month ago. How on earth had he gotten her so wrong?

The ocean breeze made springy locks of hair bounce around her face and fall across her cheeks like stray ribbons of confetti left floating around after a celebration. She used the backs of her wrists to shove them off her face. He could almost hear her mentally cursing whoever had decided to do this to her hair.

Their eyes met and her cheeks colored. For all the complexity of her brain, there was such a simplicity to her. And he'd missed it, no matter how much it had smacked him in the face.

He walked toward her, and she pressed a fist into her belly, trying to affect calm with that straightening of her spine and squaring of her shoulders that he had mistaken for uptightness. "Thanks for agreeing to speak to me," he said.

Her eyes brightened then dimmed in quick succession. Hope and tentativeness. Had she always laid down her armor around him like this? And he had returned it with pushing her away. Insulted her so much the fact that she was standing here with him felt like a miracle.

"Is it Emma?" she asked.

He shook his head. "Emma's fine. Healing fast. Can I thank you again for everything you did for her?"

She nodded fiercely, those curls they had teased out of her usually softer waves running amok around her head. "DJ, please. Don't thank me for doing my job."

He reached for the hand she was pressing into her belly and she started at his touch. But then she pushed into it. "It wasn't your job to find Jane. To give me chance after chance when I didn't heed your warnings about Julia." He took her hand and loosened her fingers, unwrapping her fist. "I was an arse."

A smile sprang to her lips. The vulnerability in her eyes made the oddest contrast with it. "I was the one who was the *arse*," she said, swallowing. "I was awful. I was all the things you accused me of being."

"Only at first. But once you'd hurt my ego, I stopped seeing you, I stopped being fair." The more unfair he'd been, the more fair she'd become. "You fought your dad. You were willing to give up your family to treat Emma."

She made a choking sound and his heart twisted painfully. "It wasn't for Emma."

He searched her eyes. She let his hand go, her fingers trailing from his grip. He felt the loss everywhere.

"I want to say it was for you. It was, a little bit. I wanted to not be the person you thought I was. But, really, Dad was out of line. To be fair I was out of line for bringing him to that point. It doesn't matter, I would have done the surgery no matter who told me not to. No matter who the patient was."

And that summed her up and summed up why he would do anything for her to give him another chance.

"Not a single thing I said to you that day at Tangent was true," DJ said. "I am so incredibly sorry. Will you forgive me?"

"There's nothing to forgive. You . . . you were right about everything. You changed my life."

"Am I allowed to say you changed mine? I was so blind, Trisha."

She swallowed and reached for his hand again, the tips of their fingers touching, stroking. "DJ, are you trying to tell me something? Because there are all sorts of conclusions I want to jump to right now. But we've done too much of that already and I don't want to be an *arse* again." She smiled but there it was again, that painful tentativeness marring her need to fly forward.

"I am. I am trying to say something." He took a step closer to her and her eyes dilated into huge pools of hope. She had the most beautiful eyes, the most beautiful lips, the most beautiful face. She swayed closer and tilted her head back, her lips parting in a way that nearly made him forget what he'd been meaning to say.

But he had to say it. "There are things we have to talk about first."

She stayed like that for a moment, leaning toward him as though the world had suddenly tilted in his direction. He could feel her wanting to argue, but then she talked herself into pulling back and letting him have his say. "Okay."

"You asked me that day what Julia was holding over my head and I lied. It wasn't the money."

"I know," her lips said, but her face said *obviously* and he almost leaned over and kissed her at that.

"Julia threatened to go to the press with something that could harm Yash's campaign if I didn't sign the release. And I knew what that would do to you, so I signed."

A strange look crossed her face, as though she wanted to throw herself at him and pluck Julia's head off at the same time. "I'm so sorry she did that to you." Then a hint of an impish smile slipped through. "Good thing I know medical law better than the two of you."

He had to smile at that. "But it's not just about signing the release. What she's dug up could be a problem," he said softly. "It's important to me that you know before we can get to the conversation we stopped earlier."

"In that case, spit it out!" She might have actually bounced on her heels and it made them both laugh.

But that's exactly what he did. He started at the beginning with how they had moved to Ammaji's in Southall after Dad died. How he grew up in that Punjabi Indian neighborhood, never relating to any racial identity. There had been a few black children in his school, but they were rich, posh folk, completely removed from his experience.

"The first time I really felt any connection at all with someone my age was when I helped a bloke with his bike when his chains came off. I had just finished school and been accepted into a few universities, but there seemed no help to be had with scholarships and the like. Emma was still in school; everything Mum made went into that, and into putting food on the table. It felt like the end of the road. It was the angriest, most frustrated time in my youth. Which is saying something.

"When I met Gulshan and his friends, it was like finding an

outlet to the sudden raw anger that had opened up inside me. They were loud and gregarious and a little bit scary. People cleared out of their way when they walked down the street. Walking by their side felt like finally being able to claim space for myself. I could be angry and still feel safe. I had nothing in common with them, but I was desperate to have something in common with someone.

"It was two weeks. That's how much time I spent with them. But Gulshan lost it when an old guy who owned a newsstand refused to make some change for him and threw in a slur. It was something that stupid, and he tossed a lit match at the newsstand. There was a car parked too close—an old clunker with a petrol leak—and it turned into an explosion. We scattered, five boys who knew their lives were over.

"When the coppers showed up at our home to take me in for questioning, my mum opened the door. It was more than she could bear. I . . . I remember her face, she was so confused. She had never even heard of these friends. It was the last time I saw her standing upright, or conscious. I heard later that she collapsed when the police car drove away with me. A stroke.

"The boys told the police the truth. That I had nothing to do with it. That they hadn't even known me until a few weeks before. They let me go, but when I came home, they had already moved Mum to the hospital. A few days later, she died. Never knowing the truth. Her insurance paid for her burial and Emma's school. Ammaji sold her dowry jewels and sent me to culinary college in Paris."

He was breathing hard but his eyes were so parched he had

to blink away the dryness. A mercy he couldn't be more grateful for.

Somewhere along the way Trisha had threaded her fingers through his. Her grip was tight, tears were running down her cheeks, and she was opening and closing her eyes in the strangest way. "Crap," she said, not letting his hand go. "There's something you should know about me, too. I'm practically blind without my contact lenses. And crying dislodges them because my corneas have a strange curvature." She started to pat her dress, which was basically the most beautiful blue thing he'd ever seen, but there wasn't much of it, no sleeves or straps. Nothing to dry her eyes with.

He untied the smock tied around his waist and held it out, thanking his stars that he had switched it out a few times over the evening.

She took it and dabbed her cheeks and the edges of her eyes in frustrated little movements. This was obviously something she hated. "Shit. This is not going to work. You should have warned me you were going to make me cry. Listen, you cannot make me cry, okay?"

He bit his lip to keep from smiling, but it didn't work. "Sorry. I didn't realize there was a crying issue. Don't you carry a pair of spectacles?"

That made her look even more horrified. "You do not want to see me with . . . with *spectacles*. And, ugh, I think I dropped a lens." Her head titled at an awkward angle and she looked miserable. "Basically, now I can only see you if you're six inches from my face."

"That can be arranged." He took a step closer and she grabbed his arms.

Holding him seemed to help her balance. "I'm so sorry," she said, head still tilted. "I can't believe what that must have been like for you."

All right, so they were talking about the Gulshan thing again. "It was a long time ago."

"But she made you relive it." Her grip on his arms loosened, then turned to a caress, the flames in her eyes burning bright and fierce. "How did Julia find out about this?"

"My assistant, Rajesh, he's Ammaji's grandson. Julia slept with him. The guy isn't really discreet. He's an idiot, but I didn't think he was malicious. Even so, I fired him. He didn't work this dinner. But he only knew what he had pieced together from neighborhood gossip, that Ammaji had saved me somehow after I'd been in trouble with the law, which I hadn't been. Not really. He probably believed that's why I was obligated to put up with him. The rest of it Julia probably pulled up from the archives of the local papers. It was a big story when it happened. It certainly can be spun to make me look like a criminal and harm your family."

Her hand moved to the center of his chest and rested on his heartbeat.

"I've never told anyone that before. Any of it," he whispered.

"I'm glad you were able to tell me."

He touched one of those springy curls. It bounced against his finger and he gave it a tug and tucked it off her face. "About that other thing I was trying to say earlier." Her hair was much softer than he had imagined. He touched it again, because he really couldn't believe how soft it was. She closed her eyes.

He supposed that was a sign that the story of his pathetic childhood hadn't altered her feelings, which filled him with relief.

"Yes, about that other thing. Could you hurry up and say what you were going to say?" Her eyes were still closed, her voice breathy.

He slipped a hand behind her head, cradling the petal-soft skin at her nape.

She gasped, and her lips parted.

"Okay?" he said against those lush parted lips, tasting her breath, tasting the anticipation at the edge of a precipice.

"Dear God, yes!" She reached up with both hands and pulled his mouth down against hers. And he fell, an anchor sinking to the ocean floor, slow and hard.

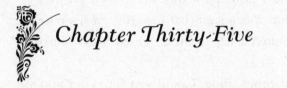 *Chapter Thirty-Five*

Before now, when Trisha had kissed she remembered looking for sparks, searching for heat. She had found both in little, hard-won spurts. Now she swam past the spasms of heat that melted her core, swam past the sparks that exploded where he touched her, and she floated into the comfort of not seeking, just feeling. His lips taking her in, nudging her apart, making her alive and right and known. That hand at her nape, that taste of his tongue, that feel of the stubble on his scalp, the long thick tendons on his neck. The bones of him, magic in her hands.

It was learning, gathering, opening up.

Even the way he pulled away was a connection, different from anything she'd ever known. His hands cradled her face, his breath continued to caress her lips, his chest rose and fell against her heart.

"Could you ask me that again?" she said, her entire body pressed tight against his. "I don't think I heard you."

He laughed and lifted her up and onto the railing. Where he did ask her again, and again until she was gasping desperate sounds into his mouth, sounds that she couldn't seem to control from getting louder and louder.

"Your family," he whispered.

"Who?"

Holy hell, her entire family was here.

He laughed again. She loved his laugh. She wanted to rub it all over herself.

"Do you have work to finish?" she asked.

"Nope, it's all taken care of. I wanted to make sure we weren't interrupted."

She looked over his shoulder. "Ambitious plan."

"I couldn't find you anywhere else."

"You looked for me?" He had looked for her?

His hand was on her nape again, his thumb stroking the one spot in her body that loved to gather tension. "All my life."

She died a little. Because she knew what he meant.

He dropped a kiss at the very edge of her mouth. "I thought you were avoiding me because I'd turned you off so completely with how awful I was to you."

Only one of her eyes was truly working but the sight of him was still overwhelming; those words he was saying made her want to pinch herself. Her hand stroked his chest. She couldn't believe she was here, doing this. "It was all true what you said. Well, a lot of it was true. But if you feel differently now, I'm not going to argue with that."

"I feel differently now." The man could smile-frown like no one else.

"And I don't."

"Does that mean we can start afresh?"

"Please."

He rested his forehead against hers, his entire body relaxing in relief. "So it would be all right to ask you if I could make you dinner sometime?"

She laughed a little desperately. "I'll tell you now that you can get me to do almost anything if you feed me your food." Her stomach felt as full as her heart. Just thinking about the food today made her woozy with wanting. Then again, his hand was moving down her spine, so it might not be the food.

His head leaned back. He was laughing again, and that chin of his, with that evil dimple, was a whisper away from her lips. She was about to kiss it when he met her gaze. "If we're going to give this a go, you're going to have to promise me something."

"That I only can eat food that you cook?" She reached out and touched his chin and he shivered, his pupils dilating in the sexiest way.

"That can be arranged. But what I was trying to say is that you have to understand that we aren't camels, Trisher. We can't eat two days' worth of food in one meal."

She nodded, a little distracted by his chin. "Not camels. Got it. So are we *giving this a go*, then?" Yes, she imitated his accent, because it was just so much fun to do it.

He laughed again. She frickin' loved making him laugh. "I'd very much like to give it a go."

She touched his chin again, just the tip of her forefinger skimming the deep notch of his dimple. A responding pulse beat between her legs. A tightening in her innermost parts. All that from touching him this way. As if he were hers to touch.

He closed his eyes, dropping a curtain over the intensity, the hunger that had just burned in there. The hunger she had made burn.

She lifted that oversensitive finger and touched his lips. They were lush and wide and still a little swollen from being sucked on just a few moments ago. She traced back down to the dimple in his chin she couldn't get enough of. He took a shuddering breath.

"Is it always so sensitive?"

He took moments to answer as though it cost him an effort. "It's never been before." Lifting her fingers, he kissed them, and then spoke against them. "It's your hands, they're magic."

Heat rose in her cheeks. "I can't believe I actually asked you if you knew what my hands were worth."

There it was again, that laugh. Deep and husky and perfect. "If only I'd known."

The lights inside dimmed and they both threw a look at the French doors beyond which real life waited.

She wasn't ready to leave the balcony. "I believe we have two problems. One, I can't see a damn thing. And two, I really am not in the mood to deal with the Animal Farm." Because they were going to be extra weird about this, she just knew it.

"I certainly hope you're not trying to tell me that your family turns into animals when midnight strikes. I mean, pumpkins I can handle, but . . ."

"It's a long story. I'll fill you in some other time. Right now I just want to get out of here."

Without taking his hand off her waist—*Yes, please, please don't stop touching me, thank you*—he leaned over the railing, which was weird to observe with one functioning eye.

"I have an idea," he said. "Turn around." He turned her around on the wide railing, her legs dangling in the air. "Stay there."

She couldn't be sure, because she couldn't *bloody* see, but she thought he lifted himself up onto the railing next to her, and then, yipes! he jumped off the balcony.

Before she could get a shriek out, she felt the tips of his fingers on her feet. "Come on, jump, I'll catch you."

She closed one eye and focused on him. "You'll what?" It was a good eight feet down.

"I'll catch you. Trust me."

And that was when she knew she had lost her mind. Because she jumped. She landed in his arms. Which were very, very nice arms to land in. Bicep-chef, indeed!

She felt like the Disney version of a princess for the first time in her life. Which made her burst out laughing.

"You jumped!" he said, also laughing into her ear, his arms still tightly wrapped around her.

"Well, you said you'd catch me."

He got all intense and serious again, but then they were smiling into each other's faces once more. "What on earth was that?" she asked finally.

"I heard that you have a thing for romantic gestures involving balconies."

"I'm going to kill Yash." But really she was going to kiss her brother.

DJ scooped her up and carried her around the building.

"You can put me down now." No one had carried her in at least twenty-five years.

He dropped a kiss on her nose. Then gave her a hard kiss on the lips. "You sure? I thought you couldn't see." But he put her down and didn't do anything that gave away how much his arms might be hurting. And she fell a little bit more in love with him.

"You'll have to lead me around. Where are we going?"

"To my car first. Then I guess we have to find you some spectacles."

"Can you please not look at me until I have my contacts in?" she said as soon as she put her spectacles on. "I'm really not comfortable with you seeing me like this."

DJ turned away from her and studied the huge painting on the bathroom wall. It was a butterfly intricately rendered in patterns of henna. Vibrant in an almost mythical way. "Will you believe me if I said it makes me like you more?"

The laugh she gave him was more of a scoff. She had all these different laughs. "You have a thing for ugly people?"

"You're not ugly. You're beautiful." He touched the painting. The patterns were thick and raised.

"Shut up. I'm not that stupid, you know."

Outside the open door of her bathroom, the walls of her room were also lined with paintings. End to end. It was like a bloody art museum. "You're not stupid at all, you're an outstanding surgeon, mate."

"Very funny. I'm an outstanding surgeon who does microsurgeries, who can't see without her glasses. I'm almost done. Sorry." She sounded apologetic and entirely too self-conscious. He hadn't noticed until now how often she did that. Actually, he'd noticed but he'd assumed it was her being uppish.

"Trisha, may I ask you a question?"

She made a sound that he took as a yes.

"You know how you said that day . . . at Naomi's . . . that you were being someone you aren't, what did you mean by that?"

"Nothing."

"Tell me. Please."

Her silence was so thick he could hear her brain working. Over the past hour they had made a leap from strangers— strangers who had hurt each other and regretted it, strangers who had wanted each other for a while but been too afraid and confused by their feelings, but strangers nonetheless—to people who had shared things they'd never shown anyone else. To people who had kissed like they were inside each other, like they'd been wanting this their entire lives.

Now she was arguing with her overactive conscience about living up to her own need to be honest, and broaching something she was incredibly uncomfortable about. She may not know which side would win. He did. So he waited.

"Nisha had prodded me that day about having the courage to let people see what I was feeling," she said finally. "Because she'd guessed how I felt about you."

"And when you did that, I was horrid to you."

"Horrid? Nah, you just told me what an insufferable snobby bitch I was. And I needed that. Because, God, how are you here right now after how I behaved that day?"

"But you're here, too, after how I've behaved."

"DJ, can this be the last time we talk about that awful day? Please."

He turned around and stepped close to her and wrapped his arms around her. "My eyes are closed," he said in her ear. "Sure, let's never talk about that again. But before we leave it behind, there is something I want to make sure you know. You are most certainly not a bitch and you are only slightly insufferable."

She elbowed him but she also pressed into him. "I'm done. You can open your eyes."

He smiled into her cheek and drank in her reflection in the mirror. "I was terribly wrong about you. You are the strongest, most generous woman I have ever met in my life. And you're also the most beautiful. Inside and out. Although right now it's the outside that's making me have trouble breathing."

He was pressing into her and the proof of how very much he meant those words was probably branding her butt and making coherent thought nearly impossible for him.

Based on the fact that she pressed back into him, harder this time, she didn't seem to mind. "Maybe you're having trouble breathing because a different part of your body is taking up all the oxygen in your system."

She was definitely going to kill him, because even when he was hornier than he had ever been in his life, he laughed. "Maybe. You're the doctor. You could, you know, investigate?"

She turned around, laughter bubbling from her, and reached for his belt, yanking it off with gusto. "Research is my first love."

"And thank the good Lord for that." He grabbed her face and took her lips. Not soft, not gentle. Her response was just as fierce, yet it softened and warmed everything inside him.

Something about the way she kissed was all consuming, like it wasn't his mouth but his entire being that her lips were claiming. And she took her time. She was such a bloody surgeon, thorough and obsessively attentive. She caressed his lips with hers, and caressed his lips, and caressed his lips, and went on until her knees could no longer hold her up and she was sliding against him. He lifted her and fitted her against him. She wrapped her legs around his hips, her feet finding purchase on his arse.

"You have a ridiculously spectacular butt," she whispered into his mouth, tracing the rise with the arches of her feet.

He groaned into her mouth, his heartbeat going insane in his chest. Her feet caressed and traced him, then hooked into his jeans and slid them off his hips. The soles of her feet found his overheated flesh through the cotton of his boxers and used it like an erotic toy.

He pulled away from the kiss and leaned his forehead into hers. She had taken him completely by surprise, and yet she hadn't. "Trisha, love, are you trying to kill me?"

Her feet stroked his butt again, and she watched him with eyes both shy and drunk on power. "All I'm saying, DJ, is that I love your butt. I love it so much I think I want to marry it."

His chest started to shake. "You're such a romantic!"

Her hands ran down his chest and slipped under his shirt. "You laugh with your chest, you know that?" Her fingers slid through the sensitive sprinkling of hair, playing him like an instrument, stroking down his chest to his abs. "And your skin. I love your skin."

His head was starting to swell almost as much as other body parts, and it felt almost as bloody good. He cupped her cheek and caressed it with his thumb. "And I love yours. It's beautiful." It was flawless and dewy, and there was a sprinkling of the faintest freckles across her high cheekbones. He kissed each one, dragging his lips against the smoothness.

"No, seriously, you don't understand your skin is like silk."

He smiled into her face. Dropped another possessive kiss on her lips. "And you haven't seen the silkiest parts yet," he whispered into her mouth.

"Any chance we can fix that soon, Mr. Caine? Like maybe tonight?" Her words were bold but she blushed. Connection crackled between them.

"You sure, Dr. Raje? Because we can take it slow."

"Can we take it fast first, and then take it slow later?" she said, pulling his mouth to hers again.

He carried her to the biggest, highest four-poster bed he'd ever seen, because his days of refusing her anything were long gone.

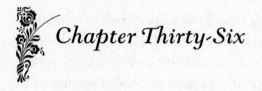

Chapter Thirty-Six

Four months later . . .

Did Aji really teach your boyfriend to make ladoos?" Vansh asked, taking the box of sweets out of Trisha's hands. And by "taking" she meant grabbing with both hands and then pulling with all his might when she wouldn't let go. The boy was skinny, but all that puttering around the world had done nothing to sap his strength.

"Thank you," he said with all the politeness befitting a Raje when she finally let the box go. Then he opened the box and stuffed three ladoos—yes, three—in his face. "Did your boyfriend really make these? You should totally keep him."

She scowled at him. "When do you go back to Zambia?"

"Zimbabwe, Dr. Clueless." He smiled and took the box with him to the patio overlooking the ocean where everyone was gathered.

They were celebrating Yash exceeding his fund-raising goal for the month twice over with a private family weekend, or minibreak as DJ called it, making her a little light-headed.

Steele had chosen to not run against Yash after all; he hadn't been able to stand up against Yash's oratory and his message of bringing right versus wrong to government. The fact that Naina had come down to fund-raise for two weeks hadn't hurt either. Californians couldn't get enough of her supermodel looks and her UN ambassador heart. She hadn't stayed for the celebration, but if Yash loved her enough to not care, who was Trisha to question things?

"I don't leave for another two months, sorry," the baby brat said. "TP needs me to save his ass with the SFPD project." Vansh had found a way to get DJ, Yash, and Officer Dunn to meet for beers at some dive bar and was working with them on a training program at the SFPD. It was still all very shaky and uncertain, but shaky and uncertain had always been Vansh's drug of choice.

He took another two ladoos from the box and then had the gall to pass the box around!

Needless to say, the sweet cream-of-wheat balls started disappearing before her eyes. DJ took her hand and pulled her into his lap. "I put some aside for you, Shasha," he whispered in her ear.

"Really?" She turned around and dropped a kiss on his cheek.

"These are seriously insane," Nisha said, placing the box on her rather rotund belly. She looked too adorable for words, but it was entirely misleading because she snarled and swatted Yash's hand away when he tried to reach for one. Neel quickly withdrew the hand that had been snaking toward the box and both Yash and he went back to their beers.

"Do you girls want some ladoos?" Trisha called to Mishka and Emma, who sat cross-legged on the grass, bent over some clay they were molding.

"They're busy," Nisha said, hugging the box, but she handed one over when Emma stood and came up the patio steps with the help of her white cane, which she wielded like a boss. She was teaching full-time with Jane now and also living full-time with her. Naturally, she held out her hand until Nisha coughed up two more ladoos.

They had retrieved all the money from Julia and Emma had returned the online donations to the donors they could trace. The anonymous donations had gone to Jane's institute. The good news was that the film had caused Emma's art sales to skyrocket, which had brought in way more money than the donations had and taken care of her medical bills a few times over. Which meant DJ had been able to use the profits from his business to rent Ashi's kitchen.

"There's moussaka in the oven. Don't ruin your appetites," Ashi said and they all laughed. Yeah, there would be no leftovers. Not with DJ and Ashi here.

"Are we waiting for HRH and Ma for dinner?" Trisha asked. "I'm hungry."

"They're at Congressman Wood's wife's book reading. If the wife is half as long-winded as the husband, I think they might come home in time for breakfast tomorrow," Yash said.

DJ seemed to relax under her. They had been together for four months and it was like he'd known the siblings and the cousins all his life, but HRH's presence still made him act like he was a cadet in a military academy and HRH was a visiting four-star general. He stood up really straight and his speech got really clipped and he tried to avoid touching Trisha, which she was happy to report seemed as hard for him as not touching him was for her.

"I'm shagging the man's daughter," he had said when she tried to talk him into relaxing around her father. "It's the strangest thing, but every time he's around, my brain kind of fixates on that fact."

She was A-okay with him fixating on shagging her. It was mutual. Especially because, well . . . suffice to say, cooking wasn't the only thing the man did as though his existence depended on it. Actually, shagging wasn't either. He loved that way too.

For his part, HRH was being HRH and still feeling DJ out. Then again, he was still doing that with Neel, and he had known Neel his whole life. Ma, dreamer that she was, insisted he was getting there.

Aji had bonded with DJ over his eagerness to learn every one of her signature dishes—something she hadn't even shared with Ashna. This might have something to do with the fact that the first time DJ met Esha he had learned all the things she enjoyed eating, then he'd researched nutrition that aided the control of epilepsy, and then he'd set up special menus for J-Auntie to cook for her. Aji was almost as much in love with him as Trisha was.

DJ had taken advantage of this fact and made Aji tell him the story of Trisha being burned in eighth grade. Trisha had threatened the siblings and cousins with death if they let it slip. But DJ, the sneak, had gone straight to the source. Aji had been showing Trisha how to temper hot oil with mustard seeds. It was the basis of almost all Indian cooking and apparently, the mustard seeds always popped open and splattered all over the place. In Trisha's opinion this was something all little children should be warned about before they were lulled into being taught to cook this particularly barbaric preparation.

"So Shasha got sprinkled with a few microscopic dots of oil and refused to enter the kitchen ever again." Every one of the siblings told DJ once Aji had let the story out of the bag.

To DJ's credit he didn't laugh. Well, didn't laugh too loudly. Also to his credit he only rarely brought it up.

"Is this the book in which the congressman's wife claims the war in Afghanistan is the longest war in history?" Neel said, rubbing the feet Nisha had rested on his lap.

"Yup. Evidently the woman has never heard of the war between the Netherlands and the Isles of Sicily!" Only Yash could look so genuinely perplexed when saying something like that.

"Nobody but you has ever heard of that." This from Vansh, who had been drinking from everyone's bottles and glasses and still hadn't decided what he wanted.

"How long did that one last?" This from the love of her life as he took his ale back from Vansh, who had the gall to make a face at it.

"Dude!" Every one of them yelled in unison. "Please do not get Yash started. What is wrong with you?"

Yash ignored everyone and addressed DJ. "Well, it was the longest war in history. It lasted from 1651 to 1986. Not a single person died."

"I'm impressed."

That sent up a chorus of groans. "You never, ever say that to Yash." Ashna poked DJ. Because, gosh, you really did not. Had the man learned nothing in four months?

"Have you learned nothing in four months?" Vansh asked.

"The shortest one was the Anglo-Zanzibar war, lasting a very dramatic thirty-eight minutes." That started a history lesson of all the wars ever fought.

DJ sipped his ale, ignoring the daggers everyone shot at him. "Why do you know all this, mate?" She loved how his mouth twisted in that lazy way when he was like this, every inch of him relaxed, his amusement coming from so deep inside it felt like delight.

"Why do you not?" they all said together as Yash said it.

Yash used the distraction to steal a ladoo from Nisha and took a bite.

"I like this one," Yash said to Trisha, pointing his ladoo at DJ.

"As opposed to which one?" This from Vansh, who finally settled on the IPA DJ had picked out for him in the first place.

Trisha glared at both her brothers but DJ was smiling in that loose-limbed way again as though he was completely at home in his skin and looking at her as though being in love for the first time at the ripe old age of thirty-two was the most amazing thing in the world, and she forgot her annoyance. He wrapped his fingers around her neck and pulled her close and she dropped a hard kiss on his lips, setting off a chorus of groans and hoots.

As usual, Vansh was right.

There had never been anyone else for her except for this one.

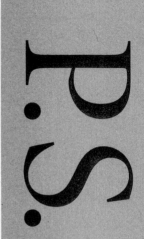

Insights,
Interviews
& More . . .

About the author

2 Meet Sonali Dev

About the book

3 Behind the Book Essay

5 Recipe: Chicken in Mugal
Cream Sauce

6 Reading Group Guide

Meet Sonali Dev

Ishita Singh Photography

Award-winning author SONALI DEV writes Bollywood-style love stories that let her explore issues faced by women around the world while still indulging her faith in happily-ever-afters. Sonali lives in the Chicago suburbs with her very patient and often amused husband, two teens who demand both patience and humor, and the world's most perfect dog. ◟

Behind the Book Essay

Someone asked me once which literary character I relate to most and my immediate response was that I think I'm a little bit like each of my favorite Jane Austen heroines. Lizzy Bennet, because of course I'm opinionated and have little patience for pretention, but also because beautiful architecture has the power to melt me in ways that even I don't understand. Anne Elliot, because I can imagine carrying the guilt of a mistake, and the constancy of an emotional connection, across time and separation. And most certainly Emma, because I might be the slightest bit guilty of feeling like I know what's best for everyone and I tend to favor the merits of intention over prudence.

The fact that I can relate so viscerally to Austen's heroines is bizarre, even ironic, given that her heroines lived in a time when her country had enslaved mine while proliferating the theme of "East is East and West is West and never the twain shall meet." But then that's the genius of Austen, isn't it? Her themes and conflicts are so human they cross cultural boundaries, and they haven't lost any of their relevance over time. The privilege people are born into and take pride in, and their prejudices, might have altered in how they present, but the underlying motivations and failings themselves have remained unchanged.

To me Austen's books are about the work we have to do to navigate social pressures and rise above conditioning in ▶

Behind the Book Essay *(continued)*

order to find happiness. Familial/societal expectation versus free will is a theme I've tried to explore in all my writing, especially through the lens of being a woman. So naturally, I've always wanted to play with Jane Austen's stories and to attempt retelling them. Not in terms of women and men in want of spouses, but in terms of people navigating the structure of society in more contemporary ways. Because look at our world: it's more heterogeneous than ever before. All these different belief systems and cultures within kissing distance of one another, more fluid rules than ever before, and all these power struggles to decide who gets to make and break the rules.

Terms like "melting pot" have been thrown around for years, but we've essentially been a salad here across most of America. Pieces of culture sitting together in their original form. Melting suggests transforming and taking on each other's properties. Is that really happening yet? I'm not sure what the answer to that question is. But I did want to poke at that question a bit.

That is where I was hoping to go with *Pride, Prejudice, and Other Flavors* and with the rest of the stories in this series. See this seemingly increasingly borderless world through the lens of an Indian American family with immense economic privilege that dreams of political power. The series begins with the oldest son announcing his gubernatorial candidacy for the state of California and ends with the election. Each story is inspired by an Austen novel and explores cultural integration and the interaction among cultures, generations, classes, and genders in America, as well as how in breaking through our conditioned perceptions we might have the opportunity to find ourselves and let love into our lives in ways that we never thought possible before. ∾

Recipe: Chicken in Mugal Cream Sauce

SERVES 4

½ cup butter
8 whole cloves
1 stick cinnamon
1 teaspoon fennel seeds (aka saunf)
1 teaspoon dried fenugreek leaves (aka kasoori methi; optional)
2 tablespoons ginger garlic paste (3 cloves of garlic and ½ inch of ginger ground with a little water to form a paste)
2 medium onions (any sweet variety), steamed and pureed
2 green chiles (any variety based on your heat preference), steamed and pureed
2 tablespoons tomato puree
1 pound skinless, boneless chicken (I use a combination of breasts and thighs, but just one or the other also works)
¼ cup yogurt
Salt to taste
¼ cup cashew paste (cashew nuts ground with water to form a paste)
¼ cup heavy cream
¼ teaspoon nutmeg
Cilantro
Rice or naan

1. In a heavy pan, heat the butter (hot but not smoking) and add the cloves, cinnamon, fennel seeds, and fenugreek leaves, if using. Let sizzle for a minute.

2. Add the ginger garlic paste and stir for 2 minutes.

3. Add the pureed onions and pureed green chiles and stir for 5 minutes.

4. Add the tomato puree and stir for 2 minutes.

5. Add the chicken and sauté for 5 minutes.

6. Add the yogurt and salt and cook over medium heat, stirring occasionally, for about 20 minutes, or until the chicken is fully cooked.

7. Add the cashew paste, cream, and nutmeg and cook for 2 minutes.

8. Garnish with cilantro and serve hot with rice or naan. ∽

Reading Group Guide

1. While the story of *Pride and Prejudice* clearly influenced this book, in what ways was it different?

2. What were your first impressions of Trisha and DJ? How did they change over the course of the novel? And how did Trisha's and DJ's impressions of each other change?

3. Family plays a very important role for both DJ and Trisha. Discuss how their familial expectations defined their characters. How did the impressions that DJ and Trisha have about their own families change as they discovered more about themselves and their histories?

4. The author has her characters explore their own prejudices throughout the course of the story. Was there anything that surprised you in their explorations of each other's backgrounds and cultures?

5. Though she was an incredibly successful doctor, Trisha had a lot of insecurity about other parts of her life. How do you think compartmentalizing parts of their lives impacted the characters' personalities?

6. DJ had a very rough childhood. Talk about how his past influenced both how he dealt with the women in his life (Emma, Trisha, Julia) and how he looked at the world.

7. Both DJ and Trisha had very specific ideas about how to handle Emma's treatment. Do you think either of them was right?

8. Discuss how the author upended some ideas of traditional gender roles.

9. Indian food is a big part of this story. Talk about how cooking, eating, and discussing food helped bring our characters together. (Which recipes made you the hungriest?)

10. What do you think Jane Austen would say about this homage to her story? ∽